Steal the Sun

Other Books by Lexi Blake

ROMANTIC SUSPENSE

Masters and Mercenaries
The Dom Who Loved Me
The Men With The Golden Cuffs
A Dom is Forever
On Her Master's Secret Service
Sanctum: A Masters and Mercenaries Novella
Love and Let Die
Unconditional: A Masters and Mercenaries Novella
Dungeon Royale
Dungeon Games: A Masters and Mercenaries Novella
A View to a Thrill
Cherished: A Masters and Mercenaries Novella
You Only Love Twice
Luscious: Masters and Mercenaries~Topped
Adored: A Masters and Mercenaries Novella
Master No
Just One Taste: Masters and Mercenaries~Topped 2
From Sanctum with Love
Devoted: A Masters and Mercenaries Novella
Dominance Never Dies
Submission is Not Enough
Master Bits and Mercenary Bites~The Secret Recipes of Topped
Perfectly Paired: Masters and Mercenaries~Topped 3
For His Eyes Only
Arranged: A Masters and Mercenaries Novella
Love Another Day
At Your Service: Masters and Mercenaries~Topped 4
Master Bits and Mercenary Bites~Girls Night
Nobody Does It Better
Close Cover
Protected: A Masters and Mercenaries Novella
Enchanted: A Masters and Mercenaries Novella
Charmed: A Masters and Mercenaries Novella
Taggart Family Values
Treasured: A Masters and Mercenaries Novella, Coming June 29, 2021

Masters and Mercenaries: The Forgotten
Lost Hearts (Memento Mori)
Lost and Found
Lost in You
Long Lost
No Love Lost

Masters and Mercenaries: Reloaded
Submission Impossible
The Dom Identity, Coming September 14, 2021

Butterfly Bayou
Butterfly Bayou
Bayou Baby
Bayou Dreaming
Bayou Beauty, Coming July 27, 2021

Lawless
Ruthless
Satisfaction
Revenge

Courting Justice
Order of Protection
Evidence of Desire

Masters Of Ménage (by Shayla Black and Lexi Blake)
Their Virgin Captive
Their Virgin's Secret
Their Virgin Concubine
Their Virgin Princess
Their Virgin Hostage
Their Virgin Secretary
Their Virgin Mistress

The Perfect Gentlemen (by Shayla Black and Lexi Blake)
Scandal Never Sleeps
Seduction in Session
Big Easy Temptation
Smoke and Sin
At the Pleasure of the President

URBAN FANTASY

Thieves

Steal the Light
Steal the Day
Steal the Moon
Steal the Sun
Steal the Night
Ripper
Addict
Sleeper
Outcast
Stealing Summer
The Rebel Queen

LEXI BLAKE WRITING AS SOPHIE OAK

Texas Sirens

Small Town Siren
Siren in the City
Siren Enslaved
Siren Beloved
Siren in Waiting
Siren in Bloom
Siren Unleashed
Siren Reborn

Nights in Bliss, Colorado

Three to Ride
Two to Love
One to Keep
Lost in Bliss
Found in Bliss
Pure Bliss
Chasing Bliss
Once Upon a Time in Bliss
Back in Bliss
Sirens in Bliss
Happily Ever After in Bliss
Far From Bliss, Coming 2021

A Faery Story

Bound

Beast

Beauty

Standalone

Away From Me

Snowed In

Steal the Sun

Thieves, Book 4

Lexi Blake

Steal the Sun
Thieves, Book 4
Lexi Blake

Published by DLZ Entertainment, LLC

Edited by Chloe Vale and Kasi Alexander
eBook ISBN: 978-1-937608-19-4

Acknowledgments

I want to thank the usual suspects. Much love to my editors – Chloe Vale and Kasi Alexander. Especially to Chloe who put up with the great capitalization debate of 2014. Thanks to my betas, Stormy and Riane, who always do an amazing job. Thanks to the bloggers like Shayna Renee's Spicy Reads and Kelley at Smut Book Junkies for getting behind this series and championing it. To Liz Berry, Shayla Black, and Kris Cook who have to listen to me whine on a daily basis. And an eternal thank you to my husband, mom, and kids who make it easy for me to work.

But this book is for Lindsey who still believes in faery tales and who I pray always will. I love you, my sweet girl. You can read this when you're forty…

Chapter One

The warmth of the midday sun shone down on the village in Faery. The sun didn't look different from the one I was used to seeing, but I was no longer on the Earth plane. I hadn't been for the hours it had taken us to walk from the *sithein* door to the village located close to the white palace, the home of the Seelie royals.

I let my face drift up, closing my eyes and pretending I was back in Dallas, standing on the balcony with Dev, waiting for Daniel to wake up.

"Zoey." Neil looked at me with big blue eyes from across the table. "They wouldn't call them brownies if they didn't taste good."

"Did you learn nothing from the pixies?" I shot my werewolf a nasty look, remembering the day not too many weeks ago that I scrubbed his scalp raw getting rid of the fleas a certain ruby red pixie had left him as payment for trying to make her a little snack.

I looked over at the next table and saw my other bodyguard. Lee wasn't even paying attention to the little brownies who were shyly watching the festivities from the doors and windows of houses. Lee and his brother, Zack, were drinking ale and guarding the coffin they'd carried into the *sithein*. Sarah's husband, Felix Day, was talking to Zack and looking around the town square with a ready smile.

Neil nodded his head vigorously, looking at both Sarah and me as we sat at a table in the middle of Dev's hometown. "Yes. I totally learned something. I learned not to eat the pixies. Those brownies look mighty tasty and easy to catch."

Sarah let her head fall to the table, and she groaned heartily about Neil's fondness for faery creatures. It didn't bode well for our stay in Faery that my best friend thought most of the inhabitants looked tasty.

I took the time to stare at my husband. Well, one of them anyway. I couldn't exactly stare at Daniel, and looking at his coffin only made me wonder if he was hot in there. So I stared at the husband who was up and walking around and wondered when I could go home. I'd been in his homeland for approximately half a day and I already wanted to be back at the penthouse. It was selfish, but I was in that kind of mood.

I like to think of myself as a fairly simple girl. I wouldn't call myself normal, of course. When a girl is married to two men, she can't consider herself normal. When those men happen to be a faery high priest and a vampire king, she can wave any thoughts of a nice, normal life good-bye.

I've gotten used to the fact that my life consists of a whole lot of subterfuge, plotting, and a liberal dose of violence. I live firmly in the supernatural world. My home might be a condo in Dallas, but I'm more likely to come into contact with werewolves than some nice accountant. Since I'm a thief by vocation, most of my human interactions involve the police, but I try to keep that to a minimum. All in all, I have a healthy tolerance for weirdness, but this was beginning to push it.

"I love you, Prince Dev!" a girl with ridiculously long hair called out to my husband. She looked like she was dressed for a medieval fair, but then we all did.

I rolled my eyes for the three hundredth time. I'd stopped keeping count or noting the hair color of the girls who screamed his name as we paraded by. It was like being married to a rock star.

Maybe I could have handled that if he was being adored for his ability to play a guitar or his amazing vocal prowess.

That wasn't what Devinshea Quinn was good at. Nope. My husband was part fertility god.

It had been this way all day. We'd gone through three towns on our way here, each one greeting the returned Green Man with pomp and circumstance and a whole lot of propositions I wish I hadn't heard.

Dev looked for me across the center of town that was now filled with all manner of curious faery creature. This village was the largest we'd visited and the closest to the palace. Dev and his brother, the future king, had walked me down the main street in a little parade of sorts, but when we reached the center he was bombarded with well-wishers and gawkers.

An officious woman who introduced herself to me as Mara, a member of the queen's staff, had met us. She was currently directing traffic around the royal twins. She had pushed or pulled the brothers this way or that in an attempt to make the most of their time in town. My group had been told to take a rest break and shoved to the side.

"He has groupies, Z." Sarah watched the proceedings with an air of shock. "This is worse than a bunch of preteens at a One Direction concert."

"There's no comparison, Sarah," Neil snorted. "Those concerts are filled with screaming virgins. There are no virgins here, thank god." Neil glanced around, his eyes taking in all the tall, good-looking Seelie commoners mulling about trying to get a word in with the newly returned priest. "Why did I have to go and make up with Chad? I could be having ridiculously hot revenge sex with some glorious slab of man. Look at them. They're all gorgeous."

They were. As a race, the *sidhe* won points for hotness. The men were all tall and well built. Their faces would grace the walls of a male modeling agency, and they didn't understand the meaning of the term pot belly. The women were tall and lithe. Their lovely bodies were made to fit into designer gowns and walk runways. And everyone was serious about their hair. It ranged from almost shock white to that deep, midnight black of Dev's. Everyone's hair was long and straight.

I stuck out like a sore thumb. I was the only redhead in the town and they were probably mistaking me for one of the aforementioned, probably-tastes-good brownies. I'm that short.

"Z, you need to tell Daniel to make a new rule." Neil pulled me out of my self-centered revelry. "Anyone who dates a vamp is also allowed one faery. It's the Zoey rule."

"Yes, I'm sure Daniel will get right on that." It had taken Daniel a long time to get used to Dev. Their first encounters had been violent and Dev almost hadn't survived them. The boys had settled into a nice friendship with some brutally hot sexual chemistry they chose to ignore and I dreamed about at night. Despite all Daniel's newfound comfort in his sexuality, I still didn't think he was going to use his power to get Neil laid.

Sarah let her head drop to her palm as she watched the crowd thoughtfully. "They seem happy to have him back."

"Yes," I murmured, watching as Dev stopped looking for me when a lovely blonde tapped his shoulder and requested a moment of his time. Dev seemed to know her but then he probably knew all of them. Biblically. Being a priest in Faery was something completely different than our world. Apparently the Fae believed their bodies were temples that should have lots and lots of visitors. "I'm remembering all the time we spent talking about how much of an outcast he was. You wouldn't believe the stories he told me. Everyone hated him because he was all mortal. If that's hate, I suppose love would be a big old orgy."

"Heh, we regular folk never had a problem with Prince Devinshea," a voice said.

I found a squat little gnome peering up at me from beneath his red cone cap. It's nearly impossible to tell age on a gnome because they get wrinkly fast, but if I had to bet, I would have said he was decades my senior. I couldn't help but wonder what kind of travel tips he could give me.

"Because he was the Green Man?" That was the reason his twin brother, Declan, had given me. Dev was an outcast with the royals because of his mortality. His status as part Green Man had made him popular with the peasants. They were the ones who had to farm, so being able to make crops grow was undoubtedly a bonus to his status among the commoners.

The gnome nodded as he looked out over the crowd. “Yes, he was a good Green Man. You have to understand that we went without for many years after his grandfather died. When the prince was found to have powers, we all rejoiced. It was more than that, though. Prince Dev, I guess I should call him High Priest now, was always a kind one. He never looked down on a single creature, not the way the other one did.”

I wrinkled my nose in agreement. He was talking about Declan, Dev’s twin and the future King of Faery. “The other one is an arrogant prick.”

The little gnome looked shocked for a moment but then threw his head back, laughing. His voice boomed and echoed across the courtyard. It was so much deeper than one would expect, but then there were many surprises in this odd land.

“Yes, he is, Your Grace,” the gnome agreed.

My fingers went straight to the gold chain around my neck that marked me as the wife of the High Priest of Faery. It was a dead giveaway. The way I was dressed didn’t exactly help me blend into the crowd. I was dressed as a royal with rich fabrics. It made a stark contrast to the working folk of the village. My husband and his brother had carefully orchestrated my introduction into Fae society. This afternoon was the parade through town, but there was also to be a series of balls and parties welcoming the newest member of the royal family. I doubted it was going to be anything as fun as a barbecue with a nice keg of beer. Of course, if it was anything like this reception, I would be able to slip out with no one noticing I was gone.

“Is there anything I can get you, Your Grace?” the gnome asked.

“Please call me Zoey,” I offered, holding out my hand. I was happy to be nice to the first person who had done something other than gawk at me. The gnome was the first member of Faery to say hello.

He looked at it not quite knowing what to do. “Your Grace?’

“Oh, it’s called a handshake,” I explained with a friendly smile. “You put your hand in mine and we shake. Then we know each other and can be friends, though you should probably tell me your name first."

The gnome stared at me for a moment and smiled gamely before putting his small hand in mine. "I am Loran. I run the gardens in town and sometimes help out my friend with this pub of his."

Sarah grinned, as enchanted as I was to be talking to a gnome. "If this is a pub then the owners probably know Dev well."

"That boy can get his drink on," Neil threw in.

Loran laughed again. "Yes, His Grace can drink with the best of them and often did. He wasn't welcome with the nobles so he spent his time with us, as much as he could. Queen Miria tried, you know. She tried to force the nobles to be kind, but when she wasn't looking they treated that boy something awful. Now, of course, the joke is on them."

"What do you mean?" I had assumed they still hated him. He was still mortal, after all.

The gnome shook his head as if the truth were so obvious. "His ascension. He bonded with an ancient god and now he has power beyond anyone's wildest dreams. He can bring us back. He can give us children again. Before he left he managed to help a few have children but not many. Now we can be fertile again. We can be great again. Thanks to you, sweet lady."

The gnome was looking at me with the greatest of hope in his eyes, and it both warmed and terrified me. These people were expecting so much from this trip, and I wondered exactly what it was going to cost us.

Dev had already taken the ancient god, Bris, into his body. On the night we married, his magic had flared, an invitation to the ancient non-corporeal Irish deity to come and sit a spell inside my husband's body. I'd become well acquainted with the fertility god on the night of my marriage to Dev.

It was the night Bris might have gotten me pregnant.

"Ah, Loran, 'tis just like you to be lazing away talking to pretty girls when there is work to be done," a deep voice intoned from behind me.

As I turned, I noticed Neil's jaw drop and his eyes widen. I tried to keep from doing the same as I came eye level with a large piece of unclothed masculinity. I wasn't sure what shocked me more, the sight of a guy's junk just swinging in the breeze, or the fact that said junk seemed to be attached to the lower half of a big goat.

I forced my head up and the chest was a nice specimen of human male hotness. Nice pecs, broad shoulders, arms that looked acquainted with gym equipment. I studied my first satyr. He was disarmingly handsome. His eyes looked almost violet in the gauzy midday light and they were set off by the darkness of his hair and beard. Unlike the sidhe, his hair was short.

"So this is Devinshea's goddess," he said in a way that made me think he approved on every level. I stood up because it seemed more polite than talking to his penis. He caught my hand in his and brought it gallantly to his lips. "I'm Ross. I own this tavern. It's such a pleasure to meet you, Your Grace. Your loveliness surpasses anything I could have imagined."

That was laying it on a bit thick, but I would take it. "You must not have much of an imagination then, Ross."

His sensual lips split in a smile of pure pleasure showing even, white teeth. "Has the little prince finally followed my advice and dumped the simpering idiots he used to prefer?"

"I don't know about what he liked here," Neil said just a little breathless as he studied the gorgeous satyr. "But I don't think Zoey's ever simpered in her life. I'm Neil, by the way. I'm her bodyguard."

Ross looked unimpressed with what I considered a bodyguard.

I knew what he was thinking. He was wondering how a boy who probably had fifteen pounds on me was supposed to protect me. I grinned because it was one of the reasons Neil was so effective. "Don't underestimate him. Appearances can be deceiving. Do you know what a werewolf is, Ross?"

"I've heard the tales, though we have no lycanthropes here," Ross murmured, casting his eyes Sarah's way. "And what do you do, gorgeous? Tell me you don't turn into something hairy."

Sarah shook her purple pixie bob at him. She'd visited her salon right before we left because she never kept one color for long. "Nothing so energetic. As for what I do, pray you never find out. Just understand, we might look all sweet and soft and human but we can handle ourselves."

"I hope you don't have to," the satyr said quietly but then he smiled again and returned to his roguish self. He'd never actually put down my hand. Now he took it between both of his and looked deeply into my eyes. "I was so happy to hear the prince had married. He is a good man. We felt his loss when he left. All of Faery is grateful to you for accommodating his ascension. It is said you performed heroically and his taking of the god would not have been possible without you."

Heat went through my body, and I was pretty sure I turned a violent shade of pink because that act he was referring to wasn't something I wanted bards singing about. Neil slapped a hand over his mouth and Sarah covered up her guffaw with a weak cough. I decided to change the subject.

"So I take it you knew my husband when he was younger?" Dev had told me about his life in the *sithein* but it was mostly tales of his life in the palace or in his temple, and I got the feeling even what he'd told me was a highly sanitized version of the truth.

Ross and Loran laughed, looking at each other, and I knew they probably had a ton of stories I'd love to hear.

"I've known the prince since he could hold a mug of ale and let a woman sit on his lap," Ross declared. "I know everything and everyone in this town. You ever want the dirt or the truth about something, my tavern is the place to come, Your Grace."

I kept a smile on my face, but his words reminded me I had a job to do while I was here. There was a folder tucked away in my luggage that contained the information about the work I had to do while we visited Faery.

I'd only been in Faery for a few hours and yet my world already seemed so far away. Just this morning I'd sat in our condo in Dallas reading through the materials Louis Marini had sent for me. He'd sent me all the information he had on the artifact he wanted me to track down while I was in the *sithein*. He also sent a cell phone with instructions to call him when the job was done. I was worried I would never be able to make that call because, as clients go, my current employer sucked. His info was crappy and he only had the vaguest idea where the Blood Stone might be. Everything he knew was based on vague rumors. He was expecting a miracle, but I needed to pull it off if I wanted Daniel alive. My payment for this job was the client not killing my hubby.

Louis Marini ran the world my husband lived in. He was the head of the Vampire Council. He was also the man who had attached a device to my husband's heart and had the detonator on a remote he carried with him. One push of that button and Daniel would be gone.

So I was going to find that stone.

"Well, Ross, I might have to take you up on that offer." I said, flirting just a little. "I think I'll definitely be spending some time here. There's nothing I like better than a good tavern and some hot gossip. I'm interested in the history of this place. After all, it's important to Dev."

"We can help you there," Loran offered with his gravelly voice. "I've forgotten more about this *sithein* than most people remember. I remember when we left the Earth plane."

Loran just might be my new BFF. I knew the gemstone Marini was interested in had disappeared around three hundred years before. According to Marini's intelligence—and I use that term lightly—I was searching for a medium-sized, blood-red jewel. It once decorated the crown of the last Vampire King and had gone missing from the vamp stronghold in Paris. He'd tracked the stone down to the *sithein* through some earthbound faeries who had seen the stone at the palace, but that was years before. "Well, I would love to hear some of those stories. I'm married to a Fae now. I should know something about the *sithein*."

"Come by anytime." Ross winked my way, a gleam in his eyes. I was certain he would love to entertain me with stories and perhaps ply me with ale. I wondered how close Ross was with my husband.

"Aye," Loran agreed. "You can find me in the gardens most of the time."

"I would love to visit with you." Sarah got to one knee to get eye level with the gnome.

He nodded with a knowing grin. "Aye, I thought you would. Ross might only see that lovely face of yours, but I know a witch when I see one. Come by and I'll teach you how to grow herbs that will make your spells spark."

"Very nice," Mara was saying as she joined us with a shake of her blonde head and a condescending stare she leveled at the group.

"It's nice that you are greeting the local color, Your Grace, but if you would not mind, there are some others who would be interested in meeting Prince Devinshea's new bride."

I could totally read between her lines. There were people with more money and power and we should be talking to them. I didn't like Mara but I suspected the feeling was mutual. When she'd first gotten a look at the lot of us, she assumed Sarah was the new bride. I guess I shouldn't blame her. Despite her eclectic choice of hair color, Sarah was much closer to what Mara would have expected. Sarah was tall and lithe with an angular face that belonged on a magazine cover. I shouldn't blame Mara for the mistake but I did.

"I think Dev's handling things just fine," I replied, looking back at him.

He was laughing at something the woman in front of him said, and I was sure he just oozed charm. He was the nerd who got to go back to his class reunion as a multimillionaire playboy. He was enjoying playing the conquering hero. I wouldn't have been quite so bitter about it if he'd included me. The minute we'd marched into this impromptu welcoming party, I'd been sent to the sidelines, watching him like a lovelorn teenager.

It made me realize how used to our ménage I'd gotten. If Daniel hadn't been relegated to his coffin, I would be sitting in his lap and wouldn't even notice that Dev was ignoring me. Danny and I would be talking about everything that was going on and I would more than likely be happy. I was completely spoiled, and I tried to remember that Dev had a job to do, too.

"I was just about to get Her Grace and her friends a mug of my finest ale," Ross offered with a flourish.

"Thank god," Neil said. "Bring on the booze. We could use it."

"Amen," Sarah seconded.

My face flushed, but I nodded and tried to look happy. I wouldn't touch the ale but I didn't want to make a big deal of it. I looked at Neil and he winked. He would make sure my cup got emptied. He would do it on the sly and maybe no one would ask those questions I wasn't ready to answer.

"I do not think this is the best idea, Your Grace." Mara looked down her patrician nose at me. "This is not the most reputable of establishments. You are a member of the royal family. I understand that you grew up outside Fae society, so you must allow me to lead you. You should not be associating with bar owners."

"Yeah, I'll mention that bit of wisdom to my husband tonight." My favorite place in the world was Dev's nightclub, Ether.

Ross and Loran walked off to get us drinks, and Mara took a moment to look at our little group. We had dressed the part of a royal retinue.

Well, not all of us. Lee had told Declan to stick it, and he was wearing comfy jeans and a T-shirt. My boobs were practically falling out of my dress, so I admired my wolf's bravado.

It was Lee who got the brunt of Mara's disappointment now. "What good are you? I was informed you are the head of Her Grace's security and yet you allow strange men to accost your charge?"

"If I beat up every weird creature who hit on Zoey, I'd never get any rest." Lee never actually opened his eyes. His head was back, with his Rangers ball cap pulled over, shading his eyes. His feet were in scuffed-up boots he'd propped on the table. He appeared to be the perfect slacker, but all I had to do was whisper and my wolf would be at the throat of whatever threatened me.

Mara huffed and turned back to me. "I was surprised to hear you do not have a social secretary. I will make sure one is assigned to you as soon as we reach the palace. You will have two hours before your meeting with our glorious queen. Please make sure you wear the dress Prince Declan has chosen for you. He took time out of his busy schedule to ensure that his dear sister-in-law will look her best. I will send a maid to help you." She said that last bit like she wasn't certain I would be able to dress myself.

I shook my head because I could feel the noose tightening. Every extra person they put on me was someone I would more than likely have to shake later. "I have a maid. There's no need to send anyone."

"I'll make sure she's properly covered," Sarah promised, sitting back down at the table. "I've been dressing Zoey for a long time."

It was true. She often picked my clothes when Dev didn't do it for me.

"See that you do." Mara looked back down at the notes she was carrying. "I will consider you to be in charge of her wardrobe. She has fittings arranged with the best dressmakers in the kingdom. Prince Declan set them up himself. Please see that she makes the appointments."

Sarah frowned because she knew that getting me to stand still while someone poked me with needles might be difficult.

Neil was up and standing in front of me before I registered that someone was coming our way. He placed himself strategically in front of me but kept his body relaxed. He wouldn't give me a reason to panic unless he thought the situation was serious, but he also wouldn't let anyone he didn't know get too close to me.

"Trouble?" Lee asked, yawning.

"I'll let you know," Neil replied.

Neil and Lee had settled into a nice partnership. Neil did all the energetic running around with me while Lee paced himself, waiting for something bad to happen before interrupting his nap. I was happy they seemed to get along well since the two were polar opposites. Neil was a flaming homosexual and Lee was a manly lone wolf. It could have been a combustible concoction, but Lee treated Neil like a little brother and Neil lapped up the attention. It was a good thing since Neil's own brother was a nasty bastard who Daniel had killed earlier this summer.

"Your Grace." A young man with dark hair and a paper and quill greeted me with an arched brow. "I am with the Royal Examiner. I have a few questions for you."

Mara shook her head and tried to shoo the reporter away. "No, no, no. Her Royal Highness was clear. Any interviews with Prince Devinshea's new bride must go through the palace. Her Grace does not speak our language and needs a translator."

"Of course I speak the language." Were they so worried I would screw up a few simple questions that they were willing to lie about my language skills? I was almost certain Declan was behind that particular royal edict. He didn't seem to have a ton of faith in my abilities, but then I had given him trouble every chance I got. I turned back to the reporter, my stubbornness threatening to get the best of me. How hard could it be to answer a couple of questions? "What do you want to know?"

The reporter gave Mara a triumphant smile, and I guessed they were old adversaries. He turned back to me and he was all business. "The rumor is that Prince Dev finds himself in an unusual ménage a trois with you and a vampire. Could you please give us some details on how you manage to keep two men satisfied?"

I felt my face heat as Mara leaned in. "The Royal Examiner is a tabloid. We tend to avoid commenting," she explained in a condescending tone.

I said the only thing I could think of. *"No hablo Inglés."*

Chapter Two

"No, absolutely not." Declan charged into the tavern's courtyard. His eyes were on the reporter, and he looked like he'd call that hidden guard of his at any moment. "Her Grace is not to be bothered by reporters. There will be a party at the palace and all of the proper questions will be answered then."

Said bothersome reporter rolled his eyes and walked away. I was pretty sure he was going to write something about the dullard the prince had married. If the tabloids worked in Faery the same way they worked in my world, they didn't need to actually talk to me to write the story. Neil and I exchanged a glance. We hadn't figured on gossip rags in our medieval adventure land. If they had them, Neil would probably get a subscription. Declan turned to fix Mara with his steeliest gaze.

"I thought I warned you about my brother's wife. You cannot let her out of your sight for a moment." Declan shook a finger at the blonde.

"You did, Your Highness. I am so sorry." Her head was down, and she listened carefully to everything Declan said.

"She will burn the town down before you blink. And do not count on those guards of hers because they will help her light the fire. Think of them less as guards and more as accomplices."

Lee shot Declan the bird, but Neil just smiled. I couldn't argue because they actually were my accomplices. We'd run many heists together over the years. Sarah, too. Lee was new and the only heist we'd run had been hard on him, but Zack was actually kind of awesome. I found Zack and his butt kissing annoying, but in the field he was a perfect partner. He never argued with whoever was in charge. All in all, they were a damn fine crew. Sure they sometimes ran away for months at a time because they were mad at my husband or on some occasions had actually shot me, but other than that they were totally solid.

"Now that we are here in Faery," Declan continued as he looked at Lee dismissively, "perhaps a more formal guard can be found. I would not want my sweet sister without a truly responsible guard. I would be a careless host if I allowed anything to happen to her."

Lee sat up, and his eyes were on Declan. My wolf had excellent instincts. The reporter had been no real threat, but my brother-in-law certainly was. It was no great love on his part for me that had Declan wanting to surround me with his trusty men. Declan was certain I was carrying a child who could save his kingdom. Just weeks ago he'd vowed to do anything to protect the baby, including make me a prisoner if it came to that. I'd kept that conversation to myself, though Lee and Neil had been there at the time. Lee had begged me to let him kill the man he thought would take away my baby. I was willing to wait to see if there even was a baby to take.

My guards were the only ones who knew about the conflict with Declan, and I was trying to keep it that way.

"I told you, brother, Zoey's wolves do a fine job," Dev said, making his way toward me. A crowd followed him, but they gave him some space now.

Lee relaxed back down into his chair. He'd gained a lot of respect for Dev after our time in Colorado, and he preferred for him to handle the politics of the situation.

Dev's mouth tugged up in a lopsided, crazy sexy smile, and my heart skipped a beat. "They've kept her alive this long, and that's saying something for them. I think they will be fine for our stay here. Besides, Zoey is used to them and they are used to her ways. A royal guard would be far too confining."

Declan's eyes narrowed, but he held his tongue. I suspected he was planning on his brother's stay being a permanent one. He was smart and knew now was not the time to argue. He had attempted to convince Dev to leave his retinue behind. Declan had argued that we should use the time in Faery as a sort of honeymoon for just the two of us, but Dev had been insistent on bringing all of our household. I was happy I hadn't been forced to fight with him. If Declan had the two of us on our own, he would find some leverage to try to keep Dev here. I just hoped it wasn't my child. I feared if I turned up pregnant, Dev might actually agree with his brother, and I would find myself a permanent resident.

Dev crossed the space between us and dropped a kiss on my lips. I went up on my toes as he deepened the embrace and slid his tongue into my mouth, turning up the heat. Dev was a big fan of the PDA. I might have been embarrassed, but I was far too busy trying to climb up my husband's body to notice.

"There's a sight I know well. Good Prince Dev is back and already seducing a beauty in my courtyard," Ross said as Dev released me and looked up at the satyr. I saw happy recognition in his green eyes. "You work faster now, Prince. You didn't even have to buy this one a drink."

Dev laughed and held out his hand in greeting. "Ross, you old scoundrel, I assure you this one cost me much more than a flagon. I paid for this one in sweat and blood and expensive footwear."

"Jerk." I gave him a strong elbow to his midsection that he pretended not to notice as he shook his friend's hand.

"Now, my sweet wife, you know it's true," he chided. "My last gunshot wound is barely healed. Since I met Zoey, I've been beaten, kidnapped, drugged, stabbed, thrown bodily into more walls than I could imagine, and shot. Just a few weeks ago I was almost eaten by ravenous wolves."

"Don't forget you were offered up as a black sacrifice to a demon lord," I reminded him. It was when I knew I loved him.

His eyes went soft with the memory. "How could I forget? Good times, sweetheart."

Ross's violet eyes were large. "You have some stories to tell, Prince Dev."

"Oh, Dev, we could tell him about that time we killed the weretiger." Neil laughed, leaning forward. "It was right after we met Dev. We were running a heist and a demon was on our trail. The demon decided to play nasty. He sicced a weretiger on us in the middle of a downtown parking garage. Dev was the best bait ever. He's faster than you would think. I was surprised he survived."

Mara sighed and looked down at Dev as he settled onto a bench and pulled me into his lap. I snuggled close to him, feeling safer than I had all day.

The royal employee shook her head. "Your Highness, you must remind your retinue to treat you with more respect. They should always address you as Your Highness or Your Grace or at the least Prince Devinshea. We must observe the proprieties or else just give over to chaos."

Dev frowned and his hands pulled me tight. He regarded the woman seriously, but kept his voice low. "Understand this, Mara, I have bled with these people. I have fought, died, and been brought back with and by these people. They are my closest friends and confidants. They will call me whatever they like so long as they call me friend. You will show them respect."

"As you wish," Mara said, but it was all for show. The minute Dev took his eyes off her she regarded us all with contempt.

I wondered if it would be this way with my mother-in-law. The Seelie court was apparently a rigid place with formalities and rules galore. My friends and I weren't big on rules.

"Besides, I never kept the best company when I was younger," he stated and a cheer went up. "And I had all the more fun for it."

"She said I shouldn't consort with bar owners," I whispered, cuddling close to my favorite barkeep.

Dev threw his head back and laughed. I noticed everyone watching us. All eyes were on him, but he didn't seem to care. He grinned down at me and stared lecherously at my cleavage.

"But you like bar owners," he said, his voice deep, and I knew he was thinking of some of the things we'd done on his bar. "I sometimes think you married me for all the free booze." He glanced back up at the satyr who was putting cups on the table. "Speaking of booze, it's been too long since I tasted this ale. It's the best I've ever had and I cannot duplicate it to save my life. Believe me I've tried. Ross, as one barkeep to another, you must give me your recipe."

Ross shook his head and crossed his arms over his magnificent chest. "That's one thing I will never share with anyone. Keeps you coming back for more. So you own a tavern on the Earth plane?"

"Dev owns several," Sarah offered. "It's a nightclub. I haven't been to the others, but the one in Dallas is awesome. The place is packed every night. It's the best music and the best bar in town."

Dev picked up the flagon that should have been mine and offered a toast. "I learned from the best. I spent much of my youth in this tavern drinking and picking up women. The picking up women part may be over, but the drinking never ends." Dev proceeded to prove his point by taking an obscenely long drink. He sighed as he emptied the large mug in a single drink. "So good, Ross. Please, if you don't mind, I'll take another. My partner doesn't believe this is the best beer he'll ever taste, and I have to prove it to him. Forgive me, lover, I've stolen your beer. Make that two, Ross."

"Just the one, please," I interrupted with a shake of my head. "I don't think I'll be drinking today."

Dev frowned, and I noted Sarah's eyes narrow suspiciously.

"Are you not feeling well, my goddess?" Dev asked, concern in his eyes.

"I am sure Zoey is simply nervous about meeting our mother," Declan offered. "I think it is a mark of her burgeoning maturity. She is a wife now. She has to present herself differently."

This was one of those times I would love to roll my eyes and get drunk just to piss off my brother-in-law. I didn't point out that I had been a wife for several years and marriage hadn't cut down my consumption. Actually marriage to Danny had refined and refocused my love of vodka. It wasn't being a wife that was curbing my drinking, but the thought of being a mom definitely was. I saw Dev bought Declan's explanation, but I wasn't so sure Sarah was sold on it. She studied me carefully, her brown eyes making connections I would, no doubt, hear about later.

"Sweetheart, don't be nervous." Dev kissed my cheek, his hands smoothing over my hair. "She is going to love you or we'll go home. I, for one, intend to drink as much as I can before having to face my mother."

"He probably should," Declan agreed with a nod. "I doubt Mother would recognize him sober."

I glanced up where the shining white palace stood. It glimmered like a jewel in the distance. That palace was going to be my home for the next month or so. It was like something out of a faery tale but there was a reason for that. This was the place faery stories had originated. I had walked into a faery tale but I suspected it would prove to be more a Grimm's tale than anything Disney would put out. I couldn't expect a happy ending here, not one I didn't purchase with blood and sacrifice.

"You're unhappy," Dev accused me softly, forcing my attention back to him.

I shook off my ominous thoughts and tried to smile brightly. The last thing I wanted to do was ruin Dev's homecoming. It was all he had talked about for weeks. "No, baby. It's like your brother said. I'm just nervous. I've never had a mother-in-law. Danny's mom died when he was a toddler so your mom is my only hope for an overbearing relationship with an in-law. Declan aside, of course."

Declan chose to ignore my comment about him. "I think you'll find Mother easy to deal with. She wants one thing from you, Zoey. She wants you to make Devinshea happy. That, and of course, as many grandchildren as your body can handle. Trust me. The moment you prove your fertility, Mother will think you walk on water."

Dev gave his brother a dark look but turned back to me. "Don't listen to him, sweetheart. You make me happy and that will have to satisfy Mother for now. I won't let her push you into anything. Our relationship is far more complex than that."

"Prince Dev." Loran walked out of the tavern with Ross, mugs of ale in his small hands. The gnome kind of waddled toward us with a big grin on his face.

"Loran, it is good to see you," Dev replied. "The gardens look lovely."

The gnome bowed slightly, pleased at the compliment. "I've had to work hard since you left. I managed to keep up the ones in town, but our fields are in terrible shape. You'll have to walk the countryside putting things to rights. You've come back just in time."

Besides his fertility powers, Dev was quite good with agriculture. Declan had told me once that when Dev walked barefoot through the *sithein*, he left a trail of green wherever he went. It would be interesting to see how his powers had grown with the taking of Bris into his body.

The gnome suddenly got to his knees and took a subservient position.

"That is not necessary, good gardener. I require no obeisance." The words came out of my husband's mouth but the voice wasn't his. I looked up and stared into solid emerald eyes. I almost scrambled out of his lap but he anticipated the move, holding my waist tightly. Bris did not come out often but when he did, he liked to get his hands on me. He was always gentle but he loved to touch me and kiss me. I was scared of just how good he could make me feel.

"Bris," I heard the Seelie whisper reverently among themselves. "It is the god."

"Hello, my sweet goddess," he said with a little smile. "Are they giving you a hard time?"

"Not so much," I lied, trying not to look too deeply into those eyes. Bris had an effect on me. I suppose I should expect that a fertility god would be intensely attractive, but I found my reaction to him disconcerting. When he put his hands on me, I wanted to melt. It was the same as my reaction to Dev, only more intense. As he had said the night we met, he was Dev and something more.

"They are an arrogant people. They tend to dismiss anyone not like them," Bris said quietly to me. "Give it time, and they will see you as we see you. We think you are the most beautiful woman here, and you should not doubt it."

He leaned in and kissed me softly, his lips brushing mine, and suddenly I didn't want to get off his lap. I wrapped my arms around his neck and let his soft magic skim across my skin. Bris's magic was like a warm wave that blanketed me. The world dissolved around us and I kissed him freely, opening my mouth under his and letting his tongue play against mine. I moved closer, wanting to meld with him, brushing our chests together, needing more. His hands were in my hair when I heard Sarah.

"Snap out of it," she said sharply, and I came to my senses.

Sarah was a good girlfriend. We'd made a deal. She wouldn't let me make an idiot of myself in public. I pulled back and Bris looked disappointed. I didn't try to break free, but I wasn't about to get lost in those eyes again.

"I apologize, good gardener," Bris said with a sigh, turning his attention back to the gnome. "I came out for a purpose and got distracted by my goddess. I find her tempting. Now, you said the fields are fallow?"

"Aye, My Lord, that they are," Loran replied soberly because gnomes took their gardens seriously. "Our crops have been weak ever since we lost our Green Man. One more season like this and we'll have trouble feeding our people."

Bris nodded. "Then this shall be our first task. Tomorrow we will tour the fields and decide what must be done to correct the problems. I shall make sure you have no issues with scarcity." He turned to me again, and his eyes were hot. "Of course, we will also be performing some fertility rites. It's another problem the Fae have been plagued with, and we must help. I'm looking forward to that, my goddess."

"I just bet he is," Dev said with a self-deprecating smile. He looked up, reassuring me Bris had gone dormant again. "Sorry, I told him he could handle the heavy agricultural lifting. He's excited about making things green. It's been a long time since he used his powers."

I doubted that was the only thing he was excited about. "So, fertility rites?"

Dev looked sweetly sheepish. "Yeah, I kinda promised we'd be doing some of that. I hope you don't mind but it is my job. You'll love our temple, though. It's beautiful and peaceful."

"Is it going to be as…intense as the last time?" We had performed a fertility rite for a large group of werewolves, and the experience had been draining, to say the least.

"No," he replied quickly. "This will be much simpler. I promise. I'll handle everything. You just need to let me take care of you."

Ross sat another beer down in front of Dev and looked at the coffin on the table next to us. "So, Prince Dev, has tragedy befallen your group? If someone has passed on, then allow me to offer my condolences."

Dev's smile became devilish as he drank his beer and eased me out of his lap. He crossed to the coffin and leaned against it. "He's not dead. He's just a lazy bastard. He didn't want to walk all this way." Dev knocked on the top of the coffin. "How ya doing in there, Dan?"

There was an angry blast like Danny had punched the coffin from the inside. "It's fucking hot in here, Dev. Move this caravan along. This thing is almost dead."

"See, he's fine," Dev said with a shit-eating grin. He held a hand out toward Zack. "You got the spare I asked you to bring?"

Zack produced the extra game system, and Dev quickly opened and shut the coffin, shoving in the needed item.

"He gets pissy when he can't play his games," Dev explained, winking my way. We had put together a "you have to spend several hours in a hot coffin" care kit for Danny. Danny and I had also done some fooling around in the small box because he said he liked my scent. It made him more comfortable when he could sense me near him. I was his companion, and we were connected on a basic level. He'd finally started asking me for what he wanted, and I worked hard to make sure I gave him what he needed.

Declan frowned and crossed his arms petulantly over his chest. "How exactly is the vampire doing anything in his coffin when you were supposed to make certain he was wrapped in silver chains?"

Dev didn't bother to look guilty. He stared his brother down. "Well, he is my partner. Those chains are uncomfortable. They burn his skin. He's also good at revenge. I wrap him in chains and I assure you he spends the entire trip coming up with some way to get me back."

"Are we there yet?" Daniel must have been screaming because even I heard him.

"No," Dev screamed back, not caring that his whole town was watching the byplay. "Suck it up, Donovan. I'm drinking."

"That beer better be worth it, Quinn!"

"Would the man in the coffin like a drink?" Ross asked, confused because unlike the tabloids, he apparently hadn't heard the rumors.

"Oh, he'd like one," Neil explained. "He just has to wait until

Dev's blood alcohol level is up."

"Working on it," Dev said, finishing off beer number two. "Keep 'em coming, Ross. I have an 'interview' with my mother in a couple of hours, and I would like to be shit faced before I have to deal with that. If I work hard, Dan can be drunk off his ass too when we finally have to deal with the royals."

I noticed Lee out of the corner of my eye. His head came up suddenly and he yelled. "Neil, six o'clock. Cover her!"

Neil was starting to leap as I saw the man on top of a building to our left. He drew back an arrow and sent it flying my direction.

I've had many people try to kill me before but this was my first assassination attempt. And I'd only been in Faery for a few hours. Yay, vacation!

Chapter Three

"Oh, god, it's in my ass." Neil fell to the ground, pulling me under him. He had done his duty, tossing his body in front of mine just as the archer let loose his arrow. Neil had leapt high, covering my torso with his body, and the arrow that would have hit my heart did indeed lodge itself in my best friend's butt cheek.

I hit the ground hard, my breath fleeing in an instant. Amid the screaming and general confusion, there was a mighty crack that split the air. Daniel kicked open the coffin and burst forth, his feet hitting the table we'd just been sitting at. I nodded at him to let him know I was all right.

"Let's go, Donovan." Lee jumped onto the roof of the tavern, moving to catch the man who had shot at me.

I lay beneath Neil as Daniel took off. Lee quickly climbed up the tavern and started leaping across rooftops in pursuit of the assassin. I turned to try to see Dev. The royal guard had appeared at the first shouts, and it was obvious they had orders. Dev had five guards on him and Declan four. They formed a protective wall around the twins.

"Let me go." My husband struggled against his guard. He tried to get to me, but they were well trained and in this case did not listen to their charge. They had one and only one duty and that was to get the heir and the spare to safety. Anything else could wait.

"I have an arrow in my butt," Neil said, his face close to mine. He covered me even as everyone around us ran.

"I know, sweetie." I wished I could see what was going on. Dev was gone, dragged away by his guard. Danny was off chasing an assassin.

"It hurts and I think it's in my left cheek," he whispered.

I raised my head slightly and caught a glimpse of the offending arrow. It was lodged firmly in Neil's left cheek. With his healing powers, we would be cutting that sucker out. "Sorry, babe. It's definitely the left cheek."

"But that's my perfect cheek," he said, resting his forehead against mine. "I'm gay, Z. My ass is my money-maker. I'm scarred for life."

He wasn't. He would heal and his butt wouldn't be any worse for the wear, but I have some experience with arrows and I knew they hurt like hell.

"Are you okay? You know, is everything okay? Even the small stuff?" He had hit me hard, trying to make sure he took the screaming arrow instead of me. He'd acted instinctively and with no thought for the fact that I might be carrying a child.

"I'm fine." I was in absolutely no pain. I was arrow free so I was calling this a win.

"Let me go!" Dev yelled, and I could hear the fury in his voice as the royal guard carried him away. They carried him bodily into the relative safety of the tavern. "Get my wife. I'm not going without my wife."

But he was. God inside or not, he wasn't proof against five immortal, well-trained warriors of the *sidhe*. He and Declan were hustled out of the line of fire. Declan obviously hadn't debriefed his full guard because he was yelling orders, too.

"Her Grace is more important," he ordered even as they dragged him away. "Protect her!"

They weren't listening and wouldn't do anything about me until their future king and their current High Priest were safe and sound. I was just some chick Prince Dev had married, and he could probably find another who looked just like me.

Sarah, Felix, and Zack rushed to my aid. Now that the place was quieter, they managed to surround me. Felix helped Neil up while Zack kept watch over the courtyard. He had a gun in his hand and his eyes moved, watching for any further trouble. Sarah got to her knees beside me.

"Are you all right?" She smoothed the hair from my forehead. "The area's clear."

"I've got a good line of sight, Zoey. You can get up now," Zack said. "Are you hurt? Neil took you down pretty hard."

Screw the royal guard. I'd take my crew any day of the week. Sarah helped me up. I struggled to my feet. "I'm fine. Neil's ass took the bullet for me."

I was used to fighting for my life but the whole assassination thing didn't give a girl much of a shot. It was a bit unsettling, and I was gratified by the fact that we were almost alone now. Even the satyr and gnome had rushed into the tavern. I stretched, making sure everything was moving, and then got to my knees to take a look at Neil's injury.

The crowd had dispersed the minute they realized there was going to be violence. Now, it was actually fairly quiet with the singular exception of my husband's continuing vitriol. I could hear him from the tavern where the guard had him under protective custody. The only one shouting as much as Devinshea was Declan.

"Zack, I'm going to need a knife." I tried to gently probe the arrow wound. It had ruined the tan pants Neil was wearing. The arrowhead must have been large because the wound was huge. I didn't want to think about what it would have done to my chest.

Neil gasped. "No, Z, you are not cutting up my butt."

Zack pulled a wicked stiletto out of his boot, offering it to me. He frowned as he stared at the tavern where Dev was proving he knew lots of cuss words. "Should I go save my boss from the people trying to save him?"

I shook my head. "He'd kick your ass for leaving me, Zack. They won't hurt him. Danny and Lee will be back any minute one way or another. As soon as they return, I assume the guard will let Dev go and try to figure out if we're alive or not. Well, they'll let Dev go or Danny will probably kill them all." Danny was a little possessive. He wouldn't like the idea of the guard hauling Dev away. "Neil, sweetie, I have to cut this out or you're never going to sit down again."

"I'll just stand," Neil vowed tearfully.

"Birds are going to perch on your ass, babe." Sarah put a hand on his shoulder.

"I like birds." He did. He liked to eat them.

Zack rolled his eyes, reached down, and with one brutal move pulled the arrow out of Neil's cheek. There was a long, loud howl that filled the courtyard.

"Zack, that was rude." I got to my feet and fixed the werewolf with a stern stare.

Zack shrugged, utterly nonplussed at my outrage. "It's like pulling off a Band-Aid, man. Do it quick. Take the pain. The anticipation is worse than the pain."

"No, it wasn't. The anticipation didn't hurt." Neil was holding his wounded buttock and asking Sarah to make sure it was healing to its normal lovely self.

Daniel hit the ground in front of me, and before I realized he was there, I was in his arms. He ran his hands all over me, searching for any possible injury.

I submitted to the inspection. He wouldn't be satisfied until he was sure. "I'm fine, Danny. Neil got hit, but I'm fine."

Daniel looked down at Neil, frowning. He could see the blood, but the wound had already closed. Neil was getting up with a hand from Felix. He looked at Daniel, but they didn't say anything to each other. It had been like this ever since Neil had come back. They circled each other and the rest of us just waited for the blow up.

Lee walked up, lugging an unconscious body behind him. He dragged the tall faery by the neck of his shirt with ease. He nodded my way. "You okay?"

I nodded.

Lee patted Neil on the shoulder. "Good job, buddy. Nice moves. It was smart of you to take that arrow in your ass. It's much easier to heal than your stomach or a lung." The older wolf turned his attention to Daniel. "What are we going to do with this asshole until he wakes up? I'd say we could lock him in the coffin but it kind of exploded."

"I didn't have time to ask nicely for someone to open up," Daniel murmured as he moved under the shade of a tree, pulling me with him. While Daniel could daywalk, he felt more comfortable in the shade. "Where the hell is Dev?"

There was both anger and a small amount of panic in the question. Daniel tended to take off without checking because he knew Dev would be there to take care of me.

"The royal guard hauled him into the tavern the instant Lee called the alarm," Felix explained. "He fought but there were five of them."

It looked like everyone was fine, so I decided it was time to go save Dev. Daniel nodded as I passed him, following behind me.

I crossed to the doors of the tavern and called out so no one shot another damn arrow my way. "I'm coming in. Don't shoot."

"Zoey." Dev was finally allowed to push his way out of the phalanx of guards. They stood down and allowed the twins to move. Several of the guards rushed out to secure the courtyard even as Danny followed me inside the tavern.

"Are you all right, sweetheart?" Dev hugged me to him, his arms wrapping around me. "I swear I'll have every one of those fucking guards in the dungeon."

Danny strode up to Declan, pointing an accusatory finger his way. "You left her out there. This is how you treat your brother's wife? You leave her out to die?"

Declan shook his head. "I did not have a choice."

"You wanted us to come in with no security, Your Highness." Daniel's voice went low, predatory. "Was there a reason for that? Were you planning on taking us out?"

Declan went pale at the accusation. "I wouldn't assassinate my own brother, vampire."

"I wasn't talking about Dev," Danny snarled. "I was talking about me and Z. I was talking about the two people in a relationship with your precious brother. Did you think he would stay here if you killed us?"

"I don't think Declan would do that." There was a fine tremble in Dev's hands as he held mine.

The guard tried to get between Daniel and Declan, but the prince wouldn't have it. He shoved them aside, preferring to get into the vampire's space. It wasn't a smart move, but no one could accuse Declan of cowardice. "I might think about getting rid of you, but I assure you I have no intention of hurting Zoey. She is…"

"Really tired," I broke in, hoping to stop Declan from running his mouth. The last thing I needed was for Declan to announce that he thought I was pregnant. Besides, Daniel was wrong. "I don't think Declan tried to kill me, Danny. He'd be more likely to kill you and hope I'd let him apply for your place in bed."

"I have thought of that on occasion," Declan admitted. "It would make things simpler. I was not behind this attempt. We need to focus on what is important. Guard, you must search the town and find this would-be assassin."

Lee walked into the tavern dragging his prize behind him. "I'll save you the trouble, Your Highness. Donovan and I took care of it."

"Is he alive?" Declan looked down at the man but there was no spark of recognition in his eyes.

"Of course," Lee replied. "He was a wimp, though. One friendly tap from the vampire and he went out. I guess you faeries aren't as tough as you like to say you are."

The way the faery's face was swelling up, it looked like more than just a love tap. That man had been lucky Lee had been there or Danny might have taken him apart. I was sure Lee had been the voice of reason. We needed him alive. I was certain Danny would get his kill in later after certain questions had been answered.

Declan flushed, embarrassed by the accusation. For all of his flaws, Declan didn't back down from a fight. It must have chafed to be treated like something that needed protection. Now he had to admit the outsiders, people he considered common criminals, had handled the situation better than his precious guard. Declan shook off his emotions and charged on. "He must be brought in for questioning. We must figure out if this is a lone, unstable person or part of a larger plot."

I was betting on the larger plot. I hadn't been in Faery for more than a day, so it would surprise me if I already had enemies. It usually took me a couple of days before I had a group who collectively wanted to kill me. This wasn't about me, though I had been the target.

Someone didn't like the royal family.

Dev was getting his feet back under him and now that the immediate threat was over, he stared his brother down. I got the feeling he was ready to fight Daniel for a piece of Declan. "You will inform the guard that I can handle myself."

"Do not be ridiculous, brother. I am not going to tell the guard to back off you," Declan declared. "You are a precious resource for this kingdom. Not only are you a royal, you are second in line for the throne and an ascended god. You must have a guard. My only mistake was not placing a guard on Zoey. I believe I tried to get you to allow it."

"Yes," I agreed. "That royal guard of yours would have been helpful."

"Finally, she listens to reason," Declan said.

"They would have been good at carrying out my corpse," I admitted. "Your guard did nothing until Lee raised the alarm. They didn't notice the assassin. My wolf did and Neil had me covered before your boys thought to show up. Keep your guards, Dec. I'll put my wolves up against them any day of the week."

I looked down at the man unconscious on the floor. His face was a mottled mess, and I could tell very little about him except that he'd pissed off Danny.

"I don't think I know him," Dev admitted.

"Neil, Zack." Lee called his little army to come forward. "Get his scent. Memorize it."

Everyone in the tavern watched as the wolves got on all fours and ran their noses everywhere. They took their time and cataloged the lightest of smells that could come in handy later.

"Why do they need to do this?" Declan frowned, watching them. "When he wakes up, we will ask him questions and he will answer."

Lee's brown eyes rolled. "Yes. He'll just tell you everything he knows because he wants to help."

"Well, I intended to torture him," Declan admitted.

Daniel looked down at the man who probably didn't have long to live. "I'll get him to talk."

Dev agreed. "Nothing you do, brother, can be as persuasive as Daniel when he gets his freak on. Trust me. One look at Dan's beast and this asshole will be begging to make a full confession. We'll handle the interrogation."

"I have to think about it." A stubborn look settled on Declan's face.

"She is our wife." Daniel's fangs had popped out.

"Fine, you can ask the questions," Declan agreed with a long-suffering sigh. "We will hold him at the palace until he recovers enough for us to beat him again. I'll get our best healer on it. I want him healthy for his torture."

The boys argued about which fun torture method would work the best, the wolves continued their scent adventure, and I couldn't help but think. No one knew about my possible pregnancy. I'd been married to Devinshea for roughly two weeks. It wouldn't occur to these people, who waited decades to get pregnant, that I might already be carrying a child. Since it was obvious Declan had kept his big mouth shut, I discounted the attempt had been made because of the child. I didn't set policy or have anything to do with politics. I hadn't even met my mother-in-law yet. So while I was the pawn, I wasn't the true target. Someone thought my death would hurt a member of the royal family.

This had to be about Devinshea.

"You're sure you don't know him?" I asked husband number two.

He studied the assassin again. "I don't know. It's hard to tell. Dan messed him up."

Neil and Zack were on their feet again. Zack looked at his boss. "If it helps I think he works with candles."

"Yeah, he smells like beeswax," Neil agreed. "It's all over his hands. He also smells like cabbage. Eww."

"Doesn't ring a bell," Dev said with a shake of his head. "Sorry."

"Well, maybe you know his wife or his girlfriend or his daughter," I pointed out with a humorless smile.

"What is that supposed to mean?" Dev asked.

"This isn't about me," I said flatly. "You and Declan were prime targets but they chose me. If they wanted to take out a member of the royal family, they would have gone for the two of you. So this is about hurting someone. They don't know Daniel so this has to be about Dev."

Dev and Declan passed a long look between the two of them. It was one of those moments when they might as well be telepathic. Declan sighed and nodded his head after a long moment. Dev looked angry but turned to me.

"It's going to be all right, sweetheart." He took my hands in his.

"Yes, it is," Daniel agreed, his face taking on that stoic look I knew way too well. "I'm going to make sure it's fine. We'll be home before you know it. I can fly us to the door in less than half the time it took to walk."

"I'm not going anywhere, Danny," I said, knowing his plan before he said it.

"We can't leave, Dan." Dev shook his head. "We have too many things we have to accomplish before we leave."

Daniel crossed his arms stubbornly. "Maybe you can't leave but Z sure as hell can. Someone tried to kill her, Dev."

"I have a job to do," I stated implacably. "You can haul me out of here, Daniel Donovan, but I'll be back the minute you fall asleep."

"Not if I lock you up, you won't." He leaned over in a useless attempt to intimidate me.

I went up on my toes so our noses were close. "You promised me you would stop doing this." We'd had a big fight about trust and I thought we had gotten past this "trying to protect me" crap.

Danny shook his head. "Not even close, baby. I promised I wouldn't leave you again. I'm not trying to leave. It's the opposite. I'm going with you. I never promised not to tie you up. As a matter a fact, I tied you up last night and you were damn happy about it."

"That was for fun." It had been a hell of a night. The boys had tied me up, blindfolded me, and made me guess who was doing what to me. I actually got hot thinking about it now, but it was a cunning distraction and I couldn't fall for it. "You're talking about actual, not sexy, bondage. Not happening, Danny. Besides, Dev already knows who did it so we'll be fine once he proves his ex-honey Gilliana is behind everything."

Gilliana was Dev's wife at one point in time before the queen annulled their marriage. I'd been told she was a bit perturbed at the thought of a new Mrs. Quinn.

"How did she know that is what we were thinking?" Declan asked, his jaw dropping slightly.

Dev smiled. "Because she's clever. Yes, my wife, I think it was Gilliana or at the least her family. We'll know more once we get this one awake and talking." He motioned to the unconscious faery.

"I knew it was someone you slept with or someone related to someone you slept with," I muttered under my breath.

Declan rolled his aristocratic eyes. "Well, Zoey, if we went by that then our list of suspects would be…everyone in the *sithein*. It is much easier to count the women Devinshea forgot to sleep with than the ones he actually did."

"That is rude," Dev shot back.

"And true," Declan responded, unwilling to back down. "We could do a hand count. Anyone who has slept with Prince Dev or had a relative sleep with him could raise their hands."

"Don't you dare, brother," Dev hissed. His fists were clenched as he spoke to his brother, but he finally relaxed and chose to turn back to Danny and me. "You knew I had a past. Anyway, it doesn't matter because it's Gilliana. No one else hates me enough to do it. I was actually quite kind to my partners."

Danny nodded. "Padric mentioned I should watch out for her."

"Excellent." Declan took control, snapping his fingers at his guard. "Then we can go to the palace and sort this all out. The guard will surround us and we will move quickly. We shall travel as true trooping faeries. I will send servants for the luggage. We shall be at the palace within moments."

"I have a problem. Does anyone have an extra pair of pants?" Neil turned around and his whole left cheek peeked through the cotton.

Dev bent over, laughing at the sight. Daniel put his hand over his mouth to try to hide his smile. Sarah just pointed out the problem to Felix.

"Oh, sweetie." She tried not to giggle. "You spray tanned before we left." I remembered the day. I'd gotten a facial while Neil got a nice glow he was sure he would need in Faery.

"Yes," he said impatiently. "I need a tan or I look ghastly."

Zack couldn't seem to stop giggling. "Dude, I pulled out a hunk of flesh when I took that arrow out of your ass."

"OMG, I don't match." Neil announced what the rest of us had already figured out. "Nice, Z. I save your life and what do I get for it? Mismatched butt cheeks."

I hugged him and smiled brightly. "We'll find someplace quiet and sunbathe nude. I promise you'll match soon enough."

"Fine," he said with a pout.

I took his hand as the royal guard began to herd us toward the exit. We would walk to the palace surrounded by a phalanx of guards. Lee pulled his quarry behind him and Danny and Dev argued about how to prove Dev's ex was behind everything. I held Neil's hand and looked up at the white palace that got closer with each step.

"I already want to go home, Z," Neil admitted.

I sighed and squeezed his hand because I knew the feeling.

Chapter Four

"She gave us three different rooms?" I asked the small creature who had guided me to what I assumed was our dressing room. Now I looked around and saw that only my luggage had been delivered.

When we'd reached the shining palace, we'd been divided up. Daniel had met with Padric and the two had decided the first order of business was to take the prisoner to the "holding cells." They actually used those words as they looked at me like they didn't want me to know there were dungeons. As I planned on visiting the dungeons later, I didn't see how they were going to keep it from me. I had some questions for my would-be assassin that I would like answered, too. With Daniel, Lee, and Zack following Padric, Sarah and Felix were shown to their room. Dev had been told he had business with Declan, and that left me and Neil looking down at my brand new social secretary.

The small troll bit her lip and looked about, wondering how to respond to me. She was dressed in the same flowing skirts as the Seelie around her, though the style swallowed her small body. She had brown hair and eyes and her long tail peeked out from under the skirt. Even as Mara had introduced her to me, she seemed nervous and on the verge of tears. She reminded me of a scared little mouse.

It looked like Mara had decided to play games with me. I should have expected it. I'd been warned by my brother-in-law that the royal court was a place of back stabbing and mind games, but I'd been hoping for something better. I hadn't missed the way Mara and her friends had laughed behind their hands as they introduced me to Bibi. I bet the rest of the royals didn't have trolls for their social secretaries.

"I am sure that Mara wanted you to be comfortable, Your Grace. You have the whole room to yourself. Perhaps she thought you would like that." Bibi's voice was tremulous.

I began to understand that becoming a social secretary to the human wife of a high priest had probably not been her idea. It was Mara's idea of an insult since the troll was obviously ill equipped to be involved in organizing a high-society social life. I wondered where Mara had picked her up. From the dirt under her nails, I suspected the gardens.

"I'm sure Mara wanted me to feel alone," I murmured, looking around. The room was airy and magnificent. Every inch of the palace was natural stone, mostly white marble. It was stunning, but it wouldn't do because I had no intention of being away from my husbands. It had been so long since I slept alone I doubted I would remember how to do it.

Neil jumped onto the bed. "Look at this, Z. It would barely hold you and me. What are these people thinking?"

He was right. The bed was maybe a queen when we were used to the oversized king in the penthouse that required specially made sheets to fit it. That bed was a monster but then it held me, Danny, and Dev, and occasionally Neil when he whined enough and Dev let him in. Neil wasn't good at sleeping alone, either.

I cocked an amused eyebrow at Neil as I walked over to the window. The view was like a painting. Everything was vibrant and green, with slate-colored mountains touching the brilliant blue sky. I could see the snow-capped peaks in the distance, but here in the valley it was summertime and the air was gauzy and sweet. I let the sunlight warm my skin for a moment before getting back to the problem at hand.

"I think you're going to have to sleep with Zack, babe. Three in a bed looks like it's going to be hard here, much less trying for four."

Zack wouldn't mind. Lee was the odd wolf who preferred to sleep alone, but Zack would think nothing of Neil crawling into bed with him. It was like that for werewolves. There was nothing sexual about it but they preferred a lot of physical contact.

Neil walked up to me and threaded his hand through mine. "That's okay. I like Zack."

I turned to him, and my question was laced with just a bit of fear. "You like Zack, or you like like Zack?"

I hoped that wasn't it. He and Chad seemed happy the one night they'd had together in Colorado. Chad was due to come home from the Council in Paris in a few months, and he would expect his boyfriend to be waiting. Vampires don't like it when you break up with them. They tend to be possessive creatures.

He rolled his eyes and contorted his face to let me know I'd said something distasteful. "No. Ewww. He's like…"

My heart warmed because I knew what he was thinking. For the first time in his life, Neil had wolves around who didn't hurt him or make him feel less. He had a small pack and it made him happy. "…a brother?"

"A real, actual one," Neil said with a shrug, trying not to get too emotional. "I guess Zack is what I thought a brother should be like. He annoys me with his butt kissing and his perfect obedience. Most of the time, I want to throttle him. But then I know he has my back. I like hanging out with him. We might not have a ton in common, but that's okay. I'm totally going to get him back for the arrow thing, though."

I nodded. Revenge was important in our world. I turned and looked at Bibi, who only reached my shoulders, or she would if she stood up straight. Bibi seemed to be trying to shrink into herself. Still, she had a job to do, and it was time she learned how to do it. "Please inform Mara that I will be sleeping with my husband. She can either move my luggage or I will move it myself. Daniel will also be joining us in whatever room Prince Devinshea has been given. They might not recognize my marriage to Daniel, but Dev certainly does."

Without a doubt, Dev would have the best room. He was a prince, after all.

"You want me to tell her?" Bibi asked, her dark eyes wide with fear. "You want me to speak to her?"

I walked back toward the troll. It was time to start making the best of things. If Mara thought I was going to bitch and complain and beg for a better assistant, then she was wrong. I sat down on the bed so I was at eye level with Bibi. "Yes, Bibi, I want you to tell Mara that she has made a dreadful error and must fix it right away. You tell her your mistress is insulted and will probably do something terrible if she doesn't get her way."

Bibi shrank back. Her whole body shook. "I will carry the luggage myself. Please don't harm me."

"No, sweetie." Neil knelt down beside her. He was sincere as he dealt with the frightened girl who was probably older than all of us combined. "You aren't getting it. She isn't going to hurt you. You're part of the team now. Zoey here is loyal to her crew. She might yank out that hair of Mara's though."

"What is a crew?" Bibi asked, shyly smiling at Neil. Her eyes were big as she took in Neil's blond hair and light blue eyes. She sighed as he smiled at her.

Trolls have no gaydar.

"It means you're with us now," Neil explained. "You work for Zoey, so you're one of the gang. If someone messes with you, then we handle it."

Bibi thought about this for a moment. Big tears shone in her eyes as she looked up at me. "But I am a gardener and a troll. It is an insult to you. They meant to shame you by placing me in your household."

"Then they did a terrible job, Bibi." They hadn't done their research on me. "Would you like to know a secret? I was practically raised by trolls. They were Huldrefolk, like you. Daniel and I spent many summers walking the bridges. You are not an insult to me. You're a cherished reminder of my home." Just the day before we left for Faery, I'd gone to say good-bye to my adoptive summer parents, Ingrid and Halle. They had been filled with advice on how to survive Faery.

"She told the others you would be upset by me," Bibi told me. "She said I would be awful and you would come begging for her help."

I was going to have to have a little talk with Mara. It sucked because my plan coming in was to try to blend in as much as possible. I was going to try to be what Devinshea needed me to be. I planned on learning how to be a member of this family, but it was looking more and more like I was going to have to be me. If terrifying trolls and going all mean girl on the new kid was what passed for family here, then they were going to get the full Zoey Wharton Donovan Quinn treatment.

"I think you'll make a fine social secretary once we figure out what you're supposed to do," I assured the troll. "That will be the real challenge because I have never been a member of a royal court before. We'll just have to learn together."

I hoped not to have to learn too much, though. I had more to do than learn royal protocols. We had a war to deal with at home, and the truth was I was anxious to get back to it. I needed to find the stone for Marini and then figure out how I could screw him over with it.

"I have a schedule," Bibi offered. "Tonight you have the meeting with the queen. I am supposed to make sure you are dressed properly. Prince Declan selected a gown for you."

There was a large closet across the room. I decided to have a look at what Declan considered "proper." I just hoped the damn dress actually had a bodice. I wouldn't put it past him to give me something that showed off way too much of me. I stared at the dress that hung alone in the massive closet.

This was what I was supposed to wear to dinner with the queen tonight? I laughed because it was blatantly obvious someone had switched it out. Declan might be a complete dick, but he had no desire to humiliate me. Declan would never have picked out that bland color or the hideous cut of the dress. He considered himself a fashionable prince. The person who had swapped the dresses must have thought I was an idiot or didn't know Declan. The prince would never in a million years have selected something that didn't leave my boobs hanging out. I wondered where the real one was but decided it was long gone.

"Ewww, Z. Did Declan lose his mind?" Neil pulled at the mucky brown fabric.

Bibi walked up, shaking her head. "That is not the right gown. The one the prince ordered was beautiful. It was made of fine fabric and the color was a lovely green. This is terribly old-fashioned. It is a gown an elderly country woman would wear, certainly not the wife of a high priest."

I giggled. I couldn't help it. I was back in junior high. I should watch out because someone was going to try to steal my boyfriend next.

Bibi looked close to tears. "It is not funny, my mistress. You will be a laughingstock. Appearances are important here. There is no time to make another and I am afraid you will not fit into the other women's dresses. They are much taller than you. This is a disaster."

But Neil was already working on it. He had pulled open the oversized wardrobe Dev himself had packed for the three of us. It had designer wear in case we got tired of the middle ages. It was a mini closet and I felt bad for whoever had been forced to lug it from the *sithein* door all the way to the palace. I'd argued with Dev that there was no way we needed designer dresses and suits and now I would have to eat my words.

"I think the candy-red Vivienne Westwood," he pronounced, pulling out the stunner with a heart-shaped bodice. "It's both hot and haute!"

"Works for me." If the mean girls thought they could get me down, they could think again. I might not fit in exactly, but in that dress I was going to stand out and not in a bad way. I hadn't worn it yet but I expected Dev and Danny would like it. Besides, the flowy styles they preferred here were for tall, lithe women. I have curves and the Westwood would hug those curves in all the right places. And it would allow me to dump the slippers in favor of heels. I was tired of being the munchkin in the room. "Shoes?"

"Oh, there's no question," Neil said as though the answer was staring me in the face. "The gold d'Orsay pumps. The Manolos. They're the perfect counterpoint to the Goddess Chain." He opened the trunk that housed my shoes, and I watched Bibi's mouth drop open.

"They are so beautiful," Bibi breathed, looking at the shoes like she was an art student getting her first glimpse of a da Vinci. She looked at me for permission and I nodded. She pulled out my purple peep-toe Louboutins. She had a good eye.

"I think she's having a shoegasm," Neil said with a smile.

"Hey, she has small feet," I noted. "She might be able to wear my shoes."

Bibi looked startled. "You would let me wear your footwear?"

"Yes, but you have to practice first." I didn't want to be responsible for her broken ankle. "Those are four- to five-inch heels. They take some getting used to."

"Yes, I remember several times my mistress almost broke an ankle trying to walk in her shoes," a deep voice intoned. "It was then I knew she truly loved my master because it seemed like torture to me, yet she did it to please him."

I smiled at Albert, who stood in the doorway holding a tray. The seven-foot demon looked stately in his white dress shirt and slacks. Our butler had traveled ahead to the palace days before. Albert had insisted he needed the time to whip the palace into shape.

"I have brought you afternoon tea, mistress," Albert announced with a smile. "It is a lovely Darjeeling with freshly baked madeleines."

My stomach reminded me I hadn't eaten earlier, and I took a seat on the couch in the sitting area while Albert served. This morning, food had just completely lost its appeal, but I was getting my appetite back. Neil looked at the cookies, trying not to salivate.

"Is there a reason you're not sharing a room with the masters?" Albert asked, his tone one of grave disappointment. Albert was a romantic. He believed married couples should cohabitate, even when the couple was a trio.

"Don't blame me," I shot back, taking a sip of the tea. It was, as always, perfect. Everything Albert did was sheer perfection. "I just went to the room I was assigned to. I'm working on remedying it right away. If I stay here, Dev and Danny will crawl into that little bed with me and I'll get smooshed in the middle."

Bibi moved from the shoes and was looking at the delicate cookies. I could hear her stomach rumble and wondered if anyone had thought to give the troll lunch. I held one out for her and she took it shyly.

"Bibi, this is Albert." I made the introductions. "Albert runs our household. Albert, Bibi is my new secretary."

Albert bowed deeply. "It is a pleasure to make your acquaintance, miss. Please, if there is anything I can do to help you, let me know. I am here to serve."

That was when Bibi burst into tears. Neil and I exchanged looks. I told him wordlessly that he could take this one. She responded well to him.

Neil looked at the little troll. "Don't let Al scare you. He's big but he's a pussy cat."

She shook her head vigorously. "No, he is nice. You are all so nice. I just wish they weren't so mean."

Neil's light eyes narrowed suspiciously. "Bibi, you're a small creature. Sometimes people don't even notice you're around, do they? They talk around you and pretend you don't exist."

Bibi nodded, sniffling slightly. "Yes, they don't care that I am there. It is like they think I do not have ears, but I do."

"Do you know what Mara is planning?"

The troll stopped, and for a moment I thought she would let her fear keep her silent. I couldn't blame her. She'd been trained to fear her "betters." After a long moment, she came to a decision, and I watched as she steeled herself for what was likely her first foray into rebellion.

"It is not Mara who is plotting," she exclaimed. "It is her cousin. She is vile. She doesn't like my new mistress and has sworn to ruin her in the eyes of the nobles."

I sighed because I could guess what was coming. "Is Mara's cousin's name Gilliana?"

Bibi's eyes widened. "Yes, and she was the one who put you in separate rooms so she could enchant the prince. She wants to force him to give her a babe. She was angry he took another wife. She thinks he will take her back if she carries his child."

I calmly set the tea down and was proud of myself because my head didn't explode, though it threatened to. Blood was pulsing through my body, and I wondered briefly if that maddening rage was what Danny felt when his beast came out. I took control of my intense, crazy-bitch rage and managed to speak to Bibi in something close to a calm tone. "Bibi, sweetie, this is important. Where is Gilliana now?"

"She is in Prince Dev's room. She is lying in wait with a spell to entrance him."

I stood, fury oozing from my every pore. Neil smiled because he knew the scene I was about to cause would stand the test of time. It was going to be legendary, and he wasn't about to miss it. I was sure he thought about getting Sarah, but I wasn't waiting on an audience.

"I'll need…" I began.

"Cold iron," Albert supplied helpfully. He reached into his pocket and pulled out a small but lethal-looking knife. It was made from cold forged iron, the true weapon to use against a Fae. "I try to be prepared for your every need. On entering the palace, I realized you would need to maim or kill someone in order to take your rightful place. These are truly dreadful people, mistress. They will not respect you until they fear you. I pulled the knife out of the luggage early this morning."

"Thank you, Albert," I managed around my volcanic rage. "Bibi, take me to my husband's room."

As we walked out, Albert was already cleaning up. "I'll have your luggage delivered to Prince Dev's room and Master Daniel's as well. Call me if you need someone to clean up the blood, mistress. I'm always ready to help."

I walked calmly through the halls of the palace, holding my cold iron knife carefully against my thigh. I didn't want anyone to raise the alarm.

When dealing with backstabbing, man-stealing, spell-using bitches, it helps to have the element of surprise. I had this with Gilliana on several fronts. First, she thought I was somewhere on the other side of the palace, far away from my probably horny husband. I was supposed to be dealing with my completely inappropriate social secretary. There should have been much time lost as I dealt with Mara, who was undoubtedly ready to take one for the team. While I handled both the room situation and the problems with staff, Gilliana would have time to pull whatever she needed to pull.

The second of her misconceptions was about me. She more than likely thought she was dealing with a lovely airhead since I'd been told over and over that was Dev's preferred type. Lovely airhead—even if she managed to figure out the plot—would just sit around and cry. She would not march into her husband's room and confront the big, scary, spell-wielding woman.

Albert was right. It was time to let these people know I wasn't an easy mark. It was my responsibility to stake a claim. This court ran on intrigue and the constant fear of someone using you as a stepping stone. After I brought my own personal stone down on a couple of their heads, they would learn not to step on me.

"This is the prince's wing," Bibi explained.

Of course he had his own wing, but Danny and I had been shoved to another part of the palace entirely. This wing of Dev's was huge with many rooms. It was obviously for his family, but Mara had chosen to leave him here alone and vulnerable to her cousin's plots. Mara didn't know it yet, but she'd been fired.

"The last room is Prince Dev's bedroom." Bibi pointed to the closed door at the end of the hall.

I looked down at the troll and thought I should probably warn her. "Look here, Bibi," I said, amazed at how calm my voice was. On the inside, I was already beating the shit out of my husband's ex. "I'm going in there and there's probably going to be some bloodshed. I intend to make quite the impression on Gilliana. If this frightens you, then you should go back and wait with Albert. I'll return as soon as Gilliana knows who the boss is."

Bibi's brown eyes lit with a happy bloodlust. "I do not mind blood, mistress. Well, so long as it is not my own."

"See, you fit right in," Neil noted. He would enjoy the fight as well.

"Then feel free to watch," I said, hearing the coldness in my own voice. "Tell everyone what you see."

I strode down the hallway and kicked the door open for maximum surprise. I walked into my husband's bed chamber and sure enough it was pretty damn awesome. It was also empty.

"This is way better than our room." Neil shook his head as he took in the enormous suite.

"Neil, focus." We were in what could only be described as a

sitting room. This was where the prince would entertain friends. I needed to know where the prince would entertain special guests.

Neil took a deep whiff of the air and immediately pointed to a door on the far wall. I started toward it when Neil warned, "They're in there, both of them. Z, you better hurry. He's aroused."

"Tell me something I don't know, Neil." I slowed down. I had an idea of what was likely happening behind that door, but I didn't know what kind of magic she was using. I was running on adrenaline, and it suddenly occurred to me that I should have waited for Sarah.

"Baby, you look so good. You're going to feel even better. Do you want what I have for you?" I heard Dev say in that voice that told me he was just about to start his happy dance.

Yeah, I wasn't going to wait. That happy dance belonged to me. I opened the heavy door and made my way inside. Afternoon sunlight streamed in through the big windows. A massive bed dominated the room. Declan had told me Miria herself had ordered the bed as a peace offering to her son. The bed was a testament to decadence and came complete with sexy curtains to shield Daniel from the sun. They'd been drawn for privacy and there was no way Dev had done that himself. He didn't give a crap about privacy. He'd screw me in the middle of a crowd if I let him.

"Give me a kiss," Dev said, his voice low and sexy.

I pulled the curtains open with one strong tug of my hand. If she hit me with a magical fireball or some shit, at least I'd stop that freaking kiss.

The two people on the bed froze like an erotic tableau. Dev was naked, his lean muscular body on display. I got the best look at his backside. He had an amazing ass. He'd stopped in the act of climbing on top of someone who looked just freaking like me. I flashed back to earlier in the day when Mara had commented on how we would have to tame my hair. She'd complained about the waviness. I'd thought it was weird when she ran her hand across my hair, but now I knew why. They needed a strand of hair to make the spell work.

I had to admit, looking down on myself in bed with Dev, I looked pretty damn hot. I always worry about that extra five pounds I carry around, but it was all curves. No wonder Danny liked to watch.

"Zoey?" Dev looked between the two of us, his gorgeous green eyes confused.

The Zoey who wasn't me cowered and held on to Dev. "Husband, it is a trick. She is a witch trying to confuse you. She will kill us both. Please save me." She clung to him and gave her role everything she had.

I rolled my eyes and promised myself I would never cower. It didn't look good on me. Gilliana could look like me all she wanted. The spell hadn't given her my personality. I looked at Dev with a flat frown. He was trying to pull away from the woman in his arms, but he still seemed a bit uncertain.

"Here's the deal, baby. I'm going to talk for a minute and you can decide which one of us is real." I looked down at Gilliana and pulled my knife. She shrank away. "All right, bitch, this is how it's going down. You get one warning and one warning only. I'm his wife. He married me and not because he was forced to screw me by some spell. He chose me. You had your chance and you blew it. Keep your hands off my husband or I'll be forced to remove them."

Dev practically leapt off the bed to get to my side. "The scary one is definitely my wife. What the hell is going on? I was about to come and look for you, but I got so tired. I laid down for a nap and you woke me up with your lovely naked body. I was quite happy to see you."

"How did you find out?" Gilliana asked, looking petulant and annoyed. "I set everything up perfectly. You should be with Mara now. You should be trying to fix the chaos."

I reached onto the bed and pulled myself out by my hair. Now the spell broke because her hair felt different from mine. Gilliana screamed as I hauled her off the bed and her glamour fell apart. I was left with a lovely, if bland, blonde. She had brown eyes and a skinny body. She probably had five inches on me, and I bet I outweighed her. The woman also had no idea how to fight. She didn't punch or try to take out my legs. She just yelled. She apparently thought screaming was going to make me let her go.

"Gilliana." Dev greeted his ex through clenched teeth. He crossed his arms, and I knew it was to keep himself from hitting her. "How dare you try this on me? I will have you imprisoned for this."

"Call the guard later, baby." I started to haul Gilliana out of his room by her long blonde hair. I had a good grip on it now, and she was surprisingly easy to drag. I had way more trouble with the friction of her bare ass on the marble than I did with her weight. Skinny bitches are good for something, I had to admit. "I have a reputation to stake."

I hauled the witch out of Dev's room, and she obliged me by kicking and screaming the whole way. Her screeching brought everyone out. Neil, Bibi, and Dev followed in my wake. Dev had slipped on his robe but followed me down the palace halls in his bare feet. He didn't try to explain anything or apologize. He knew there was no need. He also knew the value of a ferocious reputation. On our home plane, Dev had a reputation as a smooth talker who would smile one minute and stick his knife in the next. He was not a man you crossed.

I reached the greeting room after a long walk, all the while gathering gawkers. There was a huge crowd waiting to see why Her Grace, wife of the High Priest, was hauling a naked noblewoman through the halls of the royal palace. There was no way this story didn't make the rounds. By the time dinner rolled around, my reputation as a badass would be secure.

I was gratified to see Mara looking on with a horrified expression on her face. I gave her my most savage smile because she needed to remember this.

"Lady Gilliana decided it would be a good idea to trick my husband into her bed," I announced loudly. "I'm going to persuade her ladyship that this was a misstep." I let her head drop to the marble and before she could move, I shoved that cold iron into her chest making sure I stayed away from her heart. It would hurt like hell, but it wouldn't kill her. I stared down into her face, which was contorted with agony. "Next time, I'll kill you."

I pulled my knife out because I wasn't going to waste a perfectly good knife on her.

Dev grabbed my hand and pulled it to his mouth. He kissed my hand gallantly, letting everyone know he approved. When I looked over the crowd I noticed Danny, Lee, and Padric had joined. Danny was laughing but Lee and Padric looked almost paternally proud.

As Dev began to lead me away from the screaming Gilliana, I realized something. It made me frown and turned my stomach a little. If Gilliana had hired the assassin, why would she go to the elaborate trouble of this plan? It was intricate and depended on flawless execution. This had been her plan, not the archer.

Someone else was trying to kill me. It looked like I had a lot of enemies in the palace and it wasn't even dinnertime yet.

Chapter Five

"Did you want to make it to dinner?" Danny asked, staring at me. His fangs were lengthening as I smiled at him.

His eyes were on the heart-shaped bodice of my dress. It was strapless and left everything from the tops of my breasts up uncovered. The only jewelry I wore was my wedding ring and the Goddess Chain. I slipped into my four-and-a-half-inch heels. "You like?"

Daniel grinned, his dimples showing. "I hope you're not hungry because you might not make it to the banquet looking that good."

The way Daniel looked at me gave me just the boost of confidence I needed to make it through the night. I went up on tiptoes and planted a kiss on his perfectly sculpted lips. "I take that as a yes."

"Oh, I like." He leaned down to nuzzle my neck. I felt his tongue stroke the long line of my jugular vein. The last several weeks, Daniel had let his freak-flag fly high, and for me that meant dealing with his love affair with my neck. I dropped my head back and let him lick me, wondering if I was going to make it to our first state dinner. It would probably be rude to skip out on my reception because I was too busy in bed with husband number one.

"Damn, sweetheart," husband number two said, coming up from behind. His big hands slid across the red silk covering my backside.

"This is not the dress Declan picked. It's so much sexier." He cupped my rear and let his tongue trace the shell of my ear, eliciting a groan from me. "Goddess, you look gorgeous."

Yep, if they didn't stop soon I was going to miss everything.

"What made you change your mind about the dress?" Dev asked, rubbing his erection against my backside and letting me know how much he wanted me. Dev's rubbing pressed me firmly into Daniel, who was in the same condition. I let my hands slip down Daniel's trim waist to his rock-hard ass. "Not that I mind, lover."

"I didn't change my mind about the dress. Someone took it," I admitted breathlessly.

Both men stopped and Daniel looked down at me, his blue eyes now serious. "What do you mean someone took the dress? Did they take it away because it didn't fit you?"

I took a long breath to steady myself. If I had known they were going to get all freaked out and stop what they were doing, I would never have mentioned it. I was enjoying the whole "worshipping my body" part of the day, but I had to be honest. "No, I mean they took the dress Declan bought, unless you think he meant for me to wear that thing in the closet."

The boys exchanged a look and Dev crossed to the closet. He held the awful dress up and shook his head. "My brother would never pick this dress. First, it's hideous and completely out of fashion. Second, it covers your breasts. He likes your breasts, sweetheart. He talks about them all the time."

"Remind me to thank him for that," Daniel said sarcastically.

"I think they'll leave me alone now." I smoothed down my dress. It looked like I was going to make it to dinner now and I wanted to be wrinkle free. "I think the word is out that I don't like people touching my stuff." I said that with a pat to Dev's behind. I turned to Daniel. "That goes for you too, mister. Some girl starts in on you and I will take her out."

"Good to know, baby," he said with a sexy smile. "And that thing we just started, don't think we're done."

I was counting on it. This was my weird honeymoon. I'd married Dev only weeks before and Daniel and I had never been on a trip where we relaxed. We needed time together, time to bond.

"Mistress," a small voice said from the back of the room. I looked over and realized I'd forgotten Bibi was here. I winced because I hadn't meant to ignore the troll. I just forgot everything when my men walked in a room.

"Yes, Bibi," I replied, hoping I hadn't offended her. I doubted the foreplay would bother her, as trolls were open-minded, but I had yet to introduce her to Danny. She'd been introduced to Dev earlier. I made amends now and my vampire happily greeted the troll. Like me, he had a soft spot in his heart for the Huldrefolk. They were a part of our childhood.

Albert had been true to his word and now we were all happily ensconced in the east wing of the palace. Once we'd gotten rid of Mara, we'd had plenty of help moving into Dev's part of the palace. I had a whole room for nothing but getting dressed and primping. Sarah, Neil, and I had spent the afternoon getting settled in and talking to Bibi about palace life. Neil had been right about the troll. She knew an awful lot about the nobles. She knew who was sleeping with whom and who was cheating. She knew who was feuding and she liked to gossip. Once we got her talking, she had gone on for an hour as Sarah, Neil, and I had all gotten ready.

"It's time for you to depart," Bibi reminded me. She had a notebook and a clock to tell time. Though her voice was quiet, I knew she was trying to take her job seriously. "You and His Highness and Master Daniel are supposed to enter last. It's a great honor. All of the nobles want to see Prince Dev's first meeting with his mother after so long a time."

"You mean they want to gawk at a train wreck," Dev complained. He was nervous. Dev was dressed in traditional Seelie clothes, the emerald color of his tunic making his eyes even more green than normal. I smoothed back the midnight fall of his long hair. It was just past his shoulders. Normally he pulled it back, but now he left it long for the more formal occasion.

Danny had gone the same route I had. Modern. Contemporary. He was in a Hugo Boss suit that had been custom fit at Neiman Marcus. His sandy blond hair was slicked back. He looked hot and dangerous. He glanced at Dev and gave him a reassuring smile. "It's going to be all right. What's the worst she could do?"

Dev blanched at the thought but took my arm anyway. Danny took my left side and we began to walk toward the formal dining room where the nobles awaited our arrival. Our friends had gone in earlier and Lee and Zack had chosen to skip the formalities in exchange for taking guard duties.

"I don't even want to think about that." Dev shook his head as if to clear it from his dark thoughts. "Are you feeling better?"

It was said to Daniel, who as a vampire should only feel crappy when he was low on blood.

"What's wrong?" I asked, startled at the thought of him being ill.

"It was nothing." Danny shook it off. "Just earlier today, I felt weird. I got weak. Maybe I'm coming down with the flu."

"You can't get the flu, baby." I touched his forehead with my hand, seeking any sign of illness. Not surprisingly it was cool. Vampires don't do sick.

"He was in that hot coffin for two hours," Dev pointed out.

That shouldn't make a difference. It might have made Daniel uncomfortable, but from what I understood, it shouldn't have made him ill.

As we approached the uniformed guard who would announce us to the party, Danny shrugged away his earlier discomfort. "I'm sure that's what it was. I feel great now. It was actually kind of cool. It made me feel almost human. If it comes up again I'll be sure to tell Z because she likes to baby sick people."

"Well, I had to," I admitted. "When you were alive you turned into the biggest baby the minute you got a stuffy nose."

Dev nodded that we were ready to be announced and then we walked down a magnificent marble staircase. Twenty steps led us into a huge ballroom that had been set for the royal banquet.

I held on firmly to both their arms because the last thing I needed was to tumble down the stairs and break a limb. I looked out over the crowd and realized Dev had been right. Everyone was hoping for a big scene. They were whispering behind their hands and gawking. They moved their attention between the three of us and the woman at the end of the hall.

I glanced around the room and got my first glimpse of my mother-in-law.

Miria, Queen of Faery, sat upon her throne before me. There was a raised platform with three chairs. Miria sat on the largest of the three in between two slightly smaller thrones. All three were carved from oak and elaborate in their design. Declan sat in one to her right, a look of aloof superiority on his face. I'd been told the seat to her left was the one Dev used. There were several people standing around the queen, and I suspected they were counselors and high nobles. Padric stood closest to the queen. It was fitting as he was both the head of security for the royal family and the queen's lover.

Miria, Queen of Faery, was gloriously lovely. I was surprised to find she had long strawberry-blonde hair. I guessed the twins got their dark good looks from their father. Miria was fair but by no means bland. Her face was delicately sculpted, with high cheek bones and a lush mouth. Her eyes marked her as the twins' relative. They were emerald green and sparkled with the same intelligence Dev had.

"Dude," Daniel said as we approached the throne. "That's your mom?"

She didn't look old enough to be his mom, but that was the way it was with the Fae. They reached their prime and just stopped aging. Miria looked to be about twenty-five. Dev was twenty-seven now and would look older than his mother or brother had he not been taking Daniel's blood regularly. Daniel's blood stopped the aging process in humans when taken on a regular basis. I'd begun noticing that for Dev, it seemed to actually reverse aging a little. The fine lines around his eyes he got when he laughed had disappeared.

Miria tried to maintain her cool composure but the closer we got the more her eyes ate up the sight of her son. I saw her eyes get glossy with unshed tears, and she reached out to Declan. He patted his mother's hand and for a moment looked less like a brat prince.

"Good evening, Mother," Dev said formally as we reached the throne. He bowed deeply.

I could see her son's formal tone was not what the queen had been hoping for. "Devinshea, it is good to see you."

Dev didn't give her anything. He nodded but chose to introduce us rather than reply. "Mother, this is my goddess, Zoey. And this is my partner, Daniel Donovan. I assume Declan brought you up to speed on my living arrangements."

That last was said coolly and with just a hint of challenge. He was just begging for his mother to say something disparaging about his lifestyle.

Miria had none of that. She smiled broadly and stood, causing Declan to quickly get his butt up as well. She wore a lovely white gown and a crown that sparkled in the candlelight. "Yes, of course. Declan and Padric both spoke highly of your wife and partner."

Declan snorted at that. He didn't like Danny. It probably had something to do with the fact that Daniel had kicked his ass the first time they met. "I certainly did not. I spoke poorly of him."

Miria ignored her elder son. She stepped off the platform and walked to us. "It is so good to meet you, daughter," she said with what seemed like complete sincerity. The queen kissed my cheek and gave me a long look before turning to Dev and laughing brightly. "Well, Devinshea, you certainly brought a beauty home. You are lovely, dear."

"She is beautiful but not obedient," Declan noted. "That is not the dress I told her to wear."

"Hush," she admonished. "The dress is stunning and suits her far more than anything in our style. Our styles would swallow her beautiful body. Declan, you were right about her breasts. They are delicious looking."

The last bit was said with a slight breathless appreciation. I felt Danny tense beside me as he tried hard not to laugh at my sudden discomfort. My mother-in-law was looking me over with a sensual smile.

"I told you," Declan said with a lecherous grin.

Dev leaned over and whispered in my ear. "Mother swings both ways. Sorry I didn't mention that before."

I gave him a "what the hell" look but Miria was moving on to Daniel.

"I should be upset with your presence, Mr. Donovan," Miria said, looking him over. "Devinshea was supposed to keep you under control until I decided if you were dangerous or not."

Dev started to argue but Daniel stepped up to the plate.

"I assure you, Your Highness, I am perfectly harmless," he said with more charm than I'd heard him use on any woman but me. Dev was rubbing off on my vampire. Daniel was imitating his smooth tones.

Miria looked Daniel up and down, from his Ferragamo loafers to his perfectly cropped blond hair. "I doubt that, Mr. Donovan. I think you could do some serious damage."

I saw Padric roll his eyes and mutter, "Not again."

"How about I promise to be a good boy?" Daniel offered, his voice a dark seduction. I stopped myself from giggling because Danny was getting good at this.

"Please don't." Miria's lips curled up. "Where would be the fun in that?"

"Mother!" Dev said sounding completely prudish for the first time in my relationship with him.

Declan snickered beside his brother.

Miria turned her attention back to her son. "Well, Devinshea, when you bring such lovely partners home, what do you expect? They are exotic and look like they would be excellent bedmates. It would be rude not to admire them."

Yes, she was definitely Declan's mom.

"The Earth plane has changed my brother," Declan complained. "It has turned him into a squeamish old woman. He refuses to even think about sharing Zoey with me. He pulled a gun on me just for cuddling with her."

"I would have done worse." Daniel looked at Declan and his fangs were long suddenly. "And I don't need a gun."

The rest of the room was startled and seemed to take a big step back, but Miria stood her ground. She went toe to toe with Daniel. She was definitely interested in those fangs.

She spoke to her son but her eyes were on Daniel. "Declan, you should know vampires are possessive creatures. It is impressive that Devinshea was able to forge a ménage with such a powerful creature and his companion. It makes a statement about his prowess. I am proud of you, son. You have done well. Tell me, Mr. Donovan, do you bite my son?"

"As often as possible," Daniel replied with no hint of self-consciousness. "I find faery blood to be quite the treat."

"Yes," she returned with regret. "Unfortunately, it is why I was forced to close the mounds to your kind. Your kind likes our blood, and we tend to like your bite, Mr. Donovan. I found it to be a combustible mix."

"Please call me Daniel," my vampire offered smoothly.

"I will," Miria promised. "And you and your companion may refer to me as Miria or Mother if you like. I am your mother-in-law. Formally, of course, for Zoey, but I completely recognize your relationship and approve. I am pleased to welcome you. You will be treated as a member of this family, Daniel."

"Good," Dev said between clenched teeth. "Then you can stop hitting on him. And for the record, while I feed my partner, we are not lovers beyond the fact that we share Zoey."

Miria looked startled. "Whyever not, son? He is attractive. I did not raise you to be so close-minded. You should …what is that human term you told me about, Declan?"

"Hit that," Declan supplied helpfully.

"Yes, Devinshea, you should hit that," Miria said seriously.

Daniel finally lost it, and there were tears in his eyes as he laughed. He leaned over, whispering to Dev. "Shit, man, we should have come here earlier. This is awesome."

Dev turned to me. "My goddess, what are the chances of the floor opening up and swallowing me whole, sending me to a blissful oblivion?"

"Not so good. Sorry." Miria made me feel better about my dad.

"I think we should begin dinner now," Padric said sourly, looking at Daniel with a shake of his head. He took Miria's arm and started to lead her to the head table. Already servants were rushing to action.

Danny just couldn't help it. "Dev, your mom's a total cougar, man."

I grinned as Dev blushed for the first time in…ever. "My mother is five hundred thirty-two years old. Cougar does not apply."

"Sabertooth, then." Daniel just had to rub it in.

Yes, it was time for dinner since we'd already put on a show.

* * * *

Two hours later, I walked up and down the gallery halls of the palace, enjoying the quiet. I glanced up every now and then at the paintings that lined the walls. They were mostly portraits, likely of past kings and queens. The whole place was lit with soft candlelight, and the moonlight seemed to flow in from every open space. There was still a low murmur that came from the great hall, but I could finally think again.

Dinner had been an event. We'd been seated at the royal table, Dev on one side of me and Daniel on the other. Both of my men had been almost immediately engaged in political talk—Dev by his brother and mother and Daniel by a duke. I'd sat there eating some sort of salad and wishing that vodka was a staple in the Fae diet. It's not. I hadn't even been offered a glass of wine, not that I could have enjoyed it. I had found myself pushing food around on my plate since my appetite was gone again. The rest of the meal was a lot of me looking out over the banquet hall at people staring. I was surprised I wasn't feeling light-headed since I tended to crash when I ate as little as I had today.

When the meal ended and the dancing began, I found myself answering many somewhat invasive questions. There's no such thing as shame in the Fae world. They will ask all sorts of things you wouldn't expect to be asked about your private life.

The hardest part had been speaking with Braden, Gilliana's father. He was a duke or something and had apologized for his daughter's behavior. There was nothing at all sincere about it and he made sure both my husband and the queen heard him do it. There was something I didn't like about the duke.

I heard a sound at the end of the hall and turned. I wasn't alone, but then I never had been. Lee had followed me the whole time. Lee nodded at me as he leaned against the wall. He wasn't going to intrude but neither would he allow me to be alone.

"That is my father," Miria, who was going to intrude, said quietly. She stared up at the portrait we were standing under. The man in the portrait looked every bit the royal, but the artist had caught the slightest hint of mischief in his eyes.

I turned to my mother-in-law, who had Padric in tow.

"Yes, I see where Dev gets his looks." I measured my words carefully. This was what I'd been dreading. The time had come to decide how to deal with Dev's mother. It was obvious she loved her son, but she had also been behind the plot to force him into marriage with Gilliana. I didn't know whether to condemn her or thank her because it was that betrayal that sent Dev to my plane. If Miria hadn't tried that desperate ploy, I would never have met him.

"Yes, the twins look much like my father," she murmured, her eyes on the portrait. "Devinshea is the one who took after him in temperament, however. My father was a stubborn man and not so quick to forgive."

I turned to face her, not quite able to stop the words from coming out of my mouth. "Well, I've been with Dev for several years now and I find him forgiving when one deserves it."

"Zoey," Padric warned sharply.

Miria shook her head. "Stay out of this, Padric. I want the girl to speak her mind. She is my only conduit to Devinshea. She is my only hope for repairing the relationship."

"Do you want to make up with Dev because he ascended?" I wondered if that was the case. She hadn't invited us back to Faery until after his ascension.

"I want my son back because I love him," she spat back at me, her mouth tightening. It must be frustrating for a queen to deal with not getting what she wanted. She'd had hundreds of years of pure obedience from her subjects.

I wasn't her subject.

"You should have thought of that, Your Highness, when you chose to betray him." There was nothing for it now. I'd started this. I should just go all in. "I would warn you not to try it again. I wouldn't take kindly to those types of manipulations. Ask Gilliana. You try some witchcraft on my husband and you'll get the same treatment."

Miria's eyes narrowed as she looked at me, and I heard Lee move in behind me. He wouldn't care that she was a queen. He would pounce if he thought she was coming after me. "I could have you thrown in the dungeons for even threatening me."

"You could try. You might get me in your dungeons, but I doubt you could keep me there. Execution is your only choice, and I don't think that would win you points with your son." I had a sudden thought. "Unless you chose assassination. I did have an attempt on my life earlier today. You could have me killed and throw the suspicion on some poor scapegoat. I'm sure you have subjects who would throw themselves on the fire for you."

"Zoey, you go too far." Just as my bodyguard had moved in close, Padric staked his place now. He stood to Miria's side, towering over me. "You cannot accuse the queen."

Lee growled Padric's way, and his hand was on my arm, ready to yank me back at the merest hint of aggression.

Miria sighed and the anger left her body. "Stand down, Padric. If you could please have your guard do the same, daughter?"

I nodded at Lee, who took a step back. I was more than willing to allow the tension to dissolve now that I'd made a stand.

"You aren't like the others," Miria said, regarding me seriously.

"So I've been told." It was far better for her to understand that now.

"I was not behind the archer this morning," the queen stated. "The men seem to think Gilliana is, but I doubt it. It is not her way." She gave me a sly smile. "And after this day's events, I doubt she will try anything again. No, I rather think this is a plot of the Unseelies to attempt to create chaos. Our relations are not good. It is one of the things Devinshea can help us with. He always got along better than the rest of us with the dark court."

I wasn't so sure, but I wanted to stay out of politics if I could. If the Unseelie liked Devinshea, I doubted they would come after his goddess. The Unseelie had problems with fertility. It would be foolish of them to assassinate their only hope, but then I didn't have the Seelie prejudices. "I'm sure that once Daniel gets through with our guest we'll know something more. He plans on interrogating the prisoner tomorrow. My vampire can be persuasive."

Miria's smile was just the slightest bit bloodthirsty. "Yes, Padric informed me that the vampire would be questioning the prisoner tomorrow. I believe I will make myself available to witness that."

I just bet she would. Danny was going to give Dev the hardest time.

"I apologize for not forcing Gilliana to return to the country,"

Miria continued. "Padric advised me to do it, but she cried and promised to behave. I felt so bad for involving her in my plotting that I am afraid I went against my better judgment. She is on her way home now."

"So the duke told me." He'd complained about how he'd had to restructure his staff to escort her home. I took a long breath and decided to air out all the dirty laundry. "Why exactly did you trick Dev into sleeping with her?"

She stared at me for long enough that I thought she would walk away. Finally she nodded and began to speak. "I don't expect you to understand, but I will tell you anyway. You are important to my son, which makes you important to me. I am not human, obviously. Fae can die, as proven by the death of my father, but we don't tend to think of our loved ones dying. I fought for hundreds of years to have a child. Even with my father's fertility powers, Padric and I were never able to conceive a child. It was why I had to try with others, why we've never married. I can't tell you the joy I felt when I gave birth to my babies. It rapidly became clear to me Devinshea was the sweet one. Declan was strong and always took the lead but Devinshea…you could not see his smile and keep your heart intact. When I realized he was mortal…"

Miria faltered and Padric took over, his hand reaching out to slide over hers. Their fingers tangled together with the ease of long intimacy. "Devinshea was young, only three years old, when he took a tumble down the palace stairs. He and his brother were always running through the palace at neck or nothing speeds. We would laugh and praise the princes because it had been so long since we had that kind of energy in the palace. And then Devinshea fell down the stairs and broke his arm. It was nothing new. Many Fae have such injuries. The trouble was he would not stop bleeding. We nearly lost him. A healer got it under control but it took him weeks to recover. We knew then that he was mortal. It broke his mother's heart."

"I'm sure it wasn't easy on Dev, either," I said. "I heard the nobles wanted him banished."

Miria nodded. "He was considered unlucky. If I had not had such good control of the royal army, I would have been ousted and beheaded. They considered me weak where he was concerned. It got a bit better when his powers as a Green Man surfaced. He was trained to be a priest and he was a good one. He took his duties seriously."

As his duties included screwing every girl in Faeryland, I wasn't surprised to discover he was a devoted priest. I still hadn't met those priestesses, yet. I wondered if they had heard the tale of Gilliana.

Lee had moved back to his wall now but I could see he was listening as Miria continued.

"As he grew, he became more reckless. He and Declan would leave the *sithein* for weeks at a time pursuing the pleasures of the human world. That plane is dangerous. I just knew he would die there someday. I wanted something, Zoey. I wanted something to hold on to when my son died. Can't you understand that? I know I went about it the wrong way, but I did it because I love him. Gilliana was fertile and there was the chance he could produce a full Fae child. I tried to convince Devinshea that it was his responsibility, which it is. We cannot survive without a Green Man. He would not listen. I took the chance and I lost. Now all I can do is ask you to plead my case."

"Why would I do that?"

"Because you know Devinshea misses his home," she said. "You know he misses his family. I am willing to welcome you and Daniel into our lives. Someday you and Devinshea will have children. Would you cut them off from half of their culture? There is much Faery has to offer even its mortal children. I have so few years with him. Even now I only have fifty or so years left before mortality takes him from me. I do not wish to spend them completely apart."

"It is a bit longer than that, Mother," Dev said, and I turned to see he had heard much of our conversation. His eyes were serious, and he walked over to slip his hand into mine.

Miria lit up with understanding. "Of course, you feed Daniel and he gives you his blood. It elongates your life. I told you vampires weren't all bad, Padric."

"Perhaps Daniel is not but I did not like the other one," Padric said forbiddingly.

"You are never going to forgive me, are you?" she asked with an indulgent grin. She turned to Dev and me. "I will tell you a secret, children of mine. I once had an affair with a vampire."

Dev sighed. "Well, I hope your foray was better than mine, Mother. My first vampire was frightening."

Dev had tried on a female vampire for size. They're rare and pretty much creepy.

Miria smiled with the memory. "It was several hundred years ago. I was a young girl and he was…lovely. He was always giving me gifts. Such a gentleman he was. It was odd though. He seemed to think my name was *cara*."

I couldn't stop the startled burst of laughter that came from my throat. There was only one vampire she could possibly be talking about.

Dev frowned beside me. "You slept with Marcus Vorenus?"

Miria smiled brilliantly. "Yes. That was his name, I believe. He was a beautiful man from Rome, if I recall. So gallant. He knew how to treat a lady."

"Well, you and Zoey should swap stories," Dev said with a pout.

Marcus Vorenus was Daniel's patron, and he had zero problems with flirting with me. He'd let me know that he was more than willing to accommodate me in any way I needed. Daniel tended to roll his eyes and wave it off. Dev pretty much hated the guy.

"I've never slept with Marcus," I protested. Dev and Marcus were polite to one another, but Dev still hadn't forgiven Marcus for trying to kill him. He also didn't like the fact that Marcus referred to him as Lancelot.

"Not for lack of trying on his part," Dev replied shortly. "He is always trying to get into my wife's pants."

"I never liked that vampire." Padric clasped a hand on Dev's shoulder in sympathy. "Vampires shouldn't be able to walk about in the daytime."

"It makes it harder to stake them," Dev replied with a nod.

Miria leaned toward me, ignoring the men. "You should have him give you gifts. He gave me the loveliest jewels. Once he gave me a ruby the size of my fist. He said it brought out my eyes."

There was more talk but I didn't notice. A ruby the size of her fist. Yeah, that pretty much summed up the Blood Stone. Inside I was shaking my head. I should have known Marcus would be behind everything. I was being forced to work for Louis Marini because Marcus needed to steal jewelry for his mistress.

Or was there something else behind it? If that jewel was important enough, he might have stolen it to get it away from Marini. I still wasn't sure that the jewel didn't have some sort of magical property. What better place to hide something than another plane? Miria later closing the mounds would only be a problem if he planned on using the gem himself. Marcus and I would be having a long talk the minute I hit the Earth plane and got cell phone coverage again. He had some explaining to do.

"I'd love to see the jewels Marcus gave you sometime," I heard myself saying. I'd been told my mother-in-law might know something about the jewel. If she could just hand it over, my job would be so much easier.

Dev stiffened slightly beside me as he followed my logic. He'd read the file from Marini as well. "Yes, that is an excellent idea. Zoey loves fashion and jewels. You should show her your collection."

Miria nodded. "Of course, though Padric forced me to give the Blood Stone away. It was my favorite. He pouted until I relented. I gave it to a woman in town. She had done me a service."

Well, that answered one thing. The Blood Stone was here in Faery. I could do the job.

"Zoey," Lee said, suddenly stirring. He started down the hall back toward the ballroom. "Something's wrong. Come on."

Dev took my hand and we ran in behind Lee. Dev didn't question him. There was no way I would ask him what was happening. If Lee told me something was wrong, I would follow him. His instincts were that good.

We reached the archway that connected the gallery to the ballroom and I saw the problem. There was a huge crowd standing to the side of the dance floor. The band had stopped playing, and every single person was trying to get a good look. Dev forced his way in, and I realized the crowd was surrounding a single body.

I watched as Zack picked up the unconscious man.

"Daniel!" I yelled even as someone was calling for a healer.

My heart took a nose dive, and Dev ran for his partner.

Chapter Six

Thirty minutes later, we were comfortably settled into our room, having left the drama of the ballroom behind us. There were still a ton of people milling about outside our room waiting for the latest gossip, but it was easy to forget about them now that we'd shut the door. It was hard to forget how scared I'd been though.

"I didn't faint," Daniel growled from his place on the big bed.

"Let's call it a manly loss of consciousness," Felix offered.

"Dude, he fainted. Just like the southern belle he is. He had a fit of the vapors." Dev sounded more like himself than he had all day. He smirked down at Daniel, but I knew he'd been worried, too. He'd taken Daniel out of Zack's arms, preferring to carry his partner himself. He'd carried Daniel all the way to our rooms and called for a healer. He'd been holding my hand when Daniel woke up.

Now they were back to their normal, deeply masculine relationship.

"Fuck you, Dev," Daniel shot back. But I noticed he didn't try to get off the bed. Daniel laid back in our enormous bed and let his head rest against my breast. I cuddled him. It was what he'd asked for the minute he woke up. His skin was pale against the red of my dress. I stroked his hair and he snuggled down. It had been like this when Danny was alive. When he wasn't feeling well, he turned into a baby who needed an enormous amount of attention. “It’s your fault. You made me get in that stupid coffin.”

Dev held his hands up in complete confusion. “I did everything I could to make that coffin comfortable for you and all you can do is complain. Do you know how hard it was to get the lighting installed so you could read your comic books? People don’t typically put lighting in coffins, man. Besides, you’ve been out of the coffin for hours. How is this related?”

“I don’t think it is.” Sarah looked Daniel over. Sarah had taken charge of the room, immediately ordering Zack about and generally keeping everyone calm because she seemed so competent.

We were waiting on the Fae healer who lived in the village. Padric had sent a royal guard to fetch the man. In the meantime, Sarah had ordered everyone to keep the noise down and to make Daniel comfortable.

“What do you think it is?” I asked Sarah.

Daniel didn’t get sick. It wasn’t part of the vampire experience to get weak and faint. No matter how Felix wanted to play it, I agreed with Dev. Danny fainted. One minute he’d been standing up and talking and the next he hit the floor. If that wasn’t a faint, then I didn’t know what was. Zack had been shadowing his master and said Daniel had grown even paler than usual right before he passed out. Luckily Zack had caught him before he hit the floor.

Sarah gave me a long look. “I have my suspicions but you won’t like it.”

“Just tell me.” The last thing I needed was to play guessing games. If something was wrong with Danny, I needed to know right away.

“Why don’t we talk about it alone?” she said quietly in a way that made my heart pound with terror.

What could be so bad that we needed privacy to discuss it? We weren’t the most private of people. Our crew tended to witness everything in our lives. When we fought we usually had an audience. Even when we did…other things, we sometimes learned someone had been watching. If Sarah thought we needed privacy, it must be bad.

I was about to insist she just spit it out when Declan walked in the room with a tall, thin man carrying what looked to be an old-fashioned medical case. The healer was a faery with long brown hair who looked around the room, his eyes finally fastening on Daniel.

"This is the vampire?" he asked, looking Daniel over.

"Yes," Declan said with a sigh. "This is the weak vampire. My mother and brother insist that you save him. However, if you allow him to expire, I will make sure there is something in it for you."

"Declan!" I wasn't sure he was joking.

He shrugged and moved away, letting the healer sit down with his patient.

"What are your symptoms?" No one had taught this particular healer bedside manner. He frowned and his words came out in a flat, couldn't-care-less tone of voice. I supposed it fit, since he more than likely didn't get to practice his profession often. Faeries tended to not get sick. This healer would mostly be used to dealing with injuries.

Daniel was silent so I spoke up. "He was tired earlier today and then after dinner he passed out."

"I will ask the obvious," the healer began, sounding completely uninterested. "When was the last time you ate?"

Dev took that one. "About thirty minutes before we went in to the banquet. Zoey was busy so I fed him. He took the normal time. Daniel doesn't gorge himself but he gets a decent meal. I haven't eaten anything strange, if you're wondering. I had two ales at Ross's but it's nothing he couldn't handle."

"I couldn't even taste the alcohol," Danny complained.

Dev rolled his eyes. "Sorry. Someone tried to kill our wife and then I forgot about our drinking binge. I'll try harder next time."

"Do you have any other symptoms?" The healer began what appeared to be a routine checkup. He examined Daniel's eyes and ears and even made sure his fangs were functioning properly.

"No. No other symptoms. I'm just tired. It's not a big deal." Daniel suffered through the exam, but he didn't like doctors. He hadn't liked them when he'd been alive. He had to be near death before I could get him to make an appointment.

"Danny, you have to tell him everything," I insisted.

Dev started to look concerned now. He knew when Danny was lying, too. He sat up and paid attention. "Yes, Dan, you do have to own up. You shouldn't be sick. If it's something serious then we need to deal with it now. Maybe there's something here you could be allergic to."

"Could he have been poisoned?" The terrifying idea hit me as I contemplated the events of the day. I held Danny even closer as I thought about someone trying to kill him. They tried to take me out. Maybe they would go after Danny next.

The healer shook his head. "Prince Devinshea is the only one you fed from today?"

Daniel nodded. I was sure he'd been planning to make a meal of me later on tonight, but we hadn't gotten there yet.

"And you are feeling fine, Your Grace?" The healer turned his attention to Dev.

Dev shifted up in the bed. He moved next to me so he could place his arm around my shoulders. I felt better having both of them close. "I'm perfectly well. I admit there was some nausea when my mother was hitting on my wife and then my partner. It welled back up when she discussed her sex life with Marcus, who I hate, but I doubt that has anything to do with poison. The only antidote is years of therapy."

That got Danny's attention. "Your mom did Marcus?"

"Lay back down, invalid." Dev ignored him. "Everything I ate before dinner was prepared by my butler's own hand. There is no risk of contamination. I didn't feed him after dinner."

The healer listened intently. He seemed much more interested now that he thought he was dealing with something more than an anorexic bloodsucker. He took Daniel's wrist in his hand. A vampire's heart pumps when their blood is up, though slower than a normal human's. He counted for a moment. "His pulse is fine for a vampire. I know of no poison that would not kill the prince before it could contaminate the vampire's system. How do you feel now?"

"Fine," Daniel said shortly. His eyes were stubborn, and I knew he was hiding something.

"Daniel," I ordered, forcing him to look up. "You tell this doctor the truth right this second. I am not going to lose you because you're a stubborn ass."

"It's nothing," he insisted and dug in.

Dev got up and took charge of the room. I looked around and pretty much everyone we knew was there. Lee, Zack, and Neil stood at the end of the bed with Felix. Sarah sat on the end of the bed. Declan and several members of the royal guard were waiting by the door.

"Out," Dev commanded. "Everyone who does not sleep in our bed needs to wait in the outer rooms. That includes you, Neil. I'm certain Zoey will tell you the tale before she shares it with anyone else. Go about your business. Sarah, you may stay, please."

"Why does Sarah get to stay?" Neil never liked being out of the loop.

"Sarah is our group's healer," Dev explained. "Whatever the healer decides Sarah will have to administer. She needs to know what is going on."

Sarah and Neil exchanged a long look, and I knew they had been talking about something. I just wished I knew what Sarah was thinking.

When the room had cleared out, Dev turned back to Daniel. "Everyone is gone. Sarah won't mention it. I'm sure healers have an oath or something. Please tell us what's going on."

Daniel sat up and ran a frustrated hand through his hair. He looked flustered and a little emotional. It made me worried.

"Danny, please," I practically begged.

"Okay, Z," Daniel finally said. "But it's not a big deal. It's just been going on a little longer than I might have let on. I've been feeling…the only word for it is drained, I guess. I've felt that way for a week, maybe."

"Wow." Sarah shook her head, and she had those lines on her forehead she got when worried. "Z, how much did you eat today?"

I wasn't sure how my daily caloric intake would help anything, but I thought about it. "Not much. I had a half a cookie but I just wasn't hungry. Maybe it was the traveling, though I usually love road food. There's no Dairy Queen here, so that might explain it."

I liked Dairy Queen. My stomach rumbled at the thought of a nice-sized Blizzard. I hadn't eaten much.

"What does Zoey's appetite have to do with this?" Dev asked. "Please focus, girls."

The healer stared at Sarah for a moment, considering what she'd said. He directed his questions to her in an obvious sign of respect. "She sleeps with both men?"

Sarah nodded. "They're in a committed ménage a trois and have been for a while now. The prince is...well, you know what his specialty is."

"Yes, a vampire and a Green Man. An interesting combination." He finally turned back to Daniel. "Vampire, this is your companion? She is a true companion?"

Companion meant something different in vampire society than it did in the regular world. I wasn't simply Daniel's wife. My blood was different from other women's. It made Daniel stronger and faster than a vampire without a companion. I had a little bit of angel DNA in my background. It hadn't helped my morality, but it did boost my blood.

"Yes," Daniel admitted. "She's my companion. Her glow is strong."

"I would bet your blood connection is strong as well," the healer said, drumming his fingers on his bag. I noted he had closed the bag as though he would no longer need it. "You love the girl?"

"I've loved her for as long as I can remember," Daniel said quietly. "I loved her before my turn."

The healer turned to me now. "And you, Your Grace, how long has it been since you last had your woman's time?"

Dev gasped a little. "Zoey?"

"I don't remember." I took a shot. I didn't have to worry about getting pregnant. I knew my period was coming when I got PMS.

But I hadn't had any PMS signs for weeks and weeks. I knew what was coming and I knew I should have been prepared for it, but I was panicking as my husbands stared at me, realization dawning on their faces.

"She's five days late," Daniel said quietly.

I took a deep breath and chose not to comment. It was one of those creepy vampire things that previously Daniel had hidden from me. So he knew my periods better than I did. Lots of women were late. It was just stress. I led a stressful life, what with the wars and vampires and numerous people out to kill me. I couldn't be blamed if my periods were irregular.

Except, they weren't and never had been. I'd always been on time. I was like clockwork.

All of a sudden everyone was looking at me like I was the patient. Dev and Daniel went utterly silent as though they were attempting to process the information. Sarah reached out and gently took my hand.

"Zoey, sweetie," Sarah said with infinite patience. "Sometimes, when a vampire has a real, true connection with his companion, the vampire will be able to sense when his companion is weak. He can share his...energy, essence, I don't know what the proper term is, but he can share it with you. It only works in chronic situations where the discomfort is constant. It's called sympathetic transference. When you're weak he can make you strong, but there's a cost to him."

Daniel looked up at me. There was a look of strange wonder in his eyes. After a moment, he turned to Sarah. "I've heard of it. Is it true, Sarah?"

Sarah's face was so serious, and for a moment I thought I caught a sheen of tears in her eyes. "Yes, I believe so. You understand the implications?"

"I do," he said, but there was a little grin on his face.

"What implications?" Anxiety began to pulse through my system. There are times when I just know things are about to change and I want another couple of minutes of blissful ignorance. The way Daniel and Sarah were looking at each other, this was one of those times and I doubted it had anything to do with whether or not I was pregnant. "I'll eat. I don't want to make Danny sick because I forgot."

"It's more than that, Zoey," Dev said, exchanging a look with Daniel.

"This is serious." Sarah looked at me. "It means Daniel isn't immortal, Zoey. He's connected to you on a base level, and it's about more than just blood. He's formed a biological and psychic connection. If he's trying to bolster your strength now, think about what happens when your body fails. No matter how long you take his blood, your body will fail."

"Danny's body will try to keep mine alive?"

Sarah nodded, thankful I was finally getting it. "And he will fail but not before you drain him of everything. When you die, he'll go with you."

Daniel should have had eternity. My heart nearly seized at the thought of what I was going to cost him. "Can we stop it? Is there something we can do?"

"He can break the connection now," the healer said academically. "If the vampire walks away now, it is possible that he could break his connection with you, but he is not going to do that, Your Grace. The fact that the connection was formed at all is proof that the vampire needs you."

"I don't want to do anything, Z," Daniel said. "I'm fine with this. I'm kind of happy about it. But baby, you need to eat. I can't take care of you if I'm fainting because you have morning sickness."

"Is she really?" Dev asked, his voice breathless. He looked at me with a mixture of joy and abject horror in his eyes.

Daniel lay against me suddenly. He placed his ear right above my pelvis and everyone got very, very quiet. I watched Daniel's eyes close as he focused everything he had on listening for that one sound. He sat up and looked at me. There was so much tenderness in his eyes, I knew what the answer was before he said anything.

"Z, you have two heartbeats." He gathered me against his chest and kissed my forehead. "You're pregnant, baby. I told you sleeping with that bastard would catch up with you."

Dev was sitting rigidly, staring at us with his mouth hanging open. "But I used a condom."

"Not on our wedding night," I corrected him. "Not when we were on the altar."

"That night's a bit of a blur, sweetheart," he admitted. "All that magic flying around kind of messed with me."

"Yes, all that fertility magic," Sarah pointed out.

"Oh, goddess, my wife is pregnant," Dev said as though he had to say it out loud to believe it. "We're going to have a baby." He turned to Daniel and there was a wariness in his eyes. "I didn't mean for this to happen, Daniel. I tried to protect her but I didn't. It's my fault."

Daniel's arms tightened around me. "You don't want a baby? I thought you would be happy about this."

"I want it more than anything," Dev admitted. "But it's not what we agreed upon. We were all supposed to decide when the time was right, if it would ever be right. I took that decision away from us."

"It was a matter of time," Daniel said. "I always knew it was going to happen. We were fooling ourselves if we thought we could control it. I'm fine with it, Dev. I am."

Dev tried not to laugh but failed and finally came up behind me, letting his head rest against my back. I was glad the boys were working through their angst because I was still numb. I was having a baby. It didn't seem real, but there was another heart beating inside my body and I was responsible for that tiny sound. It was mine. It was mine, I decided. It was mine and Dev's and Danny's. Our baby might end up being a fertility god, but he or she would be ours first.

"Well, it seems Her Grace is in good condition." The healer stood, clutching his bag as he walked to the door. "You will need a midwife. Until I can find a good one, the witch can make do. It is fine for you to feed your vampire, Your Grace, so long as he is not greedy. If you take his blood, you should definitely continue to do that. It will strengthen you and the child. And intercourse is permitted though, please, one at a time."

"We will take good care of our wife," Dev promised the healer, his hands going around my waist.

Sarah got up to go as well. "I'll leave you guys alone to let it all sink in. Daniel, as long as Zoey starts eating again, I think you'll feel stronger. I'll make sure Albert makes her some ginger tea in the morning. We'll get a couple of good meals in her and it should help."

Daniel's head suddenly came up. "Sarah, am I going to go through labor with her?"

Sarah bit her lip, trying hard not to laugh. "If only I could make that happen. No, you aren't going to feel her pain and you won't ever be able to take pain for her. This connection works to give her strength over long periods of time. It helps her to survive when maybe she shouldn't. But I could try to work out a spell…"

"Don't you dare," Daniel muttered.

Sarah slipped quietly out. I let myself fall back on the bed, and Danny and Dev took their places beside me. We let our hands find each other, and I knew I wouldn't go through this alone. A thought struck me. "Danny, you only heard one extra heartbeat, right?"

"It sounded like one," he assured me.

"Good." I let out a relieved breath. "Knowing Dev, I could have been having a litter."

"I shall try hard to never give you a litter." Dev's hand slid over my stomach and rested there. "But twins would be nice."

I looked at Daniel. "We have to find a way to stop this whole transference thing. I don't want to be the reason you die, Danny."

Daniel cuddled up, his hand joining Dev's on my stomach. "Baby, what did you expect I would do when you're gone?"

I tried to come up with another answer but I knew. He wouldn't want to go on. "What were you planning to do?" I asked because the sun wouldn't kill him now. He couldn't just walk into the light.

"I have orders to stake him," Dev offered cheerfully.

"What?"

Dev shrugged. "I've been practicing. I think I can do it in one thrust. I hope he doesn't explode. Anyway, that's the plan. After Danny's gone, I'll drink myself to death and we'll all be together again."

I laughed because they looked so serious. "That's a horrible plan."

"Yes, it was," Daniel admitted. "Dev will probably drink himself to death long before he has a chance to stake me and then I'd have to do it myself. It's better this way. I'm not going anywhere, Z, at least not until you do. I love you. You're my life, and now I get to go with you."

Daniel tilted his head down and kissed me softly.

The door opened, and Declan stuck his head in. "The healer and witch will tell us nothing. Has my brother figured out that he impregnated his female yet?"

I sat up and tossed a pillow at the prince's head.

He managed to duck. "Well, then I offer you congratulations. I look forward to being an uncle."

As Declan closed the door, Dev sighed. "Forget what I said about twins. One of them always turns out to be an asshole."

Chapter Seven

I woke to soft lips on mine, hands stroking me gently. I was lying on my side, cuddled down on the soft bedding. The night's drama had exhausted me, and I'd fallen asleep shortly after the healer had left. Dev and Daniel had been talking about the implications of my pregnancy and I'd done what I always did when they started in on politics and crap. I drifted off.

But they also knew how to wake me up. I shivered as someone drew the covers off me. I wasn't cold for long. The blanket was quickly replaced with the heat of a hard body cuddling up to mine.

"Good morning, Devinshea." I let my head drift back to nestle against his chest as his arms came around me.

"Good morning, my gorgeous goddess." He kissed the shell of my ear, a soft touch, but I already could feel his magic warming up my skin.

The curtains were drawn but light still filtered in, a soft glow that made our little world gauzy and dreamlike. It was easy to pretend this was a vacation and we were just a normal everyday threesome having some intimate time together.

I reached out for Daniel, running my hand along the slightly cool skin of his chest. His hand came up and covered mine, letting me know he was awake.

Dev gently turned my head toward his, his lips soft against mine, his tongue begging entry. I moaned a little and let his tongue slip into my mouth. Dev held my head still as he explored, letting our tongues play against each other with velvety languor.

"This is how every morning should begin," he said with a slow smile as he flipped me onto my back. "Unfortunately, we have a problem."

I didn't see the problem. We could stay right there in bed for all I cared. Dev's hands found my breasts, plucking at my nipples.

"Hey, don't take forever, man," Daniel warned.

Dev sighed, his mouth turning down. He rolled a nipple between his thumb and forefinger. "That would be our problem, lover. Our vampire is weak and surly this morning. It's troublesome because he has some torturing to do and I fear if we don't feed him properly, he'll be unable to perform."

"I need sex," Daniel said with a self-deprecating grin as he leaned over to kiss me. He was heart-stoppingly beautiful in the soft light. His sandy blond hair needed a cut, but I wouldn't say a damn thing because I loved the way it had started to curl over the tops of his ears.

"You need sex." I pushed my fingers through that thick hair, brushing it back.

His dimples were on display, and I got the sexiest hint of fangs as he smiled. "We've been busy. I haven't fed off the magic in a couple of days, and I'm feeling weak, baby. All that sunlight yesterday nearly did me in."

One of the ways our threesome worked was the fact that Daniel, like most vampires, could feed off of sexual energy. It was why the feeding process was almost always followed by a good long session in bed. Dev, being the fertility god he was, had a sort of supercharged sexual energy that when Daniel fed off of it, allowed Daniel to handle sunlight. He still didn't like direct sunlight and he'd been exposed to plenty of it yesterday. He was probably feeling weak.

"So Dev offered to make the sacrifice?" I asked sarcastically.

"You know I will do anything to keep the three of us strong." Dev gave me a lecherous grin. He bent down and licked my nipple before sucking it into his mouth. I let my eyes close and my hand find his hair. I had a hand on both my men. I was a happy girl.

Dev sat up all of a sudden. "Seriously? I don't know that he's going to go for that. You can do that?"

I stared at my faery prince.

Daniel shook his head. "That freaks me out a little. He's started having these whole conversations with himself in the middle of talking to me."

Bris. He was talking to Bris.

Dev rolled his eyes. "We'll get better at it, Dan. Eventually I'll remember I don't have to talk out loud."

"Yeah, so you'll just zone on me. That's going to be so much better," Daniel complained.

They were ruining my perfectly happy morning. "Dev, what is Bris saying? Or better yet, why doesn't he just say it himself?"

"He isn't sure he should come out during intimate situations." Dev frowned.

Daniel huffed. "Uhm, he's a little late for that. Pregnant wife, anyone?"

"That was a ritual," Dev pointed out. "Obviously we need him for those. He's not nervous about Zoey. He's nervous about you, Dan. He doesn't want to offend you with his presence, but he has a solution to our problem."

"I thought sex was the solution." I kind of liked that solution.

A slow, sexy smile crossed Dev's face. "Sex is always the solution, my goddess."

Daniel sat up, moving much more slowly than usual. He settled his back against the headboard of the bed. Now that I looked at him, it was easy to see how tired he looked. I'd done that to him. My heart ached. "If he can help out, then please bring it on."

Dev's eyes changed in a heartbeat, his body relaxing, becoming more languid, his features softening slightly. I'd begun to see that there were subtle differences between Dev and the Irish fertility god who had taken up residence in his body. There were not so subtle differences as well, and that included his eyes becoming fully green without a hint of white.

"Hello, Daniel." He turned to me, his expression infinitely warm. "Hello, my goddess. You are happy about the pregnancy?"

"Have you known about it?" He was a fertility god. He might just know when he'd done his duty and aided in population growth.

He frowned. "Yes, but I thought it best to allow you to discover the truth on your own. I understand now I made a mistake. You did not want children. I apologize."

Daniel held up a hand. "Stop. No apologies. We weren't ready for kids. No one ever is. We'll welcome this child with open arms, all three of us."

"You aren't angry with me?" The ancient god turned his eyes on Daniel.

"It's your nature, but we have to talk about what happens after this one. She can't stay pregnant all the time, man."

That was a horrifying thought. "What?"

Bris's laugh was as rich as the darkest chocolate. "I can protect her. The small devices humans use are remarkably helpful."

"Are you talking about rubbers?" Daniel asked, his lips quirking up. "That's kind of low tech compared to other methods of birth control."

"Ah, but those methods manipulate a woman's hormones. Believe me, I can manipulate those far better and more accurately than any chemical. I can have a woman ovulating in no time at all. Trust me, those rubber things are your best bet against my magic." He turned serious. "I don't want to give you more children than you want, Daniel. But I can help you with your current problem."

I leaned forward because our current problem included Daniel's inevitable death. "You can fix the problem with the transference?"

Bris shook his head. "Oh, my goddess, he doesn't want that fixed."

"I don't." Daniel put a hand on my shoulder. "We went over this, Z."

"I don't have to be inside Daniel's body to see through to his soul. He's happy about the transference, though he has to know to protect you all the same. It won't work if someone uses one of those guns on you. Barbaric weapons. So put it out of your head. No, I was talking about our vampire's weakness. Even if she eats, the pregnancy will be hard on her. And by hard on her, I mean hard on you, Daniel. Her weaknesses will affect your ability to daywalk."

"So even if I feed properly I'll struggle?" Daniel asked with a long sigh. "I'm not used to being weak. It's been a long time since I felt so human."

"Like Devinshea said, sex is the solution." He held his hands out, showing off Dev's body. "I am sex, Daniel."

My ears perked up. Well, my whole body perked up because I would pay so much to see that show.

Bris chuckled. "That wasn't what I meant, my curious goddess." He turned, his right palm facing us. "I can channel the energy through Devinshea's hands. I can give you a boost that should last several days."

That was disappointing, but it could be helpful all the same.

"I'm up for that, man. I hate feeling like this. I've gotten used to seeing the sun. It was hard to wake up this afternoon." Daniel struggled to get to his knees.

"I'll have you waking with the dawn if you like, Your Highness." Bris got to his knees as well.

And I just kind of watched because they were both naked. Pretty, pretty naked men. My men.

"What should I do?" Daniel asked, sounding uncertain for the first time.

Bris closed his eyes, taking a long breath. It filled Dev's chest, accentuating his every muscle. "You just get ready, Your Highness."

He touched Daniel, his big palm going right over Danny's heart.

"I thought we agreed you would call me Daniel. God, is that supposed to happen? I don't think that's supposed to happen." Daniel started to move away.

I got up on my knees behind him after seeing exactly what was freaking my vampire hubby out. He had a hard-on to end all hard-ons. His cock was standing straight up, reaching almost to his navel.

Bris stared at him, his face slightly flushed with embarrassment. "Again, I apologize. I did not mean to make you uncomfortable."

Daniel stilled once I put my arms around him. "It's just…it's not that way between me and Dev."

His slight hesitation gave me hope for a kinky future. "He's not trying to have sex with you, Danny. He's just going to touch you."

"I wasn't mad, Z. I'm just adjusting again." Because it was

pretty inevitable. He'd said it to me himself. You could only have a fertility god in your bed for so long without dealing with the consequences. In my case, that was getting pregnant. In Danny's, I was pretty sure it meant exploring his sexuality in a way he hadn't planned on before. I, for one, would buy pom-poms and cheer on the day. His hand came around, his fingers threading with mine even as he gave his attention to Bris.

"Forgive me, Bris. No matter how much power I claim, I seem to still be just a man, and I fear change sometimes. Even when I know there's nothing to be afraid of. Please touch me. I won't cringe. Believe me, cringing ain't what I'm afraid of. I'm going to like this, aren't I?"

For once Bris looked almost human. His grin was so sweet. "I'm afraid so, Daniel." He touched Danny again, but this time they made a connection.

I watched as a visible pulse of energy went from Dev's body to Daniel's. His hand tightened around mine and he groaned, long and hard. His whole body shook, but it was easy to see it wasn't from pain. I let my free hand wind around Danny's waist to touch his cock. He came instantly, coming in my hand in long jets.

"Fuck. Yep, that's what I was afraid of." He couldn't help himself. He laughed as he kept pulsing in my hand.

Bris finally broke the connection and Daniel dropped over, his body hitting the bed. Bris reached out to touch my face, his fingers brushing my skin. "He should be fine for several days, perhaps as long as a week, and I'll check in on the babe. Take care of yourself, my goddess."

Suddenly Dev was back, his eyes normal again. There was a devilish grin on his face. "That was awesome. Dan, you okay?"

Daniel didn't move, simply gave Dev a thumbs-up. "Yep. I'm good."

Dev growled and I was suddenly in his arms. He pulled me close, our chests coming together. His cock rubbed against my belly. "I'm good, too. I'm fucking fantastic. And Daniel still needs a bit of blood. You know what that means."

Daniel pushed himself up. His face was still pale because he hadn't had enough blood, but it was obvious he was feeling better from the smile on his face. "Only if you're feeling up to it, Z."

"I don't know," I said with a laugh. I put my arms on Dev's shoulders and spread my knees wide. "Do I seem like I'm feeling up to it?"

He knew what I wanted and slid his hand down my body. His fingers gently opened the soft flesh of my pussy and rubbed. It didn't take long before his fingers were soaking wet. He held them up for Daniel's inspection. "She seems to be feeling up to it."

Daniel's fangs were fully out and despite what had just happened, his cock seemed ready to play again. "I should take a shower."

He did have stuff all over him.

Dev didn't give a flying shit. He just rubbed himself on me, completely uncaring that I had Danny's come on my hand. "You know what they say, Dan. Get dirty before you get clean. No one is bothered here. I swear, I'll get you to toss out that unneeded self-consciousness if it's the last thing I do. There's no place for embarrassment in our bed."

Daniel moved in, reaching for me, his eyes darkening. "Well, you know I try to follow your lead when it comes to this." Daniel pulled me down to the bed, settling in beside me.

Dev parted my knees, making a place for himself between my legs. "Why don't you work on those luscious tits everyone in my family seems to love so much and I'll pay particular attention to this sweet little pussy."

Daniel kissed me before dropping his head to my breasts and brushing them with his tongue. His fangs scraped along my skin, drawing just the tiniest bit of blood that he licked up with a grateful moan before suckling my nipples one after the other.

My eyes nearly rolled to the back of my head as Dev laved my flesh with affection. His tongue slid over and over, licking every part of my pussy. He spread my labia and sucked on each petal while his fingers worked into my channel, rubbing deep inside. He licked and sucked, his tongue darting here and there.

Daniel plucked at my nipples, rolling them between his fingers. He licked at my neck, his fangs scraping again in little bites that made me jump. It was just the right side of pain, just enough to get my heart racing, and then Danny's tongue would come out to soothe the ache.

He finally moved up, bringing himself level with me. He brought his wrist to his mouth and bit down. "Open up, Z."

"You should feed first." He was still too pale for my liking.

Dev pinched my clit, nearly making me scream. Yeah, that was still the right side of pain, but just barely. "He gave you an order. He wants to feed you. Bris just pumped a ton of sexual energy through his system. If he wants you to drink, you drink or I'll stop what I'm doing and we'll talk about discipline."

I can't lie. When Dev got that dark voice, I softened and my whole system heated up. I let Daniel place his wrist over my mouth and I drank.

Warmth filled me. Daniel's power flowed through me.

I gave myself over as Dev fucked me with his tongue, his clever fingers finding a rhythm on my clitoris as his tongue plunged in and out and his magic started to hum across my skin. I felt Daniel sigh against my breast as the magic hit him again. I'd felt Bris's magic up close and personal. It was addictive. This magic was filtered through Dev and therefore a bit gentler. It still felt like heaven. It rolled over my skin, warming me everywhere.

Daniel finally pulled his wrist away, his smile telling me how much he'd enjoyed sharing blood with me. "I'll make us strong, Z. You'll see. Dev and I will take good care of you."

"Goddess, you taste so good." Dev moaned against me and I could feel he was getting restless. He pushed my legs farther apart, giving him full access and leaving me completely bare to him. He switched now, working two fingers into me as his tongue tormented my throbbing clit.

Daniel moved up and kissed me, our tongues playing around his fangs. He took over the kiss, his tongue matching the rhythm of Dev's plunging fingers, and I came apart. My arms wound around Danny's neck as I held onto him while the orgasm rolled over me.

Before the first one had fully registered, Dev was up on his knees, working his erection into me.

"It feels so good," he moaned. "I'm going to like not wearing a condom, lover. You're so fucking tight and hot around me."

Daniel moved in behind me so my back was against his chest. I could feel his cock hard against my back but he did nothing about it. He pushed me up and wrapped his arms around me. "I love you, Z," he whispered in my ear as he reached around and gently played with my nipples.

I let my head fall back against him because I was already building toward release again. Dev worked his thick cock into me, handling me with care. He pushed in and out with such a soft, sweet rhythm, I thought I would go crazy.

"Fuck me harder," I demanded because I was oh so close.

"I don't want to hurt the baby," Dev insisted, keeping up his torture. "I like this, Zoey. I can keep this up all day. I want to do it. I'll just fuck you all day, just like this. We never have to leave this bed."

"Don't you dare." I wanted that heaven that Dev kept just out of reach. I shoved against him, and the pressure sent me blissfully over the edge. I held him close and cried out because it felt so good.

"Well, if you're going to be that way," Dev said above me with a disapproving frown. He picked up his pace and adjusted the angle. His head fell forward and he let himself go.

Daniel groaned and I felt his fangs tease my neck as the magic hit him full force. He bit down and I nearly screamed. Pure pleasure coursed through my veins. Daniel sucked and Dev's cock hit that perfect place again and I couldn't stop the wave. I felt the hot wash of Dev's orgasm as he flooded me with his come. He was breathless above me as he finished with a groan but tried to keep his weight off me.

Daniel took one last swallow and licked my neck, helping to close the little wounds though I didn't need it. I'd had his blood. I could heal just about anything.

I reached up and kissed him. "The two of you are going to treat me like a china doll, aren't you?"

"We want to take care of you and the baby." Dev panted as he let himself fall to the side. "I have no intention of being celibate, though. Dan and I will just have to take turns for a while. I think that was satisfactory for all concerned. When it's Daniel's turn, he can bite me and I'll be perfectly happy. We're going to rotate days."

"We have a system worked out," Daniel acknowledged.

I leaned back against him, loving how safe I felt in his arms. "You're really all right with the whole baby thing, Danny?"

I was worried. He wasn't the biological father and could never be one. I didn't want this to make him feel like an outsider.

He measured his words and that was for Dev as much as me. "I worry about it. What's my place, guys? Am I the uncle?"

"No." Dev sat up, looking at Daniel seriously. "We're the fathers. You can be papa and I'll be daddy or the other way around. I don't see what the problem is. It happens all the time."

"Here it does," Daniel argued. "I know our relationship is perfectly normal in Faery, but we don't live in Faery. In Dallas, we're kind of freaky. I think we need to talk about it. How is the kid going to feel when he goes to school and talks about his two dads?"

Dev laughed. "Our son will have much bigger problems than having two fathers. What happens when all the teachers at the school find themselves pregnant? Including the ones who have gone through menopause? That might cause a bit of concern. Or when he plays with the plants and they overrun the gymnasium?"

"Oh, I can see the parent teacher conference now." I swallowed because I didn't know if I was ready for a regular baby much less a magical one.

"Don't worry, sweetheart," he assured me with a laugh. "He won't be going to public schools. There are enough strange creatures on our plane that we have schools to handle the more magically inclined children."

"Nice," Daniel said, his dimples making an appearance. "Our kid's going to Hogwarts."

"Something like that. Rest assured he won't be made fun of for having two dads. The other children will be far too afraid that his vampire dad will defend his son," Dev stated.

"And I will," Daniel said with a nod. "And if it is a girl, I will make sure my beast is there to greet anyone brave enough to date her."

"Oh, god, if it's a girl, will she be a companion?" I had a new biggest fear. Some vampire was going to come after my daughter. They would try to sell her. They would put her up for auction and she would go to the highest bidder. I would die before that happened to my daughter.

Dev cuddled me close, his voice turning serious. “Zoey, we don’t know for sure that she would be a companion. We do know that she would be the daughter of the *Nex Apparatus*, and when we’re done she will be the daughter of the acknowledged King of all Vampire. I doubt they’ll be stealing her off the street.”

“I’ll take apart the first one who looks at her and then the others might learn something.” Daniel’s voice had gone guttural.

Dev leaned in and kissed me. “I love you, sweetheart. It’s going to be fine. Like I said, Daniel and I will take such sweet care of you and our children. Now, I have some fields to make green and lush. I see our vampire is back to his strength, so I leave you in his capable hands. Perhaps tonight we can go to the temple. It’s where our child will be born.”

Daniel laid back in bed. “God, Z, please eat soon. I don’t want to lose this energy. It feels too fucking good.”

Dev laughed as he pulled back the bed curtains. “I’ll have Albert bring the tea in if he hasn’t already. Oh, hello, Bibi. Good morning to you.” His voice was amused as he glanced back through the curtains. “Sweetheart, your secretary has taken up residence on the chest at the end of our bed. I hope she doesn’t mind nudity.”

She didn’t. Bibi smiled shyly and toted her notebook that was far too large for her small hands. I poked my head out of the curtains and greeted my assistant.

“Good morning, mistress,” she said. “You seemed to be involved with your husbands. I did not want to interrupt you so I waited. Mara tried to dismiss me this morning, but I told her you wanted me and she should train me or you might be angry and take your vengeance out on her. She was scared. I have notes.”

“Excellent,” I said, happy that the troll was taking charge of her life. I just kind of wished she hadn’t been listening in to mine. “How about finding me a robe?”

“Of course,” she agreed. “And the large red person has drawn you a bath, though he says you will have to be satisfied with merely warm instead of scalding. I don’t know what that means but he said he didn’t want the baby to boil. I’m very excited about the baby.”

"So everyone knows?" I wasn't sure how I felt about my private news being made so public. I wished I'd had some time to process it before everyone started planning the birth. It was inevitable. There wasn't a lot of privacy in a court like this. It ran on rumors and innuendo. With the fertility problems of the Fae, my pregnancy was going to be big news.

Bibi nodded. "Prince Declan made an announcement last night at the banquet. All of Faery is excited. They believe it bodes well for Prince Dev's fertility powers. Queen Miria cried. She wanted to see you, but Prince Declan said you needed time alone. There is a tray of tea and toast when you are ready."

I stretched and decided to enjoy my role as a royal for once. "I'll take my breakfast in the tub."

I kissed Daniel, slipped on my robe and began the day.

* * * *

"Daniel is obviously feeling better, Z," Sarah said, walking into the opulent bathroom after going to check on her patient. "What's this I hear about Bris helping out?"

I grinned up at her. "He can funnel his magic directly into Daniel's body."

Her eyes went wide. "Seriously?"

"Yep. That was a good couple of minutes." I let the warm water heat up my skin. I was feeling damn good. Danny seemed to be all right with the fact that we were having a baby, so I was settling my mind around it. It also made me think about the fact that I was having a faery child. I should try to fit in. I made a vow to myself to attempt to get along with the court. No more hauling naked noblewomen around by their hair, I promised myself. I would try to be a lady.

"I'm just wondering how Z is going to make it through nine months without a martini," Neil mused with a devilish grin from the other side of my overly large tub. It was more like a small pool complete with steps to get in. Neil grabbed the soap. He gestured for me to turn around and started soaping my back. "It could affect the entire Dallas bar scene. I wonder how many bars will go under without their best customer."

"It's more than nine months, buddy." Sarah sat on the ledge, letting her bare feet dangle in the water. "How about breast feeding? Although with Dev's DNA, the baby might actually come out of the womb with a discernible blood alcohol level."

I decided to switch the topic. Maybe I wasn't ready to confront the whole baby thing. "Where are the other wolves today?"

"Zack is going to some farm with Dev and Lee refuses to come into the apartments until he's sure you're clothed," Sarah explained with a smile. "He said he was going to the dungeons to check on our would-be assassin. He seems eager to start the 'questioning.' Maybe I should go down there and make sure they observe the Geneva Convention."

Neil snorted as he sank back in the warm water. "Honey, Switzerland doesn't exist on this plane. I assure you what Daniel is going to do to that faery will make Guantanamo look like Disney World."

Sarah sighed. "I don't want to know. After all that time on the Hell plane, I come down firmly on the side of no torture."

"You're in luck then, Ms. Day," Padric said darkly from the doorway.

I ducked down and hid my boobs under the ledge of the tub. "Hello, naked here."

"Yes, Your Grace," Padric said. "People usually bathe nude. It's nothing I haven't seen." It wasn't. He'd seen all of me and from various angles because Dev liked to switch positions. Faery marriage ceremonies came complete with witnesses to the consummation. Padric and Declan had been mine. He did, however, look surprised that I had a guest. "Is the boy your maid?"

Neil shook his head. Unlike me, he couldn't care less that he wasn't wearing a stitch of clothing. "Nope, I'm the bodyguard. I'm patrolling these dangerous waters. Can't let sharks get Her Grace."

Padric was not impressed with sarcasm. "I wouldn't worry about sharks, young man. You have far more to think about. The prisoner was found dead."

Daniel was in the room almost instantly. He'd gotten out of bed damn fast. "What do you mean, he's dead? He was fine last night. When we left him he was moaning about his headache but otherwise he was fine in his cell. The healers said he would be all right and ready for questioning today."

"Did he kill himself?" Neil asked, getting out of the tub and drying himself off. He was perfectly professional now and ready to be serious.

"No," Padric replied. "The healers believe someone poisoned the archer's breakfast. We're questioning the staff, but no one seems to know anything. The boy who delivered the food this morning is missing."

"Lee can track a man for miles." Daniel's color was back to his normal pale and he seemed much stronger from his morning feeding. "Do you have anything that belonged to the boy?"

"I will check but it will have to wait." Padric's face went dark, his eyes trailing to the large window on the opposite wall. "We have bigger problems. The Unseelie are here."

"With an army?" Daniel asked.

Padric shook his head. "No, they sent an envoy. The messenger said they merely wanted to visit in an attempt to restore our previously good relations. They wish to celebrate the marriage of the prince. Prince Dev was well liked by the Unseelie. If we refuse them, it will be a grave insult."

"But you don't think that is the real reason they are here?" I asked as Daniel held my robe up. He made certain I was covered as I walked up the steps of the bath. He wrapped it around me.

"I think the timing is interesting," Padric admitted. "They come just as someone is attempting to kill Her Grace. There is nothing we can do but welcome the envoy and watch him like a hawk. Please get Her Grace properly dressed as well as yourself, Daniel. The queen wants all of you at her side when we greet the envoy. Zoey, please wear the dress Declan left for you. We retrieved it from Mara's room a few minutes ago. She will not be working at the palace any longer."

"I will make sure Her Grace is prepared for the meeting," Bibi said with enthusiastic confidence. "And I will make sure Master Daniel is in proper costume as well."

Padric stared down at the troll with surprise. "See that you do." He turned back to me. "Your husband is already in conference with the queen and his brother. They will defer to him when dealing with the Unseelie. It is important that you and Daniel support him."

I nodded. We had just been told to behave. I would object but I had come to the same conclusion myself just a few minutes before. This was Dev's world. He understood it better than we did.

"We'll be what Devinshea needs us to be," Daniel promised. He owed Dev. Dev had played whatever role Daniel needed while he was trying to secure his own crown, so backing up Dev was no big deal.

Padric was almost out the door when he turned back. "And Your Grace, keep your wolves close. The Unseelie are not to be trusted. You should never be alone with them."

With those ominous words, the head of the royal guard left us to prepare. As Sarah and Bibi went to get our clothes ready, Daniel and I moved to the window. In the distance we could see a small party making their way from the mountains. I looked out, trying to get a glimpse of the man at the head of the group.

Daniel hugged me from behind, his hand going protectively over my belly. He was quiet as we watched the Unseelie move ever closer. "It's going to be okay, Z. You stay close to me. Dev has to do his thing, so it's my turn to protect you."

On our plane, Daniel trusted my protection to Dev, freeing him to do what he needed to do. It was obvious Danny intended to give Dev the same treatment in Faery. I leaned on Daniel, enjoying having him to myself for once, even if our time was going to be limited because that procession was getting closer and closer.

My eyes were probably playing tricks on me but I would have sworn the man leading the party had enormous antlers.

It was going to be an interesting day.

Chapter Eight

I held Daniel's hand as we stepped out of the palace and onto the white steps where the royals watched the Unseelie approach with suspicious eyes.

While I had been pushed and pulled into my dress, Bibi had patiently answered many of my questions concerning the dark court of Faery. The Unseelie had their own king who had been on his throne for two hundred years longer than Miria. Dev's mother was considered a young queen and many Seelie nobles had been waiting for the dark court to test her will. The Unseelie king was named Angus and he was half *sidhe* and half goblin. It was said he was descended from Balor and like the legendary warrior, he had a third eye which when opened could kill a man with a single glance. Bibi had explained that the envoy would be one of two ascended gods who served as Angus's seconds, and the identity of the selected ambassador would be telling.

The queen looked approvingly on Daniel and me as we took our places behind Devinshea and Declan. She reached behind, pulling my hand into hers. "Hello, daughter. I am so happy to see you well. And you, Daniel."

Daniel nodded her way. "We're happy to stand beside you, Your

Highness."

Dev winked at me.

"All of Faery rejoices at your fertility, daughter. You have brought such joy to our house."

Daniel's arm went around my waist, his mouth coming to my ear. "You always bring joy to our house with or without a child."

He knew exactly what to say. My vampire made me feel secure and safe. He loved me without a care to my ability to produce a child. I knew Dev loved me, too, but I needed to hear it from Danny.

Miria reached for Daniel. She took his hand in her free one. "Daniel, I want to congratulate you. I know you will be a wonderful father. I cannot thank you enough for everything you do for this family. I am proud to call you son."

Yeah, she was making it hard for me to hate her.

Declan made a gagging sound. "Must you, Mother?"

She gently slapped the back of his head. "Quiet."

Really hard for me to hate her.

Unlike our parade to the palace, the Seelie were silent as this caravan marched through the town. The villagers were out of their houses and businesses. They lined the streets but their silence spoke volumes. They were wary, watching every move the small party made.

Bibi had explained that a door located past the great mountains to the north connected the *sitheins* of the Seelie and the Unseelie. The door led to a vast plain travelers must cross to eventually find the entrance to the Unseelie *sithein*. She told me that the envoy more than likely had traveled across the plain by riding an eddy wind, but once on Seelie land, they would be forced to walk. The plain between the *sitheins* was there as a buffer and had once been the sight of many battles between the light and dark courts.

"Can you see who it is?" Declan asked.

I heard Dev let loose a great sigh of relief. "Yes. I would know those hounds anywhere." He turned back to me. "It is all right, my goddess. They sent Herne. If they meant to start a war, they would have sent the other one. Come, he is a friend. Well, his vessel is my friend. The Hunter can be difficult. We will meet him. Daniel, bring the wolves. Herne will appreciate them."

I steeled myself because he'd stopped using contractions. It meant he was definitely thinking about playing the part of the Seelie royal and I needed to back him up. Dev took my hand as Daniel motioned for our bodyguards to join us. Dev looked at his brother. "Can you be civil?"

"As long as he doesn't sic those dogs of his on me," Declan allowed. He nodded his mother's way. "We will greet the Hunter. I suppose it is good news, though I cannot stand the man."

"Please follow your brother's lead for once," Miria said in an irritated voice. She called for one of her assistants and began making arrangements for the envoy's stay.

Dev smiled broadly and began to lead us down the steps. The name they mentioned began to sink in.

"You're telling me that man is Herne? As in Herne the Hunter?" My father is Irish, a Galway boy. He never forgot the old country, and my childhood stories had centered on the Celtic myths and legends. From what I could recall, I didn't see how this was a good thing. If Herne the Hunter was the good one, I didn't want to think about who the Unseelie might have sent instead.

"Yes," Dev replied. "You'll love him. He's interesting."

My slippered feet hit the grass and Daniel took my other hand. He'd heard the same stories. "Yes, I'm sure the Wild Hunt is interesting to the people it hunts down and drags to the Hell plane. How is this good?"

"Don't believe all the faery stories," Dev said. "The Wild Hunt hasn't been used in many years, and then only when a noble breaks his vows. And they aren't dragged to the Hell plane. It's so much worse than that." He stopped briefly and gave his brother a dark look. "You haven't done anything, have you?"

Declan rolled his green eyes. "Would I be walking toward the Wild Hunt if I had? I assure you, I would be running the other way. I have heard the stories and, though I know it would be futile, I would still try. I have no wish to be taken apart by flying beasts."

The flying beasts were a part of the small but deadly army that according to legend made up the Wild Hunt, and Herne the Hunter was the Fae who led it. They sought out oath breakers and made them pay for their lies. It was not something to be wished for.

Dev appeared mollified by Declan's answer. "Good, then he's here because we're friends. He'll want to meet my goddess, and perhaps I can mend the fences you tore down."

"Are those true black dogs?" Daniel pointed out the huge creatures walking beside the man with enormous antlers. Black dogs are a myth on the Earth plane. On the British Isles, there were stories of huge black canines who usually foretold a death. On the Faery plane, however, they were just pets.

"Yes, they are," Dev said, picking up the pace. "It's another good sign. He left the *Cŵn Annwn* at home."

"Those are hell hounds," Declan provided. "The black dogs are sweet little pets compared to the hell hounds. I won't even go into the *Cù-Sìth*. They're huge and green with flames for eyes. The dark court is a place of monsters."

The black dogs were roughly the size of a calf. There were two of them, and they lumbered along on either side of the Hunter. Their long tongues moved in and out of their mouths as they panted in the midday heat. They were so black that in the light of the sun, they appeared to be blue. Behind the Hunter and the black dogs were several goblins who were well armed and appeared to be the Hunter's bodyguards.

"I hope he did not bring the sluagh," Declan griped. "We will be forced to feed them and they make the worst mess. The palace will stink for days."

"This is why we are in this quandary," Dev shot back. "You have no tolerance."

I was kind of with Dec on this one. I didn't want to meet the faery host. They were reputed to be even worse than the Wild Hunt.

I heard Lee start to growl behind me. Dev stopped at the edge of the palace grounds to greet the Hunter. I turned to my chief bodyguard and his eyes were dark and predatory.

"Don't you start something with those dogs," I warned. He could be a little territorial.

He merely gave me a stubborn look and continued to growl. Neil and Zack were getting antsy, too, as the black dogs approached. It was instinctive. They didn't like non-pack canines in their territory, and certainly not around their mistress. It wasn't like I was the alpha bitch or anything, but they took my protection seriously.

The black dogs caught the wolf scent in the air and suddenly they were growling, too, and the hair on the back of their necks was standing at full attention. I started to worry that we would have a fight on our hands.

"Shuck, Barghest, down," the Hunter commanded, his voice deep and filled with his will.

The black dogs sat back on their haunches but kept their eyes on the wolves.

"You keep interesting company, Prince Dev," Herne said with a friendly smile. He was a large man, broader than most of the *sidhe* I'd met, and even taller than Dev. He was six seven at the least. His sable-colored hair only reached his shoulders, but it was mostly obscured by the antlers he wore. Now that I was closer, I could see it was a headdress, but he moved with complete ease as though they were an actual part of his body. I reminded myself that this man was like my husband. He'd taken the non-corporeal hunter god into his Fae body and coexisted with the deity. Unlike Dev, he had given up his own name and chose to be known only as his god. "It's been many years since I was in the presence of a werewolf, yet you travel with three."

"I find they make fine bodyguards on the Earth plane." Dev held his hand out and the ambassador came forward to shake it.

"It's good to have you back, friend," Herne stated, tipping his antlers gracefully. "I began to worry the Earth plane would keep you forever and we would be the poorer for it. Things haven't gone well since you left. Now that you've returned, perhaps we can avoid bloodshed."

"Why shed blood when we could get gloriously drunk?" Dev asked and Herne laughed.

"You always were a lover not a fighter," Herne said, proving the Unseelie nobles were so much less formal than the Seelies. I just liked the fact that he used contractions.

Herne politely acknowledged Declan, but his distaste was easily read. He turned to me and a look of surprise crossed his tanned face. "You finally found your fertility goddess. You'll have to forgive me, Your Grace, but your husband was forever bemoaning the lack of curves in our women. Many times he dragged me to the Earth plane to visit brothels because he needed to bury his face in a soft bosom. When he described his preferred choice of mate, he could have been talking about you specifically."

"Herne," Dev said, blushing just a bit, "I would like to introduce you to my goddess, Zoey, and my partner, Daniel Donovan."

"Very interesting." Herne's dark eyes took in the two of us. He scented the air deeply. "The rumors are true. Your partner is a vampire. Odd. He's walking in the sun."

"It is one of his powers," Dev acknowledged. "Have you ever met a vampire king?"

Herne's eyes widened. The term "king" in this case referred to a trick of Daniel's DNA. Once every thousand years or so a vampire of immense power rose and shook things up. Daniel was working on the "shaking things up" part. "I've met few vampires, though I was impressed with the ones I have come across. They're fierce predators. Arawn will be eager to meet this one."

"I'm sure he would," Dev said in a way that made me think we wouldn't be meeting this Arawn person if Dev had the choice.

"I would prefer to meet your wolves," a deeper voice said.

I looked up even as Daniel placed a steadying hand on my shoulder. There was no doubt who we were speaking with now. His eyes were completely brown, deep and mysterious. Though his face was calm, I could feel the potential for violence. Herne the Hunter held his hands out and Zack and Neil were suddenly furry. They nudged their way around us and greeted the Hunter. They appeared to be happy as they leapt about and wagged their tails, but I didn't like it.

"You forced them?" There was no other answer. They wouldn't have changed on their own.

Herne turned those brown eyes on me. His hands reached down and petted the white and brown wolves almost absently. "They are mine as are all hunters." His stare came to rest on Lee, who was the only one who kept his form. "You resist."

"I have but one mistress," Lee said, a strain in his voice. He was still fighting the urge. "I won't leave her unguarded because you want to fuck around and show off."

Herne cocked a bushy eyebrow as he contemplated my lone wolf. "You need to be tamed, dog."

Lee growled behind me. I stepped up because I'd had enough. "Stop it," I said flatly to the Hunter. "You will leave him alone. He is mine. Is this the way the Unseelie treat their hosts?"

I had his full attention now. "Human, you host nothing. You're not even Fae. You're a vessel for seed and nothing more."

"You will not speak to Her Grace in such a manner. You will remember that she is the wife of our High Priest and deserves respect," Declan ordered and now the black dogs were restless again. Neil and Zack looked from one group to the other, not quite knowing what to do or who to protect.

"I'm afraid I have to take exception as well," Daniel said darkly.

But Herne ignored Daniel, preferring to bare his teeth toward Declan. "Ahh, Your Highness, have you forgotten so soon what happened the last time we met? I believe Barghest took a pound or two from your hide. Are you so eager to lose another?"

Declan flushed and looked over at the growling dogs. "You are in my kingdom now, Hunter. Do I need to call the guards?"

"I don't think that will be necessary, Your Highness." Bris took my hand. He brought it to his lips and gently wound his other arm around my waist. He turned his fully green eyes to the Hunter. "The Hunter will remember his manners around a pregnant lady or he will leave. He's insulting my goddess and I won't stand for it."

The Hunter stopped and looked at me, obviously startled. "Bris, I had heard the prince had ascended. I didn't realize it was you. You've been dormant for a long time. I apologize. I overstepped myself. That one," he gestured to Declan, "angers me. Your Grace, I sincerely ask your forgiveness. If you're carrying the prince's child, then I honor you, of course."

"I assure you, my goddess is full," Bris said, looking at the Hunter. "It's early, of course, but she carries a boy and he'll be important. You should be careful around his mother if you wish for the child to share his gifts with the Unseelie. Perhaps it would be best if we allowed our hosts to handle this. And I would definitely let those wolves go. My goddess is attached to them. It is an insult to her that you took them over."

A boy. I was having a boy.

Herne bowed deeply, but I wasn't sure how much I liked being respected for the simple fact that my womb worked. "You have my deepest respect, Your Grace. I much enjoy spending time with your husband. I meant no harm to your wolves."

Bris smiled down at me and nodded and then he was Dev again. His lips turned down. "I apologize, sweetheart. If I'd known he would insult you, I would never have introduced you."

Neil came to my side and sat while Zack went to Daniel's. They remained in their wolf forms in deference to the fact that their clothes had pretty much exploded. Lee relaxed a bit, and I knew he didn't have to fight anymore.

The Hunter's host looked slightly embarrassed. "I'm sorry, Dev. The Hunter and your brother had words when he visited. It didn't go well. I'm happy to hear your news. Congratulations to all of you." He grew serious. "If this child is what he could be…he could help all of us. The goblins haven't had a live birth in nearly twenty years."

Dev put his arm around me. "I have no problem performing fertility rites. I understand my magic is rare and will happily share it with the Unseelie."

Herne frowned at Declan. 'That isn't what your brother promised. He said you would withhold the rites unless the Unseelie made some unfavorable trade concessions."

Dev sent his brother a dirty look. "While my brother is to be king someday, he does not have control of the temple. My temple is open to all Fae. If it's more convenient, of course, we will travel to the Unseelie *sithein*. My wife is a great lover of the strange. She would find your ways interesting."

"Not if that mean old hunter is an example," I said crossly, leaning over to stroke Neil's head. He thumped his tail but seemed like he was still a little disoriented.

"Barghest, Shuck," Herne said, leaning down to speak to his dogs, "Her Grace seems like a woman who could use a kiss."

I was suddenly assaulted by two huge dogs. I fell back on my butt as they licked my face and looked far cuter than any death omen should. They panted and nudged me with their great noses, begging for me to play. One of the black dogs sniffed Neil's backside and he ran to hide behind Lee. I laughed and ran my hands through their coarse hair. I did love strange creatures, especially when they were as sweet as the dogs seemed.

Dev shook his head and looked at Daniel. "She'll want to take one home."

Daniel was watching me with a smile. "Let's not let her get around the *Cù-Sìth*, then. We would look strange running around Dallas with a green dog with flaming eyes."

"Yes," Herne said with an indulgent smile. "I think Her Grace would fit in with the Unseelie. Let's have an ale. I'll get to know your partner, and perhaps we can find a way to mend our friendships."

* * * *

I finally slipped away from the men two hours later. Herne was having lunch with Dev while Daniel sat in and listened as they told stories of the hunt. While listening to stories of the Hunter killing small creatures might be interesting to the men, I had other objectives to pursue. I also wasn't sure exactly what kind of meat they were eating and after my cat taco experience, I was more careful. I liked to be sure what my lunch was made of. I approached the kitchens with Lee and Neil, who had just rejoined us after finding clothes since his had sort of exploded. Faery was turning out to be hell on Neil's wardrobe.

Sarah had gone into the village to speak with the gnome and Felix had followed his wife, but Neil ambled beside me and he'd finally made friends with our new guests. The black dogs seemed to like me, and Herne made no move to stop them when they trailed after us. They were perfectly well behaved and hadn't tried to hump anything, so I was comfortable with my escort.

Lee, on the other hand, was a little grumpy.

"Stop," he commanded as Shuck nudged him with his huge nose.

"He's just trying to play with you." I scratched Barghest behind his big old ears.

Lee growled and if dogs can pout, that's what Shuck did. He ran over to me and presented his head for a pet.

"Don't take it personally," I told him. "He won't let me pet him either. He's not playful."

I heard a ruckus from down the hall. Someone was shouting and there was a great clanging noise. Neil and Lee both moved quickly to secure me. I found myself up against the wall with Neil covering me.

"Watch her," Lee ordered.

"Like I don't do that all day long," Neil muttered.

"He likes giving orders." I was pretty sure we were safe. The argument sounded like it was coming from the kitchen. It wasn't the best place for an assassin to hide.

"He's a drama queen." Neil sighed, watching Lee disappear behind the doors. The black dogs set their backsides down, their tails thumping against the floor as they looked between us and the door.

"Don't let him hear you say that." Lee could be surprisingly sensitive. My tummy rumbled, and I hoped he dealt with the great cooking tragedy before I used up all of Danny's energy again.

"I hear everything!" Lee yelled. "Zoey, get your ass in here. This is all your fault."

Or it could be all my fault. That happened more than you would expect. Neil and I exchanged a look and followed orders, getting my ass into the kitchens as quickly as possible.

I was presented with a small but important battle. Albert was on one side of the kitchen, looking entirely professional in his white dress shirt and black slacks. He had a very masculine apron on. All he needed was a chef's hat, though I wasn't sure how we would fit it over his horns.

Bibi was sitting on the kitchen counter close to him, her legs and tail dangling. I had wondered where Bibi was spending her time when she wasn't with me. I now discovered she made her way to the kitchens and aided Albert with his preparations. I had no doubt she'd been talking his ears off because once Bibi felt comfortable, she could talk a mile a minute. She was flushed with anger and looked across a marble island that was filled with fresh fruit.

Her adversary stood his ground on the other side. He was an officious-looking faery with his long brown hair in a neat bun at the back of his head. He was dressed to cook and looked at the demon and troll with utter disdain. Bibi, for one, was having none of it.

"This is Her Grace's personal cook," Bibi explained, and from her tone, I could tell it wasn't the first time she'd gone over it. "He has every right to be in this kitchen. He has to make sure Her Grace eats properly for her baby."

The faery sighed and it was easy to see he didn't think talking to these creatures was a good use of his time. "These are my kitchens. I am the head of the palace's chefs. You are not needed in here. I assure you I can handle Her Grace's nutritional needs far better than this demon can. He is not Fae. How could he possible know how to nourish a faery child?"

My secretary shook her fist. "If you don't allow Albert to do his job, I will call my mistress in and then you'll be sorry. She will show you."

I, for one, was interested in knowing how I would show the faery, who was at least a foot and a half taller than me.

"She is fierce and cruel," Bibi continued, her voice promising all manner of torture. "She commands the wolves and they will hunt you down should you cause her a moment's distress."

Neil snorted at the thought and suddenly everyone looked our way. Albert shook his horns, appearing grim and put upon. Bibi flushed, her whole face going pink, while the faery chef looked down his nose at me.

I told myself for the four hundredth time that I was going to be a lady.

"Your Grace, is there a reason you have brought hounds into my kitchens?" the faery asked, frowning at the black dogs.

"I'm sorry. They just kind of follow me around. They're really well behaved." They were. They were politely sniffing around Albert now, who suffered through it all with dignity.

Bibi was past her initial embarrassment and chose to continue her tirade on my behalf. "Her Grace can go wherever she wants. Who are you, a servant, to tell her what she can and cannot do?"

"It's all right, Bibi." I needed to make a few concessions. "I am sure the chef is good at his job. I can just eat whatever the others eat."

Albert sighed deeply, his disappointment an actual weight in the room. "Very well then, mistress. I will allow him to toss out my cilantro with the trash. It is what began this sad situation. He doesn't view it as a proper herb."

Now he had all of our attentions. Neil, Lee, and I were all Southwesterners. We liked our cilantro.

"Just what were you making with that cilantro, Al?" Lee asked, and I could hear his stomach rumble. Lee was always ready to eat.

The demon shrugged coyly. "In honor of my mistress's blessed state, I thought that I would make a lunch of enchiladas, rice, and beans. It's my mistress's favorite. Sadly, the palace chef doesn't believe Tex-Mex is worthy of his kitchens. I should warn you, my mistress, that he's also told me I'm not allowed to fry anything. He doesn't understand your cultural need to fry everything possible in hot grease."

"What the hell are you making for lunch?" Lee asked the faery chef.

His superior smile said it all. "I am creating a summer salad of all the freshest ingredients. It will be topped with morning dew I collected from the finest flowers of our royal gardens." All of this was said in hushed tones as though this was a great and honored meal fit for kings or queens.

Unfortunately, I had to feed wolves. They weren't big on salads.

Neil looked at Lee with desperation on his face. "He has to go."

Lee turned to me. "It's your decision, Zoey. You're the one who has to deal with the consequences." He shook his head at Neil. "No, we have to trust Zoey. She'll either pick the nonconfrontational route that gets all of us a meal of freaking morning dew or she'll go with beef and cheese."

"Please go with beef and cheese," Neil pleaded. "I don't think I'll like morning dew. It doesn't sound filling. Is it anything like Mountain Dew?"

"Did I mention the chocolate pie I made earlier that he wanted to throw out with the cilantro?" Albert asked.

"Faeries do not eat this chocolate of yours," the chef informed me with an aristocratic huff.

"Dev does," Neil pointed out. He did. Especially chocolate sauce since he liked to lick it off my body.

"You," I said to the chef, raising my voice in my most regal fashion. "Out."

My need to be ladylike completely lost to my need for chocolate. I had nine months to eat whatever I liked and fool myself into thinking my body would just bounce back after the baby was born. I wasn't about to waste that time on morning dew, which I was pretty sure didn't have anything to do with Mountain Dew.

"I shall take this up with Her Majesty," the chef promised as he turned and huffed out.

I looked at Albert. "You, start frying tortillas."

Albert smiled, completely satisfied. "It's already done. I merely need to bake the entrée, mistress. In the meantime," he began, placing a large platter on the table, "I took the time to make an appetizer of pulled pork nachos. Please enjoy."

Neil actually drooled as he and Lee started in on the nachos. "I love you, Albert."

"And I'm fond of you, Neil." Albert checked the temperature of the ovens with his usual air of competence. He put the platters in and turned to me with a suspicious look as I tried to hide the fact that I was feeding the black dogs under the table. "Mistress, you wouldn't happen to know why the brownies have suddenly stopped their routine cleaning?"

I shrugged because I was totally at a loss. I savored the greasy goodness of the nachos while Shuck thumped his tail, impatient for another. "Why would I know that? Besides, my rooms were perfectly cleaned."

Neil nodded and answered around a mouthful of nachos. "My bed was made this morning and it wasn't me or Zack."

"Apparently the brownies have gone to the head housekeeper and they are demanding something they call 'flavors,'" Albert said, his mouth turned down.

"Oh, crap." Yeah, that was me, too. I had to hope the Seelie wanted this baby or I might get us all tossed out. I decided to try to feign innocence. "Would you believe me if I said I know nothing about it?"

"Not at all, mistress," Albert intoned with a patient sigh. One hoof tapped along the marbled floor.

I tried to come up with a way to tell the story that made me look as innocent as possible. I hadn't meant to cause a revolt, after all. "Well, you know how the brownies clean up and all you have to do to keep them happy is leave out a small bowl of cream?"

"Yes, I'm aware of the exchange."

"I thought it might be fun to leave them shots, like what you get in a diner to put in your coffee," I explained. "So I might have gone to Costco and brought in a couple of crates of flavored cream. I might have exchanged it for their regular cream. I mean the poor things have to eat the same damn cream every day. Let's switch it up, people. Right? It's no big deal, Al, just a little hazelnut and vanilla cream. Maybe some caramel."

Albert shook his head. "Mistress, I hope you brought enough. They all wish to try the flavors. If you continue to feed strange creatures, we will be returning to our home with a menagerie. We'll have to start a zoo."

Barghest whined at my feet, proving Albert's point.

Just at that moment the door swung open and two goblins entered. They were short but fierce looking, with leathery skin and red eyes. They swaggered in, their eyes going directly to me.

"We demand flesh and blood," the tallest one said.

"Okay, I'll go with my patent response of ewww," I said with a glance at my wolves, who seemed to not care that two fierce warriors had accosted me. They were far too busy downing nachos.

"We're hungry, human," the shorter one said. "We demand our midday meal as is our right. You're our hosts. You'll give us flesh and blood. We don't eat greenery."

"Amen, brother," Lee said with a growl and a manly belch.

"I don't have any flesh and blood." I looked down at the goblins. I doubted Albert had thought to bring along packets of blood and hunks of flesh. Though now that I thought about it, it might have been a good idea.

They looked me over with toothy grins. There was no lust in their eyes. I think they were wondering how many burgers they could get out of me. "You certainly have plenty of flesh, my lady, and you're full of blood."

I reached out and slapped him right on his scraggly head.

His clawed hand reached up and massaged his forehead. "The human hit me."

"She did," the other goblin replied, looking at me curiously. "Does she intend to start a war?"

"No," I said, hitting the other one just as firmly. I didn't have to play the lady with the Unseelie. They would just see it as a weakness. "But I'm not going to be intimidated and I'm certainly not going to be your meal. Now, you're welcome to join us for our lunch if you can behave. We're having enchiladas."

Lee slapped at the table, giving me a stern frown. "Yeah, a small portion if you keep inviting people in. You're already planning on feeding those damn dogs."

The taller goblin gave me a disdainful look. "We don't eat anything called enchiladas. Seelie food is distasteful. It's shit."

I rolled my eyes and picked up a particularly pork-filled chip. While the goblin was complaining about all things Seelie, I shoved it in his mouth.

He sputtered and choked and then finally managed to chew for a moment. He looked at his friend. "We're staying for lunch."

Albert sighed deeply. "We'll have to begin an Unseelie wing in the penthouse," he warned. "Please, mistress, do not feed the sluagh the skittles I know you smuggled in. I have no wish to clean an aviary."

I chewed my food and promised nothing.

Chapter Nine

Neil was quiet as we moved from the banquet hall into the grand ballroom later that night. He'd been contemplative most of the day after the episode with Herne. Zack had managed to blow the whole thing off but Neil had issues. He'd been nearly silent the whole rest of the day, preferring to be my bodyguard rather than the BFF role he usually took. He'd stayed by my side, but I caught him glancing warily Herne's way from time to time. I knew he was thinking about that time in Vegas when Daniel had been able to force his will on him.

He stood in one of the open doorways, looking out over the water. The grand ballroom was open to the night and overlooked a field with a winding stream that gleamed silver in the moonlight. In Faery, they didn't worry about mosquitoes or rainstorms. The night was merely another lovely setting and they took advantage. Neil watched the fields in the distance, but it didn't seem to calm him. The moon was only half full but I wondered if he wanted to run.

"Is he all right?" Sarah asked, her eyes worried.

"I don't think so," I replied. "I think Herne is bringing back bad memories. He didn't have a choice. One minute he was Neil and the next minute he was a wolf with a new master."

"It's creepy." She looked back to where Dev and Danny were

seated with Herne. The three were talking and laughing and generally getting along. The Hunter had been silent and his host was a jovial man.

"I'm sure it felt that way for Neil."

"I was talking about the whole 'sharing your body with a god' thing. I hadn't thought about it before. I mean, Bris is so gentle," Sarah said, watching Herne. "Besides being constantly horny and having no qualms about public sex, he's helpful, you know. I was having trouble with the basil in my garden and he was so sweet about it. I can't imagine that hunter guy is helpful. And from what you told me, he's a Neanderthal. Join the twenty-first century, dude."

"I don't think you can think of him as a dude, Sarah. He isn't a man and he never was. He's the spirit of the hunt. The way it works, the vessel and the god have to be somewhat well matched or they can't bond. It's one of the reasons it took Bris so long to find a proper vessel. Dev and Bris are similar. No matter how nice Herne may seem, he has a lot in common with the Hunter or he wouldn't be in there."

"Are you all right with Bris being the father of your baby?" Sarah never shied away from the tough questions.

"Dev and Daniel will be the fathers," Neil corrected. He'd come up behind me and laid a hand on my shoulder.

"I was talking about the fact that Bris was inhabiting the body when Zoey got pregnant," Sarah clarified.

Neil shrugged. "So, who gives a crap? There's a lot more to being a dad than two seconds' worth of orgasm. The big question is who's going to take care of the kid once he's here and the answer is Dev and Daniel. Don't try to make this into one of those daytime talk shows where they shock the baby daddy with surprise DNA tests."

"Neil, it's nothing that hasn't crossed my mind." I understood why he was so touchy. His own father had been horrible. He'd kicked Neil to the curb and then sent the pack to torment him because he'd been different. Neil wasn't too big on biological fathers.

He smiled as his brain took him in strange directions. "Though it would be a funny episode. Once they told Dev he wasn't the biological father, do you think he would beat the crap out of himself?

How would the bouncers handle that?"

"Let's not find out," I murmured, wincing because the Duke of Ain was approaching.

"Your Grace." The duke bowed obsequiously. Apparently the more they scraped the floor, the more respect they were showing. "I was thrilled to hear the news of your delicate condition. It is such a boon to Faery that the prince will have a child to pass on his magnificent magic to."

I didn't like Gilliana's father. He was lean with blond hair and cold blue eyes. When he looked at me, I felt like he was sizing me up. I'd been told by Bibi that Braden was a cousin of the queen and considered important throughout the realm. He held vast lands to the north that were crucial both agriculturally and in trade. He'd also wanted to get rid of the queen's son when he was proven mortal. I was having a hard time smiling and placating the man. The only reason he tolerated my husband was that "magnificent magic" of his.

"Thank you." I gave him my fakest smile, hoping to get this encounter over with in a hurry. Perhaps I could use this whole "baby mama" thing to my advantage. I could talk about how tired I was and go cuddle up with one of the books I'd brought. "It's early, though. I hardly feel pregnant at all except for the exhaustion."

Sarah and Neil looked at me with suspicious eyes. I'd been energetic all day.

"I am sure you will feel the pressure soon enough, Your Grace," Braden said snidely, to my mind.

"Pressure?" It was an odd choice of words.

He nodded. "Well, all of Faery will anxiously await the birth of this child. Our fertility is practically nonexistent. It is better on the Seelie side, of course. We are the blessed court. Providence favors us. The Unseelie haven't seen a new generation for many years. If your child is truly gifted with his father's fertility magic then we have hope. It must be a great burden to have a whole kingdom's fate resting in your womb."

I was still getting used to the idea of having a baby at all. I was getting used to the idea of changing diapers and breast feeding and not sleeping at night. I was wondering how easy it was going to be to raise a kid when we lived over a nightclub. I was picturing Albert settling into his nanny duties. I wasn't ready to think about the fact that my baby had political implications.

"Don't scare my sister-in-law," Declan ordered, coming in from the field where he had been "walking" with a pretty brunette. They split up now, but she glanced back at him with the hint of a smile as she walked off to join her friends. There was still grass in his hair, and I wondered how he could ever smooth talk a woman into lying on the ground for him. I supposed he could always use that whole "I'm going to be your king" thing. He might just order them to. I wouldn't put it past him.

"I was merely letting Her Grace know how much I admire her for taking on the challenge," Braden said with the smooth tones of a courtier.

Declan frowned, his mouth turning to a pout. "Well, it is not a grand talent. She spread her legs for my brother, he spent his seed, and nature took its course. She is human. They breed like rabbits. I am much more impressed with her fellatio skills."

I reached over and punched my brother-in-law on the arm. "You're such a jerk."

He shrugged. I was sure he'd been called worse. "Well, I only speak the truth. While I am thrilled with your fully functional sex organs, I am not going to worship you for your womb."

Braden ignored our immature fight. I was sure having been around Declan all of Dec's life, he was used to the brat prince. "I was merely explaining that her child could be important to the Seelie."

Declan's green eyes narrowed. "Don't even think it. My brother would never allow that to happen."

"What's he talking about?" The subtext eluded me.

"He is pointing out the fact that the Unseelie have no priest," Declan explained. His words were slightly slurred. "They have no fertility magic. In the past, they had one or two priests, but almost all of them were half Seelie. Over the years, the two courts have grown more insular. We rarely interbreed. The Unseelie lost their last priest over two hundred years ago. They survive because of our priests. My grandfather was a tolerant man."

"A great man," Braden corrected.

"Yes, yes, he was a great man but he was friendly with the

monsters, too," Declan continued. "He spent as much time in the Unseelie *sithein* as he did in his own. He was more than willing to perform the necessary rites. There has been talk among certain factions of withholding our blessings from the Unseelie."

"This is what Herne was talking about." I finally understood exactly why the Unseelie were so upset. "You threatened them. You told them Devinshea wouldn't work with them."

"You have no idea what they are capable of." Declan stared down at me, anger plain in his eyes. "You have no idea what it means to be at their mercy when they have none. After what Devinshea went through, I do not see how he can stand to be in the same room with them, much less help them to make more monsters."

Dev had his grandfather's tolerance. "He doesn't judge the whole of the Unseelie for the actions of a few."

"Do you know why we were there, Zoey?" Declan asked. I'd heard the tale, seen it with my own eyes on a quick trip to the Hell plane. He and Devinshea had lived with the Unseelie for a year when they were seventeen and Dev had been assaulted.

"Dev told me your mother sent you to test your strength." The exact words Dev had used, however, had been that she sent them there to be tortured.

Braden took up the point now. "It is an old rite of passage. It had to be done. Miria was furious when Devinshea chose to go with his brother, but she could not talk him out of it. If Declan had refused to go, he would never be able to be king."

"This child you carry, he will be important," Declan said, his words softer now. "But he will be a priest. He will not be asked to take that rite of passage, nor will any brother of his. My son will. So I say let them fade. Bring on the war that finally separates us once and for all so I never have to stand at the gates and watch my son as Mother had to watch me."

Declan turned and walked away.

"You will have to forgive His Highness," Braden requested. "His time with the Unseelie left him…unsettled."

I watched as Declan walked to the tables and ordered a drink. He grabbed the bottle straight out of the servant's hands and took a long swig as he watched his brother talking to Daniel and Herne. There was something dark in his eyes that made me worry.

Glancing back at Neil and Sarah, I started to walk toward my brother-in-law. "I'm going to talk to him. The way he looks, he might start a fight and that's the last thing Dev needs. Stay here."

"Lee will kill me," Neil protested.

"I'm not leaving the ballroom." Lee was attempting to track down the servant who had brought breakfast to the archer this morning. He was tracking his scent through the countryside. "I'll be fine. I just want to talk to him."

I crossed the full ballroom, making my way around the edges of the dance floor. Miria was dancing in Padric's arms, but her eyes constantly strayed to Dev's table. It was like she worried if she took her eyes off of him he would disappear again. I made it just in time. Declan was watching that table, too. He cursed as he set the bottle down, and I could see he meant to go and have a word or two with someone. I was pretty sure he wasn't planning on talking about the weather. It wouldn't go well and a fight would set back any progress Dev had made. I reached out and grabbed Declan's hand. He whirled on me. "What do you want, Zoey?"

"I want you to not make an ass of yourself." He didn't get to be annoyed with me when I was so busy being annoyed with him.

I tried to pull my hand back but he held it firmly. "Fine, then you will have to give me something else to do, Your Grace. Making an ass of myself was the only plan I had for the evening."

He hauled me onto the dance floor and settled his free hand on my waist. He held me closer than decorum dictated, but I was just happy he could stand. He must have started drinking early in the afternoon to have gotten to this point. I looked around for one of his servants to see if someone could help me get him to his rooms.

"I'm fine, Zoey," he insisted, reading my mind. "Welcome to the royal court. This is what we do. We have parties and get drunk and plot behind each other's backs."

"It sounds like a charming life."

"It was," he said quietly. "I was perfectly happy until about eighteen months ago."

That was when Devinshea had chosen to leave the Faery mound. There was a strange phenomenon that occurred between the Earth plane and the *sitheins*. Time moved differently in the *sithein*. Dev had experienced almost seven years of maturing on the Earth plane while his brother was still twenty-two. There was a big difference between twenty-eight, married with a kid on the way, and twenty-two and single, still rolling around with strange women in the grass. Devinshea now had much more in common with Daniel than he had with the brother he'd shared a womb with. It must be difficult for Declan. His brother had returned an entirely different person with different priorities.

"What I cannot understand is why I am being punished." Declan stared down at me. "I had nothing to do with the plot. I helped Dev leave when I was certain it was what he needed. If I had known what Mother intended, I would have warned him. Why is he so distant to me?"

"He's a different person, Declan," I tried to explain.

"But I am not different. I am the same brother he loved before. I am the same brother he used to play with and drink with and whore with. It was a good life."

Declan maneuvered us around the edges of the dance floor and before I knew it, I found myself hauled into a small room off the ballroom. It was lit only with moonlight and had the same view of the field and stream as the east wall.

"Zoey." Declan pulled me in with him. I noted the room's door was a simple curtain that Declan let drop. It was furnished with a large couch that could certainly double as a bed. He pulled me close. "Let me in."

"Dec, what the hell is this?" I asked, trying to get away from him.

"It's a room for privacy," he explained. "You said you wanted to talk."

"No, I wanted to keep you from starting a fight." I could guess that most people who wanted privacy weren't interested in talking.

"Then give me something better to do," he insisted.

Now I planted my feet, a bit of fear creeping in. I was in a terrible situation. I didn't want to scream, but I knew I might have to. "Declan, don't do this."

He drew me to the couch. "What am I doing?"

"If you try to force me, I swear…"

Even in the moonlight, I could see how his face went pale. He dropped my hands and put some distance between us. "You think I was going to rape you?"

"Well, you dragged me into a convenient little room," I replied. "What am I supposed to think?"

Declan put his head in his hands, unwillingly sobering up. "I have no idea what happened to me that my pregnant sister-in-law thinks I would drag her into the night and force myself on her. I was going to do something much worse, Zoey. I was going to beg."

"Beg for what?" I settled down, fairly certain I wasn't about to be assaulted.

He shrugged, and his wry smile reminded me so much of his brother. "Well, I was going to beg for sex, but I wasn't going to force you. I would be very gentle given your condition. If you let me in your bed, Devinshea would be all right with it. It would bring us closer. You'll see it would be the best thing for our whole family. It is what we always planned, Zoey. We planned to find a woman we both liked and settle down."

"That's ridiculous, Declan," I said, disgusted at the thought. "Dev wouldn't be all right with it and Daniel would kill you."

"Well," he admitted, "my plan does require getting rid of the vampire. You have to think clearly now, Zoey. I am sure the vampire has been exciting and he is probably a pleasure in bed, but you are a wife now and you carry a faery child. Your ties to Faery are much more meaningful than anything the vampire can give you. You owe us."

I stood up, ready to plead exhaustion and be done with all of this for the evening. If Declan wanted to start a fight, then maybe I should let him. "I don't owe you anything. I married Daniel and I'm happy with him. Dev is happy with him."

I was almost out the door when I heard his sad response. "Devinshea replaced me."

I saw Neil open the curtain, but I shook my head to let him know I was fine for the moment. He let the curtain fall back but I knew he would listen in. He would stand beside the entrance and wait for anything strange.

Declan had lain back on the couch, and I could see the pain in his eyes.

"He didn't replace you." I said the words, but I wondered if I was lying. Dev and Daniel had become close. Sometimes they worked together so flawlessly, I wondered if they weren't halves of a whole. I knew beyond a shadow of a doubt that Dev was happier sharing me with Daniel than he would have been having me to himself. I doubted, however, that if Daniel were suddenly gone, he would immediately ask his brother to be our third. Whatever the brothers had shared before, Dev had moved on.

"Yes, he did," Declan stated surely. "I should have gone with him. When he left, I should have followed him. He would have followed me. I have lost him."

I sat down beside him, and when he moved to put his head in my lap, I let him. He was that pathetic. He didn't even try anything sexual. He just rested against me. "You could try talking to him. You could try listening to him. I know he loves you."

"But he doesn't like me much," Declan whispered.

I wasn't sure what to say to that so I let him rest. I placed my hand on his head and wondered what he was going to do when he realized we meant to live on the Earth plane. I got the sneaking suspicion that my pregnancy was going to complicate our living arrangements. So far the boys had been talking like we would go home and raise the baby there, but I had a feeling Miria and Declan thought something different.

The music stopped and suddenly there were lovely female voices. At first I thought it was just one and she seemed far away, but after a moment, I could hear at least three and the sound was stronger. It was haunting and beautiful, filling the space like a wind rushing in and getting caught. It seemed to whirl around me. I felt a great sadness well up inside me as I listened and then Declan sat up suddenly.

"Oh, goddess, no," he said, his voice a small prayer. "Please, no."

Neil pulled back the curtain and he and Sarah rushed in the room. I could hear the sound of many footsteps scrambling across the floor outside.

"Something's happening," Neil said. "Everyone's freaking out."

Declan rushed to the open windows of the room. He stared out and I saw him stiffen. "No."

I followed him and my eyes could make out three women in the distance. They were the source of the mournful song, for I recognized it as a lament now. They kneeled by the stream and seemed to be washing clothes.

"What are they?" Sarah stood behind me.

"Why is everyone terrified by women washing clothes?" Neil asked.

"*Bean si*," Declan whispered as though he didn't want to say the name too loud.

Neil and Sarah looked at me, confusion plain on their faces. Declan had used the Irish name for the washer women. He could just as easily call them by their Scots name, *Bean sith*, for it all meant the same thing. These women popped up in all Fae worlds.

I shook, a chill blanketing my body because I knew the name. I looked at my friends and used the term they would understand.

"Banshee."

Chapter Ten

"So these women sing and wash stuff and then kill someone?" Neil asked, staring out at the banshees. We had moved out of the small room and back into the ballroom where we had a much better view of the stream.

The three women were dressed in white and each had flowing blonde hair. I couldn't see their mouths moving, but I knew the song emanated from them.

"No, wolf. The banshees warn of coming death. They are not the ones who carry out the deed." Miria looked pale as she watched the women. The queen stood beside us, at the front of the crowd that had gathered.

The entire ball had stopped and everyone stood at the open windows, staring out at the sight. The sound of their voices was oppressive, as though it had weight and motion. Their song filled the ballroom as the previous music couldn't. It vibrated along the marble, and I could feel it on my skin.

"They are not harmless, though." Herne watched the scene with dark eyes. The goblins guarding him were the only ones who looked excited at the current events. Their red eyes danced as they looked around, probably wondering which of the *sidhe* would be a corpse soon. Herne's voice was serious. "I wouldn't approach them if you have a set of balls. They don't take kindly to men in their space. Apparently grief is women's work."

"Don't stand too close." Daniel tugged on my waist. He tried to pull me away from the window.

"Yes, why don't we take her back to our apartments?" Dev suggested, his face tense. He didn't like the banshee's appearance any more than Declan had. "She's probably tired, and I don't want her around something so unsettling."

"I'm not unsettled, Dev," I said irritably. I was going to fight them for nine damn months. I was pregnant, not an invalid. I had no intention of spending the next nine months of my life in a bubble. "I am, however, curious."

"Yes, Your Grace." Braden looked strangely aggressive when everyone else was cowering a bit. "I find it curious that the banshee wail not a day after the Unseelie invade our territory."

"It was hardly an invasion," Dev argued. "They sent an envoy."

"What exactly are you accusing me of?" The vessel was completely gone, his personality wiped out by the dominance of the Hunter. His brown eyes pinned the duke, who had to look away.

"I was just making mention of the coincidence in the events," the duke said, fooling no one.

Declan was far stupider than the duke. He stepped straight up to the Hunter. "You know damn well what Braden is saying. You show up with your demon dogs and suddenly one of us is going to die. I do not think there is anything coincidental about it. I think you planned it this way."

The Hunter's smile was savage. "You think it's going to be you, don't you, Declan? You think I'm going to kill you."

"Well, the thought had occurred to me," Declan replied through clenched teeth. "You've threatened me often enough. Perhaps I should try taking you out first."

They were almost at each other's throats when Padric pulled Declan off and Devinshea tried to talk to the Hunter. "Let's stay calm. There's no reason to believe Declan is the one who's going to die. That's just his paranoia. It could easily be one of the villagers."

"No, son," Miria said quietly, but with a resolute firmness. "There are three. The Three would not show up for a villager. It is an important death. It is more than likely someone of royal blood."

The hall erupted in conversation. Everyone speculated on which of the royal family would die and what the cause would be. Arguments began and escalated quickly to the point of violence. Immortals didn't handle the potential end of their existence well. I personally was wondering how they thought that yelling at each other was going to solve the problem. As far as I could tell, it would only possibly make the prophesized death happen that much faster. I had an easier way to stop the speculation.

"Neil, could you give me a hand down?" I asked quietly while all the attention was elsewhere.

His light eyes widened. "Zoey, you can't go down there."

"Why?"

"Because," was Neil's intelligent reply.

Daniel caught the last of that conversation. He knew me well enough to easily discern my next move. "Absolutely not, Zoey Donovan. Put it out of your mind. You are not going down there."

"Give me one good reason," I challenged him and Dev, since he was now standing beside Daniel, looking outraged at the thought.

"I'll give you three," Dev said, pointing to the women.

I put a hand on my hip. It's something I do when I'm feeling particularly stubborn, and it should have been a signal to the men in my life that I meant business. "What are they going to do? Sing me to death?"

"Yes," Dev replied. "When they want to those banshees can shatter human bones with their voices."

"Come on, Z," Daniel said seriously. "You've read *X-Men*, baby. That's some serious shit."

It isn't easy to argue with a true geek. He always has some pop culture reference. Danny was wary of the damn goblins because his World of Warcraft character always got killed by them. It was so much easier to deal with Neil, who wouldn't know a goblin from a leprechaun because the *Real Housewives* didn't cover those topics.

"Why shouldn't I ask them a few questions?" I decided to try logic. If that didn't work, I would wait until they turned around and run the other way. "They want to come here and wail then they should be ready to answer a few quick, politely asked questions."

"That is not how it works," Declan replied as though he was speaking to an unnaturally slow child.

"Zoey, we do not question the *bean si*," Padric explained. Though I was sure he knew it would do no good, his hand was on the hilt of his sword. It was the unconscious habit of a warrior. "We do not bother the washer women. We merely pray that they do not touch our house."

"As plans go, that one sucks." Was I the only one who wanted answers? I sure as hell wasn't going to just sit around with my thumb up my ass, hoping they weren't singing about me. "Look, why would they stand around and wail if nothing anyone can do is going to change things? It doesn't make any sense."

"They do not have to make sense." Declan was subdued now. He watched the women sing and crossed his arms protectively over his chest. He was nervous and had moved away from the Hunter now. He inched closer to his brother, though he did not attempt to speak to him.

"What happened to the last person who tried to talk to them?" I should probably at least know what I was walking into. I've discovered that when walking into dangerous situations, knowing how the last idiot to attempt it died helps me to avoid her fate. I might die a brand new horrible death, but at least it would be my own.

There was a telling silence as everyone looked around. I was greeted with a multitude of blank expressions. I shook my head at all of them. "Seriously? What is wrong with you people?" I threw a leg over the open window sill.

The Hunter smiled even as Dev and Danny started to protest. "She is completely insane. I like her. It's a shame she's probably about to die."

"Not helpful," I shot back at him. Daniel leapt over the sill and Dev was thinking about it. "Not on your life, mister. You heard what the guy with the horns said. No boys allowed. I'm all full on vamp blood so if they try to take my head off, Sarah will just run down and hold it on until it heals. I'll be fine."

Daniel and Dev gave each other a long look.

"If they are willing to talk, and I'm not saying they will be, but if they are, they won't do it around a man," Dev said. "I don't think they'll harm her if she's careful. And polite. Try to remember the polite part, my goddess."

"Fine," Danny said, crossing his arms and planting his feet. "But I'm waiting right here, and if one of them even starts to make anything like a sonic boom, I'm coming. All right?"

I nodded shortly. "I'll be back in a minute."

There was a collective shudder as the queen appeared at the window and asked Daniel to help her down. He gracefully lifted Miria over the sill and onto the grass. She smoothed out her dress and joined me.

"Miria." Padric said her name with all the masculine indignation he could muster. It was sad because even though she was the Queen of Faery, she still had to put up with some man trying to protect her. I knew the feeling well.

Her hand was already in mine as she turned back to her lover. "If my new daughter can be brave enough to face them, then I can find the strength to go with her. Wait here, Padric. She is right. This is not a place for men. I will return."

We started down the hill and the lights from the palace waned. We were left with the moonlight shining brightly off the stream. The water flowed from the mountains past the palace and into the valley below. We followed the stream downhill, and in the moonlight, it looked like things were moving in the shining waters. I almost stopped when I saw what looked like a horse's head staring out from the reeds in the water.

"Do not look for long," Miria instructed. "There are kelpies in these waters, and they will try to lure you down."

I shuddered as we passed the water horse and its shining eyes. It whispered to me, but Miria's hand was firm and she led me away.

I was thankful now for my "proper costume" because it included slippers. If I'd worn my normal formal stilettos, I would be going barefoot and I didn't want to know if the black dogs had been playing in this field.

"Why three?" I asked to break our tense silence.

"They represent the three sides of the goddess." Her strawberry-blonde hair looked lighter as we moved away from the palace. Her skin glowed as though the moonlight allowed her to shine. "They are the maid, the matron, and the crone. They rarely sing their songs together. When they do, it is usually an important death."

On the Earth plane, it is said the banshee will only wail for the five most important families in Ireland. On the Faery planes, they wailed for the royals and the highest of nobles. I was hoping for a noble because the royal family was small and even Declan's death would have horrible consequences for me. Declan's death would place Dev closer to the throne, but more importantly, it would make the son growing in my belly a direct heir to the crown. I didn't want that.

We stopped at a polite distance. Strangely their song seemed quieter here, as though proximity diluted the sound in an illogical fashion. I got my first real glimpse at the keeners. They looked to be the same woman but at different times of life. The young one was, perhaps, sixteen. She was lovely, with an unblemished face and a youthful body. The matron appeared to be in her early thirties, and she was ripe with child. The crone was wrinkled, but there was still an odd beauty to her countenance. Their eyes were the sliver of a full moon.

I heard my mother-in-law take a steadying breath beside me. I let go of her hand and stepped forward. Polite. Dev had told me to be polite, and I was determined to follow that particular edict.

"Hello," I said with my most gracious voice. "First off, I would like to thank you very much for the evening's entertainment. It wasn't even pitchy."

They all three stopped what they were doing and, in perfect synchronicity, turned toward me. Their heads cocked to the side, and I could tell they were surprised by our appearance.

"Good evening, Your Highness," the matron said. Her voice was even and strong. It sounded nothing like her ethereal singing voice.

Miria gathered her courage and stepped forward with a regal bow of her head. "Good evening."

The matron smiled, though there was no humor in her face. "I was not talking to you, Miria, Queen of the Seelie Fae, though you are certainly welcome. I was speaking to Zoey, Queen of all Vampire."

Miria was startled and looked at me, her eyes wide with shock. "Daughter?"

"Well, I don't exactly have a crown or anything." I was deeply uncomfortable with the distinction. Daniel was the uncrowned King of Vampire. I was his wife and still unsure what my place was.

"You do not sit upon your throne, yet, Your Highness, and it is not certain that you ever will," the crone intoned. Like the others, she wore a white dress, but it hung upon her frail frame. "It is up to you. You are a piece of the cloth that remains unknown."

"You are a nexus point," the maiden explained, her voice soft and lyrical. There was a garland of white flowers in her hair that marked her virginity.

Miria again seemed startled at the pronouncement, but I was just confused. "What's a nexus point?"

"It means you are important." Miria's voice shook slightly. I could easily tell she was wondering what her son had gotten them all into. I was wondering the same thing.

"You are a person who holds her own fate," the matron explained. "Because your fate is unwritten, the fate of all around you is dependent upon you."

"Their fates flow through the decisions you make," the crone continued. "The pathways you choose change the fate of those you love. I give you an example…"

"You changed the fate of Daniel Donovan by loving him," the maiden said. "If you had not been in his life, he would have lived to be an old man and when he died, the Council would have aided him in walking into the light. Because he loved you, he found himself on the road at night. He turned early and all of Vampire was changed."

Daniel died in a car accident while he was getting dinner for me. I've heard talk of latent vampires dying earlier because they were involved with women who were companions. I've heard it said that having a companion close makes the latent vampire more reckless.

"Devinshea Quinn should have died on the Earth plane when his business was robbed." The matron moved toward me now, and it took everything I had to not back away. "Now he lives and Faery has a chance to thrive."

On my first date with Dev, I'd uncovered a plot to rob his

business. I'd made him aware that a group was coming to steal from him and he'd been ready. Had I really saved him that night? And I had been the one to cause Daniel's death?

"All of this is interesting." The thought gave me chills, filled me with fear. I didn't want the responsibility, and I certainly didn't want to think about how I had changed my husbands' lives—killing one and saving the other. "I'm grateful to you for sharing these stories, but why are you here tonight? Why do you sing this evening?"

"We sing for him," they said in chorus.

I was proud of myself because I didn't roll my eyes. I hate the whole prophecy rigmarole. It would be one thing if said prophet ever did a girl a solid and just pointed and said that dude in the red shirt is going to die. They can't do that. It goes against their union rules. They have to make their prophecies into a code you have to crack. I think it's because an awful lot of prophecy comes after said prophet gets high. They often sounded like they had taken way too much peyote to me.

"It is a man who will die?" Miria asked, her voice thick with emotion.

"He is, indeed, male," they said.

"Could you cough up a name, maybe?" I asked.

The three heads tilted, and Miria gave me a look that told me to behave. I had to try.

"He is important," the maiden said.

"He is the second child of his mother, though she carried only once," the matron continued.

"He will not be," the crone finished.

Miria had fallen to her knees, and I heard her sob. "Devinshea."

I felt my own tears because he was the second son of a mother who had only ever carried the twins. I reached out and felt her grab my hand. I faced the banshee even as the tears started to fall. I couldn't fall apart. I had to figure out how to save him. "Is it my husband? How does it happen? Is someone going to try to kill him?" I used the word "try" because I couldn't face anything else.

The matron stepped forward and looked at me not unkindly. "We have said what we can. I only know that Faery will mourn but in the spring life will come again."

"The baby," Miria said tearfully.

My baby. She was talking about my baby, who might be down one dad soon. I couldn't let that happen. If I was this nexus point thing, then I had some say in this. They said my choices changed things. I was definitely choosing to not lose Dev. "What do I have to do to stop it?"

The matron, who was definitely in charge now, reached out to take my hand. Her flesh was cold against mine but her strength was steady. "There is nothing you can do this time. It is written."

"Then why are you here?" I asked bitterly. Inside I was raging against the thought that it was written somewhere that Dev was going to die. I was going to find that damn book and do a rewrite. "Why bother with this show? Is it just to torture me, to make my last days with him hell? I'll spend every minute waiting for him to die. How is that helpful?"

The crone and the maiden took steps forward, their faces darkening. The matron held one hand out while keeping mine in the other. "She loves. It is powerful and we should make allowances. After all, she is the only one in many years to brave our presence. She is a warrior. She will fight this battle no matter what we say."

The crone looked sad as she watched me cry. "And she will lose."

The tears were burning my eyes. "Why?" I asked more politely now. "If I can't save him, why tell me he's going to die?"

"You cannot save the one who will die," the matron said, looking deeply into my eyes. "But you can stop the war his death will begin."

"You are the only one who can stop it," said the crone.

"You are the only one who can save both sides of Faery," the maiden finished. "The sun and moon will meet in battle, and it will be the last one."

"If you fail, something precious will fade from this plane forever," the matron explained. "Find the Blood Stone. It will lead you to the truth. It will lead you back to yourself."

"The Blood Stone?" Miria asked. "What does that have to do with anything?"

But the matron released me, taking a step back to join the others.

"You must go now. We have work to do. You will figure it out, Your Highness, and you will make your own fate."

"Wait," I called out because I couldn't leave it.

Miria was on her feet, using her strength to drag me away. "No, daughter, they are done. You will not help Devinshea by angering them. Think of your child."

But I wasn't thinking of my child. I turned from the river where the women took up their washing once more, and their mournful song could be heard through the valley. I turned from my mother-in-law and I ran. I ran up the hill, holding that dress up so I didn't fall because I had one thing I needed to do. I had to hold him. I had to know that he was alive. The banshees were wrong about me. I wouldn't give a crap about Faery if Dev died. They could fight all they liked if he died here. They could take their war and shove it because I would be gone.

I tripped halfway up the hill and the sobbing started. I let loose, my grief making the banshee wails seem a weak thing. Daniel got to me first. He pulled me up and looked me in the eyes. His blue ones registered my loss, and he pulled me close.

"Tell me it's not Dev." I could feel him shake. "Zoey, tell me it's not Dev."

"She can't, Daniel," Dev said quietly from behind. "Everyone stay calm. It will be all right."

Padric ran up and Miria threw herself into his arms, sobbing her grief as well. Declan looked pale and shaken as he fell to his knees. He looked even worse than he had when he thought it was him.

I pushed away from Daniel and he let me go because I needed Dev in that moment. He wrapped his big arms around me and held me so tightly, I could feel his heartbeat against mine. I wept into his chest. I held onto him with such force I was sure I would leave marks.

"You'll be all right, Zoey," Dev said, stroking my hair. "I love you so much, my wife. Daniel will take good care of you."

"Screw that," Daniel said. "You aren't dead. Just because some weird women say it doesn't make it so."

"History disagrees with you, Dan," Dev said quietly, the only calm one on the lawn.

"Fuck history," Daniel shot back. "We fight this. You lay down and accept this, Dev, and I will never forgive you."

"All right," Dev agreed. "Tell me what you wish me to do and I will do it."

Daniel nodded, though he had no idea what he wanted Dev to do. He only knew we had to do something. It was not in Daniel Donovan's nature to calmly accept fate. "We'll figure something out."

Dev nodded but his hand strayed to that tiny heart that was beating deep in my body. He covered it with his hand and laid his head against mine, and I knew deep in his heart that he didn't believe it.

Chapter Eleven

"Oh, thank the goddess. That could be anyone, Zoey," Dev said with a relieved sigh.

I looked up at him, surprised at his reaction. It was an hour after my talk with The Three. We were safely ensconced in our private rooms, having fled the shocked scene in the ballroom. The Seelie nobles were having a distinct "rats on a sinking ship" reaction to the news that the newly ascended god had been elected to be fate's bitch.

There had been a lot of crying and yelling. There was also some irrational blame being tossed about. Many of the nobles were certain the Unseelie had something to do with Devinshea's impending death. It was the reason Dev asked the Hunter to return to our apartments with us.

When Dev had finally gotten me to calm down, he'd requested the full story of my episode with the banshees. I was sure I was red-faced and puffy, but I recounted everything I could remember about my conversation with The Three, hoping it would help Daniel figure a way out of this. Dev had been unimpressed with my tale. He'd taken an academic view of the entire quandary.

"Well, it couldn't be me," Declan offered. "I am a first born."

"Fine, it couldn't be you, but it certainly could be Braden," Dev pointed out.

Daniel's head came up. "How could it be Braden?"

Dev turned to me, ignoring his partner for the moment. "Please repeat what the *bean si* said, sweetheart. It's important you get the wording right. If they're anything like the other prophets I have dealt with, then the words will be precise, though they can have multiple meanings."

"How many prophets have you dealt with?" Daniel asked curiously. Danny and I have dealt with many an odd creature, but they were usually the fangs and claws kind, not the irritating psychic kind.

Dev shrugged a little. "Oh, it's a typical business start-up expense. If I hadn't listened to a prophet, I would have built Ether right under a site where the city council is now building a train station. Can you imagine the noise? It did take Albert and me a while to decipher the prophecy though. It was something about great steel horses and the multitude of humanity stomping across the plains. It sounded bad so I changed locations and I'm happy to have done so. That's the way these things go."

"This was fairly simple, Devinshea," Miria said from her place on the settee. She was still pale. "They stated that the victim was to be a male. He was a second born, though his mother had carried only once."

Dev nodded. "Yes, that's what I thought. Like I said, it could be any number of Fae nobles. We rarely have more than one child so most of our women have only had one pregnancy."

Declan slapped himself on the head. "Of course. That makes much more sense."

Even Miria looked hopeful now. She reached up and grabbed Padric's hand. He squeezed it reassuringly. "Well, I do not think it means it is not Devinshea, but it does open up other possibilities."

"Someone explain this to me before I scream," I announced, frustrated at being out of the loop.

"It's why I mentioned Braden," Dev explained calmly. "He's the second child of a mother who bore only him. He's the child of a relationship similar to ours. His father took two wives. His first wife bore a daughter and the second gave birth to Braden. As Daniel and I will be fathers to the child in your belly, so the wives shared their children. Braden's mother claims his older sister as her own though she isn't the biological mother."

It made sense but there was something inside me that was still wary. "They said this man was important."

Declan relaxed back against the sofa. "Oh, I assure you, the Duke of Ain is important, indeed. He's responsible for vast acres in the north. His armies patrol the gate between the Seelie and Unseelie *sitheins*. His lands provide much of our trade with the Unseelie. His death would leave a huge power vacuum." That last brought the slightest smile to Declan's face, as though he highly anticipated a chance to fill that power vacuum.

"Could it start a war?" Neil stopped pacing briefly to ask the question.

"It would depend on the circumstances of his death," Miria replied, warming to the idea. Her eyes had a calculating look in them and I wondered briefly if she was thinking what I was. I was wondering if killing the Duke of Ain would fulfill the banshee prophecy and protect Dev. I didn't like the bastard anyway.

The Hunter, who had been staring out into the night, now turned. His face was serious as he contemplated the room. "We're on the brink of war anyway, Your Highness. It wouldn't take much to push us over that line. The nobles on my side wish for Seelie blood and I can see it's the same here."

Dev had a big smile on his face as he pulled me off my chair and into his arms. "You see, my wife, it could be any of a number of people. They didn't use my name so we have to consider the fact that they were talking about someone else." He tipped my chin up so I was looking him in the eye. "So you and Daniel should wipe the morose looks off your faces. I have no intention of dying. I just got married and we're having a baby. I promise I won't die before I get a chance to be a horrible influence on our son. I have to live or Daniel will turn him into a comic book geek."

Daniel grinned, obviously buoyed by the possibility that it wasn't Dev. "I'd like to see you stop me."

I let Dev pull me close, but I thought he was wrong. There had been something personal about that prophecy. Why had the matron touched me and spoken directly to me, as though we had a connection? They had been much more interested in me than in the Queen of the Seelie, whose territory they were in. She'd been more of a distraction than anything else. They had spoken to me and I knew deep down that their prophecy would have a direct impact. I wouldn't weep for the Duke of Ain. I wouldn't fight for him.

I turned my head and saw that Daniel was still wary as well. I knew what his first instinct would be. He would want to take me and Dev and get the hell out of Dodge. He would prefer to take us all back to Ether where he felt more in control. But the prophecy would follow us wherever we went. We needed to figure this out here. I just wished I knew how long we had before whatever was going to happen came to pass.

"I am going to contact our best soothsayers." Miria stood, her decision made, and shook out her strawberry-blonde hair. "It is what I should have done the minute the *bean si* began their song." She turned to Padric. "I believe one of the women in the village has shown great potential as a medium. Perhaps we can ask the spirits to guide us."

The royal guard nodded. "I shall go and fetch her myself, Your Highness. If you would have the temple prepared, we can hold a séance as soon as I get back and we can try to get to the bottom of this."

Miria turned to Sarah, who looked pale and sat quietly holding Felix's hand. "You are a witch, correct?"

"I am, Your Highness," she replied.

"Would you mind overseeing the preparations? You will know which herbs to use and which candles to burn."

Sarah stood and bowed her head. "It would be my honor to do this for you. I know exactly which herbs to use. We must cleanse the space before we begin."

Everyone was up and moving about as there were preparations to be made. It was like a great weight had been lifted because we now had something to do. Dev kissed me and once again promised me things would be all right before joining his mother and brother. They began to plan what questions they should ask the hopefully non-corporeal dead. Sometimes these things went awry and the corporeal dead showed up and they tended to be pissed off and usually carrying weapons of some sort. Daniel pointed this out and they all began to argue the probability of their conversation with the dead beginning the zombie apocalypse.

I watched as they plotted and felt distant from all of them at that moment. I let my arms cross and rested against the wall, watching Dev and Daniel and wondering just how far I would go to protect them.

"You don't believe this shit any more than I do, Your Grace," the Hunter said quietly. His brown eyes regarded me seriously. His voice was quiet. As Neil was caught up in the undead argument and Zack was patrolling, I doubted anyone else could hear our conversation.

"I still think it's Dev." There was a knot of anxiety that told me this loss was mine, not all of Faery's. It would hurt my heart the most.

"I agree." He leaned casually against the wall next to me. To the rest of the party, it probably appeared to be a meaningless conversation. As the Hunter continued, I knew it was anything but. "I know more than I have said to this point. Celebrating your marriage is the least of my reasons for being here. It would do nothing to help if I bring up my information now. It would only confuse the issue and stop me from coming to his aid."

"If you know something, you have to tell me," I whispered back urgently.

"I will," he promised. "I need your help. The *bean si* were right. You are the only one who can stop this war. If you want to know how, I will tell you in an hour. Be ready when I come for you."

My heart skipped an anxious beat. "When you come for me? Are we going somewhere? I don't think my husbands are going to let me go anywhere alone with you."

"If you want to save Prince Dev, that is exactly what you will do," he hissed my direction.

"How will my being alone with an Unseelie noble help my husband?" I shot back at him. "That sounds like an excellent way to start a war and perhaps to lead Devinshea into a trap."

I watched as the Hunter receded and Herne took his place. I noticed that they tended to function like this. They traded places whenever one seemed to fumble. This time the Hunter couldn't handle a touchy female, so he tagged out and brought in the charmer.

Herne was gracious. "I apologize again, Your Grace. The Hunter is anxious about certain events, and it does nothing for his already questionable manners. He very much wants to avoid war. It's not that he minds bloodshed but rather that he fears no one will win this battle. He's an old and venerable spirit, but he's still dependent on us. It brings out the worst in him at times when he's reminded of his flaws."

I accepted all of that. It must be difficult to have such power yet be forced to deal with the limitations of a human host. The Hunter could strengthen his host, could give him amazing powers, but he was still limited. "Why does he want to meet with me?"

"We need you," Herne said firmly, trying to convince me of his point. "You are the only one who can stop this war. If you will aid us, I believe we can have everything settled by morning."

I sighed, wanting to believe him. I wanted to think that there was something I could do to fix this. I was just like the rest of them. I needed to feel like I was doing something useful, but holding hands in the dark and hoping someone from beyond would show up just wasn't my thing. Herne was offering me another option. "Fine. My wolf and I will go with you."

"No, it must be the two of us alone," he explained quietly and with compassion. "I'm sorry but that's the way it must be."

"You want me to lie to my husbands and ditch my guard to run away with you?" I said the words and they were improbable even to my own ears. The last time I'd done that I'd gotten into big trouble.

"It's the only way to deal with the problem," Herne insisted. He frowned and looked down at me. "Zoey, Devinshea is my friend. I'll do anything I can to aid him. I promise that I intend no harm to you."

I sighed because I knew what he was doing. Promises are important to the Fae. Bad things tended to happen when they broke their vows. If Herne lied to me, then I could call the Wild Hunt and they would aid me, even against their master. If he was willing to make an oath, then I had to consider his proposal. "I have your oath?"

"Yes, Your Grace, I give you my solemn oath that I mean for no harm to come to you," he replied with all the sincerity he could muster.

"I want his, too." I wasn't taking any chances. I wasn't sure how the rules worked concerning ascended gods and their hosts, but I was going to cover all the bases before I trusted these two.

Brown eyes blinked. "You have my oath. I intend you no harm."

"Then I will go with you." I looked at my party. Even with all the activity going on around them, Daniel and Neil were looking my way every couple of minutes, likely wondering exactly what I was saying to the Hunter. "How am I supposed to get away?" Daniel and Dev would be working on the whole *Ghost Whisperer* episode they were about to enact. It wouldn't be so hard to get away from them, but Neil was an entirely different story.

"I do not know. That is your dilemma," the Hunter said with no sympathy. "I will be at your windows in an hour. Be prepared for a walk in the woods."

The Hunter made his good-byes and departed.

So, he was going to be helpful. I watched him close the door. I faked a yawn and let myself sink onto the couch. It was time to make the whole "knocked up" thing start working for me. I looked at Dev and smiled my tired soldier smile.

"Sweetheart, you look exhausted," Dev said soothingly as he fell right into my trap.

"It's been a long day." I managed a nice yawn while gesturing at the activity in the living room. "How long do you think this will take?"

His mouth turned down in chagrin. "The better part of the night, my goddess. I'm afraid it isn't a good place for you."

"No pregnant ladies!" Sarah shouted from across the room. "Sometimes non-corporeal beings look for new bodies, and a tiny soul is just too tempting. Zoey needs to stay in the palace."

"Oh," I said, mustering my disappointment. "Really?"

"You heard her." Daniel frowned. "They'll have to make do without us. We can just go to bed and they can tell us all about it in the morning. You need your rest, baby. You've had an emotional night."

"Danny, I'll be fine." I started to panic a little. There would be no way to get away from Daniel. None. He would be a brick wall, and there was a good chance he would behead the Hunter for even suggesting I leave with him.

"Actually, I need you, Daniel." Sarah instructed Felix on which herbs to ask Albert for and then turned to complete her thought. "If things get bad, I have a spell to banish just about anything but it requires a certain type of magic. You're the only one here with a plentitude of death magic."

"And I wanted to be loved for my good looks," Daniel muttered. "Fine. Lee hasn't gotten back yet. I expected him back before now. How far could a kid get? Anyway, Neil can stay with you."

"Of course," Neil said, sitting down beside me. "We'll pop some corn and watch some *E*. Oh, yeah, we're in 'medieval world' where they don't have TVs. Trust me. It will be so easy to watch Z since I don't have anything else to do."

"See that you do," Daniel said, his voice a low rumble. Neil turned his eyes away, and I could see his mouth was tight. I decided that after I saved Dev, I was going to go to Felix and set up some family therapy because the cold war between Danny and Neil was starting to get to me.

I patted Neil's hand and tried to look pathetic. "I just want to go to bed, sweetie. I need some alone time. I need to process, if you know what I mean."

"You need to cry," Neil replied quietly. "You know my shoulder is always there for you. I'll stay out here. Do you want to know a secret, Z? I smuggled in a battery operated DVD player. If you need something to take your mind off things, I brought along some movies."

I wanted to kiss him because Neil being out here and involved in some flick watching was perfect. He would still be able to hear me if I yelled, but his senses weren't what they used to be. Since he stopped taking Daniel's blood, he'd become more of a regular wolf than the superpower he had been. I wondered if it hurt him. I knew he'd been proud to be so strong. Now Zack was the one taking the vampire blood and reaping the benefits. As for Lee, he was a freak of nature and didn't need anything to help him out. I bet it bothered Neil to be the weakest in his pack.

Danny knelt down. “Sarah says she needs me. God, I hate the magic crap. Give me something to behead any day of the week. I love you, Z. I’m going to fix this. I’m not going to let Dev die on us. You get some rest. I’ll tell you what we find out in the morning.”

I nodded and let my arms wind around his broad shoulders while he kissed me soundly. Dev was right behind him. When Danny left to join Sarah, Dev scooped me up and started to carry me toward the bedroom. “I’ll be right with you,” he said to the group. “I want to tuck my goddess in and say good night.”

Declan snorted. “I will bet that is what you want to do. Take your time, brother. I will do your part while you say good night.”

Dev pushed through the door and carried me to the bed. He crawled in with me. His eyes practically ate me up. “I love you, Zoey. I will fight this. You know I will, don’t you?”

Those stupid tears were back, clouding my vision. “I know. I love you, too.”

“But if anything should go wrong…”

“Don’t.” I didn’t want to hear any of it.

He put a finger on my lips to silence me. “You should know this. If anything goes wrong, I have a will filed on our plane. Albert has all the information on the attorney. It leaves everything to you. Daniel knows where all the money is. He knows how to run the businesses or he knows who to call. He can handle everything, but you will be well provided for.”

“I just want you.” I didn’t care about the damn money or the club or any of it. It wouldn’t mean anything if he was gone.

He pushed me back onto the bed. “I know. But I want you to be happy, Zoey. I want you to go on with Daniel and I want the two of you to raise this baby if anything should happen to me. Now get some sleep and before you know it we will be crawling into your bed and begging you to do all manner of dirty things with us.”

He kissed me and pushed himself up. I was suddenly in the presence of Bris. His eyes and demeanor changed faster than I had ever seen it.

“Goddess, I have only a moment while my host is disoriented,” he explained. “I am not foolish. I know you plan something with the Hunter. I know him well and he would not have spoken with you had he not intended to use you. I won't tell my host. I know you seek to help him, but be careful with the Hunter. He isn't evil but he is a predator."

"I have his oath that he won't harm me," I said.

Bris nodded. "Excellent. He won't break an oath. Good luck, goddess." He went still for a moment and then his smile was sweet. I knew that Dev was aware now. "I have no intention of leaving you either, goddess. I will do whatever I can to keep my host healthy. You have my vow." He leaned over and kissed me, running his hands over my nipples and making me wish we had more time. "Sleep well," he said before walking out.

I frowned after him. Every nerve ending in my body was ready for more of his touch and he told me to sleep well. I was suddenly glad I had somewhere to be because I would never be able to sleep now.

Lying back on the big bed, I waited for the sounds in the outer room to die down. After a long while I heard Sarah say good night to Neil and the outer doors close. When I was certain Neil had time to retrieve his bit of home, I climbed carefully out of the bed and made my way to the small backpack I'd stored in the closet. I pulled out my cut-off denims and black tank top and, more importantly, my Nikes. I'd brought along a couple of articles of clothing from home strictly for comfort. I knew the denim would be an odd sight in this world, but it was better than running around in a dress I'd already tripped in once tonight. I wasn't going gallivanting through the woods looking like a refuge from Shakespeare in the Park.

After getting comfy, I opened the chest at the end of the bed. It was stuffed full of Dev's two favorite things—sex toys and weapons. I ignored the vibrators despite the awful state that mean old fertility god left me in and went straight for the guns. After I retrieved my Ruger, I found the cold iron rounds and loaded up, shoving an extra clip in my pocket. I didn't care who knew I was carrying here since they didn't exactly have a concealed handgun law, so I slipped a shoulder holster over my tank top. Never one to rely on merely one weapon, I strapped on two thigh sheaths for the knives I selected. One was cold iron because it worked like magic on faeries and the other silver because that worked on just about anything else. Once I pulled my hair into a ponytail, I was ready to go.

I was pulling the curtains shut in case Neil looked in on me when Barghest and Shuck popped their heads over the window sill. I put a hand to my lips and the dogs stayed silent. As quietly as I could, I threw a leg over the opening and suddenly found myself in Herne's strong arms. He lifted me to the ground and had a smile on his face as he steadied me. "This is an interesting costume. It will make it much easier to move than your dress. Are you ready then, Your Grace?"

I took a deep breath and nodded because I was as ready as I was going to get.

Herne the Hunter took my hand and we ran off into the night.

Chapter Twelve

"Where exactly are we going?" I asked once we got past the palace walls. We had to be quiet as the whole palace was guarded. We'd waited in some bushes while the guards made their rounds. The minute they went past us, we leapt over the high white walls that separated the queen's abode from the valley. Well, Herne leapt. I kind of tried to rock climb. Finally Shuck took pity on me and let me climb on his back and then over the high wall. If Herne had wanted Spider Girl then he'd come to the wrong place.

He motioned to the woods in the distance. "There. We're going to a place deep in that forest."

"And what, exactly, are we looking for?" I probably didn't want to know, but I asked the question anyway.

"An ogre."

Nope, I didn't want to know. An ogre is a big, nasty creature that likes to gnaw on human flesh. Oh, it would pretty much eat any flesh it came across, but it was particularly attracted to flesh that talked back to it. Its pet peeves included anyone walking into its territory and anyone thinking about walking into its territory. The ogre's likes included eviscerating those foolish enough to walk into its territory. It's important to stay out of the big dude's space or he will polish you off with a nice side salad.

I'm joking about that last part. He would never eat salad.

"Are you insane?" I stopped my forward progress since every step brought me closer to the *No Trespassing* sign.

Herne turned and the dogs sat back on their haunches. "Look, Your Grace…"

"Call me Zoey." I wanted to be on a first name basis with the last person I would probably see.

"All right then, Zoey," he said with a satisfied smile before continuing his explanation. "As far as I can tell, to this point the ogre has remained undetected. It has probably eaten anyone who might have reported its presence. The ogre shouldn't be in these woods. It's not a Seelie creature."

"So, there are a lot of non-Seelies in this *sithein*."

Herne nodded. "But they have the queen's permission to live here. For the most part, they're fairly helpful creatures. The ogre is neither helpful nor would it be welcome."

I got that. Creatures who liked to eat people were not welcome. "So Miria doesn't know there's an ogre currently laying down roots in her forest?"

"No, and I intend to make it so she never knows." Herne seemed to think that was enough of an explanation so he and the dogs started back up the hill.

I rolled my eyes and gathered my patience. I had to run to catch up. "So how did Shrek get here?"

He looked at me curiously.

My extensive pop culture knowledge was lost on these people. "The ogre. How did he get here?"

"Oh," he said, finally understanding. He nodded and began walking again. "That remains a mystery."

Yeah, I bet it was. I was pretty damn sure there was more to the story. "I doubt it just popped into existence in the middle of a Seelie *sithein*."

"Fine. The ogre was ours," he conceded. "It's lived in the woods outside of Angus's stronghold for as long as anyone can remember. It served a purpose there as a sort of defense mechanism. We've always made sure he was properly taken care of. We fed him regularly and even treated him with condemned prisoners to feast upon. He had a good life."

"Nice," I said, but my sarcasm was wasted on him. "So ogre boy is living the high life but he just up and leaves one day? Maybe he got lonely and went looking for an ogress to call his own."

"It doesn't work that way. He wouldn't think to seek a mate. He would take a female if we managed to produce one, but he wouldn't leave to look for one. You must understand that the ogre is first and foremost a stupid creature. It's a miracle that it ever learned how to wield a club as a weapon. It doesn't think beyond eating and taking a nice long nap."

I kept my mouth closed because he could easily be talking about Lee, too.

"It does nothing on its own." Herne's long legs ate up the distance, and I jogged to keep up. He was dressed in brown pants made from some sort of animal skin and a linen shirt. He had tall leather boots on and a cape with a hood over his shoulders though it was a warm evening.

"So it probably wouldn't have gone for a long walk and crossed into the Seelie sithein?"

"No, Zoey," Herne said with a frown. "It wouldn't leave its territory on its own. It must have had help from someone."

Things started to fall into place. There was only one real reason to smuggle in an ogre. "It had help from someone who wanted to start something with the Seelie."

"If by something, you mean the war to end all wars, then yes, they wished to start something."

"Yeah," I commented. "We had one of those wars to end all wars on the Earth plane. Didn't live up to the name. We're still fighting."

"Well, you did not do it right, then. I assure you, when the fighting starts this time, we will kill them all and they intend to do the same to us," Herne said bitterly. "We Fae tend to be thorough."

"Why?" Not even Dev had been able to explain the real animosity between the two tribes. Declan had personal reasons, but there were Seelies who had never even met an Unseelie yet they called for their blood at the merest provocation. "I know you're different but you come from the same place. Why do you hate each other so much?"

He stopped. We'd reached the start of the forest. We'd been walking for thirty or forty minutes and now he pulled out a flask and settled down on the ground. "Sit for a moment, Your Grace. We still have much ground to cover." I dropped down beside him, and after a moment he began to speak. He took a long drink but didn't offer it to me. I was betting it wasn't water. "I think it's a lot of things that cause our hatred. My people are straightforward. They say what they mean and mean what they say. The Seelie are anything but. They play with a person mentally. They compliment, but their words have two meanings. They skirt the definition of a lie. We don't understand them so we keep ourselves apart in a way we didn't when we were all on the Earth plane."

"A couple of years back I met a group of faeries who claimed to be Tuatha Dé Danann." The Tuatha Dé Danann were a legendary group of Fae who led the second settling of Ireland and who, if you believed the legends, left the Earth plane altogether when they were defeated in battle. Well, most of them left. The ones who stayed behind built the mounds attached to the Earth plane, like the one I was sitting in. The Tuatha Dé Danann had traveled by passing through the veil between worlds. It was a talent that had been lost to this plane.

Herne grunted, a manly sound. "We haven't seen nor heard from the old ones in many a generation. Why were they on the Earth plane?"

It was my turn to skirt around certain issues. "They were traveling, you know. Doing that thing where they pass through the veil. They were moving a transference box from one tribe to another. I helped them out." I hadn't really. I'd stolen the transference box, which had been full of magic passed on to the tribe as a gift. Daniel and I had accidentally primed said stolen box, which took the gift and formed a living creature from the magic. I skipped over that part, though. It wasn't my shining moment in life. "Why did the tribes here stay behind? Why would someone like the Hunter not follow the old ones?"

"I was born in my sithein." His eyes studied the forest around him. "It was many years after the old ones left us behind, and the ones who can remember the time rarely speak of it. I have two theories on the matter. One is that the Fae left behind were weak and the mighty ones didn't want the weak to contaminate their tribes on the new planes."

"That's awful." It didn't go along with the impression I had of the older faeries. They'd been just when dealing with me. They could have simply killed us all, but they'd taken the time to hear me out. I'd been weak, but they healed me. I still thought often of the small magical child they had taken with them to their plane. Sometimes that baby girl haunted my dreams, a vision of what Daniel and I could have had.

I shook off that old ache.

"My other theory has to do with my god," Herne continued thoughtfully. "The Hunter isn't weak. He's the spirit of the hunt. He came into existence on the Earth plane and he must return from time to time. He's connected to the plane on a base level. You see, Zoey, the non-corporeal gods who stayed behind all had a deep connection to something on the Earth plane. The Hunter is connected to the forest and the predators of this plane. Bris is connected to the fields and the women of the Earth plane. Arawn is probably more connected than any of the others."

Now I found that name in my brain's repository and I sent a startled look to the faery. "The Welsh god Arawn is in the Unseelie sithein? The death god?"

Herne nodded as though he was just a guy he hung out with, not a person who used to be the Lord of all things Dead. "Oh, yes, his host is my best friend. He's a funny man. Not at all what you would expect the death god's host to be. But my point is he needs humans the same way Bris needs the fields of his birth and the Hunter needs his forests. Perhaps we stayed behind because we were more connected to the Earth plane."

It made sense. What good could a death god be if he was always surrounded by the immortal? Herne was proving to be a veritable fount of knowledge and I was curious. I had questions I hadn't gotten around to asking Dev about the god who now shared his body and our bed. "Did you choose the Hunter?"

"Oh, no," he replied. "A host does not choose his god. We open ourselves and if our magic is compatible, then we're accepted. There is a ceremony, but it changes from god to god. My ceremony was a hunt. I tracked a mountain troll who'd gone insane and begun to kill for no reason. We fought for days, but I was victorious. I cut out its heart and when I feasted, the Hunter came into me."

"Eww, that's way grosser than what Dev had to do." What Dev had to do had been me.

Herne's smile was all masculine appreciation now. "Yes, well, we can't all be that lucky. You should have had an Unseelie witness, you know. He's our priest, as well. I heard Devinshea's challenge was a pleasant experience for all concerned. Though you should know, it wasn't your technique that tempted the fertility god to inhabit Dev."

"What do you think attracted Bris?" The way I understood it, it was Dev's magic that called to the fertility god, but I was certainly interested in hearing what Herne thought.

"According to the Hunter, Bris has had many chances to bond with a host. In the end, it isn't merely the magic that calls to the god, but also the personality and life of the host. Bris is concerned with love and passion. The Hunter tells me that when Bris was corporeal, he had but one goddess and he loved her with all his heart. He seeks to feel that again, though he must feel that through his host now. Bris turned down several when he realized they would use the magic he gave them to attract many women. None of the previous hosts wanted a settled life. Dev is the odd man with sex magic who is willing to settle down."

I smiled brightly, feeling better about the god in my husband. "It's nice to know Bris isn't a player."

Herne looked confused. "Sometimes when you speak, I don't understand you."

"Well, Herne, I think you've spent too much time in the forest. The next time you hit the Earth plane, you'll have to visit Dallas and I'll show you around. I can even set you up on a date." I had several female werewolves begging to be set up. I was turning out to be quite the matchmaker. "Unless there's a lady huntress, of course."

Herne snorted his frustration at that thought. "Are you kidding me? Do you know how hard it is to get a date with this man inside me? He isn't smooth. He doesn't know how to talk to women and he won't listen to my advice. I'm a strong, talented warrior. I have the spirit of the hunt coursing through my body and…"

"You can't get laid," I finished for him.

"I can't. Even Arawn has a girlfriend." He stood up and lent me a hand.

"We'll have to work on that, Herne," I promised with a smile. He turned all kinds of serious now as he helped me to my feet.

"I must leave you, Zoey. The time has come to walk the forest, and he prefers to be in control. This is his place of power." Herne smiled down on me. "Don't take offense. As I said before, he doesn't know how to deal with women. I've enjoyed my time with you. Don't judge me by his actions."

The Hunter was now staring down at me. He looked me up and down and there was disapproval all over his face. "Is there a reason you chose to be naked in my presence, Your Grace?"

I looked down to make sure everything was covered. I didn't have anything hanging out, so I wasn't sure what the problem was. The tank top was even black so I knew he couldn't see anything I didn't want him to see. "This is what I wear when I go hunting. It's very Tomb Raider."

"I can see all of your limbs," the Hunter noted as his eyes roamed across my body. "And much of your skin. It looks creamy and soft in the moonlight. It makes me want to rip off what little clothing you have on and pound myself into your softness."

Okay, ewww. "I wouldn't try it if I were you."

"I am not going to do it. Prince Devinshea is a friend. I wouldn't dishonor him in such a fashion. I just thought you should know that dressing like a trollop has an effect on men. If you want to be treated like the lady you are then you should be properly covered." On that pronouncement he began to hike. The black dogs followed along happily.

"Yes, because I don't deserve respect for just being a human being," I replied bitterly, following after him.

"Of course not." The Hunter sounded pleased that I understood him.

"Can I get the other one back?" I grumbled more to myself than to him.

"No. I'm better in the woods. Why would you wish to be led by an inferior guide?"

"Well, he's less of an asshole, for one," I muttered.

"What does an anus have to do with…oh, you have insulted me," he said with a frown, catching up. "Well, I did call you a trollop."

"I've been called worse."

"Let me ask you something, Your Grace." The Hunter began to lead me through the heavily treed forest. "Are the knives for ornamentation?"

"No, the knives are for killing things."

He stopped and looked at me like I was crazy. "Do you think I won't care for you? I gave you my oath. Do you think I won't defend you?"

"I'm hoping you will, but I'd like the opportunity to defend myself should the need arise," I explained, surprised by the question.

"Your men don't defend you?" His question was tinged with outrage. He lived in a different world.

I laughed at the thought. "My husbands spend altogether too much time defending me, but one of the ways they protect me is to teach me to defend myself."

It was true for all the men in my life. My father hadn't cared that I was a girl. He taught me his trade and he was the first to put a knife in my hand. Danny took me to the gun range and taught me everything I knew about guns. Devinshea spent time teaching me how to fight with a sword. It would never occur to them that I should be helpless simply because I was female. In their minds, I was more vulnerable and should damn well know how to strike back.

"Seelie noblewomen keep a knife on them so they may fall upon it if they are dishonored."

I gaped at him. "Seriously? What the hell kind of women are they? And what man wants his woman to choose death over dishonor? Let me tell you something, Hunter, if someone raped me I wouldn't feel any dishonor. You know what I would feel? I would feel pissed off. I would feel like revenge. And I know neither of my husbands would want me to cry and fall on my sword. They'll take me 'dishonored' or not."

The Hunter smiled slowly, the emotion tugging up one side of his mouth in approval. “You are not like Seelie women. You’re more like a goblin female.”

I wasn’t quite sure how to take that. “Well, if the goblins let their females defend themselves then I’d rather be a goblin.”

The Hunter laughed, and it was a surprisingly pleasant sound. “Oh, the goblin males quake in fear of their women when they’re angry. A goblin female in a rage is truly a sight to be seen.”

“Good to know.”

The Hunter’s eyes gleamed. “I just thought that Prince Devinshea’s bride would be a noblewoman. Though he always seemed more comfortable with human females, I assumed when the time came he would attempt to please his court and marry a proper Seelie.”

“I don’t think Dev married me for my good breeding.” He’d always liked the fact that I could take care of myself in a fight.

“Not at all.” The Hunter agreed far too readily for my satisfaction.

I wasn’t exactly poorly bred. I knew which fork to use. Albert had slapped my hand every time I used the wrong one until it finally sunk in. I tried to dress properly for an event. I couldn’t help it that I’d grown up with a thief for a dad, who was way more concerned with my professional skills than etiquette.

“I guess that’s why the nobles don’t like me.” It sounded pathetic even to my ears.

“You mistake me, Your Grace. I was not judging you poorly. I was merely reassessing you. I’ve been judging you based on the fact I thought you were trying to be a Seelie noblewoman. If you aren’t then I will judge you based on yourself. As I said before, you remind me of the goblin females of my acquaintance. They don’t wear many clothes, either. I apologize for thinking you were trying to tempt me into fornication. This is merely your traditional dress. I like you much more now that I realize you’re a straightforward female.”

“Well, good then,” I said. “I’m glad we got that out of the way. So someone lost an ogre and now you have to get him back? How exactly are you planning on making the ogre go back with you? Do you leave a bunch of detached body parts like a trail for it to follow back to the Unseelie *sithein*?"

The Hunter stared at the trees as though trying to select the easiest path to his destination. We veered left. "I hadn't thought of that. It's a good plan, though. You have a devious mind."

"Dude, I was joking."

"I've been wondering exactly how the culprits managed to get the ogre to follow them out of our sithein," the Hunter explained. "You've given me a reasonable explanation. But taking the ogre back isn't my mission."

If he wasn't going to take the ogre back to the Unseelie lands then that left only one possibility. "You're going to kill it then?"

"Yes. I'm going to kill the ogre."

His job would be easier if he'd brought along a few more people. It was just me, the Hunter and two dogs—albeit incredibly large dogs. He should have let me bring Danny along. I would put Danny up against an ogre any day of the week. It made me wonder why exactly he thought I would be helpful. I supposed it was the banshee prophecy. They said I could stop the war and obviously the presence of an Unseelie ogre could start a war. I hoped how I was supposed to stop this would become clear to me.

The Hunter led me into a small clearing. There was a pond and the moonlight was reflected off it, giving the whole place a lovely silver glow. He looked around as the dogs sniffed the air and started to whine. "Yes, my friends, this will do nicely."

"Okay." I took a deep breath because I knew something was about to happen. I was about to meet my first ogre and I sincerely hoped I survived the experience. I knew I was risking a lot but I couldn't sit by and let Dev die. What was I supposed to tell my child one day? Was he supposed to understand that I had a shot at saving his father's life but chose to stay in bed? "What do you want me to do? How do I help you kill this thing?"

The Hunter chuckled, and he set his pack on the ground. He pulled out a long strand of thick rope. He walked toward me. "Your Grace, your job is simple."

I found myself with my hands tied behind my back before I knew what was happening.

"I need bait," the Hunter explained.

Chapter Thirteen

"You son of a bitch!" I shouted as he turned me around.

"I don't think that applies," the Hunter said seriously. I tried kicking him and caught him once on the shin before he stepped back and out of the way. It sucks being short. "I don't think I had an actual physical mother so she couldn't have been a bitch."

"Fuck you." Since he hadn't tied my feet, I started to run as he let go of my arms.

"I thought we decided I shouldn't do that." He gave chase.

I didn't get far. He was on me immediately, his big hands a vise around my waist. His body pressed against my back. He felt like granite. I struggled, but there was no way I was getting away from him. "Stop fighting me, Your Grace. I'm trying to keep you safe."

"Keep me safe?" I practically shouted the question. "You're going to keep me safe by tying me up and offering me to a flesh-eating ogre as some sort of human sacrifice?"

"I have no intention of sacrificing you. You can't believe I brought a human female along with me on this venture as a partner. I always intended to use you as bait. You see, the ogre isn't smart but it is an instinctive creature. If he thinks a great hunter is in the woods, he will hide rather than show himself. This is why the *bean si* said only you can stop the war. You will attract the ogre and then keep silent about the fact that he was here."

The Hunter hauled me back into the clearing. The dogs panted at my feet as I forced the bastard to drag me the whole way. I did not go quietly. I kicked. I screamed. I cussed like I was starring in a Martin Scorsese film.

"Very good, Your Grace," the Hunter said approvingly. He looked around as though he expected the creature to show up at any moment. "This racket will definitely bring the ogre out, though I don't think he understands our language so you don't have to curse."

I closed my mouth. He was right. I was going to have every predator in the woods curious about me if I kept the current volume set on maximum. He pulled me back toward a tree with a nicely rounded trunk. "Oh, I'm cursing, you can count on that. I'll just be quiet about it. You just try to stop me. You know what else I'm doing? I'm calling you an oath breaker, Herne the Hunter. I call for the Wild Hunt. It's my right as Her Grace, the wife to the High Priest of all Faery. I demand you call them and hold court."

He released the restraints on my hands but kept one locked firmly in his grip. I took the opportunity to slap him upside the head as hard as I could. His head snapped back satisfyingly, but he wouldn't let my other hand go. I tried again but he ducked this time, ready for the move. He pulled me until my back was against the tree trunk and caught my other hand easily. "There's no need for violence. It won't help us in attracting the creature. Your screams are good enough. I don't wish to exhaust you. After I kill the creature, we still have to walk back to the palace. You should save your strength."

I rolled my eyes and tried not to scream as the Hunter successfully managed to retie my hands behind my back. I made as big a fist as I could while he tied me and pulled my hands as far apart as my strength would allow. "I wasn't trying to attract the creature, you bastard. I was trying to hurt you and get away from you because you're a psychotic idiot."

He seemed happy with his work and walked around to face me. "How does running away help our cause? I thought you wanted to aid me in killing the creature so we can stop the inevitable war that will occur when Queen Miria discovers someone from the Unseelie has unleashed the ogre on them."

"That was when I thought you wanted my hunting skills." He snorted as though the idea was insane. I continued my tirade. "I wanted to help you before I was cast as the goat from *Jurassic Park*. Just so you know, that damn goat dies!"

"You aren't going to die, Your Grace, and I won't be bringing any dead goats in, though I'm not sure what they have to do with anything. They would distract the ogre and he would eat them quickly. I need live bait." He pulled more rope out of his pack and started laying it out.

"Where is my hunt?" I asked, stubbornly pulling on my bindings. The ropes were hot against my skin.

"I'm not going to call a Wild Hunt on myself when I've broken no oaths," he replied, working diligently. The dogs came up and sat down beside my well-restrained body. "I promised you I had no intention to cause you harm. I firmly intend to defend you. I need a reason for the ogre to ignore the fact that I'm in these woods. As I said before, the ogre is not intelligent, but he has an excellent sense of self-preservation. The only way to get around that is to overwhelm his senses with very vulnerable prey. You are human and female and pregnant. I can't think of anything the ogre will like more. He'll be so attracted to you that he'll forget about the danger I pose."

"Good to know I have my uses." I hated him in that moment. He was using my child to attract a dangerous predator who would probably kill me despite the Hunter's best intentions. I'd come out here to save Devinshea only to lose my own life and that of our child. "You understand my husband is going to kill you."

"Devinshea will understand," the Hunter said. "We're doing this to save him. It's likely that the ogre is the one who would kill him. It makes sense. It would inevitably start a war between our people. You're doing exactly what the *bean si* said you would do. You're the only one who can stop the conflict."

I didn't mention the fact that the banshee had said following the path of the Blood Stone would lead to me stopping the war. "I wasn't talking about Dev. I was talking about my vampire. He won't understand and no explanation will make sense to him. He isn't going to like the fact that you tied me up and offered me to an ogre."

Of course, he'd also probably be pretty angry with me.

The Hunter seemed to think about this for a moment as he covered the ropes with leaves he found on the forest floor. "Perhaps. But here is the way I see the situation. If we persevere then you won't wish to tell your vampire of the adventure since he'll be angry that you traipsed through the forest with a strange man after lying to him about where you intended to spend the evening. If we perish, then it won't matter."

"What happens if I die and you manage to kill the monster and live?" That was the most likely outcome of our current endeavor.

"Then I'll probably attempt to cover up your death," he admitted with a straightforward stare. "It would do your vampire no good to kill me in revenge. It wouldn't bring you back and it would only kill my host, who was against this plan in the first place. I would survive. You'll agree that if that scenario happens, it's better for everyone if the vampire never knows what truly occurred."

"I hate you."

"That's a sad occurrence since I actually find you to be quite interesting," he said seriously. "I think you could be important. You could do more to bring our people together than anyone else. The Unseelie will find you fascinating and the Seelie will eventually accept you because they need Devinshea's magic. You could be a conduit between the two faery worlds. Now be still. I don't wish for the rope to harm your skin."

He fell silent as he continued his work. He tied a long length of rope around a tree opposite me and gracefully climbed up its trunk. Though I couldn't see what he was doing, I watched as the tree shook and I thought about my quandary. I had to hope that the Hunter was as good as he thought he was or I was in deep shit. That ogre would make a beeline for me. It struck me as odd that the ogre had made its way this far without the Seelie army noticing his passage. Maybe I didn't understand the geography of the *sitheins*.

"How far are we from the door?" I asked quietly.

The Hunter dropped to the forest floor again and adjusted his ropes. "We're deep in Seelie territory. Like the Unseelie, the Seelie built their palace far from the door. It's a defensive strategy. You don't want an army to be able to come through the gates and immediately attack your stronghold. You want advance warning."

"Is the gate guarded?"

"Of course. I had to go through much security to be able to enter."

"Yet someone got through with an ogre?"

He thought for a second. "That does not make much sense, Your Grace. I follow your line of thinking. You believe someone from the Seelie is working with someone from the Unseelie, and this is the way they managed to bring in the ogre undetected."

"Let me make myself clear, Hunter." I was going to put my theory out there. If I got eaten, I wanted someone to know who to send the dinner bill to. "I believe that the Duke of Ain or someone close to him is working with someone from the Unseelie. It's the only thing that makes sense. He controls the lands surrounding the gateway. It's his army that allows passage from the Unseelie *sithein*. How else would they get an ogre through the gates and deep into Seelie territory? Someone wants a war and they're willing to work with the enemy to get it."

"Then we are dealing with traitors on both sides," the Hunter agreed, his eyes dark. I wouldn't want to be the traitor because I was betting the Hunter had plans for him. "It's an astute observation. I will speak to my king about it."

"Your king doesn't want a war?" It wouldn't be the first time a ruler used subterfuge to get the war he wanted. Propaganda and misdirection were the games of kings.

"No. He's adamantly against it," the Hunter said firmly. "He believes Devinshea's ascension is a sign that all of Faery has a chance at renewed life. Like the Seelie, many of the Unseelie have faded over the last hundred years because our fertility is gone. We need children to give our lives meaning. It might be different if the priest was someone else, but the Unseelie believe Prince Devinshea will treat them fairly."

"He might not if you get his goddess and unborn child eaten by an ogre," I said sourly.

He sighed. "I won't let you be eaten. Please relax. All we have to do now is wait. If you would like, you should feel free to scream. I believe that might attract the creature. Crying might have the same effect."

"I'll take a pass." I wasn't about to help the damn thing find me. I would be quiet as a mouse if I thought the ogre would ignore me.

I stood there with my hands tied behind my back as the Hunter took his place hiding behind the large tree with the ropes he'd secured earlier. I wasn't sure what those ropes were supposed to do but I hoped they did their job and caught the ogre in a stranglehold. The Hunter kneeled down and settled in like he thought it might take a while. My hands already hurt. The next time I had to deal with something like this I would be much more careful about the wording of the oaths given to me.

I saw the Hunter stand quickly, though he made almost no sound. He'd heard something and every muscle in his body was primed for action. Every muscle in my body was worried about becoming an entrée. I listened intently but couldn't hear what had caught the Hunter's attention. My eyes roamed the dimly lit forest and finally I saw a woman in white appear from the tree line across the pond.

I relaxed since she was obviously not an ogre. From my viewpoint, I saw a woman with platinum blonde hair and a white dress that did nothing for her pale complexion. Girlfriend needed some color or at least a spray tan because she was all kinds of washed out. She sort of floated along the ground, and I gave her points for grace. It took a lot to walk through the forest in a long, flowing gown and not trip all over the place. There was an odd air of fragility that clung to her, and I started to hope that maybe the ogre would eat her first.

"Good evening, Hunter," she said in a strange singsong voice. She paid no attention to me or the dogs, who looked at the woman curiously but obviously didn't see her as a threat.

I expected that this would be the time the Hunter clocked her over the head and pulled her off to safety so she didn't screw up his carefully laid plans. He hadn't shown any weaknesses where women were concerned. He was all about the hunt, and she was a monkey wrench to be dealt with.

"Hello." The Hunter left his perch and walked toward the woman in white. He seemed much more relaxed now, as if he'd had a little too much to drink and all his inhibitions had fallen away, leaving a man ready for pleasure. I didn't need a man ready for nookie. I needed a man ready for some serious ogre killing.

"Hey," I said, trying to get his attention.

"Is she your mate?" The woman spared me only a second's glance. Even in that moment, I could see that there was something off about her eyes. They were deep and black and far too large to be normal. She was something magical, and I doubted it would come to any good. It was like my dad always said, nothing good happened in faery forests after midnight when you're tracking an ogre.

"She's of no consequence, beautiful one," the Hunter said, his voice deep and seductive. I huffed because if this was the way the man treated his precious bait, then I would hate to see how crappy he was to his prey.

"Then she won't mind if you dance with me." This was said in a little girl voice that made me want to puke. And I minded. I minded a lot.

"Hey," I tried again. "Don't you have a job to do? King Angus gave you a mission to complete. I didn't realize you had a date in the middle of our special time with a hungry ogre."

But he only had eyes for the ridiculously pale skinny chick who circled him in what looked to be a weird-ass paso doble. I only know that because Neil made me watch *Dancing with the Stars* and let me tell you, Bruno would have been all over the Hunter's footwork. It was awful but the weird woman didn't seem to mind. She was too busy doing something with those odd eyes of hers that drew the Hunter in further. They circled each other with no thought to anything but their dance.

She moved her body sensuously, her breasts and hips flowing in time to some music only she and possibly her prey could hear. I used the word prey at this point because I was pretty sure that was how she was viewing my male companion. It was the only thing that made a lick of sense. I doubted that hookers prowled the forest hoping horny hunters had a little cash on hand.

I watched in complete disgust as the male and female continued their dance. It became somewhat frenzied as the woman's magic took over. I racked my brain trying to figure a reason why this woman would try to dance a man to death and then the word finally came to mind.

"*Baobhan sith*." I have to admit that I was in awe of the rare creature I found myself in the presence of. I've seen a lot of freaky shit in my time, but this was something totally different.

She stopped suddenly and turned my way. "You know my race?"

I did, though only through stories from my adopted summer parents. Ingrid and Halle had given me a rundown of all the creatures of Faery I should know. The *baobhan sith* were only mentioned because they thought Daniel would find them amusing. They were the faery version of a vampire. The *baobhan sith* were all female. They roamed the forests at night looking for wayward men, so in some ways my prior hooker theory held true. She would exchange her body for what she wanted. But she wouldn't take a quick hundred for a hummer. She wanted her payment in blood, and unlike the Earth plane's vamps, she almost always killed her donor.

"I know what you are." I felt no great fear talking to her. From what I understood, she wouldn't attack a female.

"This one is hunting in my forest," she explained even as the Hunter swayed close to her. "That makes him mine."

"Look, lady, here's the truth of the matter," I began, hoping beyond hope that logic could sway her. "I don't care. If you want to eat that asshole, I'm more than fine with it. Hell, if I had a fork, I'd give it to you, but how about giving a sister a hand? Why don't you untie me and I'll take the puppies here and leave you to your dinner?"

It was a good plan. I couldn't care less that the guy who wanted to use me and junior as lures would die. If the crazy vamp was willing to cut me free, then I could shag ass out of this forest and get Danny. Danny could handle the ogre with one hand behind his back and he wouldn't need to tie me up to do it. If Herne the Asshole had let me in on his plan in the first place, I would have gone straight to Daniel.

"The woods have been full of hunters tonight." Her strange eyes glazed over in memory. "I've tasted the sweetest blood."

"What other hunters?" My skin crawled. If she roamed the forest a lot, then the Fae likely knew to stay away from her. My people didn't. Some sort of sign might have been helpful or a pamphlet.

She smiled serenely. "I found another earlier. His blood was so sweet I spared his life. It's why I need this one. I must have more but I wish to make the shapeshifter last a long time."

"Damn it!" I let my head fall back against the tree trunk. Now I couldn't just run for my life. "Seriously? Are you sure about that? Was he about six foot tall, with curly brown hair and a righteously crabby disposition? Because if we're talking about the same guy then I have issues because that one is mine."

"If he's yours then he should not have been hunting in my forests at night," the vampire chided me. "He should have been at home in your bed as a good husband should. The fact that he was out at night means he was up to no good. I'm doing you a favor. Find a more easy to control male."

Nice. I was tied up in the middle of the forest and crazy bitch was giving a lecture on scene control. "He isn't my husband. He's my bodyguard."

She looked me over, ropes and all. "He's not doing a good job."

"Well, I can be rough on a guard," I admitted. "He was just doing his job so I need him back. As for this one, go crazy. The dinner bell's a ringing."

The Hunter was at her back. He was still swaying but now he ran his hands down her arms and he let his face rub into her hair. She moved with him, keeping him in a state of wanting though her real attention was focused on me. "I think you're not in a position to demand anything. Why should I give up my lovely treats to a girl who was silly enough to get herself tied to a tree?"

"Girl power?" I offered. "Come on, don't we chicks have to stick together?"

"Why do you refer to me as a baby bird? I'm not soft and sweet." She turned toward the Hunter now, who let his hands find her breasts. "I will show you."

Baobhan sith don't have fangs. She held her hand up and showed me what she did have. Her index finger sported a long, sharp talon. She drew it brutally across the Hunter's neck and I got sprayed with a fountain of blood. The dogs growled now but even as she pulled him close and fastened her mouth against his neck, the Hunter's hands came out to quiet his pets. They whined and moved close to me as though the tied up pregnant human would protect them.

The vampire feasted. She sucked and made noises I was sure Danny didn't make when he ate. Even from the outside looking in, watching Daniel feed was a sexy thing. This was kind of stomach turning. For the most part, feeding a vampire is a fairly neat experience. Even the two times that bastard Louis Marini has caught me for a snack, he didn't ruin my clothes. This girl vamp didn't seem to care that she was letting a lot of her meal go to waste. Girl needed some table manners. She seemed to have skipped vampire finishing school. The Hunter was bleeding and it was going everywhere. It was on him. It was on her. It was on me.

Even as I thought it, I could see the flow slowing. The vampire pulled back, startled, and checked her prey's neck. It was closed now and though the Hunter seemed the tiniest bit woozy, he was still on his feet.

"What magnificent prey I have found this evening!" she exclaimed with a happy sigh. "He's like the other. Their powers of healing are amazing. I'm full yet they live to feed me again on the morrow."

"I'm happy for the two of you. Now, how about we celebrate your newfound interdependence and untie me?"

Her mouth was covered in blood and it dripped down her white dress but she was surprising unselfconscious. "I think not. I think you would attempt to save the shapeshifter. I think you would fight me."

"Absolutely not," I promised, lying through my teeth. "Take 'em both. You were right. He was a crappy guard or I wouldn't have ended up here."

She moved in close, and I could smell the stench of decay on her. I tried to move away from it, but there was no place to go. "Be careful, little girl. We do not take kindly to liars."

I took a deep breath and prayed she didn't use that nasty, needed-a-manicure, finger on me. "All right, I'll tell you the truth, then. If you give me my wolf and let me go free, then I'll leave your forest and I won't return." I left out the part about sending Danny back to deal with her, but I doubted seriously she could handle Daniel.

The vampire looked at me. "And what do I get in return for giving you my prize?"

I looked into her dead eyes and I was extremely serious about my offer. "If you give me my wolf and untie me, in exchange, I promise not to hunt you down and kill you."

Her laughter rang through the air, breaking the quiet of the forest. "You're most amusing, human. I would enjoy watching the large ogre chew on your bones, but I'll allow you a private death. I need to take my new love to my home and settle in for a nice long evening. Good luck to you."

She turned and when she walked back the way she'd come, the Hunter followed her without a single glance back at the woman he'd intended not to hurt. I was left alone in the middle of the forest, staked out and bloodied. I was the perfect feast for a hungry ogre.

Barghest whined beside me. He obviously wondered if he should follow his master, but I assumed that last hand gesture had been a stay command and though there wasn't much the dogs could do to help, I was glad I wasn't alone.

Shuck lay down on top of my feet and closed his eyes. At least someone was getting something out of this.

The Hunter and his new lady friend disappeared into the wilderness. I made note of the direction they were going because I had every intention of making good on my promise. I was going to hunt down that vampire and I was going to get Lee back.

There was a rumble in the distance and it sounded like something big was walking my way. I started pulling at my bindings in earnest now because the ogre was coming and I was almost out of time.

Chapter Fourteen

I looked at Barghest, the dog not asleep at my feet. "Hey, buddy," I said in my brightest voice. "You want to pull that knife out of the sheath and cut through these ties? I'll give you a treat."

Big black eyes looked up at me with zero intelligence in them. He did that doggie smile thing and popped up to lick my face. It was sweet and not helpful in our current situation. At my feet, Shuck began to snore, his enormous body rising and falling with his deep breaths. I was in a place filled with unique and magical creatures and I got stuck with two dumb dogs.

Closing my eyes, I started to work on the bindings on my hands. I had tried to hold them apart to make the loop as large as I could while the Hunter was tying me up so I would have some wiggle room when I relaxed. I was happy to find that this ploy, unlike everything else I had tried tonight, worked. I had a small but significant amount of slack to work with. The rope burned, but I continued my struggle. If I bled, it would just serve as a handy lubricant to grease the wheels a bit. I managed to get the ropes almost down to the first joint of my thumb when I heard something moving in the distance. The sound came from the direction the Hunter and I had entered the woods earlier in the evening. I picked up the pace, working the ropes hard because while I thought the ogre would come from the opposite direction, I'd already had an encounter with a nasty-ass vampire, so I wasn't taking any chances. These damn woods were more crowded than Ether's dance floor.

The dogs sat up and thumped their tails happily, barking to let me know that a friend was coming. Shuck ran off to greet whoever was walking our way.

I was happy to see it was one pissed-off werewolf.

"Zoey Donovan." Neil strode out of the bushes looking incredibly out of place in his perfectly pressed sky blue pajamas and red velvet smoking jacket. He looked like he should be in a Doris Day film rather than walking through the woods looking for a wayward charge. He stood staring at me for a long moment, his slippered feet tapping against the forest floor. I tried to speak, but he gave me an imperious shake of his index finger that told me he needed a moment. After what seemed like forever, he finally spoke. "The funny thing is, of all the things I thought I would see when I caught up with you, this was number three."

I thought about that. "God, Neil, what were one and two?"

"You don't even want to know." He crossed his arms over his chest and stared me down with his icy blue eyes. "I'm going to kill you for this."

"Kill me later. Untie me now." I said it with a smile because of all the people to come looking for me, he was the best. He could yell at me all he liked if he saved me from being something an ogre had to pick out of his teeth and then chose not to mention the incident to either of my husbands. I was going to owe him big time.

"Oh no, sister." He stood before me, his face a mask of indignation. "You're going to stand there because I don't know who did this to you but I know why. You were intensely obnoxious and whoever tied your ass up got tired of dealing with your shit. My only regret at this point is that they forgot to gag you. It was a serious misstep on their part."

"Neil, sweetie," I started, keeping my voice calm because I deserved his lecture. I deserved far more than that, and I hoped he would calm down when he realized I wasn't going to argue with him.

"I went to get you a nice cup of tea," he said, stomping his slippered foot and completely ignoring my pleas. "I made Albert get up out of his comfy bed and make you a hot cup of chamomile since you'd had such an awful day. I was going to massage your poor pregnant feet and listen to you tell me all about how hard it is to have two gorgeous, filthy rich men who love you. Do you want to know what I found when I quietly entered your room?"

"You found I had left the building?" I asked because the answer was so obvious but seemed to require a response.

"You were gone," he said as if I weren't even speaking. "Oh, you made sure to pull the curtains closed so I spent a good five minutes talking to an empty bed. It was a nice touch. I tried to coax you out by revealing the deepest parts of my soul to you. I had a long conversation about how worried I get about Chad being with the Council and in Louis Marini's clutches. I worry every day about losing him just like you're worried about losing Dev. It was a bonding moment for us. Unfortunately, one of us was missing."

"We need to go, Neil."

"Do you have any idea how hard Daniel will come down on me when he finds out you gave me the slip? Why the hell would you sneak out on me? You're a pregnant married lady. You have to stop giving your bodyguards the slip so you can go parading through the woods doing god knows what. Daniel is going to kill me. He's going to bring in some other wolf to be your guard when Lee isn't around. How do you think that makes me feel, Z? Are you trying to hurt me? Is this because I left and you died in Vegas?"

"No, Neil." I never meant to cause turmoil between the two of us. Sometimes Neil was my only touchstone. There were times when I couldn't talk to Danny and Dev, and that only left Neil. He was my best friend. "I was being stupid, babe. This has to do with me making dumbass moves not with me being angry with you. I don't blame you for anything. I was just out here because I thought it would save Dev."

Shuck started to bark and Barghest joined in, but Neil and I were too busy working on our relationship to really pay attention. "Daniel blames me. He blames me for what happened in Vegas. It's why he won't talk to me except to bark orders since we came home from Colorado."

"Danny will come around," I promised. I meant it, too. Danny had to come around because I knew deep down he cared about Neil. There were years when no one in Daniel's life had known the truth about him, but he'd trusted Neil and Neil hadn't broken his trust until Chad had decided to become Daniel's spy. It was easier for Dev to forgive Neil since he wasn't as invested in their friendship. Dev had forgiven Neil because he knew it would make me happy. Danny's feelings about the situation went a lot deeper than that.

"I doubt that he's going to come around if he hasn't already. You just have to face facts. Daniel is done with me and we just have to be civil for your sake." He was quiet for a moment before relaxing slightly. "So, let's have the story. How exactly did you end up playing a bondage girl? Have you found a fourth to tie you up and play dirty games with?"

I thought about that for a moment. "Would he be a fourth or a fifth?"

Neil smiled. "Oh, yeah, I forgot about Bris. I don't think he should count since he looks just like Dev."

"If you think about it that way, then Declan would be a freebie."

A look of complete horror passed over Neil's face and he shuddered at the thought. "Oh, there's nothing free about that hot mess. He looks exactly like Dev so he's hot as hell but god…not even I would go there. Now stop trying to derail my important venting session with sex talk," Neil commanded as both the black dogs were now on their feet, growling low in their throats at something in the distance.

"Neil, it's time to head out." I pulled and tugged at the ropes in absolute earnest. I trusted the black dogs' instincts.

"Furthermore, what made you think you had to lie to me? I can see lying to Daniel and Dev. They're just husbands. They cause all sorts of trouble. But me? I'm your best friend."

"Neil," I growled as I saw the trees start to move across the pond.

"I'm the guy who helped hide the whole 'I'm probably pregnant' thing until you had to ruin it by actually being pregnant. I'm the guy who didn't tell Danny it was you who 'accidentally' left a Justin Bieber CD playing full blast on his stereo while he was in a dead stupor and couldn't get up to turn it off. And you hit repeat. I'm the guy who didn't tell Dev that the boo hag who took up residence in Ether last year was your client."

"You're also the guy who's about to be eaten by an ogre if you don't stop bitching at me and get me the hell out of here," I explained to him in a bitter groan as I saw the shadow of the ogre moving toward us.

"What?" Neil practically screamed the question and then did what he should have done in the first place. He breathed in the night air. He let it saturate his senses, and it was obvious he didn't like what he smelled. He shuddered. "You followed the Hunter out here and he tied you up to feed you to an ogre and there's something else, something rotty and gross."

Now he was trying to get me untied. He tugged as hard as he could. "The Hunter didn't mean to feed me to the ogre. He meant to use me as bait. The rotty gross thing is Lee's new girlfriend, who also happens to be a *baobhan sith*."

"Honey, I don't know what that is." He pulled one of the knives out of my thigh sheath. He brought it around to my back, slicing through the rope. "Use your English words."

I sighed as the rope went slack and my hands were finally, blissfully free. "It's a faery vampire. She lures hunters away in the night and has her way with them. She has both Lee and the Hunter."

Neil looked over my shoulder as I massaged my wrists, trying to get them to come back to life. I took the cold iron knife back because Neil wasn't big on weapons. He preferred to use his claws and teeth. "Holy shit, that's big. We should run, Z."

I pulled the gun out from the back of my denim shorts and clicked the safety off. "Running won't help. He knows we're here. He'll follow us. You should change now, Neil."

The dogs were seriously agitated. The hair on the back of their necks was standing straight up and they were in a crouching position, getting ready to pounce. The ogre moved toward us, though he was moving slowly. He would adjust his speed to match ours. As long as we didn't run, he wouldn't overexert himself. Even moving carefully, I could hear him. He sounded like a herd of buffalo, and he was definitely a mouth breather.

Neil started taking off his clothes. He stepped out of his slippers and shrugged out of the vintage jacket. He then took the time to neatly fold it.

"Hey, Monk, no time for neat," I taunted as I got behind the tree I was previously tied to. "Just do that thing where you change and your clothes kind of explode around you. Let's go."

Neil huffed as he continued his OCD ritual. As he spoke, he painstakingly unbuttoned each pearl fastener on his pajama top. "If you had been where you were supposed to be, you would know that my boyfriend gave this to me and I don't want it to be in a million pieces on the forest floor. He said the red made a lovely contrast with my eyes. That was part of our one-sided conversation. Do you know how much of my wardrobe I have to toss out because you need me to do a quick change? Of course, if you'd been where you were supposed to be, we wouldn't be dealing with that. OMG, that is nasty."

The ogre was standing not twenty feet away from us, and even I could smell the nasty thing. It smelled like rotting meat and atrocious BO. It stood at least nine feet tall and had to weigh close to five hundred pounds. Someone had made a type of tunic for it to wear, but it had seen better days. It mostly hung in tatters around the ogre's strong frame. The pieces that were together were stained and unsightly. He hunched over and from my vantage point, I could see his back was humped. His hair was scraggly and he was missing a couple of teeth. It wouldn't matter, though. He still had plenty left to do a fine job of chewing me up.

Neil stood beside me, finally naked, having protected his precious PJs that I was pretty sure Chad would have bought him more of had he understood our dire circumstances. Neil's hands were on his well-sculpted hips as the ogre looked us over. "Shouldn't he be doing something? What is the thing in his hand?"

"I think that's a tree," I noted. The ogre did, indeed, appear to have hijacked a small tree to use as a blunt instrument.

As if on cue, the ogre lifted his club and roared. The dogs jumped into action. They each took a side and started working in tandem to torment the creature dead set on having them for a late-night snack. One would grab his attention with barking and growls and the other would rush in and take a quick bite out of a handy target. Before I could even think to line up a shot, Barghest and Shuck had taken several hunks out of the ogre's feet and legs.

"Don't think this discussion of ours is over." Neil sent me a forbidding look just before he changed.

His muscles moved and flowed impossibly. He leaned over and with a preternatural grace shifted from human to wolf. Neil's wolf was the most beautiful I'd ever seen. He was arctic white and he stared at me with his glacial blue eyes. He barked and even though he couldn't speak when he was in wolf form, he had no problem making himself understood. That one bark told me to stay put and let him handle the situation. He joined the black dogs just as the ogre tried to bring his tree trunk down on Shuck's head.

I wasn't going to be able to follow Neil's admonition, I realized as I watched the scene from behind the tree. The dogs just couldn't make enough of a dent. The ogre was still interested in me. He was moving my direction, and I didn't think that was going to stop anytime soon.

Neil barked and started in on the ogre's backside, but the ogre swatted at the trio like they were pesky mosquitoes. If I didn't do something soon, one of them was going to get seriously hurt.

I stepped out from behind the tree, leveled my Ruger, and took a firing position. I popped off three quick rounds to his chest and realized I'd probably made a huge mistake. If I had thought the big dude was interested in me before, now he was obsessed. My cold iron bullets were apparently much more painful than the doggy love bites, and the ogre roared.

I backed up instinctively, but hit the tree I'd been tied to previously. I tripped over Neil's slippers and fell to the ground, landing on my butt just as the giant homicidal tree-wielding ogre took a swing at me. I heard a mighty crack as the tree above me took the full force of the club and split in the exact spot where my head would have been.

I rolled to the left, getting out of the way of his second attack.

Neil was swiping at the ogre with his claws when he was thrown off his prey's back and landed right on his spine with a hurt bark. I winced, but he was up in no time, growling threateningly as he circled the ogre, trying to make himself into the target.

I stood still as the ogre watched the dogs and Neil. He suddenly moved his hands and swiped the ground with his club. Barghest and Shuck were struck full on by the enormous tree trunk and they landed somewhere in the forest with a thud. Neil was more agile than the black dogs and he leapt gracefully over the sweeping trunk. The ogre was plainly unhappy that his prey had avoided the trap.

He roared, his shout of rage causing the trees around me to shake their leaves. It also had the unintended effect of leaving the ogre standing still. He was a perfect target and I took advantage. I stood up and fired three more times into his huge body.

It was at this point I discovered that ogre bones are stronger than human bones. If you shoot a human straight in the sternum, said sternum will usually oblige and break under the force of the bullet. Not so with the ogre. The ogre's sternum chose to reject the bullet and send it back to its original owner. I felt the bullet sting my right thigh before it buried itself somewhere in the forest.

I was bleeding but even without taking the time to look at it, I knew it wasn't as bad as I'd dealt with before. I could still move the leg, so I called this round a draw.

Neil sank his teeth into the ogre's thigh and held on for dear life. The ogre tried to shake him off, but Neil was persistent. I watched his furry body swing from side to side as the ogre slung him around. It occurred to me as his spinal column was sent shifting in new directions that his birthday was coming up and I knew just what to get him. I was going to have Dev buy him his own personal chiropractor.

Raising my gun again, I tried to take aim at the monster's neck. Hitting him in his thick skull was an invitation to more painful ricochets, so I would go for something softer. I fired a couple of times before hitting my target. The bullet found a meaty part of the ogre's neck and released a fountain of blood. Neil was drenched before he realized what was happening. He let go and stared at me like I had meant for the blood to hit him.

"Sorry," I shouted across the woods.

The ogre staggered, shaking his head. He was still as strong as a bull but the black dogs were back and they were two mad pups. They leapt into the fray, not at all worried about being covered in blood.

They reveled in it. As the blood coated their fur, they seemed to be drawn into the fury of the kill. They gnashed at the monster's flesh with their sharp teeth and held on with their claws.

The ogre swatted at them, trying to get them off his body. He stumbled back, knocking the dogs against the trees around him.

Shuck and Barghest were having none of it. In fact, it seemed to make them dig in even more. As his foot hit the place where the Hunter had left his long circle of rope, I heard a small snapping sound and then the ogre was hoisted into the air by one leg. He was caught in the Hunter's trap, his massive body dangling over the ground.

The black dogs, satisfied they had done their job, let go of their prey and came back to me, thumping their tails happily. They sat back on their haunches and looked up at me, probably hoping for a treat. I'd made a serious error not smuggling in Snausages.

Neil changed again. Now he was a lovely human coated in thick ogre blood and so obviously not happy about it. "Thanks, Z. I look like Carrie at the prom."

"Again with the sorry." I watched the ogre sway back and forth. He tried to pull his body up to reach the rope but he was a tubby ogre despite his obviously low carb diet. His arms just wouldn't reach. The rope creaked, though, and I was worried it wouldn't hold his massive weight for long.

I approached the swaying ogre, his blood flow slowing but not stopping. As a creature of Faery, he had decent healing powers, but the cold iron I had managed to pump into his body affected him. He groaned and when he looked at me his eyes were sad, like he didn't know quite what was happening but he knew it was bad.

"Don't you dare, Z," Neil said, coming up behind me. "That thing tried to kill all of us. Just because he bats those big, ugly eyes now doesn't make him any less a killer. Get it over with."

I knew Neil was right, but I still felt bad as I leveled my Ruger and took aim. If he'd been left alone, he would be at home in his Unseelie forest where everyone knew not to roam about. He would have been fed and taken care of. Here he was a pawn and like all pawns, I had to sacrifice him.

I squeezed the trigger and the cold iron entered the ogre's brain through his large eye. There was a mighty twitch and the tree holding him shook. Within seconds, the light that animated him was gone, leaving nothing but blankness on his face.

Lowering the weapon, I sank down to the ground and finally took a look at the wound in my leg.

"How bad is it?" Neil asked, wiping blood off his face with the back of his hands. He knelt down and took a look himself.

"It's already healing." That vampire blood I took from Daniel every couple of days always did the trick. The bullet had torn a hunk of flesh out of my thigh but it was closing nicely.

The dogs jumped happily around Neil, and he smiled as he batted them down. They had enjoyed the play and liked running with him.

"Down, boys," Neil tried commanding in his best alpha voice. The dogs just licked at him. Neil isn't and never would be an alpha. "Fine," he said, giving up. He walked back toward the pond. "I'm going to get the ogre blood off me and then we can discuss how we're going to save Lee from his new lady friend."

Neil walked off with the dogs and they all jumped into the pond.

I watched the ogre sway and wondered how many more unique creatures would be sacrificed before we uncovered the traitor. I only hoped one of them would not be my husband.

Chapter Fifteen

"Why do I have to carry them?" I asked, following Neil through the forest carrying his precious vintage pajamas. They had looked kind of starchy since Neil liked his clothes perfectly pressed, but the fabric was quite soft. Chad sprang for the best for his boy, so it seemed.

Neil stopped and the black dogs followed suit. All three were quiet for a moment, scenting the air and looking for those clues that completely got past the old human sniffer. I stood there, holding my cargo, completely unnecessary at the moment. It was kind of nice though. With Neil there had been no discussion of going back for reinforcements or dropping me off someplace safe. In his mind, I was the reason his ass was out here in the first place so I was damn sure coming along for the ride. I was also being forced to play the role of sherpa. It was a trade-off. Neither Danny nor Devinshea would ever have asked me to lug their crap around, but they would have fought like hell against me coming along on the "let's save Lee from the creepy chick" mission.

"You have to carry them because I need all my senses. So stop your bitching."

"No, you don't," I shot back because I liked my bitching. I was good at it. "All you need is your nose. Have you caught it yet?"

He pointed in a direction that led across the woods and up a steep hill. "I'm getting the distinct scent of cheap beer and laziness coming from that direction. It smells like home."

He began trudging his way to his destination, not caring that he was walking perfectly naked through a strange forest with two dogs at his heels. I felt much more self-conscious, but that had nothing to do with my clothing and everything to do with the scary undead thing at the end of this quest. I could only hope she'd done what she promised and kept my wolf alive.

"What's Lee's place like anyway?" Unlike Neil, I'd never been invited in. Lee lived in the same building I lived in, but the boys and I had the penthouse and Lee had a single two floors below us, next to Zack's apartment. Dev owned the building so the small apartment was one of the perks of working with me. Actually, now that I thought about it, I kind of owned the building, too. I was married to Dev, so that made me Lee's landlord. I was going to have to rub that in.

After I rescued him.

"It's about what you'd think. There's lots of beer, an old television. The only real furniture he has besides a bed is a Lazy Boy. It's surprising he keeps the women just coming on through," Neil commented. "I guess he's packing some serious heat under his lazy exterior. I offered my design skills, but he politely turned me down. Well, he growled a lot and told me to mind my own business."

"Women? As in plural? More than one?" The thought of Lee and a string of women was somewhat unsettling. I always kind of took Lee for a monk. He was the definition of emotionally unavailable. He was a lone wolf and by his nature tended to push people away.

Neil turned briefly with that know-it-all smile he got when he knew the good gossip and I didn't. "He's considered the stud of choice among the unattached Dallas she-wolves. I'm sure his number is in the women's restroom of the local wolf bar with the tag line 'get it here.'"

My mouth dropped open. "Are we talking about the same wolf? Lee isn't exactly a ladies' man. He's the most charmless man I've ever met. He doesn't even look at women."

"Well, honey, I don't know about looking," Neil said, taking back up his naked hike, "but he sure likes playing with them. I'm kind of lying though. I know what it is about Lee they all like."

"Spit it out." I wanted to know.

"Okay, so like most of the odd non-human creatures, werewolves have trouble with fertility. Unless you and Dev get it on in close proximity, it can be hard to get a wolf pregnant. Not surprisingly, this makes a lot of wolves slightly obsessed with having babies. Also not surprisingly, there's a small faction of female wolves who don't want to be broodmares for the next generation of puppies," Neil explained. "Most of the male wolves I grew up around measured their masculinity by whether or not they could impregnate a female. It's an instinct. When I was fifteen, my dad tried to pair me with another fifteen-year-old. Unfortunately, my proposed mate's name was Jane instead of John and it just didn't work for me."

He'd been kicked out of his pack for his refusal to mate with the females. I hadn't realized how young he'd been when he was expected to try to become a dad.

"Lee doesn't have that instinct," Neil continued. "Take Zack, for example. He's been dating Lisa for a month or so and they aren't using anything. He's actually hoping she turns up pregnant so they can get married."

"Wow, that's fast." It wasn't unheard of for two wolves to get married without first proving their fertility, but it rarely happened. They tended to like to know they were compatible first.

He shook his head. "No, it's not. It's normal in the wolf world. You humans take your fertility for granted. Anyway, Lee is willing to use protection and he doesn't get obsessed with the women he screws, so he has a parade of happy women coming in and out of that sad apartment."

"I had no idea." It was odd to think of Lee having a life outside of work. He had a whole second job as the she-wolves' booty call.

"Yeah, I think he wanted to keep it that way," Neil allowed. He shook off his guilt at having let me in on the secret. I was surprised he managed to keep it from me for this long. "Of course, if he really wanted to keep it that way, he shouldn't have gotten himself made into a love slave and forced me to walk through the woods to save his ass. Zoey, seriously, don't give him a hard time about it. He's private. It would bug him if you knew."

"He knows everything about me." He did that thing where he sniffed me from top to bottom at least twice a day. It was invasive and I'd strangely gotten used to it. Now I didn't even stop what I was doing, but it had the side effect of him knowing every bit of my business. He knew how often I had sex and with whom.

"That's his job, Z. He takes it seriously. He considers you to be his responsibility. I think he loves you a little. You're like the sister he didn't know he wanted. Zack told me their mom died when they were young. Their dad kind of drifted in and out, so Lee had to raise him. It's second nature to protect the people he cares about. I think he's happy with his life right now."

"I'm glad you like him." It warmed my heart that Neil finally had a father figure. My dad had been good to Neil, but he needed another wolf to look up to.

"I like him a lot, Z. I didn't expect him to accept me but he did. He even asks me how Chad is doing from time to time, and I never give him too much information. He's a good man." Neil stopped and pointed. "He's also in that scary house about two hundred feet that way."

I took a deep breath and got ready for my second fight of the evening. "Okay," I said, putting down my cargo. Neil wouldn't want it any closer to the fray. "I promise that once we save him I won't give him a hard time about becoming a female vamp's love slave."

Neil looked at me like I had lost my damn mind. "Are you kidding? I was talking about his string of one-night stands back home. We're so giving him a ton of shit about this. We'll be giving him hell about this night forever."

"Agreed," I said with a smile as I changed the clip in my gun. I was happy because it would have been hard not to tease the crap out of him about this particular incident. The good news was the cold iron should work on this faery vampire as well as it had on the ogre. She didn't care about silver, unlike the Earth plane's vamps. In this case, her Fae nature was more important than her undead status.

I studied the small house in the middle of the forest. It was completely incongruous against the wild nature around it. The cottage had been painted white and stood out starkly against the greenery. It was like a lighthouse for people lost in the woods at night. I was sure many a roaming hunter had thought he could get a hospitable meal and a place to sleep when he came across this small *brugh*. Of course, it wouldn't be long before he became the dinner and settled here for the longest of sleeps.

It struck me that the *baobhan sith's* residence could have been any number of houses in the woods from faery stories. *Hansel and Gretel*, *Little Red Riding Hood*, all could have been set in these woods, and it wasn't just the structures. There was a feel to the forest here in Faery. It was as though it was a living creature all on its own and it hungered. It called to the wild things of the world and let them know they had a home here.

I suddenly felt very much a stranger in this strange land. Despite my misgivings, I forced myself to follow Neil.

We moved quietly forward. I was aware that both of the men in the house had crazy strong senses. It remained to be seen if those senses came into play when under the *baobhan sith's* spell. The rest of the Hunter's personality and will had seemed to go by the wayside, so it was possible, but we had to be careful.

Neil moved silently though the thick trees and I followed, doing my best to move as quietly as he did. The dogs caught on to the game and became serious. One took to my side, Shuck, I think, and the other stayed with Neil.

Flattening himself against the side of the cottage, Neil made his way around toward the door. When he reached the open window, he stopped and took a careful peek in. When he turned back, his eyes were wide and he motioned me to come over. He leaned close and whispered straight into my ear. "Forget what I said earlier. I know why the chicks dig Lee."

I moved in, getting close to Neil. There was a fire in the hearth, and it gently illuminated the windows of the cottage. Lee was standing in the middle of the room. Oh, holy crap. I knew why they liked Lee, too. Lee might be a werewolf, but he was hung like a horse. It took everything I had not to giggle at the erotic tableau before me. It was like walking in and finding your dad with his girlfriend. I finally understood why Lee freaked out when he caught me without my clothes on. I tried looking anywhere but at that pretty damn big part of him.

The vamp was having some fun with her newly acquired harem. Apparently this part of the woods was clothing optional. The female vamp was kissing Lee, her tongue plunging into his mouth while she held his head back with one hand. With the other hand, she stroked that part of Lee the ladies liked, and it was ready to play.

The Hunter, for his part, watched the scenario in a daze from one side of the bed. Since he had no creepy vampire to play with his junk, he was flying solo. He had worked himself into quite a state. I didn't want to see that either.

"He's going to kill me," Neil said under his breath.

"What does he expect us to do? Leave him there?"

"He would probably prefer death to you seeing him like that."

"Too bad," I said because that wasn't going to happen. "I have a promise to keep."

I walked around to the door and kicked that puppy open with the flat of my foot. All eyes flashed around to me.

"Hey, how you doing, guys?" I said with a cocky smile.

I've found that when faced with weird creatures that are probably going to kill you, it's always best to go in with a positive attitude. Pessimism doesn't do anything but bring you down in a fight, so I put on my happy face and held my gun out. "Surprised to see me? Well, Vampira, I told you I want my wolf back. Why are all you faery bitches trying to steal my stuff? You want a wolf? Go find your own. That one is taken."

If he hadn't wanted me to claim ownership, then he shouldn't have made a blood oath to serve me. That oath went both ways. It was an old vampire ritual, but I took it seriously and I knew Lee did, too. Lee had promised to follow me and lay down his life in service of me. I promised to treat him fairly, and part of fair in my book was saving him from a lifetime's slavery to a vampire chick.

"I'm shocked you managed to get away, though I see you found some help," the aforementioned vampire chick hissed as she turned and looked back and forth between me and Neil. She stared at Neil, and it made me think twice about having brought him along with me.

The black dogs moved to their master. The Hunter seemed dazed, but let his pets come to his side even as he moved to protect his new friend. He and Lee took up protective stances around the *sith*.

The vampire smiled now, her lips turning up in a sly grin. She gestured toward Neil with an exceedingly confident smile. "Another hunter looking for prey. We're not so different, little girl. We both use men to do our bidding. We both know they're but helpful tools to be used and discarded."

Neil snorted. "That's Zoey's problem, lady. She can't discard any of them. She just keeps marrying them. If she doesn't stop soon, we'll be looking for a bigger place."

The vampire was paying close attention to Neil, who was already obligingly naked for her. She held out her hand and the boys let her pass. She wasn't doing anything threatening and I'd already killed once this evening. If I could talk her into giving up Lee, I would still leave without firing a shot.

"What's she doing?" Neil never took his eyes off the *baobhan sith* as she started to sway her hips and move toward him. Her body rolled in an impossibly sensuous dance and, for the merest of moments, I worried. She called to hunters and Neil was a hunter. He was a predator. Despite his sweet looks, he had the heart of a wolf beating inside his body, and I wasn't so sure she wouldn't call to that.

"Sweetie," I heard myself saying as I laid a hand on his arm to start to pull him away. The last thing I needed was Neil to find the hetero within. I already had one wolf to save. "Maybe we should stash you somewhere."

"Z," Neil whispered, still watching the vampire do her mating dance. "I think she's calling to me. She wants me to come to her, to love her, to feed her."

My insides clenched at the thought of losing Neil. I was going to have to make a move and fast. I was just about to level my gun at her when she reached out to touch Neil's face. Her mouth was slightly open in a lusty show of desire. Just before she caressed him, his hand shot out and stopped her.

"Not happening, sister," Neil said with a disgusted groan. "Unless you have a hot brother stashed away somewhere, that shit ain't working on me. Now, keep your skanky hands to yourself. I have a boyfriend. Trust me, I've turned down some super-hot male tail because I love Chad. I'm certainly not going to start my own episode of *Cheaters* because some ho-bag faery vamp can make me hear music."

"What's wrong with you?" She hissed the question as she looked him up and down, trying to see the problem.

"There's nothing wrong with me," Neil said simply with no hint of animosity. He didn't care what anyone thought. He had people who loved him and they were enough. "I just don't find you even vaguely attractive. I like boys. If I were going to break down and fuck some chick, it would be Z."

"Thank you." I was flattered that I was at the top of his list. I had always kind of thought it would be Sarah.

"You're welcome," he said with a coy smile. "I'd do you because you have so many hot dudes going through your bed, I'm sure one of them will eventually slip up and take me instead."

The vampire obviously didn't like being turned down. Her face was a mask of rage, and she drew that nasty finger back to slash it across Neil's throat. Without the aid of her victim being drugged by magic, she was no match for Neil. He slapped her hand back and she found herself on her ass.

"Protect me," she commanded and Lee and the Hunter moved forward.

"Oh, shit," Neil said under his breath as we moved backward in perfect time with each other. "I don't know about the other one, Z, but Lee can kill me and not even break a sweat."

"I think the other one can, too." I felt the back of the wall and we had nowhere else to go.

The Hunter gave the dogs a closed fisted gesture and they began to growl.

I took a deep breath. The problem with this whole scenario was that I didn't want to kill any of the people or animals who were about to come after me. Shuck and Barghest didn't want to hurt me, but they were the Hunter's creatures. They had to do his bidding. If I wanted to get everyone out intact, I was going to have to get creative.

"Think about this, Herne." I didn't make a single threatening move. "What you are about to do will hurt me. You intend to hurt me if you sic those dogs on me. You will break your oath and my friend will call down the Wild Hunt. They'll come, Hunter. They'll come even for you. They won't care about the spell you're under. Your oath holds no matter what. It can't be broken without penalty."

He stopped and even through his magic addled brain, my logic seemed to penetrate. It went against everything he was to break his oath. He was the keeper of the Wild Hunt and the Wild Hunt was about justice. If he harmed me, he was doing an injustice, and that he could not handle.

I turned to Lee, my voice strong and righteous. It was a voice Lee would understand and relate to. "I own you, wolf. You're my creature or you're an oath breaker as well. You promised me. You made vows, Lee Owens. You made vows to me, not this creature before you. Search your brain and you'll know I speak the truth. The hunt can come for you as well. They can come for royals or nobles who break their oaths or those who commit crimes against them. I am your queen. Don't make me call them down on you."

He seemed to fight with everything he had. His muscles bunched up, his eyes closing as though he was in pain. Whether he was fighting to come with me or to stay away, I didn't know. I only knew which instinct won out. Lee calmed finally and took his place at my back.

The *sith* backed away and stared at me, suspicion in her eyes. "What are you? Why do you glow so brightly?"

I'd wondered if that shine I had was visible to the faery vampire. I had met one female vampire in my life, and while she could see my glow, she wasn't particularly taken by it. I used the *sith's* ignorance to my advantage. "If you were on the Earth plane, you would know me well. I'm the Queen of all Vampire, and pray you don't meet my husband. Your wiles won't work on him and he'll kill you for even trying. These men are mine. I take them back now."

"You're not a vampire," she insisted even as she backed away.

"I'm something more," I said, using Bris's words. They sounded pretty impressive to me, so I tried them on her. I moved forward, staring down at the vampire. "Do you doubt me? I killed the ogre. I own the wolves. My servant is unaffected by your unique brand of magic. I walk the forest with no fear. If you choose to test yourself against me, then you will lose. I'll enjoy the exercise. It's your choice, nightwalker."

"You said I could keep the other," she argued, pulling back even as she tried to negotiate. She dropped to her knees, her head falling forward into a submissive position. Unfortunately for her, that time was done. I was through bargaining.

I pulled the cold iron knife from its sheath and knelt down so we were eye to eye. It was time to use those faery stories to my advantage. "That was a deal I was willing to make should you have aided me. You know how these tests go, vampire. If you had aided your queen, I would have showered you with gifts. You chose to show me no hospitality. I'm well within my rights to take your life."

She believed me. She began crying bloody tears, another way she was different from her Earth plane brethren. "I am sorry, Your Highness. I will aid my sisters from now on. I was just eager to get back to my prey."

"And that's why you failed," I said, standing up. "I leave you with your life, *baobhan sith*. Remember the lesson. Now go. We will need this cottage for an hour to prepare for our return to the palace."

Her eyes were downcast as she rose. "I'll go and sleep in the caves. The house is yours until tomorrow." She gave one last long look at the men in the room and then she was gone, disappearing in the night.

"Wow, Z," Neil said with a look of approval. "That was an Oscar-worthy performance."

I cocked my eyebrow. "Why? I technically am her queen. She's a vampire and I have it from the *bean si* that I'm the Queen of all Vampire. I didn't lie. I did all those things. And bitch really did fail the sisterhood test." I looked at the boys, who were kind of in a fugue state. "Do you think she broke them?"

Neil waved a hand over Lee's impassive face. "I hope not. I can probably drag one of them, but we'd have to leave the Hunter dude behind."

Lee suddenly took a deep breath and intelligence came back into his eyes. He glanced around the room, shocked at finding himself in a completely different place from the last one he remembered. He frowned when his eyes settled on me.

"Zoey, what the hell is going on?" He put his hands on his hips like he was going to launch into a lecture, but the minute he felt bare skin he blushed all over and I mean everywhere. His hands left his hips and cupped his privates. He should be happy he had big hands.

"Nice to have you back, Lee." I located his jeans and tossed them over.

"What happened? Where the hell am I? Why am I here? Why aren't you back at the palace?" Lee barked questions as he tugged the jeans on. I turned away to give him as much privacy as possible because he was still trying to cover up with one hand. I heard his zipper go up and turned around. "And why the hell was I naked?" He practically yelled the question and naked came out sounding like nekkid. I loved it when he sounded backwoods. It meant he was way passed pissed off.

"Are you done yelling at me?" I asked. "If you are, I'll answer your questions. You met a hottie in the woods and decided to come back to her place for a little action. This is your new girl's pad. You're here for some loving and a nice blood exchange, since you suddenly have the hots for a vampire. It's okay. I understand. They can be persuasive. I'm not at the palace because the asshole next to you decided to make me ogre bait before he joined in on your threesome. As to why you were naked, well, I think that's the state you're usually in when having hot sex with a vampire. Daniel insists on it."

"So does Chad," Neil added helpfully.

"I did not have sex," Lee stated, offended.

Neil shrugged. "He can lie to himself but not to his nose."

Lee took a deep whiff and blushed again. "I can't believe I had sex with a vampire."

"Welcome to the club, buddy," I said with a grin.

The Hunter was starting to come out of his stupor. "Why am I…"

I rolled my eyes. "Hush and I'll give you the Cliff Notes version since you slept through the lecture. You, *baobhan sith*." I made an *O* with my left hand and shoved my right index finger in and out in a junior high gesture, accompanied by a creaking mattress sound.

Lee groaned and sat down on the bed with his head in his hands, but the Hunter eyed me curiously. "I was with you in the woods and the ogre was close. I could feel it in my bones. Then I woke up here. You're saying it was a vampire that lured me here?"

"And you loooved her," I said with a smile that made Lee moan again.

"I certainly did not," the Hunter said seriously. "I was enchanted by her. Did I kill the creature? Is that how I escaped?"

"You didn't escape," Neil pointed out. "Zoey saved you."

Lee's head came up and there was a horrified look on his face. "Why didn't you just leave me to die, Neil? How could you let Zoey save me?"

"Well, it's not exactly a fate worse than death." He could be more grateful.

"Oh, yes, it kind of is," Neil replied. "Zack is never going to let him live it down. He can give his brother hell."

I wasn't sure what the problem was. "Well, it's not like Lee is the first. I've saved everyone. I saved Daniel and Devinshea many times. I saved you from your asswipe brother when he tried to kill you. I saved Sarah from Hell. Why should Lee be any different?"

"You haven't saved Zack," Lee said sourly.

Now that I thought about, it was true. While Zack had saved me from a demon last year, I'd never had a chance to return the favor. "Huh, I guess it never came up."

"Hence the hellacious ribbing Lee is going to get from his brother. It'll be constant, Z. He won't ever let up," Neil said with the tiniest bit of malicious glee.

The Hunter frowned at all of us. "How is this conversation aiding us? Your Grace, I have no idea how you escaped, and I'm grateful you're alive, but our problem still persists. I still need bait to lure the ogre out."

Lee was suddenly on his feet. "What did you say? Are you telling me you dragged my charge into the woods to use her as bait for an ogre?" He was baring his teeth at the Hunter even as the black dogs started to growl.

"It doesn't matter," I injected to try to stop the inevitable fight. "I killed the ogre."

Both heads turned and looked at me with complete disbelief.

"Well, I had some help."

Neil smiled. "She didn't need much." He always had my back.

The Hunter invaded my space, searching my face for the truth. "You truly killed the ogre? You dealt the death blow?"

"Yep." I wasn't about to let him intimidate me. I'd had quite the night. I crossed my arms. "And by the way, is there a reason you're naked in my presence, Hunter?" I asked, tossing his words back at him. "Are you trying to tempt me into fornication?"

He looked down, realizing he wasn't dressed, and when he glanced back up, he was Herne once more.

"Coward," Herne said to the god inside him. He smiled down at me before going in search of his pants. "Nice going, Zoey. The Hunter is now slightly afraid of you. It's the greatest compliment he's ever given a female. You made him run and hide."

"Good to know. Now, if you'll get dressed, I need to sneak back to the palace before anyone realizes I'm gone." I looked at Lee, who seemed hopeful for the first time that evening. "Yes, I'm keeping silent because I don't want the hubbies to know I was out for the evening."

"Thank god for that," Lee said before frowning Neil's way. "Where the hell are your clothes?"

Neil shrugged. It was a question he often had to answer. I was satisfied that I'd managed to keep all of my clothes on for once.

It was the only great satisfaction I would get from the endeavor because thirty minutes later, as we approached the palace, I realized there was no way to sneak in.

The entire palace was lit up and the army seemed to have been called in. There were people everywhere.

Declan charged up on horseback, and even as we left the woods, he was calling the royal guard down on me.

Chapter Sixteen

"Hand her up," Declan demanded as the royal guard separated me from my own guard.

Lee growled and started to shove his way through the bodies surrounding us.

"Lee, Neil, stay back." I was sure Declan wouldn't hurt me. The only thing that would come out of a fight would be one of my friends getting roughed up. I'd spent most of my night trying to protect the people I cared about, so I was willing to go with my brother-in-law.

"Zoey," I heard a voice saying. Zack changed from his wolf form. He put his hands on his naked hips and frowned at all of us. At least I now knew how the guards had found me. "What the hell are you doing out here? Lee, where have you been? You should have been back hours ago. We were terrified."

Whatever Lee said to his brother was lost as I was lifted up and placed in front of Declan on his big, black horse. I felt awkward as I wasn't allowed to straddle the horse. I was more or less in Declan's lap and completely dependent on his strength to not fall off. He wrapped his free arm around my waist and glanced down at my party. "You all have a lot to explain. You have been called to the palace where you will answer for this night's idiocy. The queen and I will expect you in the throne room in one hour."

With that forbidding declaration, he turned the horse around and started back toward the palace. The rest of the guard mounted and followed closely behind.

"It wasn't their fault." I hated that I felt the need to wrap my arms around his chest, but I wasn't comfortable I wouldn't slide off his lap. "I left with Herne and Neil came after me."

"Then Neil should have kept his eyes on you." Declan didn't look down at me but stared at the palace. "He should know you well enough to know what you are capable of."

"Why didn't Daniel come after me?" If anyone was going to rush in to save the day, I expected it to be Danny.

Declan's handsome face was coldly furious. "The vampire is currently up to his knees in dead bodies."

"What?"

"Unfortunately, the dead bodies are moving so he must kill them again," Declan said, his disgust plain. "The witch made several mistakes and we are being forced to clean them up. When the zombies rose, we all worried that this was the way my brother was to die. Would you like to know what his only concern was? He cared nothing about his own life but fought his way through herds of the walking dead to reach you and ensure your safety."

I felt my heart clench. It was bad enough he knew I'd slipped out, but he'd probably been terrified.

"Is Devinshea all right?" I would never forgive myself if he was injured fighting his way to save his wife, who wasn't even there.

"He is unharmed. He was mounting a horse to search for you himself when one of the guards recalled seeing you running across the fields with the Unseelie ambassador. He meant to alert us before then but he was knocked out by those pesky zombies. Needless to say, Devinshea was surprised that his pregnant wife would run off with another man. He shouldn't have been. You were cheating on Daniel with him. He should have thought about that before he chose to bind himself to you."

"I wasn't starting an affair with Herne," I said because that should have been self-evident and I never considered what Dev and I had to be cheating. I slept exclusively with Dev until Dev had asked to bring Daniel into our relationship. It was only through Dev that

Danny and I reconnected. "I was trying to save my husband."

"Well, I know how you like to save men, Zoey."

I turned up to face him. He looked so much like Dev it hurt to have his contempt directed my way. "Someone led the Unseelie's ogre into the forest. Herne was worried that the ogre would be the thing that killed Dev because it would most definitely start a war."

"Yes, Zoey, if the Unseelie sent an ogre to kill my brother it will certainly start a war."

"You aren't listening to me. That ogre couldn't have gotten in without Seelie help. Are you telling me that something that big and that stupid managed to make it all the way to the forests outside the palace and no one noticed?"

"Well, I would believe that before I would believe that a Seelie would aid the enemy," Declan said stubbornly. "I suppose you have some proof of this ogre? Or am I to just take you at your word that you didn't sleep with the Hunter?"

"Well, I killed the fucker so I guess the body might be my alibi." I let go of Declan's waist and forced my hands into my lap. If he wanted to keep me on the horse, he could just work that out himself. I wasn't going to touch him.

"Damn it, Zoey," Declan swore as he tightened his hold. "Do you want to break your neck?" I stayed still in his arms. "Did you really kill an ogre?"

"Yes." We reached the courtyard. Every lamp and candle in the palace seemed to have been lit. "Dev didn't want to come get me himself?" I supposed that Declan could have stopped him, but I doubted that was the case.

"He asked if I wouldn't mind retrieving you and taking you back to your room." Declan replied.

A sick feeling took hold of my stomach. "I suppose you told him what you thought I was doing."

"I did not," Declan admitted. "I thought it was evident and I did not wish to rub his face in his folly. It is not that I hate you, Zoey. I am actually rather fond of you. I simply think you are not suitable to be the wife of a Seelie prince. You would be a fine mistress, but that is where Devinshea should have kept you."

I went silent because I had nothing further to say to my

husband's brother. I sat as still as the horse's movements would allow and held myself as far from Declan as I possibly could. The real trouble was I was wondering if Declan wasn't right.

I didn't fit into Devinshea's world. The nobles didn't know what to make of me. I behaved more like an Unseelie, and the Seelie would never accept that. Our marriage had seemed like a good idea when Dev was estranged from his family and his world. He was back now and they accepted him as they never had before. I was a bit of an inconvenience.

The courtyard was littered with corpses, and I had to try not to breathe to avoid puking. I saw Sarah being led through the yard by Felix, on their way to their rooms. Her face was red, her eyes puffy from crying.

Felix rushed over and gave me a hand down. I was happy because I didn't want Declan to touch me any more than he had to. Felix hauled me gently down and then Sarah was hugging me.

"I'm so sorry, Z." Sarah sobbed into my shoulder.

I hugged her tightly. I had no idea what had happened, but I was sure that she hadn't meant to plunge Faery into a remake of *Night of the Living Dead*. "It's all right."

"Yes," Declan said, his sarcasm flowing. "It is fine that you turned our palace into a graveyard. We do not mind at all."

"Shut up, Declan." I sent him a frown.

"I got the incantation wrong." She sniffled, wiping her tears away. "I'm out of practice."

"Yes, you're out of practice with black magic." Felix gave Declan the dirtiest look a former angel from the Heaven plane could muster. "They should never have asked you to try it in the first place. Let's go to bed, dear. It's been a long night."

Sarah pulled away and gave me a sympathetic look. "Dev is upset, Z. Danny tried to tell him you were off somewhere coming up with an insane plan to save his ass, but he wouldn't listen. He left. I don't know where he went."

I nodded as she walked away with Felix. Declan took my arm, and I pulled away as hard as I could. I'd had enough of him. "I know the way to my rooms."

I just wondered if Dev would show up in them.

Declan was a stubborn ass. He reached for me again. "You know your way to your rooms, but you have no idea where Devinshea is. Luckily, I do."

I let him pull me along because it seemed easier than fighting him. "Why would you take me to Dev? You might get your wish, Declan. Maybe Dev will talk to your mom and she can annul the marriage."

He led me toward the temple, crisscrossing the courtyard to avoid the bodies. I recognized the fluidity of Daniel's work. The zombies were in neat piles because if Daniel could take them out in groups, he would greatly prefer it to singular kills.

Declan walked fast, as if it were important we made it to the temple quickly. "Mother will never annul the marriage, Zoey. You are pregnant. You are perfectly fertile and your compatibility has been proven. We just have to make the best of things."

"Screw you, Declan," I said bitterly, pulling my hand out of his.

"Things would be infinitely easier on me if you would. Look, Zoey, Devinshea loves you. He does not want your marriage annulled, but he is angry. For the most part my brother is not hotheaded, but when he gets angry, he can burn down his own house without thinking of the consequences. He is a storm of emotion tonight, and you taking reckless chances was the last straw. Daniel took your side and that did not help things either. I worry Devinshea is about to do something he will regret."

My heart rate picked up. Declan was right. When Dev got really mad he could be irrational. He would say things he didn't mean just to lash out. "What's he going to do?"

Declan frowned and walked faster.

"Tell me." I wanted to know what I was getting into.

"I believe he is going to call for his priestesses," Declan finally admitted as we opened the door to the temple.

I came to a full stop. His priestesses were there for one thing and one thing only. Their job was to please their priest sexually and aid him in his fertility magic. I turned back to go to my rooms. Jealousy burned in my gut. "If that's what he wants, then who am I to stop him?"

"You are his wife," Declan said savagely, hauling me around.

"You are supposed to love him so much, Zoey. Well, prove it. Get in there and stop him from making the biggest mistake of his life. He will never get over losing you. I will not let him fade because your pride left him alone."

Declan pulled me through the gilded halls of the glorious temple. He stopped at an ornate door. "This is the priest's chambers. Go and fight for him. He would fight for you. Prove me wrong, Zoey." He pushed the door open and I found myself in Devinshea's private pleasure dome.

The marble room was lit with soft candlelight from wall sconces. I was in some sort of entryway. I could hear feminine whispers and the sound of water running. The entryway was separated from the rest of the rooms by a series of filmy curtains. I could see the outline of a group of women standing around.

Tears pricked my eyes. He had done it. He'd actually called for them. I took a deep breath. If he was going to burn our marriage down then the least I could give him was a witness to the act.

"He thinks he's going to die, Z," Daniel said quietly from a bench a couple of feet from me. I hadn't noticed him sitting there. He looked incredibly tired and he was beyond filthy. "I wouldn't take anything he says or does seriously." Danny reached out and briefly squeezed my hand. "I'm sorry I let Declan find you. I just finished with the last of the zombies."

"I wouldn't want you to leave his side right now." If something was coming for Dev, Daniel was his best bet.

"I can't leave either of you. This stunt tonight, Z…" His jaw clenched down.

"I was trying to help him."

Daniel damn near stared a hole through me. "I tried to explain that to him. If you do it again, I swear I'll lock you up. I can't take care of both of you."

I touched his face. "I'm sorry."

He nodded, letting go of his anger. "It's over. You're alive. He's alive. Just fix him, okay? He won't listen to me."

"And if he's in there fucking his harem?" I was kind of surprised Danny would ask me to accept that.

Daniel shook his head, squeezing my hand. "Dev would never

do that. He's posturing. He's scared and angry at the world. If I know him better than you do, we're in trouble."

I stepped away and pushed back the curtain quickly because I needed to see where he was at before his mask came down. I caught a quick glimpse of Dev as he sat in what looked like a hot spring flowing through the room. It reminded me of the grotto in our penthouse, though this stream had been caught in a large pool complete with steps leading down to it. Dev was sitting in the water alone. There were four women whispering among themselves as they looked down at their priest, obviously wondering what they were supposed to do now. For his part, Dev didn't look like a man who was anticipating a five-way with some hot chicks. His face was blank, like a man who was about to lose everything and he couldn't figure out how to stop it.

The minute he saw me his mask fell firmly into place and his gorgeous face took on the countenance of a dude who couldn't care less. His eyes went a stony blank and quickly shifted from mine.

He could pretend all he liked, but I knew the real Dev. He was terrified and when he got that way he would fight because it was infinitely easier for him to yell than cry. What he didn't seem to understand was that if he couldn't cry, I would do it for him.

"You look like you're down a couple of priestesses." At one time they numbered six.

Dev arched an eyebrow, his voice lazy and uncaring. "The trouble with the Unseelie sent two of them home. I will miss them terribly, of course. They were unique and a pleasure to fuck."

"I'm sure they were," I said under my breath, not wanting him to know how it hurt me to think of him with anyone else.

"You look like you've been hunting. Did you have an interesting evening, lover?" Dev's voice held a hard edge.

I noticed the large bed dominating the room. The bed was fit for way more than two, and there were armoires and a dresser. I crossed to the bedroom portion of the room. "It was trying. How about you?"

He sighed. "Oh, the usual. We called the undead to us and my wife lied to my face and ran off into the night, placing our unborn child in the gravest of dangers. All in all, just another day as the husband of Zoey Donovan Quinn."

So he was going to play the martyr. I would rather he just yelled at me. "I was convinced I was helping you. I didn't just run off for fun."

"Deception is always a helpful way to manage a marriage." He shook his head and crossed his arms over his naked torso. "You're never going to settle down, are you? You're never going to be a proper wife and mother. My brother told me. I should have listened."

"Yes, you married me for my skills as a housewife," I said bitterly, feeling those damn tears bubbling up again. "I tricked you, Dev. You can't blame yourself. I presented myself as perfect-wife material." I stood up and looked down at him, completely ignoring the women who huddled together, their perfect faces turning between me and their priest like they were watching an emotional tennis match. "I have never lied to you. I told you the first night we met what I did for a living and then proceeded to nearly burn your club down when a job went bad. If that wasn't a hint that I was trouble then I don't know how I should have let you know. I've never hidden who I am or what I wanted, but I have to wonder if you've given me the same courtesy."

His eyes narrowed. "What is that supposed to mean?"

I shook my head. "It means that if you wanted a proper wife, you should have found someone else. It wasn't fair for you to marry me and then try to change everything I am."

I expected him to yell, to scream, to say some truly awful things. It was the way he fought. Instead he turned and snapped his fingers.

"I need help with my bath." He commanded the women and they obliged him by entering the tub, not bothering to take off their shifts. "Perhaps you are right, Zoey," he said in an imminently logical voice as he let the women begin to soap his body. "We are from two completely different worlds. It was a mistake. I am trying to change you and you have already changed me into something different. If we separate, we can go our own ways and be the people we were meant to be."

"How have I changed you?" I asked curiously because I wasn't afraid of this conversation anymore. He told me all I needed to know with one glance at his body. My incredibly horny, always ready to go at it husband, had eight soft female hands on his body and he wasn't sporting even the hint of an erection. I didn't know what he was looking for from me, but I intended to find out and give it to him. He needed me and I wasn't going to let his stubbornness tear us up. If he wouldn't listen to reason from Daniel, then I would have to appeal to his other instincts.

He gestured around him as though the answer was evident. "I am used to the attention of many women, Zoey. It has been difficult to remain monogamous."

I couldn't help the small smile. "Yes, I can see it's been boring for you."

I pulled my tank top off and let it fall. He couldn't possibly know about my earlier conversation with Herne. I had been reminded that the reason Bris had accepted him was his willingness to remain faithful to his wife. I kicked off my sneakers and unbuckled the sheaths on my thighs, placing the knives on a table by the bed.

"I am used to variety, wife," Dev said and I noticed he had not once looked at the lithe bodies around him. His gaze was steady on me as I undressed. "I allowed you Daniel but I am held to monogamy, though my nature runs against it."

I shimmied out of my bra. Why he was lying to me I had no idea, but it didn't matter. I could win this war and I wouldn't have to fight. I let my underwear drop to the ground and walked to the spring. Tossing aside the band that held my hair in its ponytail, I let it flow down my shoulders. I knelt down and cupped my hands. Filling them with warm water, I showered my breasts.

He frowned my way. "Do you have to do that here?"

"I've been in a bloody fight too, Dev. I hope you don't mind." I looked down and now my non-monogamy loving husband was sporting an enormous erection. One of the priestesses tried to run her hand down his chest, and Dev seemed startled at the action. He moved away before remembering the game he was playing.

"I mind, Zoey," he said, his attention focused solely on me. "I mind that you could have killed our child."

"And I mind that my child might lose his father. I won't let you go without a fight. I won't raise my child that way. If you want someone who will hide in a closet for nine months, then you should start knocking up some of these women."

He looked at me and practically snarled. “If I was doing my duty, I would impregnate them all.”

“I thought you tried that once.” I lobbed that grenade back his way because he was seriously pissing me off. “It must not have worked out since I don’t see a passel of tiny Devs running around.”

His eyes heated and I knew I’d made a mistake. He wanted to fight. He was practically begging for it. A long slow smile crossed his face, but it held no humor. “You know what they say, lover. If at first you don’t succeed…Besides, now I have Bris and I assure you, if I wish to fill them up, I can do it.”

It was time to tone down the rhetoric. I wasn’t about to engage him. The thought of him doing that could make me crazy, and that was exactly what he wanted. He didn’t mean a word of it. It was time to say things we did mean, and it looked like I got to go first this time. I walked into the water and straight up to him. “I love you, Dev. You recognized that I needed Daniel and I’ll always be grateful for that. If you need these women to make you feel complete then I’ll still love you.”

He gripped my arms, hauling me to his chest, warm water surrounding me. “Are you offering to be one of many, my wife?”

“Declan thinks I make a better mistress than wife anyway,” I said quietly, letting my insecurity show. There was no place for posturing here. “If being a proper and traditional priest is what’s best for you, then we can make it happen. I don’t fit in here. Doesn’t a mistress get her own place somewhere where she won’t insult polite society? I’m not a good wife, Dev. You should have talked to Daniel before you made that mistake.” I let my hands trace his chest. I loved his chest. I loved being pressed against it and feeling the strong beat of his heart. I couldn’t imagine a world without him.

“Fight me.” He shook me slightly, and I knew he was close to breaking.

I wrapped my arms around his waist. “I would much rather make love to you.”

“Damn you,” he cursed me. He looked at the women around him. “You are no longer needed. I meant what I said earlier. I expect you to take other lovers. I’ll no longer be available. I have one goddess, no matter how much I want to strangle her from time to time."

As the confused women got back out of the spring, Dev pulled at my hair, forcing me to look up at him. "Declan is a fucking idiot, wife, and the next time I see him I'm going to punch him in the face."

My nipples immediately sprang to attention, my body softening. "I thought you were mad at me."

"I am." His hands slid down my sides to rest on my hips. He brought our bodies together, and I felt the long line of his erection pressed against me. "I'm so angry with you I can barely see. Do you understand what you did?"

Couldn't we just get on to the makeup sex? "I did what I thought was best, Dev. I did what I needed to do to save you."

"With no thought to what I need, which is to keep you safe."

That was an easy thing to reply to. "No, I was selfish because I don't want to live in a world without you in it and I'll fight with everything I am to keep you here with me and Daniel. I'm scared out of my mind. I can't just sit back and do nothing."

His eyes grew heavy. "You don't play fair, Zoey. I want to argue and scream and rage and all I can think about is getting inside you. Know this, my wife. I love you. I don't want a mistress and I don't want a proper wife. I want you. Even when you're a raging bitch, I still want you." He covered my mouth with his and his tongue demanded entrance. I softened under him and let him plunder. He cupped my ass and pulled me against him, grinding his erection against my pelvis. "I don't want to die. I don't want to leave you."

Now I let the tears flow because we'd come to the heart of the matter. Dev always struggled with his real fears. He'd grown up in this court where any fear would be seen as a weakness, so his default state was to posture and fight. He had to realize he was safe with me. I let my hands find his face and looked deeply into those emerald eyes. "I can't let you go."

I didn't care what the *bean si* said. He wasn't going to die.

"I need you," he groaned against my skin. "I need you and I need Daniel. I should never have brought us here."

"I asked you to bring us here, Dev," Daniel said. He'd been sitting out in the hallway just waiting for a chance to come in. It probably killed him to have to wait. Patience wasn't Danny's strong suit. He stood at the edge of the pool, staring down at us.

Dev pulled me close as he looked up at the man he considered his partner. "If you're worried I blame you for the mess we find ourselves in, I assure you I don't."

Daniel's face turned grave. "I wouldn't be surprised if you did. I've been blaming myself for hours. I'm the reason we're here. I need the ties to Faery if I'm going to take over the Council."

"And I need you to stop blaming yourself. We're a team. You didn't order me. I came up with this plan." Dev lifted me up and suddenly I was sitting on the edge of the tub, my legs dangling in the water. The marble was strangely warm against my naked skin. "I don't want to think about this anymore tonight. Besides, I've decided I know what will kill me. It took me a while, but I figured out where the real danger lies."

Daniel's whole body tightened as though preparing to act against whatever threat Dev pointed out. "What is it, Dev?"

"Our wife is going to give me a heart attack," Dev said with a wry smile.

Daniel rolled his eyes. "Asshole. This is serious."

Dev arranged my legs, completely invested in his task. He pulled me this way and that until he was satisfied. His finishing touch was to pull my hair forward so it just touched the tops of my breasts.

"Stay that way," he demanded, taking a step back and admiring his work. I was completely spread and open to his gaze. It wasn't terribly uncomfortable, and I got the feeling I was in for a couple of hours of Dev's demands. I'd put him through hell and he would want some payback, which usually meant sexual servitude.

Sometimes I misbehaved just to get him in this mood. I wasn't about to fight him because I got the feeling we could all stand to blow off some steam.

Dev continued staring at me while talking to Danny. "I'm serious, Daniel. I'll expire one of these days because Zoey will finally have pushed my poor heart to its brink." He glanced up at Daniel. "Are you going to stand there or are you planning on helping me torture our wayward wife?"

Danny was out of his clothes in record time. "I wasn't able to get my torture on this morning, so I'm up for it. Literally," he said, unselfconsciously pointing out his glorious erection.

Dev looked slightly horrified as he caught a glimpse of our vampire. "You're covered in gore and bits of dead people."

"Well, he…" I started.

"Hush, woman." Dev immediately shut me down. "How can I objectify you if you keep talking?"

Danny's hands were on his hips as he frowned down at Dev. "I'm sorry I'm offensive. I killed like a thousand zombies. It's not exactly the neatest of professions. I didn't stop to take a shower."

"Get in here and clean up. Stand in the stream side though so it can take the filth away," Dev told him, handing him a jar of something I was sure would smell good.

Daniel stepped into the water, careful to move to the part where the stream ran the swiftest. I sighed as he started to spread the soap across his chest and down his six-pack. He looked at Dev, obviously more amused than irritated. "You're the bossiest person I've ever slept with."

"Well, that's not saying much, Daniel." Dev turned slightly, and I didn't miss the way he took in Daniel. "Everyone you have ever shared a bed with is currently in this room. Perhaps I'm normal. You won't ever know."

Dev went back to staring at his favorite piece of female anatomy as Daniel sank into the water to wash the soap from his hair.

He surfaced, slicking his hair back with big hands that I was pretty sure would be roaming all over my body soon. "Are you the one who got her to wax?"

"Yes," Dev acknowledged. "I like to be able to see my sweet little pussy when I fuck it."

"I begged her to shave and she kept putting it off," Daniel complained.

Dev shook his head. "That's because you were asking, Daniel. Zoey prefers to be told what to do when it comes to sex."

"Hey," I started because I didn't like the way that sounded. Even though it was probably true. Mostly true. Mostly always.

"Shhh," Dev shot back and he walked up to me. I was seated above him, putting him in the perfect position to play with me. He stepped between my legs, letting his mouth linger over my pussy, his breath a warm temptation. "For the next several hours, you will speak only when spoken to. And I think I would like to be referred to as sir." He dropped a far too light for my liking kiss on my clitoris. "How about you, Daniel?"

Daniel sent me a heated look. "I think that sounds like an excellent idea. I've had a shitty night. I think some submission from our wife might help turn it around. I do have a couple of questions for her, though."

Dev was breathing deeply in, luxuriating in the arousal he was pulling out of me. "Ask away. I'm sure you'll find her perfectly truthful now that her scheme is over."

Dev started placing chaste kisses all over my wet flesh, and I whimpered because I needed a hell of a lot more than his lips. I wanted to beg him to use his tongue on me, but it wouldn't do any good. Dev was going to enjoy his bit of torture, and the truth was I did like to be told what to do in bed. I loved it when they tied me up and I had no control over what they did. I knew it only worked because I loved and trusted the men I slept with. I certainly didn't want them telling me what to do outside of the bedroom, but the thought of submitting to their desires always made me wet.

"Why don't you explain how you thought running around in the middle of the night with the Hunter would help Dev?" Daniel asked, catching my eyes. He stood in the deepest part of the stream, the water up to his waist.

"There was an ogre in the forest." I tried to fight the instinct to move against Dev's mouth. I bit my lip as he used the tip of his tongue to delicately flick at my engorged clit. Dev's fingers came up to play with my nipples, sending shots of pleasure/pain through my system. "Herne told me he thought it was what the *bean si* were talking about. He told me I was the only one who could help."

Dev stopped what he was doing and looked at me expectantly.

"Sir," I added quickly, hoping it would placate Dev and he would go back to what he had been doing.

Dev gave me a look that told me to behave and rewarded me with a long, luxurious stroke of his tongue. I was already so wet. All I needed was a little suck, maybe some firm pressure, and I would go off like a rocket.

"How were you supposed to help Herne?" Daniel asked. "I would think if he wanted backup in fighting an ogre, he would come to me."

I should have lied. I should have, at the least, massaged the truth a bit, but Dev was distracting me with his teeth and his tongue. His fingers spread open my labia so he could taste every centimeter and I just answered without thinking. "Turns out I was bait."

Dev's head came up, and I didn't like the expression on his face. His eyes darkened, his jaw forming a stubborn line.

"I was bait, sir," I tried.

He turned and started to stalk out of the pool. I had a strong suspicion where he was planning to go, and I didn't like his odds in that fight.

I scrambled down from my perch and wrapped my hands around his waist to stop him. "Danny, help me. He's going to go do that thing where he slaps the shit out of someone and then they fight."

He'd started the process with his brother when we were all in Colorado. It was apparently a traditional way to resolve differences in Faery.

"Why the hell would he do that?" Danny had his arms over his chest, a fierce frown on his face.

Dev stopped and turned, utterly ignoring the fact that I was still hanging on to his waist. He just moved like my weight was no concern to him. "That man tried to use our wife as bait for an ogre. I cannot let that go unanswered. I will challenge Herne for what he did."

"And he'll kill you." I looked desperately at Daniel, who just stood there. I was pretty sure that Herne's god could kick Dev's god's ass. If it had been a competition based on sexual prowess, Bris could win hands down, but this was combat and he was a lover, not a fighter.

"What's up with you, man? Ever since we got here you've been acting like some fucking eighteenth century gentleman," Daniel complained. "Did this asshole inform us of his intentions to sacrifice our wife? Did he give us fair warning? Why the hell would you make a public announcement of his future ass-kicking? What happened to the man who didn't play fair? You never have with me. I don't expect you to do it now."

"What do you suggest?" Dev asked.

Daniel's fangs had popped out, a sure sign of his rage. "Well, I thought I'd give him a day or two to feel comfortable then we can jump him when those dogs of his aren't around. I intend to beat him to death, unless that will start a war, then I'll think about leaving him alive but I assure you, his balls won't work after I cut them off and shove them down his fucking throat. Or we could have some pansy-ass duel that will probably get you killed and fulfill the prophecy Z was trying to avert."

"Fine. You're right. Don't you dare jump him without me," Dev said and his body relaxed against mine, content that he would have his revenge. He turned back to me. "Did I give you permission to leave your place?"

"No, sir." I rushed to get back to where I was supposed to be. I shot Daniel a grateful look. I was comfortable with Dev beating on Herne if Daniel was there to make sure he was all right. I tried to remember exactly how he had me and my hands brushed against my pussy. Dev slapped at them.

"None of that," he said, pulling my hands firmly to the side. "That belongs to us."

I smiled. "Yes, sir."

"Daniel, turn around," Dev commanded, picking up the soap again. "You have something all over your back. It's probably some distant relative of mine."

My mouth started to water and I was sure my eyes were as wide as saucers as Danny turned around and allowed Dev to run his hands across the skin of his back. Dev's strong hands ran down Daniel's spine and I couldn't help my reaction. Dev soaped his back, carefully cleaning him. They were so fucking gorgeous together that everything below my waist tightened.

Daniel's head came up, and I knew he had caught my sudden interest. "Seriously, Z? This gets you hot?"

I could only nod my head as I watched.

"Is our wife having those thoughts again?" Dev asked, brushing his hands across Daniel's broad shoulders and pronouncing him finally clean.

"You can't tell? I can smell it from here." Daniel practically growled. "And her heart is beating like a race horse."

"Should we try an experiment?" Dev suggested.

Daniel looked at him, wary. "Are we ready for that?"

"Nothing too out there," Dev promised. "I just want to see if our wife is interested or if she just thinks she is."

I could have just told them the answer to that question. I was really interested, but I kept my mouth closed because I wanted to see what Dev had planned. He had a creative mind, and I liked to watch a master at work.

Dev walked over to where the soap had been. There was a small tray with soap and washcloths and a straight razor. I was sure Dev had already used the razor as his face was perfectly smooth. He picked it up now and turned back to Daniel. "One of the perks of being a fertility god is knowing what turns people on. I knew from the moment I met Zoey that she needed some light, playful domination. As a man who enjoys dominating a woman, I was more than willing to provide the service. Don't think I don't know what you want, Daniel."

He brought the edge of the razor to his perfect lips and quickly drew it across his mouth in a shallow cut that had blood welling out of it.

Daniel's reaction was immediate. He was in front of Dev before I could see him move. He crowded Dev, their bodies close but not quite touching.

"You are a bastard, Dev," he growled and I watched him try to control his lust.

"Don't, Danny," I begged, moving again. "You promised not to hide anymore. It isn't wrong."

I moved in behind him. They were standing so close, and I knew if I could break through this, I might get what I wanted. I wanted them to love each other as much as they loved me. I wanted a true threesome. I wanted them to enjoy each other and I didn't see why that was bad or wrong. We loved each other. We were faithful to each other.

"Fuck," Daniel cursed right before slamming his mouth over

Dev's.

I moved to the side where I had the best view of the action. I placed a hand on each of my boys and watched as Daniel's tongue lapped up the blood running to Dev's chin. He ran his tongue from just where Dev's neck met his chin, upward to the cut on his lip. There was nothing soft or sweet about it. He was dominating Dev, his hand running up to Dev's hair and sinking in so he couldn't move. He pulled Dev's bottom lip into his mouth and sucked deeply. Dev groaned and I felt his hand reach down to cup my ass and pull me in closer even as Daniel's hands held his head still.

Dev's fingers were hot on my skin, and I felt the tingle of his magic start. That hot lust rolled over my skin, and I couldn't imagine what it was doing to Daniel. He wasn't just crowding Dev at this point. Their bodies were flush, chests and hips touching. The water was sitting at their waists, but it was clear and I was close enough to see those big cocks nestled together. Danny sucked at Dev's lips, his lips and tongue drawing up that sweet blood.

"It's not enough," Daniel growled and turned Dev around forcefully.

He held Dev firmly against his chest with one hand and wrapped the other in his dark hair, forcing his head to the side. I moved to Dev's front and let my hands wrap all the way around his body to clasp Daniel's waist. My nipples were hard nubs against Dev's chest and his hands came up to play.

"I think she wants it, Dan," Dev said with a decadent laugh. His cock was hard as a rock, and it moved restlessly against my belly. The air was so thick with lust and magic I could barely breathe.

Daniel was past talking. He looked at me, his blue eyes a dark promise that I would get mine later, and he sank those fangs into Dev's neck. He held Dev still as his throat worked, feeding, drinking Dev down so he would walk around all night with Dev's blood pumping through his body.

Dev's fingers tightened on my nipples and he panted. "Zoey, wrap your hand around me. Stroke me."

I did as he asked and reached down between us. He was so hard I couldn't make my fingers meet when I held him. I pumped his cock in my hand, lusty magic rolling across my skin.

"Suck me harder," Dev commanded as he put his hand over mine and started to rub his cock forcefully. "I'm not Zoey, Daniel. I can handle it. I want it. I want you to be rough with me. I'll fucking love it."

Daniel groaned and I saw him sink his fangs in deeper and draw harder than he ever could with me. His eyes rolled back as he enjoyed letting his instincts lead him for once. He was always so careful with me, treating me with a delicacy he didn't use with Dev. Dev gave him something I couldn't. Dev wouldn't break. He wasn't as strong as Daniel, but he was strengthened by the god inside him.

Dev's hand tightened impossibly on mine as he raced toward orgasm. "Faster, Zoey, I'm going to come. Please, don't fight me."

I relaxed my hand and just let him use it. Within ten strokes, I felt him jerk against me and his magic washed through the room. Daniel released his vein, his hands going around Dev's chest as he held him up.

"Told you she wanted it," Dev said to his partner with a sigh. He didn't fight Daniel, simply allowed him to drag him along.

Daniel set Dev's boneless form down on the marbled steps. "Can you sit? I don't want you to drown. I'll be damned if you die because I took too much." He stared at the spot on Dev's neck where the puncture marks were already healing. He reached out, touching them as if to reassure himself.

Dev's hands came up, covering Daniel's. "It would be a good way to die, but you would never hurt me. I know that. She knows that. You have to learn that. We trust you."

"Then be ready for more of that because it felt fucking good." He turned to me and his beast was loose. His eyes were sapphires burning through me. He held a single hand out. "Come to me, companion."

I didn't hesitate. Daniel rarely allowed his dark half to take over. I'd seen this pure vampire side of Daniel only a few times before, usually when he was close to death. In the years since, I've learned so much about vampires. The beast, as I like to call it, comes out when the vampire's instincts take over like in times when he's fighting for his life or when he's protecting his precious blood. A vampire is a deeply possessive creature, and Daniel felt that this particular evening. At first he'd been scared of losing Dev and then me, and now he needed to put his stamp on both of us, needed to know we belonged to him and we were both alive and warm and ready for him.

None of those instincts mattered to me. I loved him. That was all that counted. I rushed through the warm water to get to him. He pulled me close and his hands tangled in my hair. He lowered his mouth to mine and when his fangs nicked me, he just groaned and lapped up the little blood before plunging his tongue in.

I wrapped my arms around him and held on for dear life. Daniel lifted my legs up until I was supported by his strong hands and he shoved his way inside me. I let my head fall forward as he physically moved my body up and down on his cock. I steadied myself on his shoulders as he plunged his dick in to the hilt.

"God, Z, how do you stay so fucking tight?" he asked, walking to the side of the pool and shoving my back against it. He stroked deeply inside me as he brought his mouth down to mine. He kissed me so sweetly I almost didn't notice as Dev pushed his way behind me.

"Hello, lover," he whispered in my ear. I felt his chest at my back, and he was ready to go again. Even as Daniel pumped into me and groaned, Dev ran his hand down my back toward my ass. "Know that if the healer hadn't said we couldn't, I would be fucking this sweet ass right now. We want to take you at the same time. It's all we talk about. You'll be so full with both of us inside you. We'll be able to feel each other, too." He slipped his hand between me and Danny and unerringly found that cluster of nerves that made up my clitoris. He rubbed firmly and my head fell back as I came. "We're going to rub against each other even as we fuck you, wife."

Daniel's strokes lost their regularity as he bucked against me, coming in hot jets of semen. He bit into my neck and sent me over the edge again before the first one had even stopped. As we both came down, he moved softly against me as he licked the wound in my neck closed.

Dev laughed behind me and held me close, which was good because I didn't feel like standing up. Danny went down on his knees and rested his head on my belly as he wrapped his arms around me.

We stayed like that for the longest time, just feeling connected and happy together. After a while, Daniel got back on his feet and he looked at me and Dev, a light happiness in his eyes.

"Carry her to bed. I'm not done yet." He walked up the steps even as Dev caught me against his chest and followed Daniel's orders.

He grinned down at me. "And he calls me bossy."

Daniel threw himself down on the soft bed, laughing.

* * * *

I lay against Dev's chest, napping just a bit as the boys talked. It was deep in the night and I was tired and completely satisfied, resting on the big bed with my men close by. If Herne had been right, then the threat was gone and I had averted a war. If he was wrong, then Daniel had a plan.

"I'm not going to let you out of my sight, Dev." Daniel leaned down to kiss the curve of my hip, resting his head against it as he stroked his hands across my skin. The warm light of the temple made everything seem golden, as though the sun was contained in the marbled walls, warming and lighting the space from within. I could hear the gentle rush of water from the pool and stream. Everything about the temple was soothing, conducive to rest and romance.

Dev chuckled slightly. "So you want to see me die?"

Daniel's head came up and those eyes were suddenly sapphire again. "Don't talk like that."

Dev put a hand up. "I'm sorry. I was joking."

"You don't joke about this." Daniel settled back down, rubbing his cheek against my skin and cuddling close. His hand moved down, resting on my belly. I wondered if he could hear the baby's heartbeat. He would likely find it soothing. "I'm going to watch you like a hawk and if you die, then I bring you back. The banshees get what they want. We get what we want. Everybody wins. The prophecy can be fulfilled. There's no reason I can't bring you back. You've died before."

I shuddered at the thought. I remembered watching him die when we were in Vegas. I remembered seeing Daniel's body on the slab of the Denton County Coroner's office when he died all those years ago. The two worst days of my life. I couldn't lose them. I couldn't. The *bean si* claimed I was some sort of hole in the fabric of fate. I'd saved Dev and simply being near me had caused Daniel's early death and his rebirth as a vampire. I had to be able to affect this scenario, too. I'd killed the ogre. It had to be enough.

"I think it would be best if we left as soon as possible," Dev said. "The situation here is worse than I could have imagined. The Seelie are ready to fight. I don't want to get Zoey and the baby trapped in a war zone. I have to visit the fields or people here will starve soon, but after that I think we should pack up and head back to Dallas."

"I think you just miss the Xbox," Daniel teased because he certainly did.

I sat up because they were forgetting something. "I still have to find the Blood Stone. I'm not leaving without it." Louis Marini had told me if I didn't do this job he would kill Daniel and I, for one, believed him. He had the trigger for the surgically implanted device on Daniel's heart. I'd seen the X-ray, and if Marini pushed that button, Danny would receive a lethal dose of silver straight to his heart. Not even a king could survive that.

"How long will it take for you and Bris to make sure people don't starve?" Daniel asked, thinking about the problem.

Dev had one of those weird, in-his-head conversations before answering. "We need at least a week, maybe two. Most of that time is travel, though. If you flew me, we could be done in five days."

Daniel nodded. "You have five days to solve the puzzle, Z."

"It shouldn't be difficult," Dev reasoned. "Everyone knows the Blood Stone is one of the things the *bean si* discussed, so people should be willing to talk. You don't have to hide your interest. Talk to Mother in the morning. She can tell you who she gave the stone to." He closed his eyes and I knew he was exhausted. "I'm reluctant to leave Zoey behind."

"So am I, but I don't see how we accomplish both tasks if she comes with us. She has all three wolves," Daniel pointed out. "If I directly tell Zack to not allow her to die then I assure you he'll get the job done. He never disobeys, unlike some others."

"Don't be mean to Neil," I ordered. "He had a tough night, too. He had to find me, help me kill an ogre, and save Lee."

"He shouldn't have let you slip away in the first place," Daniel pointed out, moving up on the bed. He settled down on the other side of me, spooning me from behind. "His senses are crap since he came home."

"Well, he hasn't had vampire blood in almost a year," Dev said reasonably. "You can't compare him to Zack."

Daniel sighed behind me. "Well, I'll deal with Neil later. I'll leave Zack explicit instructions. Between Zack and Lee, she'll be fine. Now hush, both of you. We have a long day ahead and I'm tired."

"Bossy," Dev said as I felt him drift off.

The boys were soon fast asleep, surrounding me with their warmth and safety, but I couldn't help but think none of this would be as easy as they were making it out to be.

Chapter Seventeen

Declan strode into the room with a smirk on his face the next morning. Or afternoon. I hadn't checked the time. I just knew it was far too early to have to deal with my brother-in-law. "Well, we all know what you were doing last night, Zoey."

It had been only minutes since Dev and Daniel had kissed me good-bye and promised to hurry their task to get back to me.

"Hey, what happened to privacy?" I pulled the covers up to my chin since I wasn't wearing anything.

"What are you talking about?" Declan rolled his eyes and threw his body on the bed. "It is not like I have never seen it before. Besides, I would love to see it again. You know I find you attractive, Your Grace. I came to congratulate you. Once again your skills in bed have saved my brother from a horrible fate. You should teach a class, you know." His face turned serious. "But we have to discuss the fertility rites situation. Give a guy a chance, Zoey."

It was my turn to be confused. "You're going to have to give me more than that, Dec."

He gestured around the room. "This is the temple of the High Priest of Faery. It was constructed to amplify fertility magic and send it throughout the palace and down to the valley below. Before, when it was just Devinshea and his priestesses, he needed that amplification to get anything at all going. Think of it like one of your radios. Before Bris, the volume was set at a ten or maybe, if the night was going well for my brother, perhaps a twenty out of one hundred."

"What was the volume like last night?" We'd done some pretty freaky stuff together last night. Devinshea had been creative, I'd been submissive, and Daniel had been insatiable. I felt a sweet ache in my backside from the spanking Dev had given me for sneaking away. He'd been serious about that bit of discipline.

"One hundred and fifty." Declan crossed his arms as he sat up. "I was sitting in the throne room giving those wolves of yours the lecture of a lifetime when Padric suddenly walks in, sweeps Mother up, and carries her away. That was when I felt it. The wolves all ran when Lee explained what was happening. He said he didn't want to be something called a 'manwhore' twice in one night and he shifted and ran away as fast as his paws could take him. I cannot shift into another body. I only have this one and I'm susceptible to lust magic since I'm already horny all of the time. I was caught up in your carnal cloud and now I might have to get married."

I laughed out loud. "Serves you right. Was it that girl you were with last night?"

"Which one?" he asked seriously.

"You don't remember?" I'd only seen the brunette, but apparently there had been more.

"There were several, though not all of them at the same time," Declan replied. "There was the brunette at the ball. I do not remember her name, but I will ask about her because she was incredibly flexible. At one point I had her ankles touching her ears and she never complained."

"Spare me the details, please." I looked around to see if someone had thought to leave out a robe.

Declan was utterly unconcerned with my anxiety. "But that is not the one I am worried about. You have to understand that when that lust magic hits, the urge is overwhelming. I ended up fucking one of the village maids, well, one of the maids and her sister. They were somewhat attractive but they have no manners whatsoever. Actually, I do not even remember if they are attractive. That magic makes me feel drunk."

I had a fun thought. "What happens if you got them both pregnant?"

Declan shuddered and blanched visibly. "Then I will have two completely unsuitable wives. From now on, you will inform me when you are going to fuck my brother so I can get out of the way. I need several miles between us." He nodded down at me and relaxed. "At this point, I am just going to plead complete ignorance if they come up with child. Maybe they'll forget. If Dev hadn't been here, I could blame him."

I sat up and tossed a pillow at his head.

He smiled. "Continue your violence against me, Your Grace, and I will get a peek at a nipple. I think they are already bigger. Pregnancy suits you."

I was about to toss whatever modesty I had left out the door and slap that grin off his face when Albert walked in carrying a massive tray. My stomach growled as the smell of bacon, eggs, and waffles hit me. There was a pot of tea in place of my usual coffee, but I would just have to get used to it. No caffeine for Baby Boy.

Declan sat up beside me, resting his back against the headboard. "Excellent. I am starving. There is nothing like breakfast in bed."

"Then go have it in your own bed," I grumbled, securing the covers around me once more.

"Mistress." Albert greeted me with a smile. He placed the tray on the bed next to me where I could easily reach it and he gracefully poured the tea. "I saw the masters off this morning. I fixed Master Dev a basket of his favorite foods and a few excellent bottles of wine. I included some eighteen-year Scotch for Master Daniel."

The boys would definitely be getting their drink on while they were away from the wife. "I'm sure he will appreciate it, Albert. It was thoughtful."

He nodded. "I'll be back in an hour to retrieve the tray, mistress, and I expect it to be empty. You need your strength. Mr. Owens informed me you might be in the village for luncheon this afternoon."

I took a long drink of the cold orange juice. "That's right. I have to talk to the queen, but she said she gave the Blood Stone to a villager, so I'll probably be there this afternoon."

"Then I will pack a basket for you and the wolves," Albert offered. He frowned. "It will have to be a large basket. The wolves eat an enormous amount of food."

Declan reached across me and stole a piece of bacon. "I will take a sandwich or two as well, servant. Also, if you have any of those sodas Devinshea likes, I will take one of those, too. I like them. They have bubbles."

"I don't recall inviting you along." I wondered if he was going to leave anything for me as I slapped his hand away from my remaining piece of bacon.

"I told my brother I would care for you in his absence," Declan explained. "I did that even after he punched me in the face for absolutely no reason. Do you have any idea why he would do such a thing? My nose is still sore."

"No idea whatsoever," I lied. It was good that Dev had remembered his brother's insult.

Albert walked around to the side of the bed Declan was occupying. "I will get on the luncheon basket right away, mistress, after I take out the trash."

Albert picked up Declan by the neck and started to haul him bodily out of the room.

"Well, I suppose I will see you later, Zoey," Declan said, taking his dismissal with surprising good grace. He didn't fight or scream, as though being hauled bodily out of rooms was an everyday occurrence. "I would yell and complain, but he is bigger than me and I do not think my brother would be happy if I beheaded his servant. An hour, then?"

His feet disappeared out the door as Lee walked in. The werewolf did a double take, and there was satisfaction on his face as he watched the prince being dragged out. It didn't last long. "Damn it, Zoey. Where the hell are your clothes?"

Zack and Neil walked in behind Lee. Neil laughed as he walked over to the closet. "I'll get her a robe."

Lee turned around, but Zack just sat down on one of the sofas. He couldn't care less what my state of dress was. He was wearing casual work clothes, chinos and a button-down. His brown hair was stylishly metro and he was impeccably groomed. He was the exact opposite of his slobby older brother, who cautiously waited for me to cover myself.

"This must be Dev's." Neil brought out a plush white robe from the armoire. I climbed out of bed and let Neil wrap the robe around me. It was enormous but it would have to do until I got back to the palace and our rooms.

"I'm perfectly covered, Lee." I sat back down on the bed and started in on my breakfast. The baby was being a good boy. I hadn't felt a moment's worth of morning sickness but god, I was so hungry. I poured maple syrup over the waffle. The way I felt this morning, I could eat a dozen.

"I don't know why he's such a prude, Zoey," Zack said with a grin as his brother looked around the room, getting the layout. "I guess you're just not his type. He prefers his chicks a little more on the bloodthirsty side."

"Fuck you, Zack," Lee growled.

"I thought we all agreed to lie to Zack if we got caught."

We'd made the decision as we walked through the woods. In order to spare Lee the humiliation, we would all say we'd run into him as he came back from his mission to track down the boy from the dungeons. That mission hadn't gone well. He found the boy's cooling corpse several miles outside of the village. He mentioned that he smelled the same candle wax on the boy as he had on the assassin.

"We might have agreed to lie, but some of us aren't good at it," Lee said with a pointed look at Neil.

Neil flushed. "It's my only flaw."

He was, in fact, a horrible liar. I was sure Zack had zeroed in on that.

"Man, I just had to take one look at Neil to know there was a whole other story," Zack announced. "I love it. I never thought big brother would fall for a nightcrawler."

Lee rolled his eyes. "I was under a spell, asshole. I wasn't in love."

Zack sat back and grinned. "I don't think that's how I'll remember the tale. I think I'll always remember your true love, the faery vamp, and how that mean old Zoey chased her away. It's Romeo and Juliet with fangs and claws."

"I'm so sorry," Neil said, looking at Lee.

"Forget about that." I had a surefire way to get Zack off his new favorite subject. "With the boys away, I guess I'm in charge. Maybe we should go over the plan for the day."

"You are so not in charge," Zack said, losing his grin.

"I'm your boss." I started in on a kind of singsong. "I am Zack's boss. Zachary Owens has to do what I say."

"Screw that," Zack said. "My master told me to keep you alive. He said nothing about sacrificing my sanity to do it."

"What's the plan, Zoey?" Lee asked because other than situations he felt compromised my safety, he let me lead him.

I gave Zack a self-satisfied smile before turning to Lee. It was going to be fun to order his ass around. "I need to talk to Miria and then we'll head out to the village if that's where the trail leads us. Apparently we'll be taking Declan with us."

"Not if we give him the slip," Neil pointed out.

It was a nice thought, but I wasn't so sure it would work. "He would just set the royal guard on our asses. He can make my life difficult without Dev here to countermand his orders."

Lee didn't look happy at the prospect. "None of this would be a problem if you'd taken my advice a couple of weeks ago and let me kill him."

Neil had liked the idea then and saw nothing wrong with it now. "If we killed him, then Dev would be the next king and your baby would be a prince. Power. I like it. He'll need his guncle to advise him."

Zack and I laughed, but Lee looked a bit lost.

"Gay uncle," Zack provided. "It's what we'll call Neil and Chad when we talk about the kiddo. They'll be the boy's guncles." He shrugged at Neil and me, silently apologizing for his brother's lack of current vocabulary.

Lee shook his head. "Two dads and a couple of gay uncles. This kid is going to need me to have a normal life. Zoey, eat up. Let's get this show on the road. I never thought I would find a place weirder than Ether, but this tops it. The sooner we find this thing Marini wants, the faster we can get home."

I picked up the pace on the breakfast because Lee was right. I wanted to go home.

* * * *

It was late in the day before we made it to the village. The sun was still a firm presence, but before too long it would be sinking into the horizon. I wondered how Dev and Daniel had fared. They'd taken camping equipment with them because some of the locations were isolated. I wondered if the boys would be sitting around a fire, drinking their Scotch and telling stories.

Miria had been unavailable for most of the morning. So had Padric. We'd been told they were recovering from the events of the night before. Once she'd been ready to take visitors, she happily provided me with the name of the woman she'd given the Blood Stone to and her direction. Luckily her last known address was for the village outside of the palace. We were looking for a woman named Hildie, and after Declan had asked a few questions, we discovered that she was a barmaid at Ross's tavern, employed there for many years.

Declan was obnoxious but also a great help in getting people to talk. Apparently being the future king meant people were more than willing to answer any question he could come up with. I wasn't sure they would have been so readily open if a human surrounded by werewolves asked the questions.

Declan's hand was on my back as we entered Ross's tavern. Though I'd been in the pub once before, I'd been too concerned about the assassination attempt to get a good look around. I corrected that mistake now. The great room was huge, the first floor covered in small tables, some shoved together for larger parties. One side of the tavern was dominated by a huge bar. Next to that was a set of stairs leading to the second floor, where I was sure the owner's private rooms were.

"Your Grace," I heard a voice call from behind the bar. The satyr was coming from the back room, carrying two plates of steaming hot food. He quickly set them in front of two customers and made his way to our party, his hooves clacking against the wooden floors. He bowed his head respectfully toward Declan. "Your Highness, it is my honor to have you in my establishment."

"Yes, of course it is," Declan said dismissively. "We require a private table, four ales, and some food."

"You just ate." We'd stopped halfway into town and enjoyed the lovely lunch Albert had prepared.

"No, Zoey, the wolves ate," Declan proclaimed irritably. "I barely snacked. All of the sandwiches were gone before I finished my first one."

"You snooze, you lose," Lee said, his eyes searching the tavern. He inhaled deeply, but seemed unfazed by it. "That stew smells good. We'll take some of that."

Declan shook his head. "You should make more, Ross. They will eat everything. They are worse than locust. Bring Her Grace some water. She has walked a long way and needs to rest."

"I'm fine," I insisted as Ross began to lead us to a quiet table in the back. The tavern was quite full even at this time of day. It seemed many people ate here rather than their own homes. I found the hum of conversations around us comforting after the relative quiet of the palace.

"You should put up your feet and rest," Declan declared. "Why my brother decided to allow you to roam around the countryside in your condition I have no idea."

"I'm pregnant, Declan." I planted myself in the chair he held out for me. "I'm not an invalid. I'm not the first woman to find herself in this condition. Trust me, if all pregnant women spent nine months in bed doing absolutely nothing, the world would grind to a halt."

"She-wolves work until they can't stand the labor pains anymore," Zack supplied helpfully. "I was told my mother was a strong bitch. She gave birth to me in between shifts at the casino. She was a blackjack dealer."

Lee smiled, nodding. "No drugs for our mom. She bit the bullet. Literally, she bit down on a bullet so she wouldn't be heard. She was paranoid about the medical establishment. She thought they would find out what we were and experiment on us."

I stared at him in horror. "Well, I'm not going that far."

"Zoey is not some peasant," Declan pointed out.

Neil had an answer for that. "Sure she is. Just because she married nobility doesn't make her a blue blood. Face it, man. Dev married a commoner."

"Hell, Dev married a criminal." Lee smiled broadly, enjoying Declan's discomfort. "Has Dev told you about the time he and Zoey got hauled in by the cops? He has a record, you know."

Declan's eyes were wide as he looked at me.

"They're teasing you, Dec," I promised him. We worked hard to make sure none of us had records.

"Well, I should hope so," Declan said. "My brother is a royal. He is not some common criminal. I would hate to think the authorities on the Earth plane would have a mistaken impression of him."

"Oh, there's no mistake," Neil said implicitly. "Dev is definitely a criminal. He has some sticky fingers, that one. He's just not a common criminal. He was in on that awesome hijacking that made like every newspaper in the country. I wish I'd been around for that one. I bet he would run a great long con, too. He's an excellent liar."

"Unlike some," Lee grumbled.

"And he totally doesn't have a criminal record," I assured my brother-in-law. "The Council cleaned that up for us. The only record of our crimes is with the Vampire Council, though I've been told it's pretty long and detailed."

Declan stared at me. "When you told me you were a thief, I assumed you stole from various shops to enhance your wardrobe. Even some noblewomen here get a thrill from it."

I rolled my eyes. "I don't shoplift. I steal certain arcane objects for a select clientele."

"Select?" Neil snorted.

"I turn people down from time to time. The point is I'm a pro, not some amateur trying to jack lip gloss. Why is everyone looking at me?" I had noticed that all the people in the room were whispering, and they kept stealing glances before turning their attentions back to their soup bowls and mugs of ale.

It was weird to be the center of attention. On our plane, I tried so hard to blend into the background.

Declan seemed surprised by the turn of the conversation and he looked around. It only took him a moment to get his bearings. He smiled slyly at me.

"Word of Dev's magic has made it to the village, then. I thought it might have. The magic itself might have made it this far. Do you want to know what they're whispering about? They're wondering what you're doing to my brother that six lovely Fae women couldn't do." Declan leaned in, his voice all soft seduction, and I knew he was making a conscious effort to sound like Dev. "I'm wondering, too."

His seduction was interrupted by Lee smacking him upside the head. God, I loved Lee.

"What was that for?" Declan practically shouted the question, rounding on my guard.

"Don't hit on the boss," Lee growled as Ross returned with several steaming bowls of stew. He set them down in front of the men, but I was full and couldn't see me fitting anything else in, so I waved him away. "If you want to be part of the crew, then you have to follow certain rules, and one of the rules is don't hit on Zoey."

"Well, I do not want to be a member of anything called a crew," Declan claimed. "And apparently you do not follow your own rules closely because I know my brother was on the crew before he married Zoey. I doubt they stayed pure until their wedding night."

I shot both of them dirty looks, and they were smart enough to shut up. I looked up at Ross, who placed a tall glass of water in front of me. "Thank you, Ross. Do you happen to have a woman named Hildie working for you?"

The satyr nodded. "Why, yes, Your Grace. She's in the kitchens right now."

"Bring her out, then," Declan ordered, pulling his bowl of stew closer to his body as Lee made quick work of his second lunch. Declan huddled over his stew as though he expected one of the wolves to steal it. "Her Grace has a few questions for the wench."

"Wench?" I had never thought of her that way.

"'Tis a common term for a person who works the kitchens." Declan shrugged off my evil eye.

"I'll let her know you wish to speak with her," Ross acknowledged and headed back to the kitchens.

"Do you have to be so rude?" It seemed to be my brother-in-law's stock-in-trade.

"I didn't think I was rude," Declan said, looking surprised. "She is a kitchen wench."

"Have you ever heard of tact?"

He smiled. "Tact is just another way of lying."

"Hello, Prince Declan. I knew you would come looking for me," a sultry voice said from behind me.

"Oh, goddess, no," Declan said, proving he really didn't believe in tact.

I watched a look of complete horror cross the prince's face, and it took everything I had not to laugh because I was sure now I knew at least one of the names of Declan's sexual partners from last night. I looked Hildie over. She was pretty but not exactly Declan's type. She was slightly tough looking and her speech was rough. I could see from my place that her hands were callused from work and she didn't care about her clothes. They were stained and torn in several places.

All in all, I approved mightily of her being Declan's future queen.

"Do ya want to go upstairs then?" she asked. "I can spare ten minutes or so for a rough tumble."

Declan looked at me, his eyes pleading.

"Sorry, Hildie, I'm afraid I'm the one who wanted to see you," I said, taking pity on my brother-in-law.

"Really? What for?"

"A couple of years ago, the queen gave you a jewel for your service to her," I started.

Hildie smiled, showing only two missing teeth. "Ya, her carriage had broke down on the road and she was beset by a couple of bandits. I fought 'em off with a club."

"Very impressive," I said, and noted the wolves were impressed as well. Only Declan was thinking about how the large woman could take a club to his head.

Hildie shrugged her broad shoulders. "Anyone would do it for her. She's a good queen, she is. And she's got some pretty sons."

I gave Hildie a broad smile. "Don't I know it, sister. High-five!" I held my hand out and she gamely did the same but didn't know to slap hands, so we just ended up waving at each other. "Anyway, I need that stone so if you could just get it for me, Dec here will pay you handsomely."

"Zoey," Declan protested. "I did not bring money with me."

"Then I guess she can take it in trade," I teased, loving the way his face went stark white.

"Damn, I knew I should have kept it." Hildie was cursing.

I reached out to grab my water but noticed that someone had placed a nice cup of tea where the water had been. I hadn't noticed when Ross had changed that but the tea smelled delicious. I breathed in that scent and couldn't help myself. It smelled light and delicious, like something that would settle my sometimes crazy stomach. I brought the delicate cup to my lips and savored the semi-sweetness of it.

"You don't have it anymore?" Neil asked the question I would have if I hadn't had a mouthful of fragrant tea.

Hildie sank ungracefully into a chair at the closest table. "No, I don't have it. It's the damn leprechauns' fault. They're a menace, they are. They run those damn card games. I won for a long time but then I just couldn't stop. Once I started losing, I just kept trying to get it back."

I sighed and took another drink. "That's how the con works, Hildie. You think you can win it all back, but you just get in deeper and deeper. So you paid your debt to the leprechauns with the Blood Stone."

"Yes," she acknowledged. "I didn't have anything else and those damn leprechauns can be mean. You don't want to owe them nothing. I always knew it would come back to haunt me. It would have looked good on my crown, you see."

"I think we should go now, Zoey," Declan said, standing suddenly. "If we hurry, we can find the leprechauns."

"Oh, no, Prince Declan. It was many months ago. They're long gone by now." Hildie winked at him. "We have plenty of time."

"Oh, I have to get back to the palace right away," Declan said. "Don't I, Zoey?"

I shook my head but something was off. I felt a small pain start low in my belly. I took a deep breath and figured it was my first pregnancy pain. I smiled to myself because for the first time, I actually felt a little pregnant. It was just a cramp and I stretched to relieve it.

"Zoey, are you all right?" Neil asked, his brows forming a concerned *V*.

Zack sniffed the air. "I smell blood. Where the hell is that coming from?"

"Yeah, I do, too." Lee turned, looking straight at me, his face grim. "Zoey, what's wrong, darlin'?"

Neil was on his feet, moving around the table toward me. All three guards stared in my direction, but I didn't see the problem.

"I'm fine," I assured them. "Who's bleeding?"

"Oh god, Z." Neil stopped as he approached my seat. "You are."

I stood up suddenly and my gown was soaked in blood.

Chapter Eighteen

I doubled over as a horrible cramp hit me. Pain filled my body, racked every inch of my flesh.

"Oh, god, what's happening?" Deep down I already knew what was happening. I was just too horrified to admit it. It had to be something else. It couldn't be that. Not my boy.

The gown that had been delivered for me to wear earlier this morning was a light yellow. It turned a dirty brown color as I continued to bleed. So much fucking blood. Like it would never stop.

I clutched my stomach, low toward my pelvis, and wondered what I'd done to cause this. It couldn't happen. Not my boy. Not my baby. It was mine and Dev and Daniel's and he couldn't be dying. He couldn't.

There was so much blood.

"She is losing the baby," Declan said quietly, looking completely terrified at the prospect.

Another cramp, worse than anything I've ever felt, struck me. My knees buckled, but before I could hit the floor Neil was there, picking me up and taking me with him gently to the ground. He had one arm around my back and the other held my hand as I squeezed through the pain. Agony shuddered through my body, every moment a fresh misery. I started to scream. I couldn't help it.

"It's going to be okay, Z," Neil promised me once I calmed slightly, though his eyes were wide with fear. He looked up at Lee, who was stark white as he stared down at me. It was the first time I could remember Lee not having any idea what to do.

I was aware of the crowd surrounding me. They looked down, their faces worried and horrified at the event unfolding before them. I heard the whispers about a curse on the Fae and that all of this was happening because their priest was a mortal. They were cursed because Devinshea was cursed.

"Shut up, all of you." Declan looked savage as he stood over me, staring down the crowd. He had his sword out, brandishing it toward the crowd. "I hear one more whisper about my brother and I swear I'll consider the lot of you traitors. I'll behead you all myself. Do something useful. Someone get the healer."

"Don't you fucking touch that," Zack yelled, and I saw a smallish man attempting to clear off the table. Zack had pulled a gun and was aiming it directly at the blond faery. "The first one of you who touches anything on this table will find out what a cold iron bullet can do to you."

"Everyone else all right?" I heard Lee asking.

"I feel fine," Declan said but then allowed, "well, physically, that is. Zoey did not eat anything. It was not the stew."

"I'm sure it was that tea," Zack said. "I don't think we ordered it, but I saw Zoey drink it."

I started crying because I was just realizing that this was truly happening. I looked up into Neil's blue eyes. "Where's the doctor?"

A doctor would fix it. I needed a doctor.

"They have gone to fetch him, Zoey." Declan kneeled beside me. His emerald eyes looked so much like Dev's it hurt. I loved Neil, but I wanted Dev's arms around me. I wanted Daniel standing over me.

"He'll save my baby?" I hadn't meant for that to come out as a question, but it did. My insides seized and I felt another rush of blood leaving my body. I barely concealed a scream. The fact that it hadn't hurt so much this time terrified me. If the worst was over, then what was left to do?

Declan looked at Neil, his face filled with pain. Neil just shook his head and pulled me close. "No, sweetie. There's too much blood. I'm so sorry, but I think the baby's gone."

"He can't be." I sobbed and now I wasn't rational. I was a ball of pain and emotion. Any ambiguity I had about wanting a baby was completely gone now that I was losing him. Now that I was losing him, I wanted nothing more than to be his mom. "I need Daniel. Where's Daniel? He'll fix it."

"Daniel can't fix this, Zoey." There were tears escaping from Neil's eyes now. I felt them hit my skin as he tried to pull me close. He tried to give me the comfort I needed.

"He'll give me blood and then the baby will be fine." Danny fixed things. I got hurt and he fixed me. I died and he brought me back. It only made sense in that moment that he could save our baby. Daniel could do anything. I just needed Daniel. Daniel wouldn't let this happen to me. I sobbed, calling out for him. Calling for Dev. Begging anyone who would listen to stop this thing that was happening to me.

God, this couldn't happen to me.

Neil hugged me to him and stood up. "It's too late. We have to worry about you now." Neil looked at Lee. "Tell the healer to meet us at the palace. I'm getting her away from this place."

Lee stepped forward. "We should wait."

"And let them gawk at her?" Neil asked savagely, turning his scorn on the people around us. "I won't let her pain be mocked and gossiped about. I won't let them use her to further their own agendas. For god's sake, Lee, one of them did this to her."

"We don't know that," Declan said, but even to my ears he sounded unsure.

"I do," Neil replied. I let him take over because I couldn't. I let myself rest in the security of his arms. "I know it deep in my bones. They got the baby but they don't get her. You hear me?" He shouted the question all around. "You don't get to take her! Get that healer to the palace. I'm taking her to Sarah."

"Neil," Lee shouted in that alpha voice of his. "Give her to me and I'll take her."

I tensed, ready to be shifted to my head guard's arms because Neil always obeyed Lee when he used that alpha tone. Neil wasn't an alpha. He followed the strongest leader in the group and that was Lee.

"No," Neil said, walking away.

"She's my responsibility," Lee insisted.

Neil whirled around. "And she's my friend. Sometimes she's been the only friend I had in the whole world. I won't give her up when she needs me. You think I'm not strong enough, well, let me tell you, I'll always find the strength for her. If you want her you'll have to fight me so just follow me and try to keep up, Lee."

Lee sighed and his shoulders slumped forward in defeat. I could see every one of his thirty-five years on his face in that moment. "Go on, then, but be careful. I'll stay behind with Zack and try to figure out what happened. I'll be at the palace as soon as I can."

"I will bring the healer," Declan promised.

Neil nodded and then we were out in the sunshine of the afternoon. It was bright and sunny and that seemed to me the biggest insult of all. I looked over Neil's shoulders and saw the trail of blood we were leaving. My heart seized because that was my baby boy's life I was leaving in a thin stream on the ground. That was all of his tomorrows. I would never know him. I wouldn't hold him and think about how much he looked like his father. I wouldn't watch him take his first steps. I wouldn't worry about his first day of school or tease him about his first date. He wouldn't have any of those things, and I clutched Neil and cried for this small thing that would never be.

This is what the *bean si* had wailed about—my child, not my husband.

I had done everything wrong. I had never seen the danger coming. I finally understood the prophecy. So much had been lost and I mourned. I mourned for both my children. My boy and a girl I hadn't realized was mine.

"Hold on, Zoey," Neil said as he started to run.

I held on to his strong shoulders. He wasn't that much bigger than me but he didn't falter. I held on to him because it would kill him to fail.

I had already failed, so it didn't much matter to me.

* * * *

I woke up a long while later in the bed I shared with Dev and Daniel in the palace. Neil slept beside me and when I looked up, I knew it was night. The room was lit only by small candles, and the gloom seemed oppressive to me. I wanted to sink back into oblivion.

It was mostly over by the time the healer made it to the palace. Sarah had done everything she could to make me comfortable, but she confirmed that there was nothing that could be done to save my son and that was the way I thought of him now. Before he'd been just a worry and then something I might be able to get excited about in the distant future.

Now that he was gone, he was my son and I would never know him.

I'd been given several different solutions to drink and if Neil hadn't been around, I would have just downed whatever was given to me. Neil had made sure Sarah watched the healer like a hawk. Neil had insisted on sniffing or tasting everything given to me. I didn't care. I took something that was supposed to help complete the miscarriage, something for the pain and, worst of all, something to clear the curse because that was what had taken my child's burgeoning life.

Through the haze of everything that had happened that afternoon, I understood what Sarah had explained to me. The tea I'd drunk contained a series of herbs that, when combined with the hex bag she found sewn into my clothes, formed a black magic curse. This particular curse purged a vessel of any magic. It could be used to render a magical sword mundane or kill a witch. In my case, my son was magical and it caused my body, which was not magical, to purge itself. It was a nasty spell, and whoever had used it on me had known exactly what they were doing.

Everyone who had been in Ross's tavern was being held for questioning by the royal guard. The man who had tried to clear away the spiked teacup was being held in the dungeons, and I heard someone say he was talking. I wasn't even mildly interested in what he had to say. They had also questioned anyone who handled my clothing.

There was a rustling at the window and I noticed a tall figure there. Sarah was asleep in a chair by the bed and I heard someone prowling in the outer rooms. I was pretty sure it was Lee. When the man turned from the window, my heart seized because Dev had come back.

"Dev." The tears started again. It was all right to cry because Dev would hold me and if he was here, then so was Danny. I could sleep between them and they could promise they didn't hate me for losing our child. I'd been reckless and stupid and we were all going to have to pay.

"I am sorry," Declan said, his voice low as though he didn't want to wake the others. Neil shifted beside me, but he did not wake. There was no arrogance on Declan's face. It was why I'd mistaken him for his brother. "It is just me."

I took a deep breath and wiped my tears away. "Sorry. I thought you were Dev."

He nodded. I noticed he was dressed in traveling clothes, his riding gloves in one hand. "I wish he was here right now. I do not mean to pry, but I have to ask the question."

I knew what he wanted. I was sure it was the question everyone was asking. I sat back, inexpressibly tired as I explained how the *bean si* curse had been about my son. "You want to know about my first child. God, I can't believe I just said that. My child. Her name was Summer. I didn't carry her, obviously. She was the product of a transference box that Daniel and I primed. I never considered her to be mine. She was an odd piece of magic. The tribe the box belonged to took her with them when they passed through the veil."

Declan thought about that for a moment. "I know a little about transference boxes, though they are incredibly rare. There must be intent of will to create a child. Was it you?"

I thought back to that day so long ago. Daniel and I had been together for the first time in years, making love over and over again. I remember my greatest hope had been to never leave his arms again. It had come as a shock to know that a child had been Daniel's deepest wish. "No, it was Daniel."

Declan nodded shortly as though he'd had some truth confirmed. "If Daniel wanted a child and that is the wish he put into the magic, then Zoey, you have to know that child was truly yours. He would not want anyone else's child. That piece of magic was your and Daniel's baby. It is why the *bean si* prophecy is clearly about this child. Devinshea is safe. I suppose it is only natural you would not have considered this child to be yours. I would have been confused as well. We do not normally form humans from the magic. That can be unpredictable."

The faeries had explained all of that to me. They normally molded the magic into something easily controllable, like a tree or a cat. We had seriously screwed up their plans by making a baby. I thought about her. She'd been so sweet but nothing like what I would have expected from a human baby. She hadn't cried or given me a moment's trouble. She'd saved me and healed me. If Daniel had believed for one second that child was truly ours, he would never have allowed her to pass through the veil, magical being or not.

It seemed I had lost two children in one day.

"I am going to find them," Declan announced suddenly. "I promise I will bring your husbands back to you. I have already sent a riding party to the farthest field to look for them. I will search the others. I cannot fly so it might take me a while, but I swear I will not stop until I find them."

I nodded.

"I apologize for insisting you come here. I should have left Devinshea to his new home. My only excuse is a need to see my kingdom safe…and I wanted my family back. I…well, I am sorry," Declan said with more sincerity than I had ever heard from him before. He was quiet for a moment before deciding what to say next. "The healer says this will not affect your ability to carry a child in the future. He says you are already healing because of the vampire blood. He doubts a poison alone would have hurt the child. It was the curse the vampire blood in your system could not handle."

"So it was someone who knew about vampires," I said quietly.

Declan frowned. "That could be anyone. The newspaper ran a story on Dev's new goddess and his partner. The taking of vampire blood was a salacious story point. I know who did this, Zoey. It was the Unseelie. The black magic proves it."

"Because no Seelie ever used black magic," I heard myself saying, surprised at Declan's naiveté.

"I am not going to argue with you," he replied with a sad frown as he took my hand. I didn't care enough to jerk it back. He squeezed it between his hands. "You and Devinshea will have other babies. You will see. I am so jealous, Zoey. Sometimes, I cannot stand it."

"I never meant to take your brother from you." I wished he would go and leave me alone with my thoughts. I wanted to think about Summer, to try to remember everything about the only child Daniel and I would ever have.

Declan got down on his knees so he was staring up at me. "I am jealous of my brother, Zoey. I want what he has. He is so in love. He is happy with you. I was in love once." Declan shook his head. "She was unsuitable. My people would never have accepted her as their queen. She would never have accepted life as a mistress. I left without a backward glance."

"Then you didn't love her." I hated the coldness in my voice but I couldn't seem to muster sympathy for him.

"I did not look back." He got up and straightened his clothes. "But I think of her often. It was the biggest mistake I have ever made and, Zoey, that is saying something."

When he reached the door, he turned back. He was Declan again, his face a mask of royal will. "Know this, sister, I will see my nephew avenged. Padric is questioning the witnesses, but I know the Unseelie are behind it. There is no question. They have pushed me too far, and I will see them wiped from this plane. I will find my brother and we will prepare for war."

Declan turned and left.

"We'll be long gone by then," Neil murmured, moving his head toward mine. "When Daniel comes back, he'll pack us all up and we can leave this place. Let them kill each other."

I said nothing, simply let myself fall deeper into the softness of the bed because no war, no amount of killing or revenge, was ever bringing back my son or my baby girl.

The *bean si* had been wrong. I didn't care enough to stop a war.

Chapter Nineteen

Grief, at least for me, has always been a private thing. In the days following my miscarriage, the biggest nuisance in my life was the string of people wanting to comfort me. I heard platitudes and metaphors all ending in some hopeful piece of crap about how I would get through this.

I suffered through Neil and Sarah telling me how I would still be able to have babies and Dev and I would make more. Miria came through with tears in her eyes and told me how hard it had been for her and that I would be all right. I was still young and had all those years of fertility ahead of me. Even Bibi patted my hand and told me the pain would get better.

Someone was always sitting in the chair by my bed or, in Neil's case, resting beside me. They took turns on Zoey watch and I knew someone had made a schedule.

It was easier when Lee was the one watching me. He didn't feel the need to talk or maybe it was that he didn't have any idea what to say to me. He just sat and watched over me while I slept, and I slept a lot. I kept my eyes closed even when I was awake because Lee might not talk much, but I couldn't stand the look of pity in his chocolate brown eyes.

I resented all of them.

After a day or two, I didn't even want to see Dev and Danny. I just wanted to be alone and sleep. My world narrowed to the confines of my bed, and the rest of life seemed a hazy mess I didn't want to deal with.

When my husbands showed up on the fourth day after the incident, I barely sat up in bed to greet them.

"Sweetheart, are you all right?" Dev knelt at my bedside. He took my hand in his, and he looked like he hadn't slept in days.

"I'm fine," I said dully.

Daniel stood behind him looking down on me with a worried expression.

"I'm so sorry this happened," Dev said, and I could tell he'd been crying. "I would do anything if you didn't have to go through this."

"It was my fault." I just spoke, saying the things I thought I should say, running on a zombie-like autopilot. I didn't see either one of them. For the last several days, most of my time had been occupied with wondering how life would be if I had made a single different choice. What would things be like if I hadn't taken that sip of tea? It seemed an insignificant thing, but that one tiny move had changed so many lives.

"Don't be ridiculous, Z," Danny said harshly. "You can't possibly blame yourself."

But he was wrong. I could definitely blame myself. I'd had a person try to assassinate me in the courtyard of that same tavern. What the hell had I been thinking drinking something I hadn't even ordered? I shouldn't have touched anything not made by Albert's own two hands. I should have been more careful because I was risking so much more than my own life.

"Zoey, it isn't your fault," Dev said, kissing my hands fervently. "It's likely there was a spell on the tea that made it attractive to you. If it hadn't been the tea, then they would have found another way. It is the Unseelie agent's fault, and I promise you I'll do everything I can to see that justice is done."

Daniel's face caught my attention. He grimaced when Dev said that. It was obvious they had been briefed on something I hadn't. I questioned him with a single look.

"Declan and Padric are quite certain that the Unseelie are behind the plot," Daniel explained, but his face told me he didn't believe it. Declan would believe the Unseelie were behind an earthquake if they had one here.

"Why?" I finally mustered the will to sit up. If there was actual evidence against the dark court then I wanted to hear it.

Dev looked like he wanted to ignore the question and he gave it a go. "It's nothing for you to worry about, my wife. We'll take care of everything. Albert says you have not eaten in several days. You have to eat, Zoey. I know it is painful, but you must keep your strength up. We need you."

I looked past Dev. I didn't want to talk about my lack of appetite. "Why are they so certain it's the Unseelie?" I asked Daniel, who seemed more willing to treat me like something other than a china doll who could break at any moment.

Daniel crossed his arms over his chest and looked serious. "The man Zack caught trying to clear away the table claimed to be an agent of the Unseelie."

"He has confessed," Dev stated firmly, and it was easy to see he and Daniel had been arguing about this before. He looked at Danny with a stubborn set to his face. "He knew about the hex bags, too. What more do you want, Daniel?"

"How did he get the hex bag in her clothes, Dev? He worked in the tavern. He'd never been inside the palace, according to the guards. Sarah thinks he was under a spell," Daniel explained. "We won't ever know though because he was executed before we had a chance to question him."

"Not big on fair trials here in Faeryland, huh?" I said bitterly. It was nice that my pain had been an excuse to commit atrocities.

"It was a mob, sweetheart." Dev spoke softly as if the tone of his voice could make it less horrific. "There were too many of them. The guard had to give him up or they would have overrun the palace. The entire tribe is incensed at what was done to you."

I rolled my eyes. "They couldn't care less about me, Dev. They finally have a reason to fight and they're going to take it. They don't give a damn about me and they didn't care about my son."

"You don't understand them," Dev said sadly. "They're

frightened and angry. They thought our baby was a sign that things would get better."

"Did they string up Herne while they were at it?" I had kind of wondered what had happened to the Unseelie ambassador. I hadn't seen or heard a word about him since we had gotten back from our adventure with the ogre.

Dev's face got hard and his eyes were cold as he thought of his former friend. "The Hunter escaped. He fled the palace after you lost the baby. Several of his guards were not so lucky."

There was something small inside me that was happy he'd escaped. Despite his deeply stupid plan to use me as bait, I didn't believe he would hurt my child. I wondered if they had killed the goblins I'd shared lunch with. "What other proof do they have beyond a spell-struck faery's confession?"

Dev sighed. "Zoey, you don't understand this world. Please, just leave this to me and you concentrate on getting well again."

"I want to go home, Devinshea." I stated my desire as plainly as I could. I wanted to leave this place and never come back. If I was ever lucky enough to get pregnant again, I would never let these people near me. I was tired of being a pawn in their war against each other.

"We talked about that." Dev nodded, seemingly happy he could give me something I wanted. "Albert is organizing the packing already. Neil and Sarah are getting everything ready so you'll be comfortable."

I smiled the tiniest bit for the first time in days. The thought of being back in our condo made me slightly energetic. I was a twenty-seven-year-old woman, but I wanted to see my dad. "Really?"

"Of course, sweetheart." Dev ran his hand through my hair, smoothing it back. "I would never want you caught up in this. I love you. You'll be home in just a few days."

There was something about the way he said it that made me suspicious. Daniel was frowning over him as well. He didn't look like a man who was getting to go home. "What do you mean by 'I'll be home'? What about you and Danny?"

Dev looked earnest, like he expected me to understand. "The wolves are going with you, but Daniel and I must remain here. We must avenge our son, sweetheart. They took our child. We can't allow it to stand."

Any joy I had felt was snuffed out like a candle. "I don't have a say in this?"

Dev swallowed nervously, trying to figure out a way to handle me. "Zoey, don't you want revenge?"

I lay back, tired again. "Revenge won't bring back my baby. It will just get you killed. Why would I want that? Why can't we just go home and try to put our lives back together? I just lost a baby, Dev. You're going to leave my care to my bodyguards?"

I loved Neil and Lee, but they weren't married to me. They hadn't made a baby with me. They hadn't lost what Dev and Danny and I had.

"You can't expect me to just walk away."

"But that's what I'm asking you to do," I replied simply because if there was ever a time when what I wanted should come first, I thought this was it. "Take me home, Devinshea."

He stood up. "No, I can't do that. I'll make sure you're safe, but I can't leave until those who did this have paid for their crime. I owe this to our son. Come on, Daniel. We're needed in the throne room. We have planning to do. The call has already gone out for the warriors of the *sidhe* to gather. They'll be here within the week."

Dev had turned his back and was halfway out of the room when I heard Daniel say "No."

"What the hell does that mean?" Dev asked, rounding on him.

Daniel frowned, shaking his head as he looked at Dev. "I can't go with you. I'm going home with Z."

Dev's eyes got wide as though he couldn't believe what he was hearing. "You can't mean that. Daniel, you can turn the tide of this war. You could be the deciding factor in whether we win or not."

"I'm not sure this is a war I want to be involved in, Devinshea," Daniel admitted, trying to make him understand. "Things don't add up. It doesn't make sense. If you were being rational, you would see it. Beyond that, we have to worry about our wife. She's been through so much. She's hurting. If she wants to go home then we should take her home."

"And our son? What about him?" The question dropped like a

land mine between them.

Daniel shook his head wearily. "Dev, she'd been pregnant for a couple of days, man. It just doesn't seem real to me. I'm sorry, but I'm much more concerned with Z than some baby who didn't seem real to me yet. You're safe. Z's alive. I have to be satisfied with that. The two of you, you're real to me."

Dev eyes narrowed and every muscle in his body went tense. "You never thought of him as yours."

"Man, I never had time to think of him as mine," Daniel shot back, frustrated at the whole situation. "I've had less than a week to digest this. I know all of your life this has been a goal of yours because your culture expected it, but I was raised a human. I'm just a guy. It's not real to us until someone puts a screaming baby in our hands and tells us to take care of him."

Dev shook his head like he couldn't believe him. "You never wanted a baby."

"That is not true," Daniel replied, getting angry himself now. "I'm just not willing to risk the people I love for a revenge I'm not even sure is justified. You want me to basically commit genocide on the word of one man, one man who might or might not have been under a spell. Your brother made sure we couldn't figure out the truth. Give me concrete evidence and the names of the conspirators and I'll take them out for you. You can't take out an entire people for the actions of a few."

Dev's whole face fell, his skin going pale like a man who just lost his footing and worried about ever getting it back again. "After everything I have done for you, this is how you treat me? I have devoted my life to your cause. I have fought beside you. I have done everything I possibly could to ensure you get what you want."

"It's not the same thing," Danny insisted, his voice even as he walked up to Dev. He was being careful. He reached out to his partner to put his hand on his shoulders. "Just listen to me…"

Dev brought his hands up, shoving Daniel's away from him. Daniel took a shocked step back. "No, it's not the same because this is something I need. This isn't about you so it doesn't fucking matter, does it, Daniel? I can pour myself into your fight. I can fucking bankroll the entire enterprise. I can provide for all of us, but the minute I need you it's not the same."

Daniel's relaxed stance turned hard, his eyes tightening. "I have money, too."

"You have chump change, Daniel," Dev replied. "You have whatever crumbs Marini sends your way in exchange for slaughtering whoever he wants you to. You'll be the Council's executioner, but you won't spare a minute for my son. Well, if I need to pony up some cash, I can do that. How much will it take to get the *Nex Apparatus* to spare me a moment of his time?"

"Fuck you," Daniel spat. Dev always knew just where to stick the knife in. It was a talent of his.

"Come on, Dan," Dev continued recklessly. "Give me a figure. How much to kill someone? You need a million? I'll get the cash. I am asking you to fight in a war, though. I'm sure that's a premium service. How about twenty million? Would that satisfy you?"

I closed my eyes, squeezing them tight. I didn't want to listen to them tear each other apart.

I heard a thump and didn't have to open my eyes to know Dev was on the floor. I did it anyway because I knew for a fact that he would never stay there. Sure enough, Dev was up and pushing against Daniel.

"How long were you going to use me?" Dev snarled as he punched Daniel in the gut. It didn't matter. Daniel didn't even grunt. "Were you going to wait until after you took over the Council to get rid of me? Would the baby have been an inconvenient reminder of the fact that you needed me once? That you wanted me once? The great Daniel Donovan can't put up with the fact that he's just a man, can he?"

All of the fight went out of Daniel and he just took what Dev was giving him. Dev punched and kicked and didn't fight fair and Daniel just silently took it. It incensed Dev even more that Daniel wouldn't fight back.

Daniel had been pushed to the wall by the time Dev pulled back. "I'm not even worth fighting, am I?"

"I don't want to fight you, Dev," Daniel said quietly, his blue eyes serious as he regarded his friend. "I don't want to hurt you. You're hurting enough already. And you're wrong about why I don't want to fight. It has nothing to do with that. Can we talk about this? Just come to bed with us. We need to rest and figure out what to do together, you and me and Z. We'll work it out. Please. We'll hold our wife and we'll discuss what to do as a family."

For a moment, Dev looked like he would give in. He stared at me and there was a slight softening.

"Devinshea, we need you," a quiet voice asked from the doorway. Declan stood there, his face serious, and I knew he'd watched the fight. "Padric is ready to begin the meeting and Mother wants you there."

Daniel reached out and put his hand on Dev's arm. His voice was pleading. "Please, Dev. Stay with us. We're your family. You belong with us."

Dev turned, and their intimacy was lost. "I am coming," he said to his brother. He turned to me but made no move to get closer than the end of the bed where we'd made love that first morning here. "I am sure Daniel will take care of you in my absence. I will join you at home when I am finished, if I am still wanted, of course."

He seemed to want me to say something but I didn't. If he wanted to leave then I wasn't going to stop him.

He finally walked to his brother and as they left, I saw Declan put his arm around Dev's shoulder. "I will fight at your side," he promised quietly.

The door closed behind them and Daniel and I were alone.

Daniel looked weary as he sat on the bed and took off his boots. He pushed his jeans off his hips and pulled his shirt over his head. He climbed into bed next to me and pulled me into his arms.

"I'm so sorry, baby," he whispered. "If you want to go home, I'll take you but I've got to come back. I have to make sure he doesn't kill himself."

"All right." It didn't matter to me. I just wanted to go back to sleep. I didn't have to think about it when I was asleep. Despite the fact that I hadn't been out of bed in days, I was so tired. A deep weariness had settled into my bones.

"Zoey," Daniel started tentatively. He turned me on my back and looked deeply into my eyes. "Did we make a mistake?"

I didn't pretend to misunderstand him. He would have worked

out the prophecy and known that it had spoken of Summer. "I don't know. I don't know anything. I think she's probably safer where she is than she would have been with us. We weren't even together then, Danny."

"Maybe we would have been if we'd kept her," he said, voicing all those useless questions.

"We weren't ready for a baby, Danny." If we'd gotten together for Summer, I wouldn't have gone back to Dev. I would have put him out of my mind. It was likely Daniel would never have daywalked and we would have been forced to remain our whole lives under Marini's thumb with no way out. Our daughter would have been just another tool in Marini's bag.

"If she's ours...god, Z, I want her back." His arms tightened around me. "She's the only child I can ever have. I'll love any kids you and Dev have, I will, but...I need to know that she's okay. She's out there, and I don't know if she's loved, if she's being taken care of. Anything could happen to her. I have to find her. When all this crap is done, I have to find her."

I nodded because it seemed the most expedient way to get him to stop talking. "Could you close the curtains?"

Daniel did as I asked, drawing the heavy curtains closed and shutting out the world. I lay back as he pulled me against him once more, not fighting him but not exactly returning the embrace. I just let him do what he wanted and was grateful when sleep took me once again.

Chapter Twenty

Daniel stayed in bed with me for a couple of days as the two factions in the palace prepared for their separate journeys. Our group organized for the long trip home and the Seelies prepped for war. Every day I heard more and more warriors had arrived. In another week, they would march toward the door that led to the land separating the blessed court from the dark court. It was on that long field that the war would play out. Word had come from King Angus that when the Seelies came for war, he would meet them with swords drawn.

I could tell from his tone and the look on his face that Daniel was worried about me, but I couldn't seem to muster up the energy to do anything about it. I was trapped in a dark, selfish place and I didn't want to leave it. When Daniel left my side, it was to consult with Albert or Lee. He was never gone for long but Dev always heard of the absence and managed to make his way to our bed. He didn't talk about the fight with Daniel. He didn't mention the plans for war. He asked me to eat and get out of bed. When I did neither, he kissed my forehead and left as quickly as he'd come.

I thought it was Dev when Daniel left the afternoon before we were to return home. Everything had been packed and we were set to leave that night. I wasn't looking forward to walking all that way but

I also didn't want to ride a horse for so long. I couldn't ask Danny to fly because he looked as tired as I felt. I'd offered to feed him but he was worried I wasn't up to it yet and I hadn't wanted to fight. I thought he was hoping getting me home would fix me. I wasn't so sure about that.

I was in bed when I heard someone moving in the room. It had to be Dev and I closed my eyes, hoping to avoid a long, drawn-out good-bye. If he didn't want to come with us, then I wasn't going to beg him. He was leaving me at the moment I needed him most.

The curtains came open with a swift pull and I opened my eyes, surprised by the move. When he came to see me, Dev crept into bed, unwilling to frighten me or disturb me with too much noise. The person opening the curtains had no such qualms. I was surprised to see Sarah's husband frowning down on me. I sighed because Felix was the one person who hadn't given me a lecture on how I would see the freaking good in life again one day. I should have expected it, though. The man used to be an actual guardian angel. Blowing sunshine up people's asses was part of their job description.

"Hello, Felix," I said with a sad sigh. I contemplated the easiest way to get rid of him.

"Not exactly," a voice that sounded like Felix's, only gruffer, said.

I sat up because that was not Felix looking down at me with judgmental eyes. "Who are you? What did you do with Felix?"

Whatever was in Felix crossed his arms over his chest and shook his head down at me. "I can't manifest on this plane. It's embarrassing, but I don't know how to do it. Felix graciously offered to host me. I shouldn't be here at all, but you're leaving me with no choice. I would never have signed up for this gig if I knew it included being your life coach."

"Oliver?" I asked with the first emotion I'd been able to muster in days. Oliver Day was Felix's "brother." He was one of a group of three angels who balanced each other and watched over their charges. I'd been told Oliver, who was kind of an asshole, was my guardian angel.

"In the flesh," he agreed. "Well, in Felix's flesh anyway. What the hell do you think you're doing, Zoey?"

"Should angels curse?" I'd never once heard Felix do it. I hadn't heard their sister, Felicity, curse either. Only Oliver seemed to have gotten a potty mouth along with his halo.

"I get special dispensation because no one could deal with your crap and not drop the occasional f-bomb. I'll ask again. What are you doing, Zoey?"

"What is that supposed to mean? I'm resting, Oliver. I've had a hard couple of days," I shot back bitterly. I didn't need a guilt trip. Now that I thought about it, I didn't want to talk to Oliver Day. He was supposed to watch over me. He hadn't done a good job.

"Yes, Zoey, blame me for everything," he said, rolling his eyes. He wasn't one of those cuddly guardian angels who soothed you and made you feel good. "I don't have to be able to read your mind to know what you're thinking. You're blaming me and everyone else for how miserable you are." He sat down on the side of the bed. "Most of all, you're blaming yourself. Give it up, sister. It wasn't your fault and it sure as hell isn't mine. Shit happens. We deal with it."

"He was my son," I said, biting off a cry. I pushed at him because I didn't want him anywhere close to me.

"And he will be again." Oliver held my hands in his and forced me to look at him. For the first time since meeting him, he had something akin to compassion in his eyes. "Zoey, that small spirit was a gift. He was a unique creation—a brand new soul. The boss doesn't give those out to just anyone. It didn't work out this time, but that doesn't mean he's gone forever. That's not the way the universe works."

"I don't understand." And I wanted to. I needed to understand this because nothing made sense.

A small smile crossed his lips. "Would it work if I told you you're not supposed to?"

I frowned.

"Fine." He sighed as though he hadn't really thought his ploy would work. He sought the words to explain it to me. "Normally when something like this goes wrong, the soul finds another vessel, one that's ready. I don't know why these things happen. That's beyond my pay grade. I only know that there is a reason. As I said, usually another vessel would be selected but Rhys prefers to wait."

"Rhys?" I asked, but I felt a smile spreading across my face. Rhys was a perfect name.

"I probably wasn't supposed to tell you that," Oliver allowed with a shrug. "That's his name. He was allowed a choice and prefers it this way. He would rather wait for his brother."

My eyes went wide. "His brother?"

Oliver smiled slyly. "Yes, Zoey, his brother. Did you think you could sleep with a fertility god and not have a couple of litters? Your firstborn children will be twin boys. But that ain't happening if you stay in this bed feeling sorry for yourself. I know it's not fair. You should probably be allowed to wallow in your grief like a normal person, but you're not normal. You don't have time. Things are moving faster than I thought they would. If you want those sons to have a chance a couple of years down the road, you need to get out of that bed."

"How will that help anything, Oliver?" I was already tossing the covers aside. "Dev is set on his course. I could try to talk to him but he wouldn't listen to me before and he wouldn't listen to Daniel."

Oliver rolled Felix's eyes. "Do you ever pay attention? I sent you three women to tell you exactly what to do. Do you have any idea how hard it is to get on the washer women's schedule? They're busy and they charge out the ass for a rush job."

I stopped, the truth settling in on me. "I have to find the Blood Stone."

"She shoots, she scores," Oliver said sarcastically. "Find the Blood Stone. It will lead you where you need to go."

"Somehow the Blood Stone can stop the war?"

Oliver shook his head. "No, Zoey, you stop the war. The Blood Stone merely gets you into the place you need to be. Just find the stone. Have a little faith."

I arched an eyebrow. "I thought that was Felix's territory."

When Felix had been an angel, he had represented faith. He had balanced Felicity's love and Oliver's justice.

"I have faith," Oliver said with a shrug. "You met me at a bad time. Felix was gone. We have a new brother now. His name is Jude, and we have found our balance. I suppose I was rude the last time we met."

"Rude? You nearly killed Danny." He had unleashed some ultraviolet light that nearly burned my vampire up. It had taken everything I had to keep Daniel alive. It had not endeared the angel to me.

He had the grace to look embarrassed. "About that…you know one of my powers is to be able to filter light around myself. It's how we do the whole 'glow like the sun, holy manifestation' thing. It works really well when I need to get someone's attention. It's kind of a parlor trick. It wasn't exactly God's light or anything."

"You know what Daniel thought, you bastard." Daniel had thought he was standing in the presence of the holy and that burning meant he didn't have a soul anymore.

"I didn't have parents so their marital state is of no consequence," Oliver pointed out. I stared at him. "Sorry. I was in a pissy mood. Tell Donovan his soul's intact. It would be helpful if he would stop all those assassinations, though. It's not getting any cleaner."

"He's planning his retirement as we speak." After Danny handled a few more key assassinations, he was planning on hanging it up. I had another question though. "Daniel wants to find Summer."

Oliver nodded. "And he will when the time is right. Like I said before, all things happen for a reason."

"Is she safe?" I couldn't stand the thought that she needed me.

A small smile lit Oliver's face. "She is giving the Tuatha Dé Danann hell and the tribe curses your name daily." He shook his head. "She is a light for them now as she will be for the Earth plane one day."

Tears pierced my eyes, beautiful, healing tears. "I'll see her again?"

"I believe so, but the *bean si* were right. You are an undone thread to the universe, one of God's true miracles. I can't see your future the way I should. I can only tell you that she is safe and loved and she knows who her mother and father are. She remembers you and hopes to reunite when the time is right." His sympathy disappeared and he was right back to frowning. "But guess what?"

"The time can't be right until I get out of this bed." He'd made that clear. My time as an invalid was at an end.

"Excellent," Oliver said and he stood up. "There's one more thing I was asked to speak with you about, though it is all connected, of course. Felicity is worried about her charge."

"Devinshea?"

Oliver nodded. "If this war is allowed to rage, she believes he will die. This war could be bad. If the faery dies…"

"No babies for me." It wasn't hard to figure that out.

"He's your mate, Zoey," Oliver said. "Your life is hard, but allowances have been made for you. Daniel can't provide you with children, so you were granted a second soul mate. Be grateful. Most people have a hard time finding one."

I smiled a real, true smile and I leaned up impulsively. I kissed Oliver Day right on Felix's cheek. "Thank you, Ollie."

"Don't call me Ollie," he groused. He shook his head and grinned anyway. "I picked you, you know. Worst mistake I ever made."

"You get to pick, huh?"

"Yep. The odds on you were like 200 to 1. The others thought I was crazy. Do you want to know what the odds are now?"

"Probably not." I never wanted to hear the odds against me. They were usually phenomenal. "They let you gamble in Heaven?"

"Yeah, it's that or harp playing, and I could never get my fingers to do that," he explained. "The odds are now 20 to 1. I am damn good, Zoey. I picked you because I knew you would beat those odds. I can be an ass sometimes, but I'm an ass who has faith in you. Now, get off your butt and do what you were born to do."

"And what is that, Oliver Day?"

"Change everything." He smiled and gave me a wink.

The door to the bedroom opened. "Are you ready, Z? Albert has everything we need. We should be leaving in an hour or so. Oh, hello, Felix. Sarah is looking for you," Daniel said as he walked into the room. He looked beyond tired. His skin was looking ashen.

"That was weird." Felix shook his head and seemed to be Felix again. "I thought I would be able to listen in, but I found myself in a waiting room. There was coffee and cheesecake and a radio tuned to someone playing Britney Spears's greatest hits on a harp."

"What is he talking about?" Daniel asked.

I grinned at him, and Daniel's eyes widened in surprise. "I'll tell you all about it, but there's something I need from you first."

"What's that?" He was ready to do anything I asked.

"I need you to eat, Danny." I looked at Felix. "He hasn't fed in days, has he?"

Felix shook his head. "We've all offered, even Lee offered."

Daniel's eyes avoided mine. "I wasn't hungry."

I moved to him and forced him to look at me. I knew why he hadn't fed. He was in a fight with Dev and he thought I was too fragile. Feeding was an intimate thing for Daniel. He would rather go hungry than share that with anyone else. My vampire was faithful even when it cost him. "You were heartsick, baby. I know the feeling, but we're going to be okay. Felix is going to go tell Albert that I need a cheeseburger and fries and you're going to have a nice snack. I need you strong because we have work to do, my love. And I have something that will make you feel like fighting again, babe." Tears fell again, but they were happy because I suddenly had faith and hope where before there had been none. I had faith that I would meet my sons, faith that my daughter was out there living a good life. "Felix, you should probably go now if you don't want to see me naked because I'm dropping this gown in five seconds."

The door slammed in three. I tried not to take it personally. Daniel pulled the gown off for me.

"What happened to you, Z?" he asked, dragging me into his arms.

"I just needed a little divine intervention, baby." I let my head fall back so the line of my neck was arched and long. Daniel groaned as he accepted everything I had to give.

* * * *

Two hours later, I'd told Daniel everything and we stood outside the "war room" with a feeling of great sadness. The palace was one big ball of stress. There were warriors everywhere, and they were all itching for a fight. I had to wonder—if this was what everyone wanted, why did absolutely no one seem happy? There was a specter of doom hanging over everything as I stood waiting to see my husband. The throne room was doubling as the war room. From what I understood, Devinshea had been sleeping in there, when he slept at all.

"Come with me." I held my hand out to Daniel.

He stood back with our little raiding party. We'd decided to travel light. We weren't exactly sure where this quest would take us, so we thought a smaller group would be best. It was me and Danny and Neil and Lee. Albert, Sarah, and Felix were staying behind and had instructions to keep their heads down. Zack was sticking to Dev like superglue. He had strict orders to not let his boss die.

"He won't want to see me," Danny insisted. He understood that I needed to see Dev before we left, but he didn't want to start another fight. There was a horrible distance between them that I hated.

"You don't know what he wants. He's in a bad place, Danny. He should know we're here even if he doesn't want to see us." Dev and I had made it clear to Danny that we wouldn't leave him even when he was being an ass. It was Dev's turn to be a stubborn idiot, but I hoped Daniel was willing to stand beside me.

Daniel nodded and followed me inside.

Declan and Dev were pouring over maps with Padric. All three men were in what looked like the Fae version of military uniforms.

Miria watched them, her mouth turned down. Her eyes seemed old for the first time since I met her. She glanced up first and her mouth became a startled *O*. "Zoey, Daniel. I am surprised to see you. I was told you were leaving to return to the Earth plane."

Dev looked up and the weariness on his face made me want to cry. "You're up, Zoey," he said and for a moment he sounded happy. Then a cloud passed over his eyes. "You are leaving, then. I wish you a safe journey." He nodded at Daniel and went back to his maps.

I wanted to run to him but I didn't think a big scene would help anything, so I stood my ground. "I'm leaving, Devinshea, but I'm not going home."

All eyes were on me now.

"I'm going after the Blood Stone." I was dressed for hunting. No more gossamer gowns for me. "I need a couple of things, though. I don't know how long it will take or where we're going to have to go.

I could use a set of camping gear. The wolves don't mind not having shelter, but I'd rather at least have a tent."

I'd rather have a suite at the Hilton, but I doubted I would find one of those out here. I had to track down leprechauns, and they would likely be working their cons in the countryside.

Declan crossed his arms. "I think it would be best for everyone if you went home, Your Grace. This is not a place for humans."

Dev shook his head dismissively. "There is no purpose in looking for it now, Zoey. You cannot stop this war. When it is done, I will help you search for the Blood Stone. Until then, it is very dangerous."

"The people have spoken," Miria said tightly. "They are angry. If I do not…"

"What Mother is saying," Declan took up his mother's explanation, "is that even if we wanted to stop the war, we could not. The people would view her as weak and we would lose the army as well. There would almost certainly be a coup."

"You see, my wife, the path is set," Dev said, his voice low and full of his willpower.

"If you're so sure I can't stop this then there's no harm in giving me a couple of tents and some camping gear. The war won't take place here. I'll avoid the plane between the *sitheins*. I doubt my target is there anyway," I pointed out sensibly.

Dev turned to me and I noticed for the first time that he was wearing a sword on his belt. I knew there would be a few knives hidden somewhere on his person as well. I hoped he was smart enough to have a gun or two. Declan would consider them to be dishonorable weapons, but they were effective and that was all I cared about. "I would prefer it if you would see her safely home, Daniel."

"She would just come back, man," Daniel replied. "She's set on saving your ass, and she thinks this is the way to do it."

"I could have the royal guard escort you to the door," Dev threatened.

Daniel frowned and now his will was fully on display. "You could do that if you wanted to lose a couple of royal guards. I'm with her on this one, Dev. If you throw us out, I'll find a way back in."

Dev's eyes tightened. "I would think you would want to see our wife safe, Daniel."

"Our wife is not the only one in danger," Daniel replied quietly.

"I will have a servant ready the gear," Declan said to his brother, who nodded his assent. "It will be waiting for you at the palace gates. I will have them issue you some soldier's rations as well. Do you need horses?"

Daniel shook his head. "Lee and Neil will run and I'll fly Z wherever we need to go."

Declan went off to order people around and Miria drew herself up, looking regal in her small crown. "I wish the two of you luck. Please be safe, all of you," she said sincerely before taking Padric by the hand. "Come, dear. Let us allow them a private good-bye."

The three of us were alone finally and the silence threatened to crush me. Daniel and I stood looking at Dev across the room, the space between us a chasm I hoped we could cross.

"I wish you luck as well." Dev looked uncertain what to do so he turned his face back down to study his briefs.

"I love you." It would be useless to say anything else.

I almost made it to the door when I was whirled around and Dev hauled me up against his body. His arms were a sweet cage holding me to his chest, my feet dangling inches off the floor. He kissed me and I ran my fingers through his hair, all the passion and love we had ever felt in that one meeting of lips.

He pulled back and rested his forehead against mine. "I love you, wife. Forever and always."

I didn't ask him to come with us. He would have said no. He was doing what he felt he had to and I was doing the same. I kissed him sweetly and gave him back his words. "Forever and always, my love."

He set me down and he and Daniel exchanged a look. Something dark sat between them, a wariness I didn't quite understand.

"Watch your back," Daniel said.

Dev nodded and we walked out. I turned back as the door closed between us. His eyes were on me to the end.

I brushed a tear away, wanting so much to destroy that door that separated us from Dev.

"It's time to go." Daniel took my hand. Neil and Lee were already moving toward the front of the palace. We would exit through the front gates and from there we would be completely on our own.

Strangers in a strange land.

I turned away. Daniel was right. It was time to change this world. I had to. My world depended on it.

Chapter Twenty-One

"Is this like the Lucky Charms guys or the ones who ate Jennifer Aniston?" Neil asked as we peeked over a hill and looked down on the small encampment. There were several tents and two large campfires. Someone was having a party down there, and it sounded a little raucous.

"I think she survived that film." This was definitely the place. There was that sucker in his green suit with his green and gold hat perched on his head. So stereotypical. Leprechauns had a uniform. They also had what looked like a roaming casino going.

"Huh," Neil said thoughtfully. "I must have fallen asleep during that movie. It would have been better my way."

"Don't try to eat the leprechaun." Daniel crawled up to us on his belly, keeping his head down. Even though it was well after dark, we didn't want anyone to see us watching. "At least not until we figure out where he stashed his treasure. Then, man, feel free 'cause I was awake for that whole movie and they get pissed off when you take their gold."

It had taken us two days, but we tracked them down. Normally leprechauns are solitary Fae creatures, but there were two down in the field working their short con. Even from this distance, I could see they had two tables of card games going. There were twelve faeries watching or playing along, and they all looked to be warriors, probably on their way to the palace. The war was already proving to be a boon to the plane's con artists.

"He can keep his gold," I muttered. "I just want the Blood Stone."

Daniel had relaxed, so much more comfortable now that it was dark. We had thought to try to sleep through most of the day, shielding Daniel from the sun and reserving his strength. Unfortunately, the only way to track the leprechauns was by following their rainbow, and it was only visible during the day. Without Dev's magic to feed from on a daily basis, his strength in the daytime was failing. He could still daywalk and the sun didn't burn him to a crisp, but it was painful. We got along by protecting Danny's skin with a black hoodie and sunglasses, but it was hot. He was so much happier now that he was able to get rid of the hoodie and gloves and pare down to his T-shirt and jeans. He was at full strength now that darkness had fallen.

"Well, I doubt the stone is down there, baby," Daniel said, looking things over. "Harry dealt with them on the Earth plane. You remember he used one for a job back in the nineties. They don't keep their treasure on them. They stash it away."

My dad, Harry Wharton, had used a leprechaun once. He'd needed a person of small stature to get through a series of caves and unlock a door for the rest of the crew. Danny and I had been kids so we hadn't been in on the heist. I just remembered how foulmouthed the little guy was and how much he'd liked beer. I also remembered that the leprechaun had buried his piece of the action. I don't know why he had been against a bank, but he preferred the hard ground to Wells Fargo.

"So what's the plan?" Neil asked, his gaze focused solely on me. If I'd hoped that close quarters would bring my husband and my best friend to some sort of understanding, I'd been wrong. They still avoided each other like the plague.

I watched as Lee prowled the edges of the forest down below. He clung to shadows and if I hadn't known what to look for, hadn't watched him work, I would never have seen him. He was being his normal, careful self. Lee never liked to walk into a situation until he'd taken a cautious inventory of every risk involved.

"Well," I said, getting around to Neil's question as Daniel settled himself down on the ground, his hand planted firmly on my ass. "I thought we would try to talk to them first. We should see if we can buy it from them."

Neil rolled his eyes. "Z, they stole it in the first place."

Danny leaned his head against my shoulder and squeezed a cheek. He didn't care that we weren't alone. Since we'd broken through his reserve back in Colorado, he never held back with the PDA. "No, they didn't. They conned her out of it. Z's right. We gotta respect a good con. If we don't, what the hell kind of criminals are we?"

"The horny kind?" I asked because he was kissing on my shoulder, working his way toward my neck.

The last two days had been illuminating. In the course of our normal, daily lives, Daniel was very busy. Back home he was responsible for training new vampires and had all the work the Council gave him. He and Dev worked on their coup plans all the time. Sex was certainly something we slipped into the schedule, but not like this. I discovered that when Danny had nothing to do, he constantly tried to do me.

"I can't help it." A wicked grin brought out Daniel's ridiculously cute dimples. No one who had killed as much as Daniel had should have adorable dimples. They always made me sigh. "I've started to think of this trip as a long overdue honeymoon, baby."

"Oh, yes, Danny, this is all terribly romantic," I whispered sarcastically. "When I think of a honeymoon, I think of Hawaii and a big comfy suite. I don't think of tents and sleeping bags and hiking through Faery forests all day. I haven't had a decent night's sleep since we left the palace."

Neil eyed me. "I don't think you've slept at all, princess. I'm pretty sure of it because you've kept me awake for two nights. I don't want to go on your honeymoon."

"How did I do that?" I'd stayed in the tent with Danny the whole night. Once we'd eaten our craptastic rations, I hadn't bothered Neil at all.

Daniel grinned lecherously. "He's talking about the noise you make, baby. You're kind of a screamer."

I blushed and reached back to firmly move Daniel's hand off my ass. "We're working. No hitting on the boss. It's a rule."

"We'll see who the boss is," Daniel whispered in my ear, not giving up his position. "I still wear the pants here, Z, but don't worry. I'll let you in them anytime you want."

I laughed and pushed at my husband because he was such a dork and I still loved him. He rolled me over until I was on top, looking down at him.

"God, not again," Lee groaned as he joined us. "Let her rest, Donovan. You would think her being one husband down, she could get some rest."

"Spoilsports," Daniel groused but let me scramble off of him.

I sat back against a tree, looking up at my bodyguard. "What's the report?"

Lee's brown eyes were serious as he looked at me. "There are only the two leprechauns. As far as I can tell, they aren't armed."

"They don't need to be." Daniel sat up and straightened his shirt. "Unless we lay physical hands on them or keep our eyes on them, they can teleport. I'm serious about keeping eyes on them. You can't even blink or they'll be gone in an instant."

Lee nodded. "Okay. We have to deal with that. They're in the early portions of the con. They've lost money at this point, so they aren't going to want to drop everything yet."

"Why don't Danny and I head down and watch for a while?" I said. "You and Neil can work your way around to flank them. When the time is right, we blow their con and if they try to run, you catch their tiny asses."

"And if they won't talk?" Lee asked.

I shared a smile with Neil. "I have ways of making them talk. Trust me. This is going to be fun."

I had plans for the evening. Daniel helped me up, his hand going around my waist.

"Have I told you how fucking hot you are?" Daniel obviously had plans, too.

I couldn't help but laugh. We'd lost so much in the last few days, but Danny had been with me. He'd held me and loved me and given me strength. Sometimes I worried that Danny and I had too much of a past, but these last few days had proven me wrong. He'd given me a comfort no one else could have, an ease. As we began to walk down toward the leprechauns, I leaned into him, finding strength there.

He leaned over, kissing my hair. "This is kind of fun, Z. It reminds me of the old days except we have a ton of sex. I prefer having the sex. It makes everything better. Do you want to stop somewhere and have sex now?"

Yeah, he pretty much never stopped. "You could be nicer to Neil." We hadn't talked about it yet.

He sighed. "It's hard, Z. It's hard to forgive because he put you and Dev in danger."

We kept walking, our feet crunching against the forest floor. I did understand that he was possessive and anything that went contrary to his nature came under fire. "Dev wasn't your partner then. It shouldn't have mattered."

His face turned away. "I'd shared you with him by then. I'd had his blood by then. It mattered, Zoey. Neil…damn it, I want to forgive him. I do. Just give me time."

The problem was vampires viewed time differently than the rest of us. I wasn't ready to wait a couple of decades to have my family whole again. Still, I had more to worry about than just Neil. "Can you forgive Dev?"

He stopped as we reached the flat valley where the leprechauns were working. Roughly a hundred yards away sat the small encampment we'd been studying. "It isn't the same."

Something had been going on between them, a distance I didn't understand. I could only think of one thing that could really come between them. "He told you to send Summer back. He actually told me to get rid of her."

Daniel stopped, turning my way. "He didn't understand, Z. Dev wouldn't do that."

I breathed a sigh of relief. I remembered that day so long ago. We'd all been confused and scared with a demon on our trail. I didn't blame Dev, but I worried about Daniel. "Then what happened between the two of you?"

Daniel's stubborn frown did nothing to dissuade me. "He's just mad I wouldn't commit genocide on his say-so. He wants to be able to point and shoot. I'm not his weapon, Z. I'm not anyone's weapon."

But there was obviously so much more and I knew suddenly that he wouldn't tell me. Something had happened when they were out in the field, but he wasn't about to talk to me about it. He strode forward, making any further conversation impossible.

Danny watched carefully as the con artists worked their game.

"Who can find the queen?" the leprechaun asked in a rapid-fire voice. "Ten gets you twenty. Twenty gets you forty. All you gotta do is keep your eye on the queen."

"Seriously, who falls for three-card Monte these days?" I stared at the crowd surrounding them. The leprechaun's hands shifted quickly, moving the cards back and forth.

"They learned it on the Earth plane, I'm sure." Daniel's eyes followed every movement. "These *sidhe* are from the country. They're only making their way to the palace for the war. They're just ripe for the plucking. What a bunch of pigeons."

"We have a winner," the leprechaun said with a frustrated sigh. He made a big deal of paying out the "winner."

"We have a shill," I commented and Danny smiled.

I watched as he caught Lee's attention across the field and gestured toward the faery we were pretty sure was working with the leprechauns. They were working a classic short con. Get a bunch of people together with nothing better to do and offer them a seemingly simple game. The shill would look like everyone else. He would pretend to not know the cons and step up to play the game. He would make comments on how easy it was. *Hey*, he would say, *look at that. The idiots marked the queen without knowing it. We can take them for everything.* For a while, the shill's words would prove true, but in the end, the fast hands of the con artists would win every time.

We stood on the fringes of the small crowd, trying to be as inconspicuous as possible. The pigeons were starting to lose, but they hadn't realized the scam yet. Unfortunately, they did realize something was wrong and, as usual, it was me.

One of the *sidhe* warriors stared at me and not in a sexy, good way. He looked at my hair, and distaste was plain on his face. He turned to his friend and whispered something that made Daniel tense beside me and then the friend studied me, too.

"Your clothes are strange, warrior," the faery said to Daniel. He didn't speak to me but regarded me with disgust. I knew I wasn't the hottest chick on the plane, but I was pretty sure I hadn't grown horns.

Daniel looked at the faeries. They'd been joined by two others. The faintest smile crossed his lips and I sighed. I was going to have to move out of the way and soon because Danny had been itching for a fight since he'd allowed Devinshea to beat on him. The sex had helped, but he was a creature of violence and nothing but a little bloodshed was going to satisfy him. It looked like the faeries were going to indulge him.

"One might think you aren't a Seelie, friend," another said, and the word "friend" was bitten off.

"I know damn well your strumpet there ain't Seelie," the third said. "She's short and her hair is red. She's a halfling of some type. Probably goblin from the way she shows off her limbs."

What did these people have against limbs? They thought nothing of boobs hanging out, but the minute they saw an ankle, a girl got labeled a tramp.

"I'm human, idiot." I would try honesty at first.

They looked at each other as though trying to see if anyone was buying what I was selling.

"We don't let humans in our *sithein*," the tallest one said.

The card game was put on pause as all of the faeries looked our way. They moved away from the leprechauns, who eyed us, obviously upset that their con was turning into an evening of mob violence.

"Z, come here, baby." Daniel spoke in quiet tones. Danny was always at his most dangerous when he was ice cold. I did exactly what he said. I moved cautiously to his side, never taking my eyes off the men threatening us.

"I think what we have here is an Unseelie spy." A big faery with dark hair frowned our way, his hand cradling the hilt of his sword.

I felt a presence at my knees. I looked down and Neil sat back on his haunches beside me, his arctic white fur brushing my legs. He barked up at me, and I knew what he was telling me without words. He had my back.

"The man is odd, too," said another. "He ain't pure. He has the look of an Unseelie."

"There's no reason to fight, men." One of the leprechauns tried in vain to interest his pigeons in rejoining the game. The evening was young. He was probably still in the hole. Danny and I were causing major problems for him and his partners. I noticed the shill hadn't joined in with the mob. He stood at the back, shaking his head.

"There's always a reason to fight the monsters," someone said.

"The war hasn't started yet, boys." The second leprechaun climbed up on his table, raising his tankard high. "They'll be time enough later for killing. Tonight is for drinking and gambling."

A particularly mean-looking faery stepped to the front of the crowd. "How about we celebrate after we string up the Unseelie interlopers?"

That got the small crowd cheering, and I wondered why we hadn't thought to bring along a note or something from my mother-in-law explaining who the hell we were. I fingered the delicate gold chain that marked me as Dev's wife, but I doubted any of these country faeries would have seen it before, much less believe that I could be their High Priest's wife. Pulling it out and using it would be a good way to lose it. The Goddess Chain was my only real connection to Dev at this point, so I wasn't willing to risk it.

"He ain't even wearing a sword," one of them pointed out. "If he ain't Unseelie, then he's a coward 'cause he's not going to the palace to join the queen and the good prince."

"If he isn't Unseelie, then what's he doing with that half-breed?" someone else muttered.

"For the last time, I'm human," I insisted, getting a little pissy.

"For the last time, Unseelie bitch, we don't let humans in." The largest one snarled, moving close.

Daniel's hand shot out and he lifted the larger man up by his shirt. He smiled and his fangs shot out of his mouth. "You don't let vampires in, either, yet here I am."

Daniel tossed the faery back into the crowd, knocking several down like bowling pins.

The crowd drew swords and rushed the man they were certain now shouldn't be among them. Neil barked at my feet and used his head to nudge me back. I followed directions as I always tried to in a fight. I can hold my own, but Daniel…there's no one who fights like Daniel.

"Get him!" someone yelled. "He doesn't even have a weapon."

Daniel actually had two guns and three knives hidden on his body, but he didn't make a move for them. He didn't need weapons. He moved into the crowd that now surrounded him. I could have told them that was a mistake. In cases like this, he preferred to have his prey in a nice neat circle.

The first warrior rushed Danny with his sword held high. Daniel punched him in the face and the faery flew back, politely losing his grip on the shiny sword. It was in my vampire's hands before it could fall to the ground.

Neil herded me back toward the tree line even as Daniel began to move. I watched intently because Daniel was a vision of violent power and grace when he worked. The crowd fell like dominoes as he twisted and whirled that sword in an arc that left not one of the men untouched. Blood began to splatter in a neat circle, saturating the ground around him. Half the men had already fallen.

Daniel stopped, his head down, sword held low and he looked over at me and winked. So fucking sexy.

I heard moaning and groaning, but not a one of them was dumb enough to get up. My vampire looked at the remaining men and smiled. "Who's next? You should be glad I'm not Unseelie because if I was, your army would be in serious trouble."

This incensed three of the remaining *sidhe*. They looked at each other and nodded, trying to flank Danny. They let out rebel screams as they rushed him. He gutted the first one, allowing the faery to keep his sword deep in his belly as he fell away. Daniel lifted the next one and tossed him to Neil.

"That one's yours," he yelled as he faced the third. I felt a deep well of love for him. Handing Neil a kill was a signal that he was softening.

Neil barked happily and then started toward the faery with a low growl.

"Nice puppy." The warrior shook his head and tried to back away from the lovely display of teeth I was sure Neil was giving him.

While Neil enjoyed terrifying one faery, the last of the three who had rushed Danny laid his sword down. There were three left who had pulled themselves out of the fray after the first assault. They chose to put their weapons down as well.

"A vampire isn't Unseelie," one of them pointed out.

"Nope," another said. "They're from the Earth plane."

"So he probably isn't a spy," they concluded.

"Then there's no need to fight him," a faery with long yellow hair said, his voice shaking even as he stood his ground. "If he ain't the enemy then we should probably buy him a drink and try to convince him to fight on the Seelie side of this war."

Daniel growled and his eyes pierced the remaining men. "And why would I fight beside men who insult my wife?"

The faeries all took up the new cause of getting the vampire to calm down. "I never believed she was Unseelie," one said.

"She's obviously a woman of good character," said another.

I rolled my eyes, but now the danger had passed and I didn't see a need for revenge. I'd been called worse before. The faery Neil was playing with was crying and I think he'd peed just a little. "Neil, stop farting around. This isn't why we're here."

Neil looked back at me and changed, becoming human in an instant. "You're no fun, Z."

I turned around and noted that our leprechauns had fled.

"Damn it," Daniel cursed.

"I'll go after them." Neil started for the forest line, but stopped.

Lee walked forward and he had both of the leprechauns, one in each hand. He held them up even as they tried to kick out at him.

"Lose something?" Lee asked with a superior smile. Something caught his eye. "Hey, is that beer?"

Neil headed toward the woods, running quickly. We'd gone over the plan and Neil ran off to do his part.

"Don't forget the package," I yelled as he disappeared.

Daniel looked at the *sidhe* around him. "Clear out. I have business with the wee folk."

The remaining *sidhe* tried to pick up the ones on the ground and started to stumble off toward their campsite. They kept their eyes on Daniel, watching to make sure he didn't make a move. I noted his self-satisfied smile as they regarded him with pure terror.

"Not you." I put my hand up to stop the black-haired faery who'd been working as the leprechauns' shill.

"Me?" He seemed determined to act the part of a completely shocked bystander.

"Yes, you," I replied as Daniel came to my side. "You were on an awfully lucky streak, buddy."

"I guess it was just my day, friend," the faery replied.

"Oh, for the goddess's sake, Tully, we've been made," one of the leprechauns said.

"Well, we certainly have been now." Tully got his frown on.

Neil returned, dressed in slacks and a polo and carrying my secret weapon. I just hoped its battery was still good or we'd be screwed.

Daniel walked up to the wee folk. "I don't give a damn about the con, guys. I could care less if you want to take those idiots for everything they have. My wife is looking for something and we think you have it."

Tully looked at me, his arms crossed defensively. "Look, lady, no refunds. If you were dumb enough to fall for the game, then you deserved to lose whatever it is you're looking for."

"I didn't lose anything. Someone else did," I explained.

"Well, then she deserved to lose," Tully replied with a frown. "We won that money fair and…well, we won that money."

"I'm not saying you didn't." I got into Tully's space. "Look, we said we didn't care about the con. I'm looking for something and I'm willing to pay for it."

"Really?" Tully stared down at me, a speculative look in his dark eyes. "Just what are you willing to pay with?"

Daniel growled and the leprechauns looked at Tully liked he'd lost his mind.

"Did you not watch the fight?" They asked the question in perfect stereo.

"Are ya trying to make the vampire angry? He said that's his wife. They don't take kindly to men hitting on their wives," the one in Lee's left hand asked.

"He could decide to eat ya, ya dolt," the right side interjected. "And I'm not about to stop him. We can find another just like ya."

"He ain't gonna eat me, Corben," Tully said with more assurance than he should have had. "If he'd been hungry, he'd have eaten all those idiots who insulted him and talked bad about his lovely bride. I did neither. I actually think she's kinda cute, if you ask me, and she's definitely a con. So's he. I can see it in their faces."

"I'm not a con," I said.

"A thief, then," Tully insisted, looking between Daniel and myself. "Ya ain't legit, honey. I know a girl on the game when I see one."

I smiled because he did have good instincts. "I'm a thief and a damn good one at that. I'm showing you some respect by offering to buy the item I'm looking for."

"How much are we talking?" Lefty asked.

"What exactly are ya looking for, darling?" Righty wanted to know.

"It's a stone." I made a circle with my thumb and forefinger, showing them the approximate size. "About this big. When the sun hits it, it looks like blood."

All three faces fell and I knew I'd lost them.

"Never heard of it," the leprechauns said in unison.

I looked at Tully, giving him a disbelieving glare. He shrugged. "We only accept coin. Right, boys?"

The little men shook their heads. "Cash only, that's the way."

Daniel took lefty off Lee's hands and brought him up to eye level. "I don't believe you."

"We know you took the Blood Stone from a woman named Hildie," I stated flatly.

"Never heard of her." Tully's expression never changed. He was a cool customer.

I was going to have to play a little rough. Luckily, I had just the tools I needed. I looked over at Neil and nodded. He brought over my cell phone. I hadn't brought it to make a call. There were no cell towers in Faery. No, I had a different use for it here. I'd brought it for entertainment, but it was about to come in handy. Neil plugged it into the portable speakers. "Danny, you should let the boys down now."

Daniel looked at Lee, who set his leprechaun down beside Daniel's. "Don't take your eyes off them. Don't even blink."

Lee watched both of them, his eyes never wavering.

The leprechauns moved closer together, obviously wary of what we were going to do next.

"What's that thing?" one of them asked.

"That's for me to know and you to find out." The menu popped up and I scrolled down until I found what I was looking for. "Just consider it an addition to your party."

I hit play and a thumping beat started.

It's a well-known fact about the wee people that they love a good party. Give a leprechaun a cold brew, some good grub, and couple of hot chicks and they are happy campers. But if you turn on some music, you get real entertainment. Once a leprechaun starts to dance, they can't stop until the music is done. And the minute the music starts, a leprechaun can't help but dance.

"What is this?" one of them asked as their feet began to move of their own volition.

Neil and I bopped along with the heavy thrum of the drums.

I looked over at Lee. "You can blink now," I told him. "They're stuck until I hit stop. I should warn you, boys, I got like eight hours of music on that sucker."

"Is it all this bad?" one of the dancers asked.

"This ain't music," the other said. "I don't know why I'm moving."

Daniel shook his head. "I'm with the wee folk on this one. I thought we agreed on AC/DC. I hate the Black Eyed Peas."

"Only because you don't dance," I said, wiggling around. He wouldn't even dance with me at Ether. He claimed vampires didn't have a sense of rhythm, but I'd seen plenty of vampires make idiots of themselves on the dance floor. The good news was Dev moved like a dance-floor god.

"I don't know what your problem is. I like it," Tully said cheerfully. "I especially like the way it makes her jiggle."

"I'm getting cranky again, Z." Daniel glared at the faery.

"Yes," Lee said, putting a tankard to his lips. "It's beer. Nice."

"Ya bastard," Lefty said, or maybe he was Righty. I had trouble because they were dancing around each other. "That's me ale."

Lee took a long swallow. "You should try it, Zoey. It's some good stuff."

A good ten minutes passed in sociable music and dancing. I gave the beer a try and pronounced it delicious. Tully sat down with a tankard of his own, still swearing he had no idea what we were talking about.

"Three wishes," one of them said.

Both of the leprechauns looked like they were tiring. The music I'd put together for the occasion was all dance music, with fast beats. They didn't have the option of waiting for a nice slow song. Their legs would go until they fell off.

"Not a chance." I hoisted the tankard to my lips.

It was an old ploy. When the leprechaun got caught, he offered his captor three wishes to set him free. But they liked to play fast and loose with their wishes. It always seemed like a good deal, but it would go bad in the end. For example, if you requested a nice chicken sandwich you would probably find yourself with a case of salmonella poisoning. It wouldn't hit until the leprechauns were long gone, but they were little cons to the end.

"Come on," the other pled. "There has to be something you want."

"Yes," I agreed. "I want the Blood Stone."

"God." Daniel groaned from where he sat on a tree stump. "Please just give her what she wants. I think Beyoncé is next. I can't handle Beyoncé."

"I'm with Donovan," Lee injected. "This is cruel. We should just kill them. I'll get a good scent trail on them and we'll find their hiding place. It might take longer, but anything's better than having to listen to whatever the hell is coming out of that stereo."

"They'll never break," Tully said surely. He looked at his cohorts. "Stay strong, boys. I know these human machines. It will run out of power soon."

"Easy for you to say, Tully," one of them panted, his legs moving.

Neil danced around and put his hands up because he considered himself a single lady until someone put a ring on it. He pulled out my spare, fully charged battery pack. We planned for all contingencies. "Three more hours! We haven't even gotten to Lady Gaga yet, Z. I can't wait to take a ride on her disco stick."

Daniel went paler than usual. "Please, just let me beat them until they talk. I didn't do anything wrong. Why are you torturing me, baby?"

"I give up," one of them said.

"Oh, thank the goddess," the other cried.

Tully cursed, but accepted it with a rueful shake of his head. My hand hovered over the pause button. Daniel and Lee each caught a dancing leprechaun and then the forest was quiet again.

"I miss Ether," Neil pouted.

"I know you do." I sympathized. I looked at the little cons. "Spit it out or I'll bring out the big guns. I have show tunes on this puppy. Who wants to listen to *Legally Blonde, The Musical*?"

Daniel pulled his leprechaun up and gave him a full view of his fangs. "If you make me listen to musicals, I'll kill you myself."

"It's in a cave on the mountain closest to the door between the *sitheins*," the one Danny was holding spat out.

"There goes two damn years of work." Tully cursed into his ale. He looked bitterly up at me. "I was going straight. I was. I was getting out of the game with that money."

"Sure you were," I said sarcastically. Once a con…

He grinned. "Nah, I wasn't. I was gonna steal it myself. You're probably saving me a ton of trouble. They can be right mean when you cross them."

Neil frowned at our talking leprechaun. "A mountain is a big place."

"It's in a cave," he said. "About halfway up on the Seelie side of the mountain. It's in the cave at the back. We hide all our profits there."

"If you're lying…" Daniel started.

"Yeah, yeah," the one in Lee's hand said. "You'll track us down and kill us with those fangs of yours."

"Nope," Daniel said with a ferocious smile. "I'll let her have you."

I smiled brightly and waved.

"Couldn't ya kill me instead?"

I pulled out one of several bags of coins Declan had been gracious enough to put in our gear. It was what the leprechauns loved—gold. "For your trouble, gentlemen. This is more than the stone is worth. And I have no intention of taking anything but the Blood Stone, so you're coming out on the heavy end of this particular deal. Good luck."

Danny and Lee let the wee folk go. They immediately went to the table and started counting coin.

"You're a generous lady," one said, giving me a wink.

At least I wouldn't have to worry about revenge. If they were satisfied with our bargain, they would leave us alone. We turned to leave.

"But you're the one who's gonna be needing the luck," the other said in an "I know something you don't know" voice.

When I looked back, the leprechauns were gone. Tully sighed and took another drink. It seemed like it wasn't the first time he'd been left behind.

"Come on, Z," Danny said, and I could see he was wary of what the leprechaun had said. "Let's get our gear. We can make it to the mountain before dawn and then get some sleep."

I followed my husband and hoped our luck would hold.

Chapter Twenty-Two

"I'm gonna kill those fuckers," Daniel said, his head all the way back as he looked up at the ridiculously imposing mountain. It made Everest look like a baby hill. Someone might have mentioned that fact to us.

"How do they get up there?" Neil's eyes were wide, his head thrown back as he looked up.

"They must be part goat," Lee commented.

I shivered because it was damn cold. The wind whipped around something fierce. "At least goats have a nice coat of fur."

I wrapped my arms around my chest and wished Declan had thought to put some parkas in the gear. I'd managed to sleep some during the day with Daniel's arms around me, but I missed Dev's warm heat mightily. He was like a furnace in bed sometimes, and Daniel and I both were missing his warmth.

"Here, baby, take my coat." Danny took off the light jacket he was wearing and wrapped it around me. "I don't even feel this."

I knew he did but not as much as I did, so I accepted the gesture. The truth was even if he felt every degree of the cold, he would insist I take his coat. The wolves didn't mind the cold at all.

Daniel looked up the mountain and made his decision. "I'm going to try to fly up. It would be a hell of a lot easier than climbing.

Come on, Z."

He hooked his arm under my knees and held me close to his chest. He took off faster than he normally would and I wove my fingers together around his neck so I had the tightest hold possible without choking him. I'd gotten somewhat used to flying with Daniel, but I still got a rush of adrenaline any time he launched us into the sky. The moon was almost full as he climbed higher and higher. I needed that parka now as the higher we went, the colder we got.

"Do you see it?" Daniel shouted the question because the winds were loud as we got closer to our destination. He nodded toward the mountain. Sure enough, there was the opening to a cave in the middle of the rocky face of the mountain. It wasn't small, either. We would have no trouble getting in and out. Given that we were dealing with leprechauns, I'd been worried about small spaces.

"Let's go," I yelled. "We can check it out and you can go back and get the wolves if we need them."

I was hoping we wouldn't. We would only need Lee and Neil if there was some serious security. The leprechauns had chosen this site because the mountain was a security measure in and of itself. It was difficult to get to and unless you were up as high as Danny and I were, you couldn't see the cave. It wasn't visible from the ground. Someone would have to be looking for it to find it. Even if the leprechauns had locked their treasure in a chest, there wasn't much Danny couldn't get through.

Looking over Daniel's shoulder, I noted that there was a castle in the distance. It was a pale ivory, much like the palace, but it looked even more medieval. There was a wall around what looked like a large village just outside the castle. Even from this distance, I could see the activities going on in the walled city. Like the palace, they were preparing for war.

Daniel's arms tightened around me the higher we went, and I realized he was trying to stay in control. The wind whipped around us in a violent wave that sent my stomach flipping, and Danny had to correct his course three times before a mighty gust sent us flying back down. Daniel lost control and we tumbled through the air, twisting like an out-of-control kite. I saw the ground suddenly coming up at an alarming rate of speed. I clung to Daniel, my heart in my throat. I couldn't scream, couldn't do anything but hold on to Daniel and pray that the end was quick. I closed my eyes, waiting for impact.

Daniel pulled up at the last second, and I felt the ground just scrape my back as I was jerked up like I was riding a bungee cord. Daniel swore as he righted us and managed to float us lightly back to the ground.

My heart did a weird skippy thing, and I just managed to avoid vomiting.

"Jeez, Z, are you okay?" Neil asked, hurrying forward.

"What the hell happened?" Lee put his hands on his hips, staring up at the mountain as though he could see the threat.

Daniel ran his hands along my back, making sure I hadn't taken any damage. "God, baby, I lost control. Those winds were hellacious. I'm so sorry. Are you okay?"

"I'm fine." My voice was shaky and my legs even shakier. "I think I'll walk from now on. Like forever."

"I'm going to try again. Maybe I can handle it better without a passenger." Daniel handed me off to Lee, who made sure I could stand up. "You rest, Z. I'll be right back."

I nodded and Neil sank down on a log, pulling me with him. I sat beside Neil and leaned into his warmth. Lee kept his eyes on the sky, watching as Daniel tried to break through that wall of wind.

Neil put his arm around me as I shivered. I'm not a cold-weather girl. I felt that cold in every damn bone. "I saw a castle while we were up there."

"We're close to the door between the *sitheins*," Neil pointed out. "We're on that duke person's land."

"The Duke of Ain?"

"Yes." Lee cocked his head to keep his eye on Daniel. "His castle is supposedly well fortified since he's so close to the Unseelie *sithein*. I overheard Declan talking about it. It's the first line of defense. From what I overheard, the queen spends a lot of money making sure this part of the *sithein* has the best defenses."

In the end, whenever you want to know who's behind anything, whether it is an assassination plot, a theft, or who stuck gum in the lock on your locker, it's necessary to ask one all-important question. Who profits most? At the heart of almost every crime is a dollar sign of some sort.

At first I'd thought someone was trying to start a war because they hated the other side. What if someone wanted to start a war for a much more mundane reason? Wars are profitable.

Daniel hit the ground with a resounding thud, leaving a crater in the dirt.

"Shit, that hurt," he said, pushing himself up.

"So flying is a no-go." Lee pointed out the obvious.

"Unless everyone wants to end up like that." Daniel pointed to the indention in the ground.

"Pass," Neil said.

Daniel sat down on the other side of me, and his big body did a wonderful job of shielding me from the wind. I moved my head from Neil's shoulder to my husband's and his arm went around me.

"Z, why don't you stay in the tent? The wolves and I can take care of this," Danny said. I gave him the look I always gave him when he said stupid stuff. "All right, baby. I was just trying to keep you warm. I'll give you a minute and then we'll go."

"Danny," I started as Lee came around and sat at my back. I was warming up rapidly now. "What do you know about the Duke of Ain?"

A long, slow smile spread across Daniel's face. "I know that if I had a shred of evidence against him I would rip his throat out."

"I couldn't get Dev or Declan to listen to me." They didn't want to look past the obvious villain.

Daniel regarded me seriously. "I tried, too. I especially tried after I found out that the Duke of Ain makes all the war machines the Seelies use. His province is also known for their candles."

"How is that not evidence?" Lee asked in a low growl. He'd wanted to kill something or someone for a long time now.

"Almost every province makes candles, Lee," Daniel explained. "I got the whole lecture when I came in. Padric took me on a tour and gave me the rundown on who did what and how the economy works."

I frowned up at him. "I was shown to the bedroom where I could fuck Dev."

Danny laughed. "They're not the most liberated of thinkers when it comes to women. I think Padric would tell you that's your job. The Seelie women won't be fighting in this war, not even the queen. She'll be there but kept well away from the fight. In these times, she cedes her power to Padric or Declan, now that he's of age to rule."

Yet another reason I was happy to live on the Earth plane. "That's shitty. I wouldn't ever cede my power."

"We know you wouldn't, Z" Neil said as Daniel stood again.

Danny reached down and helped me up. "We're climbing."

I groaned but got my butt off the log. I looked down at my Nikes. They were good for running and supposedly something called cross training, but I doubted that included complex mountain climbing. I'd also noted the snow started about halfway up to where we needed to go. I doubted my jeans were going to prove a good barrier against that frigid white powder.

I was more of an urban thief.

Lee was already taking off his shirt and he gave me a frown. I turned around so I wouldn't see anything I'd already seen in action. Neil didn't care. He passed me his polo to fold and then his jeans. He never bothered with anything as silly as underwear. When he was ready, he smiled and waved and changed in the blink of an eye, his transition from man to wolf a smooth slide. He barked cheerfully and ran to Lee, whose brown wolf was enormous. Lee's wolf seemed larger than his human body. When in wolf form, Lee could give the black dogs a run for their money.

"Go on ahead," Daniel said. "We'll wait for you on top of the first ridge then we'll continue together." Danny picked me up again. He started to float and I hung on. "I can at least spare us the first leg."

He made it to the ridge quickly and set me down. We waited, watching the wolves make their way up the rocky incline. Daniel hugged me to him, but his body didn't provide the warmth that a human's would. Still, I huddled close.

"It's going to be all right, Z," Danny said, and I heard the smile in his voice. "If it gets too cold, I'll slit Lee open like a tauntaun and slide you inside for warmth."

"Dweeb," I shot back. Only my husband would be making *Star Wars* references at a time like this.

He laughed as the wolves caught up. We started the rest of the climb together.

* * * *

I clung to Danny's neck as he dug his claws into the rock face. He tried once to swing his leg over the cave's ridge but couldn't quite make it. After we had gone as far as Danny could safely fly us, he'd put me on his back and made quick work of the climb. The claws he could pop out of his hands helped enormously. He'd clawed and scratched his way to the top. I was sure my weight on his back held him up, but he convinced me it was the easiest way to get this done. So I held on for dear life, my arms around his neck and legs hooked around his waist.

I felt a warm presence underneath me, and Lee pushed his back against Daniel's legs. Wordlessly communicating, the vampire and the wolf got on the same page. Daniel stepped as lightly as possible on Lee's back and managed to swing us up over the final hurdle. We landed in a heap and had to scramble to get up. Daniel leaned over the rock face and helped pull the wolves.

"God, he's heavier than he looks," Danny groaned as he hauled Lee over the ridge. "And he looks heavy." Neil he only had to use one hand on. The wolves stayed in their furry bodies as we entered the cave, padding cautiously across the cave floor.

My hands shook as we moved carefully. I let my eyes adjust to the dark of the cave before carefully pulling out the small flashlight I'd placed in my pocket. It was a penlight, illuminating only a few feet ahead of me.

"Keep that down, Z." Danny shielded his eyes when the small light hit them. He didn't need anything so technological as a flashlight to see in the dark. "My eyes already adjusted and I'm sure the wolves' have, too."

I held the light down, shining where I was walking because my eyes wouldn't adjust to being able to see in this blackness. It wasn't always easy being the only pitiful human in the group. I took inventory of the cave, careful to keep my light away from preternatural eyes.

From what I could see, the cave was large, though the ceiling seemed to taper down after roughly a hundred feet. I bet we would find what we were looking for in the back of this cave. I found my footing much firmer as we hit rock. The ground was even this far into the cave, and I caught a glimpse of something metallic shining. It was just a shimmer, but that was all I needed. Bingo. X marks the spot and all that. I tripped slightly and fell to my side, hitting something kind of soft and…furry.

"Danny." I spoke slowly, not moving at all because whatever I had hit was breathing in and out.

"Z, what the fuck are you doing? Get up. We have work to do." Daniel moved close, reaching out to me.

I scrambled up and away from the now shifting body.

"Shit," Danny said as an enormous eye opened. Even in the dark I could tell it was red and angry. It glowed like a stoplight.

The leprechauns had neglected to mention their enormous guard.

Chapter Twenty-Three

All of the trolls I've ever met personally are the type who could almost pass for human. They tend to be of Scandinavian descent. They're not the only trolls to come from the north countries. There are a small number of trolls who used to rule Norway and Sweden before the humans hunted them down and they passed into legend.

I fell into one of those legendary frost giants, and when he sat up, the mountain moved.

"Holy shit," Daniel yelled as the frost giant stood up.

The giant had to be at least twelve feet tall and he weighed what an eighteen wheeler would. Daniel looked like a leprechaun next to him. Lee growled and Neil moved in beside him, the hair on his back standing at rigid attention.

Daniel reached into his pocket and pulled out his handgun. I was wondering what he was going to do with it besides annoy the enormous frost giant. The bullets would be like mosquitoes to the giant. "Move your ass, Z. Get what we need so we can get out of here."

I stepped back from the gigantic shadow against the cave wall. My penlight could only help me see bits and pieces of the enormous creature. He had white, mangy fur that looked like it could use a good conditioner and a blow out. As I moved the light up, I caught a glimpse of razor-sharp teeth. The giant took way better care of his choppers than the ogre had. They looked like his pride and joy. It was easy to see why the leprechauns had felt their treasure was safe here. Even if a thief could find their hiding place, they would have to deal with the frost giant—who did not like having his nap disturbed.

"What are you going to do?" I asked Daniel as the frost giant regarded us carefully with his red eyes.

"Distract him," Daniel said with more confidence than I would have had.

"How?"

"I don't know. I'm probably about to do a nice impression of a toothpick. Could you hurry up this heist?" Danny held the gun in his right hand and aimed it at the frost giant, who was still curious about the odd creatures who had invaded his home. He reached down and plucked Daniel up, hauling him into the air.

"Now would be a good time!" my husband yelled as he fired off three quick rounds.

The frost giant's howl shook the world. Seriously, I think it moved my liver around.

I picked up the pace and started to the back of the cave. "I would aim for the eyes if I were you." I shouted my helpful advice over my shoulder.

Daniel shot off four quick rounds. The giant roared again. Exactly as I knew would happen, the bullets just stung him and pissed him off because Danny hadn't hit him in the eye. The whole cave shook with the force of the giant's rage, and I had to clasp my hands over my ears because the sound was so loud. The echo after it did nothing to assuage the assault on my hearing.

I couldn't see more than snatches of the fight. I heard something hit the ground with a low huff.

"Did you hear the stuff about the eyes?" I shouted my question as I caught a glimpse of Daniel rolling away from the giant's attempt to squash him like a bug. I heard Lee's growl and briefly saw Neil nipping at the giant's heels. The cave shook as the giant's fist narrowly missed its target.

"I heard you," Daniel yelled irritably. "Woman, I am working here. Give me a break."

I rolled my eyes. Men never listen to good advice. They have to make all the mistakes on their own because they just know better. "Fine, but don't say I didn't warn you. I tried all this stuff with the ogre. The only thing that worked was cold iron straight through the eye, into the old brainpan, and this guy is way bigger than the ogre. So shoot him in the damn eye."

"Did I ask for your advice?" Daniel screamed.

There was a volley of gunfire and another gut-shaking roar. I jumped back as a bullet whizzed past me. I turned to my husband.

"Nice, Danny," I said with some irritation of my own because I warned him about the dangers of bullets on large faery creature's bones when I told him how I killed the ogre. "Ricochet. Do you listen? I told you that could happen."

"This is why I don't drive anywhere with you, baby." Daniel growled through the darkness. I could hear he was on the run. "I don't know how Dev handles it with you constantly giving him instructions. *Speed up, slow down. Why are you taking the scenic route?* It's annoying, Zoey. It makes me want to pull out my hair."

There was a loud thud and then the giant roared.

"Dev is a gentleman," I continued once it got quiet enough to talk again. That last roar had made me drop the flashlight and it had gone out. I got on my knees and felt around for it. What Dev was really good at, I admitted to myself and myself alone, was tuning me out. When we drove somewhere together, his conversation consisted of saying "uh huh" and "yes, dear" a lot.

"Neil," Daniel screamed. "Go with her! Get the freaking job done. If you don't, she's just gonna stand there and bitch at me because I'm not working fast enough for her."

I frowned in the darkness. Put like that, I did seem kind of controlling. I had to admit I was harder on Danny in these situations than I would have been with Dev and that wasn't exactly fair. Danny deserved praise, too. Right?

"I think you're doing a wonderful job, baby." I used my best cheerleader voice. I found the flashlight and now Danny crawled up the creature's torso and was trying to punch him in his probably sensitive nose. "Just like a shark," I commented, letting my appreciation for his technique show through. "Very clever."

Daniel groaned as he was tossed off and Neil was there growling at me, looking thoroughly annoyed. He used his nose to push me forward.

"Fine." I knew why he was mad. He wanted in on the kill, and he'd never tasted frost giant before. "I was only trying to help."

Neil and I made our way through the cold darkness. The cave's ceiling eventually sloped down and I had to stoop as I got closer and closer to the back. I moved the flashlight around, searching for the glint of metal I'd seen before, but I couldn't quite remember exactly which direction it had come from.

Neil scented the air and then put his nose firmly to the ground. He looked up at me and yipped shortly. It was an order. He had the scent he wanted. I trained my flashlight on his white tail and followed. When I heard his happy bark, I knew he'd found what he was looking for.

Even in the gloom of the cave, I could see the gleam of gold. Wherever my light hit, the color washed across the walls, glittering in the darkness. The leprechauns had been right to be worried. This was some cache of treasure.

"God, Z, it's like a pirate treasure." Neil was suddenly a naked man. He still didn't seem to mind the cold. He reached down and picked up a handful of gold coins and let them drip from his fingers. "We'd never have to work again."

"No, we wouldn't," I commented with amusement. He was forgetting a few truths about the leprechauns. "We would never have to work again because we would meet with some nasty accident before we could ever spend it."

Neil pouted up at me. "That sucks. If we're smart enough to steal it we should be able to spend it."

"Doesn't work that way, buddy, at least not in Faery. Those leprechauns will be in here soon making sure I didn't take anything we didn't agree on. If they find a single coin missing, they'll be after us." I looked at the chest in the middle of all that glorious gold. I ran my hands over it. It was solidly built and there was a heavy chain around it. I felt the well-made lock holding the chains together. It whispered to me, like all locks do. It begged me to wiggle it and play with it and pick it open.

“I want my own money, Z.” Neil looked forlornly at the wealth around him. “I’m not married to Dev. He shouldn’t have to give me an allowance. I would rather he just let me pick his pocket. At least I would feel like I was working for it.”

I heard another volley of shots as I pulled my lockpicks out of my pocket. Daniel was obviously having a good time with the frost giant. “You are working for it. He’s paying you to be my bodyguard. It isn’t an allowance. It’s your salary.”

“Lee is your bodyguard,” Neil said with a sigh. “I’m just your playmate. I don’t even cook anymore. Albert kicked me out of his kitchens. I just hang around the house and go shopping with you.”

“And take arrows in the ass to save my life.” I rubbed my hands together vigorously to get some feeling in them. I needed my hands warm and working to feel the give and take that came with raking the lock and holding the pins in place. Lockpicking is a delicate business and requires a deft touch that one doesn’t normally get from frozen hands. “The minute we get back, I’ll look around for a job. I’ll make it small time so it can be just you and me.”

“Promise?”

“Promise.” I was sure my dad could come up with something. He was retired for the most part, but he still had good connections. I wondered though if Chad wouldn’t have something to say about his boyfriend’s criminal activities. Neil and Chad might not be married but Chad was incredibly possessive. I held the lock in my hand and started to gently glide the pick in.

Neil looked up from his perusal of the gold and gave a startled laugh. “Seriously?” he asked, looking at the picks in my hands. He reached down and pulled the chains apart with little effort on his part. He tossed them aside and opened the chest.

I frowned. “You have no appreciation for a soft touch.”

Arctic blue eyes rolled. “You have no appreciation for speed, honey. That frost giant out there is about to have himself a Daniel sandwich. We need to pick up the pace.”

“Fine.” I agreed with him even though I doubted Daniel would ever let himself be made into a sandwich in a nonsexual way. There was a whole lot of roaring, and not all of it came from the frost giant. Daniel was doing some yelling of his own. He was obviously getting impatient. I sat down beside the treasure. Neil and I sifted through the contents of the chest. This was where the leprechauns kept the good shit. It was full of jewelry and gold and silver housewares, and what looked to be the deeds to land and houses. It had been stuffed with anything a gambler could use to pay off his debts.

"Wow," Neil said in a reverent tone. He held up an unmounted stone.

"That's the Blood Stone," I said with no small amount of awe. It was beautiful in a freaky way. I shone the light directly on it and the reflection filled the cavern. It made everything look like it was bathed in rich, sweet blood.

"Creepy." Neil handed the stone to me, shivering just a little.

I shoved the stone in my pocket and we both stood up, leaving the rest of the treasure regretfully on the floor. I heard a single gunshot and then a triumphant laugh.

"Take that, fucker!" Daniel's yell echoed through the cavern.

I looked at Neil with pursed lips. "What do you want to bet he just shot that frost giant straight through the eye after he tried everything else?"

Neil held his hands out. "I try to stay out of your marital arguments."

"No, you don't." I made my way back out to the front of the cave. Neil followed after me. He was naked, so I knew there was no chance he'd palmed that sapphire I'd seen him looking at. I wasn't concerned about the stealing—that came naturally—but those little leprechauns really would come after us.

It was easier to see in the big part of the cave. The moonlight made everything glow in a silvery shine. I could see Daniel trying to push the now-dead frost giant off Lee's wolf body. With a great grunt he managed the task, and when he turned I noted his shirt was covered in blood. I wouldn't be able to tell if it was his or the giant's since he healed so quickly.

"You just had to try everything else, didn't you?" I shook my head as I studied them. There was a neat little hole in the giant's eye. "You couldn't just take my word for it."

Lee changed and groaned as he tried to get up. "God, Donovan, is she always this way? How the hell did you work with her?"

My husband grimaced as he looked down at Lee, trying to ascertain the extent of his injuries. "You want to know something, Lee? She's been this way since we were eight freaking years old. She used to tell me how to play Monopoly. She'd roll her eyes anytime I made a wrong move. I think your pelvis is broken."

"You broke my wolf?" I asked, shocked.

"He'll heal," Daniel shot back.

"Not like this I won't." Lee groaned. "Somebody's got to reset it." I started to open my mouth to offer my services. "Anybody but Zoey."

Neil ran forward. He got in behind Lee and maneuvered his arms under Lee's armpits. Daniel took his feet. They nodded at each other and Daniel realigned the bones. Lee proved he knew lots of cuss words.

"Better?" Daniel asked.

"If you can call it that." Lee laid back on the cavern floor. "It's going to be an hour or two before I can move." He turned his head to me. "Did you get it?"

I pulled out the stone and tossed it into Danny's waiting hand. He held it up and the moonlight hit it. My little flashlight hadn't done the stone justice. Now we were all covered in its bloody beauty.

"This is mine," Daniel said with a possessive sigh. "This belongs to me."

I walked up and put my hand on his back. His arm went around me out of habit. "According to the information Marini gave me, it has something to do with the last king."

"What does it do?" Neil asked.

We were all damn certain it did something. It was a powerful object. I could tell that just by touching it.

I shook my head as Daniel watched it, mesmerized by the glow. "I'm not sure but I think I know who to ask. Marcus gave it to the queen. I think he was smuggling it out the best way he knew how."

"Marcus has some explaining to do," Daniel commented, his attention still on the Blood Stone.

"Daniel, we're going to have to give that stone to Marini." It was the plain truth of our situation.

He pocketed the stone. "Like hell we do, Z."

"Daniel, he could kill you."

"We don't have any proof of that," my husband replied, a stubborn look on his face.

I put my hands on my hips. "Oh, and that X-ray of something shoved surgically into your heart proves nothing, huh?"

He shrugged a little. "It proves Marini can bluff, baby. Just because he has some box he carries around doesn't mean it works, and I'm not turning that stone over to him because it doesn't belong to him."

"No, it belongs to me." This was my job. I'd done all the background for it. I would be damned if I let Danny decide to change our entire plan because he liked the stone. "I'm the one who found it."

"Yeah, you could have run this job by yourself…"

"Shut up!" Lee shouted from his place on the floor. "How do you two get anything done? You're either fighting or fucking. God, I never thought I'd want the faery back."

Daniel and I stopped and looked at each other. It was true. Daniel and I both had big personalities that often rubbed each other the wrong way. When Danny had been human, he'd had much better control of his temper. His vampire DNA had taken over, and we fought a lot since his turn. I was just now considering how Dev balanced us. If Dev were here, he would have steered us away from the fight. He would have suggested other options or said something ridiculously outrageous and turned our minds from our stubborn positions.

Danny pulled me back into the warmth of his body. "We'll figure it out, Z. Let's get back to the palace and find a way to stop this war so we can get Dev and go home."

I nodded.

Daniel looked back down at my broken bodyguard—who probably wouldn't have gotten all broken if Danny had followed my advice in the first place. "I'm going to take Zoey back to the tent. She'll be warmer there while we wait for your bones to heal."

"It won't take more than an hour or two." There was an unnecessary apology in Lee's eyes.

Daniel leaned down for me to hop on his back. I jumped up and wrapped myself around him. He looked back at me. “It’s just until we get past the winds and then we’ll fly the rest of the way. Neil, stay here with Lee. I’ll be back for the two of you in an hour if you aren’t down the mountain by then.”

Neil nodded and Daniel leapt out of the cave. He made his way down much faster than we had come up. I was thankful when Daniel stopped and let me down briefly before cradling me to his chest and taking off for the final part of our journey.

“We’ll be back at the palace tomorrow, Z,” Daniel promised as we floated toward the ground. “I’ll fly us as far as I can before dawn tonight and then we’ll be there after the sun goes down. We’re not going to let him kill himself.”

“Thank you, Danny.” I was so grateful to have him with me. I grinned up at him. “I’m cold. I can’t feel whole portions of my body. How am I ever going to get the feeling back?”

His smile was all male promise. “I think I can help you with that particular problem, baby. You just show me where you’re having sensitivity issues and I’ll make sure all those parts are functioning.” He leaned down and kissed me, his tongue making a brief, sweet appearance across my lips. “I’ll warm you right up. We have an hour. I can’t think of any way I’d rather kill some time than making sure you’re hot.”

We hit the ground softly and his hands were already delving into my shirt, his mouth back on mine in a possessive kiss. I went up on my toes to deepen the kiss and started backing us toward the tent and our somewhat comfy makeshift bed when Daniel’s head came up.

“Zoey, run,” he yelled as the arrow slammed into his torso. He flew back and was impaled on the trunk of a tree, his body stuck and unable to move.

I turned as fast as I could and saw a group of *sidhe* warriors advancing on us. They were led by a single female who had the nastiest grin on her unfortunately familiar face.

“I would not run if I were you.” Gilliana was wrapped in a fur-lined cloak and looked comfy. “I will order my men to kill that nightcrawler you are so attached to. They missed his heart. Barely. I could make sure they do not this time.”

I moved backward, standing beside Daniel and not letting that bitch out of my sight.

"Don't, Zoey." The tight tone of Daniel's voice gave away the amount of pain he was in. "It's silver tipped. I can't move, baby. Just go."

"She is not going anywhere," Gilliana said. "Well, not anywhere she would want to go. I will take whatever weapons you have on you, please. Or I will order my men to fire. We can take you out with arrows, too. You should understand we're prepared. After we heard you were looking for the leprechauns, I set my trap. Everyone in this part of the kingdom knows where the leprechauns hide their treasure. We've lost more than one citizen to that monster who guards it. I rather hoped he would eat you, but I do have a backup plan."

I gritted my teeth and slowly pulled my gun out and laid it on the ground. There were too many of them to try taking a shot and Daniel was a big target. I pulled the knives out and gave them up, too. "What do you want, Gilliana? Killing me isn't going to endear you to Devinshea."

She sighed. "Yes, I'm afraid I got caught in that little web of Miria's. Who would have guessed a mortal could be that good in bed? Trust me, if I had known what that fluffy piece of impurity could do to me, I would have begged Miria for a betrothal earlier." She shrugged. "Some things do not work out the way we could hope. I had planned on getting him back with a baby. You ruined that. Father came up with a much better plan. I lose Devinshea, but at least you do not get to keep him."

"Turn the Seelie against the Unseelie." It was exactly what I had decided they were doing.

"That was the easy part," she admitted. "The common folk hate the Unseelie. So does that idiot prince. Getting the queen and our good priest to agree to a war was the difficult part. Father is clever, you see. He knew the only way the priest would ever push for war was to engineer a very personal loss for him. He tried to take you out, but the baby proved easier."

Rage pulsed through my system, and the only thing that kept me from tearing her throat out was the fact that Daniel was vulnerable. I wanted to, though. She'd taken my child, killed my baby. Dev had asked me if I wanted revenge and I did, but I couldn't risk Daniel.

"I'm going to kill you, bitch."

"I am sure you would try." Gilliana looked back at her guard. "Wrap the vampire in the silver chains. I would be careful if I were you. It might be best if one of you held a knife to his wife's throat to ensure his compliance."

I quickly found myself hauled against a body with cold steel at my throat.

"I'll cooperate," Daniel promised tightly.

"I know you will." Gilliana turned back to me. "I would rather kill you, but I am afraid Father needs you alive. Even as we speak, Devinshea is weakening. The people will listen to him. The army will listen to him. I have to make sure he wants this war. He will be incensed when he realizes the two people he is closest to in the world have been taken as slaves by the Unseelie. I hope you like it rough, Your Grace." Gilliana walked right up to me and slapped me as hard as she could. I tasted blood but refused to show it to her. "That was for humiliating me."

"All of this for money?" I had visions of slicing her open and playing in her entrails going through my head.

She looked down at me. "This is not about money, Your Grace. This is about power. Father has been trying to kill Miria for decades. That guard of hers is good, but things happen on the battlefield. We will take out Devinshea and Declan, and then we will make certain that Miria meets an accidental arrow. The battlefield is chaotic. When we win, my father will take the throne and we will rebuild the Seelie into a pure haven for the *sidhe*."

She glanced back at something I couldn't see. I saw only that Daniel moaned as they pulled his body off the arrow and quickly bound him in heavy silver chains. He remained still, though he could have fought. His flesh smoked where his skin met the metal.

"I hand you off to your Unseelie hosts, Your Grace," she said to me before addressing someone behind me. "I think you will find these two will get you a good price on the slave block. The vampire is exotic and can do the work of ten men, though precautions must be taken, of course. As for the girl, consider her a well-trained pleasure slave. She kept a sex god satisfied, so I think she can be called an expert."

The voice behind me was scratchy, as though it hurt him to speak. "They'll never make it to the auction house. I've already secured a private buyer to take them both."

"Excellent," Gilliana said. "I hope he is well satisfied with the purchase. I will make sure that the tale makes the rounds on this side of faery."

"I have no doubt," the voice said. "It may be time to up the rhetoric, my lady. King Angus is talking about negotiating."

"He will have no choice but war after news of Her Grace's enslavement is known. It is better than merely giving them a dead body." Gilliana turned back to me. "I wish you joy in your new profession. I assure you serving that vampire of yours has not prepared you for the roughness of an Unseelie lord. They are barbarians. I will be surprised if you survive the night. Knock her out."

Something hard came down on the back of my head, and I was down for the count.

Chapter Twenty-Four

I came back to consciousness gradually, having the most delicious dream. My body was warm and safe. There had been no confrontation with Gilliana and no one was going to take me to an auction house. Dev was with me, his tongue laving my nipples with the greatest of affection. My breasts were heavy, the nipples taut as they stood up begging for his attention. I didn't have to do anything but let him pleasure me.

He sucked gently, more sweetly than ever before. Usually with Dev there was a certain amount of domination. He liked to show his strength and I got turned on by it so we all won. This was a new side to him and I sighed into his gentle touch. I would have thought Bris was with me, but I didn't feel the rush of lust roll over my skin. There was a laziness to his tongue, like he had all the time in the world and he was content to play forever.

"God, that's hot," Danny said from somewhere in the darkness. I smiled in my sleep. He always liked to watch when Dev made love to me. He liked to join in, but sometimes he would just sit back and enjoy the show. I was naked and the world was warm with Dev's love and care surrounding me.

"You like that do you, vampire?" Dev asked but his voice was strangely…feminine. "I'm surprised. I'd heard vampires were extremely possessive. It was a worry of mine when I made the deal."

"Yeah, well, I might be a vampire, but I'm still male." Danny laughed, a deep sexy sound. "No male is that possessive. Besides, you're very much not what I expected. Why don't you let me join you?"

There was a sweet tug at my breast, and I felt myself getting soft and wet. I sighed because I didn't want to leave this dream. Somewhere in the back of my head I knew I would wake up and be forced to deal with the fact that I'd been sold to a goblin, or something like a goblin, as a sex slave. I would be used roughly and Danny would be forced to watch, and he'd probably be killed when they realized he couldn't be controlled. Dev would fight his war and he would die. I would live my life out on this plane in agony, so I didn't fight the dream of being gently made love to.

"I don't know if that's a good idea, but I do know what you're talking about," Dev said in that strange, sweet voice as his mouth moved to the other breast and his hand sought out my soft center and rubbed so gently I moaned. "She's so responsive. This is why I had to buy a girl. My boyfriend would freak if I played with another guy. I just…like girls. They're so soft and sweet. I can be gentle with a girl. With my boyfriend, it's all strength and power and dominance and that's fine most of the time."

"But sometimes you just need a little sweet pussy, right?" Danny asked, his voice low, and I knew he was ready to go.

There was a soft sigh. "Oh, and it is sweet. I'm not going to hurt her, you know. I really do promise that."

Something small began to play with private parts of me and my eyes flew open. Even in my craziest dreams there was nothing about Dev or Danny that was small and soft. I looked up into the eyes of my Unseelie captor, who was supposed to be a brutal, barbarian overlord.

"Hello," the small, sweet-looking female said with wide eyes. "Welcome back. I hope they weren't too rough getting you from…well, wherever you came from. They didn't tell and I didn't ask."

I couldn't estimate how tall she was, but she was slender and her breasts were small but spectacularly formed. Dark-brown hair curled around her face and gave her the appearance of a gorgeous pixie with violet eyes.

I knew her breasts were pretty because she was right next to me and she was naked.

"You're not wearing any clothes," I said because I wasn't sure of anything else.

The pretty pixie smiled, a decadent grin spreading across her expressive face. "That's all right, gorgeous. Neither are you."

I shoved my head up, which was a mistake because my brainpan felt like it was going to split in two. I rested it back down, but I'd confirmed the fact that she was telling the truth. I was naked and spread out for the world to see. My arms were over my head and I was pressed into a soft mattress, apparently tied to the headboard.

I moved my eyes to the left and the right, but all I could see was a softly feminine bedroom. The walls here were wooden, and I suspected I was in some sort of cabin. The only sound I could hear beyond my own labored breathing was a dog barking somewhere.

"What am I doing here?" I wasn't where I was supposed to be. I doubted Gilliana had meant to sell me to anyone who looked like this girl. She would be flustered at the prospect.

The woman sat up. She smiled down on me and let her hands run across my torso. "Well, sweetie, I kind of bought you. Don't freak or anything. I'm not going to hurt you. I just want to play with you for a while. I was promised you're experienced at giving and receiving pleasure."

"I'm not a whore." God only knew what Gilliana had said about me. I might have a strange sex life, but I'd slept with exactly two men.

She frowned and touched my face gently. "I didn't say you were. I said you were an excellent lover. At least that's what I was promised. Goddess knows you are extremely responsive. You got wet the minute I started rubbing your pussy."

"Well, you should stop that." I was sure my entire body went red with embarrassment. I would have crossed my legs but my feet were tied to the posts at the foot of the bed.

"God, please don't," I heard a familiar voice plead.

"Daniel!" I nearly shouted and I looked around again. If I

stretched, I could catch a glimpse of him. He was stuffed in a corner, but he had a view of the action.

"Sorry, Z," he said with a shake of his head. Even from where I was lying I could see that his fangs were out. "I'm just a guy and I didn't even get to watch you and Sarah do it last month."

"We were keeping Neil warm," I explained for the thousandth time. We certainly hadn't done it.

"Baby, you were naked with another girl in a big old bed. If Neil was there, I've blocked it from my memory," Daniel admitted in a husky voice. "All I remember is four pretty breasts rubbing together and both of you looking at me and begging me to join you."

I looked up at the smiling woman staring down at me and shook my head. "That was a fantasy of his, a product of his horny male imagination. I didn't sleep with Sarah…well, I slept with her but I didn't…" She slid her fingers down and gently played with my clitoris, parting my labia and rubbing with perfect pressure. I gasped. "Yeah, I didn't do that with her." I tried to get a little oxygen into my lungs. Girls really know where to touch other girls.

"I can teach you what she likes if you just let me out of these chains, sweetheart. I'll tell you this much. She likes it when you rub little circles," Daniel commented.

"Shut up, Daniel," I hissed even as I proved I really liked little circles.

"I'm sorry, baby," my vampire apologized. "It's just this is so much better than we expected. This isn't a bad place. We can relax here. She's not a bad person, Z. I need you to know, I'm doing this for us. If she plays with you a little longer, I think I might be able to cut through these chains with my dick."

The brunette threw her head back and laughed long and hard. "He's hilarious."

Her right leg rested on the lower half of my body. She was certainly a girl comfortable in her own skin.

"Yeah, he's a laugh riot," I said sarcastically but I was happy she'd stopped playing with me. My body apparently didn't care that she was female and not married to me. If she'd played a little longer, I would have gone off like a rocket. I blamed my husbands. When you've had that much amazing sex, your body gets conditioned to it.

I decided it was time to ask a few questions. Since I wasn't being tortured by a goblin and Daniel was with me, we might have a shot at getting out of this. "Who are you?"

"My name is Nim," she introduced herself. "The hot vamp over there told me your name is Z."

"Zoey," I corrected.

"That's pretty." She moved her thumb lightly across my lips. If she'd been a nasty old barbarian goblin I would have been tempted to bite her and set our relationship on a proper footing. I found myself strangely reluctant to hurt the dark-eyed girl who looked down at me with an amused fascination.

"So you bought me?" It wasn't the first time someone had tried to buy me. There were several vamps out there who had offered cash to Daniel for me. It was just the first time someone had succeeded.

"For a pretty penny, too," she admitted, wide eyed. "I've been saving up. I'm afraid I haven't found anyone over here who does it for me. I mean my boyfriend does, but the women here tend to be a little fierce. They're actually kind of scary, if you ask me. I like soft. There's one female but she isn't into girls. I guess she's my best friend. She actually has awful taste in men. Her last boyfriend was an asshole. You look like her. It was a bonus in my book."

I wasn't sure what that had to do with anything, but I nodded. "So you thought a slave could do it for you?"

She smiled brightly. "Oh, I made them describe you, but I knew the minute they said they had a human female that I was finally in luck. Human females are so sweet. The vampire was just icing on the cake. My boyfriend is going to love him."

Now it was my turn to smile as I heard Daniel swallow nervously. I'd been planning our escape but it just might have to wait an hour or two. Turnabout was fair play. My vampire had enjoyed my sexual servitude. It was only fair that I enjoy his. "Nim, I'm going to have to watch that."

"Wait just a minute now. I only knew about Nim," Daniel was saying.

Nim laughed, her lilting amusement an infectious thing. "He's not going to want to have sex with you, silly. I told you. We won't hurt either one of you." She brought her attention back to me.

"Though I don't personally see anything wrong with it. It would be hot. They would look good together, but every time I bring it up that I'd like to watch him with a lovely man, he just rolls his eyes like it's the stupidest thing ever."

"I know." I was rapidly getting altogether too comfortable with my captor. We had a lot in common. "I have two husbands and all I've ever managed to get them to do was kiss."

"That was not a kiss, Z." Daniel huffed, a sound filled with masculine indignation. "That was food. There was blood involved."

I smiled sweetly up at husband number one. "That's not the way I remember it. I seem to remember tongues and hard cocks rubbing together and the two of you begging me to join you."

"Two husbands, huh? I can't get the one man I have to marry me. It's the story of my life," Nim said with a little pout. "Is the other one as pretty as the vampire?"

I sighed at the thought of husband number two. "He's so hot. He's the filthiest man ever. The horniest one, too. I miss him already. He has the dirtiest mind ever created."

"I don't know about that. There's this guy in the Seelie *sithein* you should meet. So is he the one who sold you?" Nim asked the question with a great deal of sympathy.

I shook my head. "No, he would never have sold us. He loves us. That was his shitty ex who decided if she can't have him no one can. I'm in the Unseelie *sithein*, right?"

She nodded. "Yes. It's where we live although I should tell you, I'm not a faery. My boyfriend is…well, mostly."

That made sense. The Unseelie accepted pretty much everyone. The *sidhe* here would be halflings or simply *sidhe* who felt more comfortable with the Unseelie. "What are you? Are you human like me?"

"I'm a lot of things," she explained. "I started out as a nymph. That was a long time ago. I got into black magic for a while and became a powerful sorceress. I kind of stumbled into immortality, wandered the Earth plane for a while, fell in love, fell out, and now I'm here."

"Nim," a deep voice said from the doorway. "What is the meaning of this?"

Nim turned with a brilliant smile on her heart-shaped face. "Hey, lover, I've got a surprise for you. I found our third. You promised if I found a girl we both liked that I could have my threesome. Isn't she pretty?"

I looked up at the man, who had to be six two. He had a startlingly handsome face, though it bore some of the scars of battle. He wore brown leather trousers and an open-necked linen shirt. There was a sword on his belt. He had dark eyes that looked me over with the assessment of a connoisseur. His annoyance faded and those eyes heated up. "She's an excellent counterpoint to you, dearest. Is her hair red? That's very exotic. She's quite lovely. I worried when you said you wanted a third that I would end up fucking some cold Seelie bitch. She's obviously not Seelie and she doesn't look cold at all."

"She's not." Nim clapped her hands in happiness. "She's warm. We can sleep with her between us."

The man smiled affectionately at his girlfriend. "Well, my lover, if this is what you need, who am I to deny you? We can keep the girl."

"Lay one hand on her and I swear to god I will kill you," Daniel promised.

Daniel suddenly had the new guy's attention. The man's eyes turned from me to the vampire wrapped in the corner. Daniel struggled against his chains and his flesh was smoking again.

Nim frowned and faced Daniel as well. "Now, see, he was perfectly reasonable when I was playing with her. He was cheering me on. Please don't hurt yourself. He won't cause her pain. I promise. We're not like that. We just want to have a little fun. We'll let you watch if you like."

The new guy's eyes rolled but it was not from sarcasm. They rolled back and he became a different person entirely. When he spoke, his voice was deeper and smoother. It was a voice that could pull you in if you weren't careful. These eyes were way more interested in Daniel than me. "Nim, my dear, don't you know vampires tend to not share? He's been trying to trick you."

Nim glanced at Daniel. "Trick me?"

The man chuckled indulgently. "Yes. He was trying to trick you into releasing him, though I doubt he would have hurt you. He's an odd sort. He has very firm ideas of morality, and you triggered his kinder impulses. This one is his companion. Am I correct?"

For a moment there was silence as we waited. All I could hear was that dog barking again. The dark man narrowed his eyes as he looked at my vampire.

Daniel's voice was hesitant, as though he were responding not entirely of his own free will. "She is my companion. No. I do not share her. I was willing to go along with Nim in the hopes that she would free me and I could run with my wife."

Coal black eyes considered me carefully. "I thought so. Tell me something. Were you going to hurt Nim?"

Daniel immediately answered, his voice a rough monotone. "No. She's no threat. She's quite nice. I would have spared her life, but I would have taken my wife from here. I can talk all I like, but I don't want anyone but myself or my partner touching her. I suffered it because I thought she might take me out of the chains."

Well, that explained a lot. "Daniel, it's going to be okay."

Daniel didn't seem to hear me. All of his attention was on the new guy. "How did you know she's my companion?"

"She glows," he replied. "Of course, all living creatures glow for me, but her shine is quite different. She's luminous. She's rare. I'm sure her blood is exquisite for you. Don't be upset. Calm yourself, vampire. I have no intention of trying it for myself. I was merely making an observation. How many vampires did you kill to keep this one?"

"I've never fought a duel for her." Daniel had stopped fighting and was still, but in a way that made me wary. His entire body seemed to have gone limp. "No one would dare. If you choose to be the first, I'll be more than happy to fight you once you take these chains off."

There was a dark, seductive laugh. "I assure you, I don't need those chains to keep myself safe from you. Right now, consider them your protection." He turned back to his girlfriend. "So you bought me a vampire to play with."

She smiled and sat up on the bed, her eyes a playful invitation. "I thought you would like him. I lucked into it. I got the girl for me and

Roarke and the vampire for you, sweetie. I know they've become rare on the Earth plane."

"I would enjoy the female as well, Nim. Roarke isn't the only one who enjoys sex. I simply think we should think about using this one." He looked back to Daniel. "Vampires are rare indeed. I remember when there was an army of undead warriors. It couldn't last, of course, but it was something to see. You, my lover, have brought me something even better than a mere vampire."

"What is he?" Nim asked, curious.

Masculine lips turned up in a smile. "I think he's a king."

"Seriously?" Nim looked at Daniel with renewed interest.

"How do you know that?" I was deeply uncomfortable with the way that man stared at my husband. Very few people outside of vampire society understood what the word "king" meant in our world. This man seemed to grasp the term fully.

"I know everything about him, companion." He reached up and touched Daniel's face. I expected Daniel's fangs to flash, but he went unnaturally still. I didn't like the vacant look in his baby blue eyes. "I know he died in a vehicle seven years ago. You were his final thought before his human life ended and the first when his vampire life began. He has killed…oh, has he killed. He's a death machine, as all kings are. What's wrong with his heart?"

"How did you know?" I asked, my voice shaking a bit. "What are you doing to him?"

Danny was so still that I knew something was wrong. I struggled against the damn ropes holding me down. The man looked at me and there was no white left in his irises, just black orbs. I knew those eyes. I'd seen them before. They were emerald green when my husband's god took over and brown when the Hunter was present. There was only one other ascended god I knew of in either *sithein*. He was the one who terrified me. I stopped struggling because it wouldn't do me any good. I decided to see if Death had a heart.

"Please," I begged. "Please don't hurt him."

Arawn, the Welsh god of the Dead, turned to me and smiled.

Chapter Twenty-Five

"My Lord, I have word that there is a small party moving toward our position," a young man said from the doorway. He didn't seem concerned that his master had a naked woman tied to the bed or a chained vampire in the corner. He didn't give a damn that I'd been pleading for my husband's life.

"That will be Herne," Arawn explained shortly. "He's on his way to discuss our current situation in regards to the Seelie. He'll be joining us in our journey to the palace to meet with King Angus. See that his needs are met." The black-haired Lord of the Dead frowned down at his servant as there was another long volley of barking from outside. "Is there a reason the dogs are so loud?"

"It's not our hounds, My Lord." The servant wrung his hands in defeat. "There's a stray dog in the yard. I've tried everything I can think of to get the dog to go away, but he just comes back. He just stands out there looking at the house and barking."

"I'm sure Nim fed him at some point," Arawn said with a long-suffering sigh. "We'll never get rid of him now. Well, perhaps if you let our hounds out he'll be frightened off."

The servant nodded and left, closing the door behind him. I wasn't concerned with Arawn's animal control issues. I had much bigger problems.

"What did you do to him?" I strained to see my husband. His head was slumped forward now and he was still.

Arawn sat down on the bed. He was on one side of me and Nim on the other. Unlike his girlfriend, he was respectful enough to keep his eyes on my face. "He's only sleeping, companion, as he should be during the day. Even those with the power to daywalk must rest for a time. He was emotional. It cost him much to pretend to be all right with what Nim was doing to you."

Nim stiffened. "I didn't hurt her."

Arawn ignored her. "I gave him respite. He will wake when the sun goes down and he will feel more like himself. It will be no more than thirty minutes."

"We lost a whole day?" It had been night when Gilliana had taken us hostage and sent us into servitude. Every day we lost brought us closer to Devinshea being in battle and potentially killed. I was on a timer and it was moving fast. I had to find a way out of this cozy domestic situation I found myself in.

Nim smoothed back my hair. She seemed intent on calming me down. "It's all right, Zoey. Arawn won't hurt your vampire. As for losing a day, well, travel can be difficult. I know you had to come across the plains, and that is a long journey. Now you can rest and relax and know that I'll take care of you."

"Yes, you can relax and tell me what is wrong with the vampire's heart," Arawn commanded softly.

"So you can use it against him?"

Arawn shook his head and he and Nim shared a long look. "She's not very trusting."

Nim shrugged her slender shoulders. "She was sold into slavery. I suppose that could make you wary. Perhaps if I untied her she would believe me that we don't intend her harm."

Jet black eyes looked down at me and after a moment, he made his decision. "We're going to unbind you, companion. Behave yourself. I would prefer to not have to punish you." He sighed inwardly. "Yes, Roarke, I know you think it would be fun to spank her, but I have different objectives. There will be time for your games later. Can I trust you not to try anything?"

"For now," I agreed, wanting much to get the feeling back in my hands. I was willing to bide my time.

Herne was on his way. Hopefully he wasn't too pissed about the whole being-blamed-for-crimes-he-hadn't-committed thing. He knew who I was and that I wasn't a slave. Then, again, I knew the way the Hunter thought. He might advise Nim to wash her hands of the whole thing. She couldn't get into trouble if no one could find our bodies.

I was untied and finally able to sit up. My wrists ached and I wondered just how long Daniel had enjoyed watching Nim play with my unconscious body. Nim reached over to her nightstand and pulled out a jar of some kind of oil. She dabbed some on my wrists and began to rub away the chafing the heavy ropes had caused.

The Lord of all things Dead looked at me impatiently.

I was still wary. He obviously had powers over my husband that I never imagined possible. I hated the feeling. I wasn't used to Danny being vulnerable. Daniel was my Superman. I just hoped we hadn't walked into a whole mess of kryptonite. "How do I know you won't use the knowledge to harm him?"

"I'm merely curious." Arawn spoke evenly, as though we were talking about a simple science experiment. "I'm interested in all things dead. He's an amazing specimen. I'm afraid I always indulge my curiosity. If you refuse to tell me I'll simply open the vampire up and discover the truth for myself."

"Well, that makes me feel better," I spat at him while Nim threw him a dirty look.

"Don't scare my pet," Nim demanded.

"Yeah, don't scare her pet," I agreed. She was working on my feet now. I decided Arawn was serious and proceeded cautiously. "It's a control measure. It's a device filled with injectable silver. They had it surgically implanted on his heart shortly after he died and rose as vampire."

"'They' being the Council, I assume," Arawn murmured, looking at Daniel. "I've always been interested in the vampires. They're fascinating creatures. Their bodies are dead, only reanimated by the blood of those they feed upon. They're so much more interesting than other dead things. They have an entire society and laws that are different from the living. Most undead creatures are solitary, but the vampires have formed their own little world. Is that

Frenchman still in charge?"

I nodded. He was up to date on his politics. "Yes, Louis Marini still heads the Council. He placed the device on Danny's heart. If he wants to, he can push a button and that device will pump silver through his system."

"Very efficient," the death god said. "I suppose he wanted to keep the king from reaching his full potential while still using him as an asset. I never liked that Frenchman. He's arrogant and ambitious. I suppose the device has fail-safes."

I nodded and raised my voice because it didn't sound like the hounds were driving off that dog of Nim's. The barking had gotten louder. "If we try to extract the device, it will go off."

"Have you considered staying on this plane? I assume the detonator only works in close proximity."

Of course, I'd thought about it. We could be safe here but everyone on the Earth plane would end up under Marini's dominion. Daniel was the only one who could stop Marini. "We have people we care about back on the Earth plane. Marini has plans. That army of vampires you talked about, well, Marini wants to revisit the good old days. He's preparing for war, first against the other supernaturals and then the humans."

"Yet another reason to stay here," Arawn said reasonably.

"No." I'd had this argument in my head a thousand times. "We have to go back and we have to fight. I won't allow them to take my home and my people. We were given the tools and strength to fight back and we will damn well use them."

"And probably die in the process."

"Probably." At least we would go down together.

Nim crawled up the bed and kissed my cheek. Her soft hands tried to smooth the tension from my shoulders. "Now she doesn't have to. She can stay with us and we'll protect her and pamper her. Why should something so pretty have to fight?"

"Because she believes," Arawn said, and there was suddenly respect in his voice. "I wish you luck against the Frenchman. He's more formidable than he looks. You must solve the vampire's heart issue, though. It will be the death of him."

"He doesn't believe it." Dev and I took the issue more seriously than Danny.

A dark brow arched. "I am the Lord of Death. I can see all possible deaths for a person. Right now, if you continue on your course, the most likely event is the vampire dying from his heart exploding." Arawn reached out and touched my face lightly. I was surprised his touch was warm and not cold. I held still but it was hard. My skin tingled where he touched me. "His death leads to yours. You will die at Marini's hands, attempting to avenge your husband."

"She won't if she stays here," Nim insisted.

Arawn ignored her. "It's what I see. You must get that thing off his heart. It's an interesting quandary. I shall think on it for a while. Stop pawing the girl, Nim. She's obviously not a slave. There's been a mistake. The vampire is important. I can feel that and she's important as well."

Nim made a little huffing sound but did nothing to stop pawing me. As her "paws" were doing a damn fine job on my bunched up muscles, I didn't protest. When she was done there, my aching feet could use a good pawing, too.

I looked at the death lord and let my gratitude show. "Thank you. My husband will be grateful."

"I'm sure the vampire will," he commented.

"How about the other one?" Nim asked.

"Other one?" Her boyfriend looked at her.

Nim nodded as her eyes lit with righteous fire. "Yes, she has two husbands. Imagine that. She has two men willing to make a commitment. I didn't think there was even one out there with the guts to step up and push aside their issues to make the woman they love feel secure."

"Yes, yes, that's sad for you," a sarcastic voice said. When I looked up, the death lord's eyes looked human again. "Give a guy a chance, Nim."

"Roarke, you've had several hundred years of chances and Arawn many more before that." She pulled the sheet up, covering both of us.

"Hey, you don't have to do that," Roarke protested because he'd obviously liked the show.

"I've decided not to share," she said, hugging me to her. I kept my hands carefully at my sides. "Tell Arawn he can go to hell. He knows the way. I bought her and I'm keeping her. I'm keeping the vampire, too. He didn't like you boys, so he can just play with us girls."

"That's not fair, Nim," Roarke protested. "Why do I get punished when Arawn is an ass? Have I ever denied you anything?"

"That's just weird," I said because it was. Roarke and Arawn worked flawlessly together. It was a completely different relationship than my husband's with Bris. When I was in the presence of Bris, it was obvious and it took a little time for them to tag team out. Herne and the Hunter were extremely different. Roarke and Arawn were like two halves of a whole. Other than the deepness of their voices and the shift in the eyes, it was hard to tell who was who. Nim and Roarke were staring at me. "Sorry to interrupt the relationship fight, but you're good with the whole ascended god thing."

Nim looked at me, surprised. "You're well informed. I was actually wondering how I was going to explain it all to you. I thought you would be a little freaked out by the two souls in one body thing."

I smiled an intimate smile, thinking of Dev and the ever-horny, gentle Bris. "I know one. He's over on the Seelie side."

Nim shot her boyfriend a confused look. "I thought it was just you and Herne."

Roarke shook his head. "Didn't you hear? Dev Quinn ascended. He took the fertility god Bris into his body. It's why we're in this mess. His brand new goddess lost their babe and they blamed Herne."

But Nim wasn't interested in war talk. Her violet eyes narrowed. "You asked if you had ever denied me anything. There's one. Dev Quinn. You denied me him. He was perfectly willing to join us and you said no."

I smiled and said a little hallelujah. I had found one female who my husband hadn't slept with. It was truly a miracle.

"You know why I wouldn't do that," Roarke replied. "Arawn and I both thought it was a bad idea. He is a Green Man. You sleep with him and you'll never want to go back. We'd never get him out of our bed."

I heard Daniel's husky laugh. "Good call, man. Once he's in, he is hell to get out. I haven't managed it yet. I've pretty much given up hope of ever kicking his ass out of our bed."

Arawn was back suddenly, his dark eyes turning. He stood and walked to the vampire. "You're strong. You should be out for at least another twenty minutes."

"I will not leave my companion alone. If you put me under again I'll fight my way out," Daniel swore, struggling against the need to sleep with everything he had. "Why are you talking about Dev? Is he here? Did he come for us?" His question was hopeful, and he shot a look my way.

"No, baby," I said with a frown, knowing exactly how Danny felt. "He probably still thinks we'll be back any minute. He's going to get worried soon. He'll be disappointed that he missed my sexual servitude."

"I'll describe it for him in vivid detail," Danny promised with a slight smile. "I'll probably exaggerate, too. He would do the same for me."

Arawn paled. He turned his head between me and Daniel and he looked a little ill as he put things together. "Oh, shit."

"So you know Dev?" Nim grinned, her face showing her great affection. "He and his nasty brother spent a year here. He was just delicious. He's the filthiest guy ever. Whoever you're married to could learn a thing or two from him."

"Nim, back away from Her Grace," Arawn ordered.

"Her name is Zoey, Arawn," Nim corrected.

I smiled up at the death lord, loving the fact that I briefly had the upper hand. "I never blamed Herne. He's an asshole who tried to use me as ogre bait, but he had nothing to do with me losing my baby."

"Goddess, Nim, what have you done?" Arawn asked.

Nim looked at me, finally catching up. "She's Dev's goddess? Well, that's unfair. I finally find a girl and she's unavailable. Or is she? I bet Devinshea wouldn't mind us playing around as long as he got to watch."

"He would mind," Daniel growled.

"You are missing the point, Nim." Roarke had taken back over. Apparently death gods didn't do patience well. "Think about it for a second. We're on the verge of war with the Seelie. You're currently in bed with a Seelie royal and it wasn't her idea. You bought the High Priest's goddess and made her your sex slave."

Nim chewed her lower lip. "Put like that it does sound bad. I didn't mean to start a war. I was just a little horny."

I laughed long and hard because I was pretty comfortable with the fact that these two probably wouldn't kill us. I still didn't like the way that old death god looked at Danny, but I thought I could handle the other two. "It's not your fault, Nim. I totally blame Gilliana."

Now there were three dogs barking. Someone had unleashed the hounds. At first it sounded like a fight but after a minute the barking and growls changed.

"I should have known something was wrong," Nim complained, standing up. Roarke held out a robe and she slid it on. "I should have been charged way more for smuggling someone off the Earth plane. Isn't Gilliana the Duke of Ain's daughter?"

I could feel my face getting hard at the thought of that bitch. "She is. She's also the one responsible for our brief foray into servitude. She gave us to whoever sold us to you. Her father is behind everything, including my miscarriage."

"I suppose no one on the Seelie side believes this?" Nim asked.

Daniel took that one. "The duke has been careful. He's covered his tracks and used the Seelies' prejudice against them. They're more than willing to believe that the Unseelie killed our baby out of jealousy."

"Jealousy of what?" Nim shook her head, obviously confused. "If Devinshea has ascended and is proving his fertility powers, how can that be bad? The child might have been a fertility god in his or her own right. Why would we be jealous of that?"

Daniel sighed. "Because it is a Seelie power. Some think to keep Dev's power strictly to the Seelie side."

"The priest would never do that," Roarke said firmly.

"Is that what everyone believes here?" I wondered if the mistrust went both ways.

Nim and Roarke exchanged a glance before Roarke explained. "Everyone who knows Dev understands that he takes his duties seriously. He wouldn't deny the Unseelie fertility."

"But…" I started because there was a big old but coming.

"The problem is with his brother." Nim's frown told me she didn't like the prince. "He came over and told us all about how Dev would ignore the temple on the Unseelie side if we didn't pledge fealty and submit to Seelie demands."

"Yeah," Danny said. "That sounds like Declan. Uhmm, now that we've ascertained Z and I aren't slaves, could I get out of the uncomfortable, burning my flesh, silver chains?"

Nim nodded and started toward him. "Of course, sugar. I'll have you out in no time. I'll sadly find something for Zoey to wear. I didn't buy anything for you because I planned to keep you naked."

"Good to know." I clung to my sheet.

Arawn made a sudden appearance. He stayed Nim's hand. "Vampires are dangerous creatures, my love. You have offended him greatly."

"I can forgive her," Daniel said, his voice slightly surly. "She rubbed my wife's boobs and got me hot as hell. At the end of the day, she would have taken no for an answer. I have no intentions of harming Nim. You're an entirely different story."

Arawn stared at Daniel and then gave him an arrogant smile. "Go on then, Nim. He's telling the truth. He means you no harm. As for me, we shall see."

"Danny," I started. "We need them. They're the only ones who can help us."

Roarke drifted back. "Help you how?"

"We need to stop this war," I said. "We need to get back to Miria and Dev and tell them everything."

"That's easier said than done, Your Grace." Nim began to carefully unwind Daniel's chains. I got up, wrapping the sheet around me to help.

"We have to do it." I ran my hands through Daniel's sandy, slightly overgrown hair. When the chains were off, I sat down in his lap and held him. Daniel's previous thoughts of beating the shit out of Arawn took a back seat to hugging me tightly as the dogs' barking reached a crescendo. Daniel put his ear right over my heart and sighed.

"What a mess." Roarke ran a frustrated hand through his long, dark hair. He walked over to the window and sighed heavily. "What is the use of having hell hounds if they make friends with every stray to come through?" He turned on Nim. "This is your fault. I tried to train them but no, Nim knew better. Nim just had to give them treats and toys to play with. Now we can't even scare off a single big white dog."

I looked up from Daniel's lap. "Did you say white dog?"

Daniel and I were at the window, shoving Roarke out of the way. We looked down because apparently we were on the second floor.

"Neil!" I yelled at that gorgeous ball of white fur.

Neil stopped his frolicking with the enormous black hell hounds and when he looked up, he changed.

"Hey, Z," he yelled up. "How's the whole slavery thing working out?"

"So far, so good. Herne's on his way. Why don't you come in and we can wait for him." If anyone could get us out of the Unseelie *sithein*, it was Herne. I didn't trust anyone on the Seelie side outside of our own household. Who knew how many were willing to follow the Duke of Ain's lead?

"I don't know about the Hunter," Neil said, his face concerned. "But what are we going to do about the army on its way here?"

Roarke pushed his way in so he had a view to the outside. There in the distance we could see a group walking in perfect lockstep, their heavy weapons held high on their meaty shoulders. Even from where I stood, I could see the way their caps glistened.

"Nim, pack a small bag," Roarke said calmly but I could hear the fear in his voice. "King Angus has sent the red caps. They're coming to execute us."

Chapter Twenty-Six

"Why would the king want to execute you?" I wasn't able to take my eyes off the sight of the red caps moving our way. They were still in the distance but moved closer every minute we stayed. It had taken us some time to get dressed and for Nim to deal with her servants and I was eager to put some distance between us and our executioners.

Red caps are a specialized type of goblin. They tend to guard things but didn't mind a little execution duty. Like most goblins, the red caps were smallish with grotesque features and little hair on their heads. The red caps got their names from their unusual choice of head gear. On the top of each goblin head sat what looked like a red skull cap. It was the scalp of the red cap's first victim. In the ritual that makes a goblin a red cap, the goblin kills, scalps his victim, and ceremoniously covers his head with the bloody scalp. The newly minted red cap must then kill to keep his cap covered with fresh blood. If the cap dries out, the red cap is executed for not keeping up his end of the bargain.

"Oh, I don't know, Your Grace. It could be just about anything," Roarke said, looking me up and down pointedly. He'd been short tempered since realizing he was about to be executed. Arawn seemed much calmer about the whole thing but that might have been a byproduct of his immortality. While Roarke was technically immortal, he could still be killed if someone, a red cap for example, cut his head off or chopped him into enough small pieces.

"How would they already know where I am? It can't possibly have gotten back to the Seelie that I was taken prisoner yet." It wasn't like I'd updated my Facebook status. *Zoey is…enjoying a little girl time with her new master.*

Nim, who was hurrying about the room shoving items in a small pack, looked up with a fierce frown on her face. "It was that bastard Con. He's always looking to make a quick buck and he's the one who offered me use of your lovely body. I should never have trusted him. I should have known something was up. You would think after all the years I've lived, after all the things I've seen that I would be wary but no, Nim just keeps trucking on like no one ever betrayed her."

Arawn made a sudden appearance at Nim's side. He stopped her and forced her chin up. He leaned down briefly, placing a light kiss on her lips. "I would have you no other way, my love. Your nature gets us in trouble from time to time, but I wouldn't change an inch of you." He turned back to the rest of us, his calm manner somewhat reassuring. "We must assume that this is all a part of their plan and that Con is working with the duke. They would immediately give both palaces the information in an attempt to create utter chaos and move the war forward."

"We knew he had to have help from this side to have gotten the ogre over," I pointed out. While Nim had fluttered around getting ready to flee, I had told them everything we'd learned about the traitors. I hoped the Unseelie would be more open to the fact that someone on their side of the *sithein* might be corrupt.

Arawn nodded shortly. "Yes, it fits. Con is a close advisor to the king. He has many who are loyal to him. He would have been tasked with finding you and bringing you to the palace. Angus trusts him as much as he trusts anyone. I'm certain Angus intends to give you back to your husband in a show of cooperation he hopes would lead us away from war."

"But we won't make it to the palace," Daniel said seriously as he looked out over the field.

"No," Arawn agreed. "The red caps are guards, but they're also killers. All Con had to do is buy one's loyalty. The minute he kills, the rest will be pulled into bloodlust. We will all be dead and Angus will be blamed. The Seelies will attack without worry."

"Well, all we have to do is evade the red caps for a little while." I tried to put a positive spin on things. "My guard is already on his way to the Seelie palace to tell my husband what happened."

There was no way Lee wouldn't get to Dev.

Neil frowned from his comfortable seat on a chair. He was dressed in too-big clothes and looked even younger than his twenty-three years. The two *Cŵn Annwn* sat on either side of him, their enormous black tongues panting. "I don't think that's going to help the situation, Z. It wasn't like we overheard the conversation with Gilliana. We stayed where we were until Lee could move safely. When he didn't come, we climbed down and found the camp deserted and trashed. Your clothes were torn up. They left the Goddess Chain behind, I guess so there wouldn't be any question who they had taken. Lee thought the worst. We tracked your scent straight to the door of the Unseelie *sithein*."

"Why didn't Lee come after us?" Daniel asked, his voice tight. He was getting ready for a fight and he was still feeling the tension from knowing Arawn had power over him. I know my husband. He didn't like feeling vulnerable.

Neil frowned because he knew that Daniel would rather have Lee here than him. "Lee is faster. We decided he should get to the palace and tell Dev so he could mount a rescue. We had no idea what had happened to you except that someone had taken you both over here. It seemed prudent to get help."

Daniel grunted. It wasn't what he would have done, but it made sense.

"So all Devinshea is going to know is that his goddess was taken to our *sithein* without her clothes," Roarke said, not happy with the prospect. "He won't mount a rescue. It would be far too risky and his mother and brother would never allow him to come over here. He will push forward with the war."

"And no doubt that was their plan all along." I was a little worried that this would work out all too well for the bad guys. Though I thought Dev might fool them all. He loved me. He deeply cared for Daniel. It might kill him to not know where we were. Still, he'd allowed us to leave without him in the first place. "I love my husband, but he's being irrational. He was heartbroken over the loss of our child. We have to find a way to get to him and tell him what we know."

"Nim," Roarke shouted. "Are you ready yet? They aren't getting any farther away."

Nim appeared in the doorway. She was dressed in some sort of animal skin trousers and a thin black shirt. "Let's go. I told the servants to run." Nim had been concerned with her servants being captured and tortured by the red caps. It was another plus for the woman in my books.

I was dressed in one of Arawn/Roarke's shirts. It was enormous, but Nim was slender and I was not. My curves wouldn't be fitting into any of her clothes. I looked down at my bare feet. The forest was going to be hard on them.

"Don't worry, baby," Daniel said, picking me. "Your feet won't touch the ground. Let's move. We need to get to the palace as soon as possible. Point me in the right direction and I'll fly me and Z."

"It won't work," Nim said grimly. "The entire *sithein* is plagued by eddy winds. Unless you know how to ride an eddy wind, we're walking. I can't and neither Roarke nor Arawn can."

Daniel rolled his eyes and slapped his head like he should have known something. "That explains the mountain. It was surrounded by eddy winds. I have no idea how to catch one much less ride one. Sorry, Z, we're walking. We should get moving."

"Vampire," Arawn said suddenly. "You should nourish yourself. I can feel your hunger."

"It can wait until she's safe." Daniel started down the stairs.

I heard the others following. I glanced about, taking in my surroundings. It was a small but well-appointed *brugh*. If I had to guess I would say it was a vacation house. They probably normally lived at the palace, as all the ascended gods did. The servants had taken Nim's orders to heart. They appeared to have fled. The cabin was quiet as we made our way through.

"The door is to the left," Nim called out behind us.

Daniel took a hard left and then he was kicking the door open, allowing the night in. He strode out with Neil following hard behind him. Nim and Roarke ran to keep up as we made it to the yard. We needed to make it to the forest where our small party would have the advantage over the heavily armed troops. They wouldn't be able to travel as quickly as we could. Daniel began running to the left, but Neil stopped him with a decisive pull on his shoulder.

"Stop," Neil yelled, frustrated that Daniel wasn't letting him go first. It was a reversal of everything we'd done before. In the past, Danny and I did nothing during a job without Neil's senses telling us it was all right to continue. The change was obviously pissing Neil off. "Will you give me a second? I smell something. It's coming from that direction." Neil pointed to the direction we were about to head.

"Watch out for the advance guard!" Nim yelled as she and Roarke made it out the door. "They always send a couple ahead of the full troops."

The red caps came into view. They carried iron pikes in their hands and the minute they saw us, an unholy gleam lit their dark eyes. They took in the scene in front of them, quick to recognize their quarry.

"By the order of King Angus, you will give us aid, My Lord. We seek Her Grace, the wife of the Seelie High Priest," one said, his voice harsher than sandpaper. "Surrender her and we shall be satisfied."

"No you won't," Nim said, huffing her disbelief.

The three smiled, their grins creepy and bloodthirsty. "No," the one said. "We won't."

Their eyes told the tale. They had full orders to execute Nim and Roarke and probably to parade the traitors' heads through the *sithein* as they brought me to the king's palace.

They began to move forward, their movements a testament to long training and discipline.

"Catch her," Daniel demanded as I found myself tossed into the air.

Neil moved gracefully under me, and I was grateful for his physical prowess as he made sure I didn't hit the ground.

Daniel struck quickly. His legs kicked out, attempting to

dislodge the goblins from their traditional weapons. He hit one hard, his foot meeting with the goblin's chins. The red cap's head flew back and his body followed, but the other two paid no attention to their weakened comrade. They were far too busy shoving their cold iron weapons into my vampire's body. One of the pikes entered Daniel's chest and the other met his belly. I was shocked not at the blood but the lack of it. Daniel's body bled weakly, and I remembered he hadn't fed the day before. Even a single day could weaken him.

"Neil, you have to help him," I said even as he was putting me down, having already determined the same thing.

Neil tossed his shirt over his head and before it had time to hit the ground, he changed and howled, calling the *Cŵn Annwn* to his aid. The enormous dogs growled and leapt into the fray. Daniel pulled the pikes out of his body, tossing one behind him and keeping the other in his hand. He wielded it against the red cap closest to him. The small, fierce goblins were more wary now as three canines approached with deadly hunger in their eyes.

Daniel surged forward, catching a red cap on his pike and shoving the cold iron home through the goblin's chest. He hauled his prey high into the air, letting gravity work its magic as the red cap fell forward, impaled on the iron. Blood dripped from his mouth and Daniel tossed the fallen foe aside.

Neil and the hell hounds moved in on the last two. They chose their targets and pounced carefully. The hell hounds gleefully tore apart the goblin, reveling in the blood and gore. The final red cap saw the writing on the wall and began to back up. He left his weapon behind and started to flee. Neil began to give chase, but Daniel called him back. The werewolf changed and looked at his former master curiously.

"It won't do any good," Daniel said, pain evident in his voice. He stumbled a bit as he walked back toward me, and I could see the blood on his clothes. He'd lost blood he couldn't afford to lose. Daniel had gotten used to a free blood supply. Most nights Daniel fed from both Devinshea and me. He'd been meeting only half his need with me the past few nights and had nothing at all the night before. "The rest will come anyway. We need to get away."

Arawn stepped forward. "The vampire is right, but there is something I can do to aid our escape." The death lord looked down at the two fallen goblins. He pointed to the one Daniel had impaled. "This one is still viable. His heart is beating. Nim, do you have a knife?"

"Of course," the brunette said as if the answer should have been obvious. She pulled a long knife out of her pack and handed it to her lover.

Arawn did not hesitate. He brought the knife down on the goblin's neck with brutal force, neatly separating the body from the head. He smiled down, satisfied with his work. "That's better." He looked to the hounds and whistled sharply. They turned their heads and ran back to their master, muzzles covered in blood. "Good job, boys."

Nim frowned as she came to stand beside me. "This part is creepy."

Daniel staggered his way back to me as Arawn held his hands out, and I felt a chill permeate the courtyard, a wave of cold that made me shiver. The leftover body parts of the ex-goblins began to quiver and shake in a way that dead body parts just shouldn't. The body stood up, not seeming to care that it had a pike through it or that its head was staring up at it from two feet away. The parts the dogs had left whole were also doing their best to get themselves upright.

I helped Danny remain standing and looked at Neil as he changed and got back into his clothes. We watched as the Lord of the Dead proved his mastery. The former goblins were joined by a couple of skeletons that looked to have clawed their way from the ground.

Nim rolled her eyes as she stared at a corpse with a little meat still hanging on the bones. "Yuck. They'll be coming here for days. I'm not cleaning this up, Arawn. You can do it yourself."

Arawn smiled, satisfied with his work. "You will block our retreat," he commanded his small army of the dead. He closed his eyes and even I could feel he was sending that cold magic out from him. "You will fight the red caps. Delay them any way you can."

I felt Daniel shake and my arms tightened around him. "You can feel that?"

Danny nodded shortly, trying to concentrate. "It's taking everything I have to not join them, Z. He can take me over. He can make me do whatever he wants."

I shot a quick glance at Neil, who knew exactly what that felt like having experienced it at Daniel's hands before. I expected at least a little hint of satisfaction that the man who had caused him to feel this way was getting well acquainted with the experience. He simply looked at me and came to Daniel's other side. He pulled Daniel's arm around his shoulder and gave his support.

Daniel leaned against Neil. He took a deep breath, his eyes tight with strain. "Neil, I am sorry. I didn't understand what I was doing. Not really. Could you forgive me?" The question was asked in a calm voice but I knew Daniel well. He was worried about the answer.

Neil simply nodded. "I promise I won't leave like that again. I'll stay and fight it out with you, but I won't leave."

I hugged Daniel's side as Nim and Arawn turned back to us. Nim frowned at Daniel. "He looks sick."

"He's fighting," the death lord replied. "He's strong but he hasn't fed. It would be easier for him to resist the effects if he'd properly fed."

"When she's safe," Daniel insisted.

Arawn's eyes narrowed. "I could force you."

"Then you'll fight all of us." There was a dark growl behind Neil's words.

"As you wish." He shrugged as though he didn't care either way. "But you should know that my concern is Nim. If your weakness threatens her in any way, I'll do what is necessary."

Nim shook her head. "He'll be fine. We just need to get to Chima's. We can make it there and the red caps wouldn't dare enter her territory."

We made for the forest even as I heard the rumble of the red caps' approach. Daniel walked on his own and picked up speed as he forced himself to move. I hurried to keep up with him and hoped this Chima person's house wasn't too far away.

Chapter Twenty-Seven

There's a reason most people who choose to hike through the forest wear pants. Pants are helpful when tromping through the brush. When one wears pants, even lightweight pants, one's legs tend to not get cut up and scraped by the aforementioned brush. Shoes are helpful as well. Shoes mean your feet don't get cut up when your hungry vampire gets driven to distraction by the blood welling up on your legs from not wearing pants. When your now surly vampire has to get downwind of you so he no longer smells those little tiny cuts and scrapes, you're left to walk along the forest floor without shoes.

I'm pretty sure Eve ate the apple so she could get a pair of boots.

"Are you okay, Z?" My surly vampire tossed back over his shoulder as he forced us through the forest at a brutal pace.

"I'm fine," I assured him from the back of the pack.

Neil was just a little ahead of me, walking along with the red-eyed hell hounds. Arawn and Nim kept pace with Daniel so they could guide him to the house we were attempting to get to. Arawn kept praising Daniel for his strength and his ability to function on little blood. No one mentioned the fact that my tummy was growling, too. I'd gone just as long without food as the vamp, but no one complimented my stamina. It might have had something to do with the unholy amount of whining I'd been doing, but it was true.

"We are almost there, Your Grace," Arawn announced and my hopes for a ham sandwich went up.

"That's great," I said with a happy smile.

"Just another hour or so." Arawn proved he had no idea what the word "almost" meant.

I growled, causing Neil to giggle a little.

"Do you need a lift, Z?" he asked, offering me a piggyback ride.

"No." Though I had new scrapes opening regularly, I would heal quickly. Daniel's blood would see to it. I wanted Neil ready to jump into action if he had to. I didn't want him to worry about me.

As we passed through a particularly thick part of the forest, I found another problem with my wardrobe. When a pissed-off ascended god plucks you from the forest floor and hauls your body up to his weird tree house, you don't want to be going commando.

I was happy the sleeves to Arawn's shirt were well made because one minute I was trudging along, grousing in my head about how much I hated nature, and the next I was hauled up by the neck of the shirt. Before I could scream, a hand covered my mouth and I felt cold iron at my neck.

"Keep quiet, Your Grace," the Hunter's voice demanded in my ear as he pulled me close to his body. He shifted, finding a better balance on the massive tree limb we were standing on. "I don't have any problem using this on you." He shoved his free hand into his pocket and dropped something that looked like sand to the ground where I had been. Then his arm wrapped underneath my breasts and he stood on the tree's wide limb with far more surety than I would have had. "If you scream, I will gut you, do you understand? We can go to my place and settle our differences or I can kill you here. I've already been convicted of the crime, so I have no issues making that a reality. If you agree, nod."

I wasn't completely sure if I was agreeing to not scream or if I was giving the Hunter permission to horribly murder me. Either way, he was going to do what he wanted. I nodded and his hand left my mouth.

"I didn't…" I began in a quiet voice.

The knife immediately went back at my throat. "Not a word."

I nodded again even as I heard Neil call my name. The Hunter held me roughly against his body and began to climb up the tree with a strength that might have matched Daniel's. He was graceful and agile as he moved through the tree, never once showing that my added weight slowed him down for an instant.

"Where the hell did she go?" Daniel asked, panic tingeing his voice.

"I don't know." Neil's voice was starting to fade the higher we went. "She was right there."

The Hunter moved silently, his weight making almost no movement as he sprang from branch to branch. I heard my husband and best friend frantically trying to find me but the sound was farther away now. The forest here was lush, with ancient trees that seemed to go on for miles. I was surrounded, my world doused in the blanket of leaves the trees made. I worried that the Hunter might be planning to take me high up in the canopy and then drop me on my head, but after a harrowing couple of minutes, we reached an odd structure.

It was a box in the air. As the Hunter hauled me into his little room in the trees, I saw that it was sparse but comfortable. There was a chair and a pallet and a single oil lamp providing a small amount of light. The only other things in the space were weapons and a canteen. I finally realized this wasn't a tree house. This was a high hide. The Hunter used it to hunt.

I was tossed on the floor of the structure and the Hunter stood over me. I had to scramble so my hoo-ha wasn't on full display. The man hadn't liked to see my limbs. I didn't want to find out what he thought of girls who didn't wear panties.

"Whatever you are thinking I did, Hunter, think again." I got to my knees because I wasn't going to let him intimidate me.

He pushed me down again and I got my first real glimpse at the knife he had held to my throat. It was enormous and wicked sharp. I quickly rethought my stance on being intimidated. "I've been kicked from my home for treason, Your Grace. I've been told that I will be executed and the Seelie wish to use a spell to not only kill my host but to trap me."

So they were serious about punishing him. I could bet Dev was behind that one. "I had nothing to do with that."

"Oh, I disagree," he returned flatly. "I was convicted of crimes against you."

"I told Declan and my husband that I didn't believe you had anything to do with it."

"I'm sure you protested my innocence mightily." He bit out his words with a sarcasm I hadn't thought him capable of. "I'm sure that you cried out my innocence to all who could hear."

"No," I said, remembering those terrible days. "I told Dev what I believed and then I went back to bed because I didn't care. I didn't care about you, I didn't care about him. I didn't give a damn that the world was falling apart around me. I only cared that my child was gone. If that's my crime then you should punish me for it because I admit to it willingly."

My admission seemed to deflate a bit of the Hunter's rage. "I was sorry to hear about your loss." He was quiet for a moment and then finally went to sit in the chair. "Did you truly tell Devinshea I had nothing to do with this atrocity?"

"I did," I replied, relaxing a little bit. "I told Declan as well, but he had a confession and that was all he needed. The man who gave me the tea confessed to being your accomplice."

"It only proves that the Seelie know nothing about us." Herne made his first appearance of the night and the minute the Hunter gave him the body, I knew the real threat had passed. "We wouldn't stoop so low as to spike a pregnant woman's tea with a curse. We would carve the babe from your belly."

"Yes, that's much better."

"You take my meaning," Herne said impatiently. "The Unseelie are a direct people. We would strike hard and with great violence. We would proclaim our crime. This has Seelie betrayal written all over it. They have put Angus in a terrible position. Now I hear that Arawn is wanted for questioning in your kidnapping."

"Oh, that was Nim," I corrected. "She bought me. She wanted a little girl-on-girl action."

"Really?" Herne asked, his eyes lighting up. "Did she get some?" His eyes rolled and the Hunter looked at me, shaking his head. "Forgive my host. He thinks of only one thing. So the traitor has managed to force Angus's greatest allies into hiding right before the war. It's clever. How can I be sure that overindulged idiot Miria calls her heir isn't behind this?"

It was a reasonable assumption. Declan, as far as the Unseelie knew, hated them and was capable of anything. "I have proof that the Duke of Ain is behind everything and is working with someone named Con."

"Bastard," the Hunter growled. "I should have known. Con has been plotting for years to move up in the court. He always speaks ill of Arawn and me to the king. He tried to convince the king that ascended gods couldn't be trusted, that we would seek to overthrow him someday in order to rule as we did when we were corporeal."

I nodded. "It's a good play. I take it Angus hasn't bitten until now."

"He has no choice at this point," the Hunter admitted. "If he wars with Miria, we most likely lose any chance we had at Devinshea performing his duties as our priest. The nobles over here will revolt. If he concedes, we come under Seelie domination and then the nobles revolt. We cannot win."

"Why didn't you call a hunt down on me?" If he had truly believed I'd called him a traitor, he could call for the hunt to execute me. It was his right. I was a royal and owed him honesty.

"It's a good thing I did not. Do you think the Wild Hunt is to be used in this manner? It's a serious thing. Had I called a hunt down on your head, I would have found it coming after me."

"Because I didn't commit the crime you accused me of," I reasoned.

He nodded. "It's a great responsibility. It's not to be taken lightly."

"Why not just call a hunt down on the duke?" I sat up straight. "I'll call it. I have the right. I have no fears that the hunt will turn on me."

He reached out and put a finger to my lips. "Hush, Your Grace. You have the right but this isn't the time. You must stand in a space with both me and the Duke of Ain and look at him when you make your accusations. You must then request a hunt of me. It would be best, however, if you allow your husband to call the hunt or the queen herself. It is not right or fair, but the Seelie will be forced to accept the sentence of the hunt if it comes from them."

I didn't care who said the words as long the Duke of Ain and his daughter met with justice. I nodded my head in agreement. "Will calling a hunt stop the war?"

The Hunter sat back in his chair and took a long swill from his canteen. "It's important to stop the war before it begins, Zoey. Once the battle is on, I can't call the hunt until the fighting stops. It's too confusing. I won't risk everyone there. We must press on and take this information to the king. Perhaps with you in my custody, he'll at least take the time to listen." He leaned the chair back and pointed to the pallet on the floor. "Take the bed. We'll sleep for an hour or two and then press on to the palace."

My eyes widened. "I can't do that. Danny and my wolf are down there waiting for me. So are Arawn and Nim. I need to get back to them and let them know what we're doing."

"No. We can move faster on our own. The vampire will slow us down. Don't worry. They cannot find us here. I left a special powder that will mask our scent. To the werewolf's senses, your trail will stop cold where I picked you up."

Maybe that would work on Neil, but it wouldn't with my husband. "Daniel won't give up that easily and we share blood. He can sense me without his nose."

Sure enough, even as I said the words, a clawed hand gained a hold on the floor of the high hide. Daniel pulled himself up with one arm. He crawled into the small room, and I suddenly knew I was dealing with that part of Daniel that was pure vampire. His hair was unruly and his eyes wild as he took in the scene.

I started to get up and go to him when I noticed another person climbing in, following Daniel's ascent. Arawn pulled himself up and then leaned back to lend Nim a hand.

"How did you find us?" The Hunter got out of his chair. He looked at the hungry vampire, and for the first time I saw he had survival instincts as well as predatory ones. "Now, vampire, I have not harmed your mate." His hands went behind him to his weapons cache and he felt around for something.

"It's true, Danny. I'm fine." Staying calm and even was the way to deal with Daniel when he was in this state. This was when he typically started throwing large objects around.

"He took you from me," Daniel said in that low growl that let me know he was close to losing control.

"He just wanted to talk."

"He tried to hide you from me." He started to slowly move toward his quarry. I moved quickly to place myself between them. "Move, companion. I mean to kill him and you cannot stop me. He took what belongs to me and I won't abide it."

"You promised Dev," I said quickly, hoping to appeal to his friendship with Dev. They were partners. They tried to always keep their promises. "You told Dev you wouldn't jump the Hunter without him."

"They were going to jump me?" The Hunter actually took a step back.

"The whole ogre bait thing," I threw over my shoulder. "You don't want to disappoint Devinshea. He belongs to you, too. You owe him."

It was the way it worked for Daniel. Deep in his primitive heart he truly believed we belonged to him. We were his precious blood. We fed him and gave him love and companionship, but it was a two-way street. He owed us. He protected us with everything he had. He was honest and faithful to us.

"He will forgive me," Daniel decided and his fangs were full as he started to move me out of the way.

Arawn placed a hand on his shoulder and Daniel ceased his movement. He stood still in the death god's grip. "Your companion may not be able to stop you, vampire, but I can. You're not thinking properly."

"Let him go." I hated the blank look on Daniel's face. "Don't do this to him."

"He was going to kill the Hunter. We need him," Arawn explained. "The vampire isn't rational because he chose not to feed. He must correct that mistake or I shall have to deal with him. His stubbornness is jeopardizing all of us."

"I can get him to feed." I looked back at the Hunter. "Give me a knife." He passed me one even as he watched Daniel warily. I looked over as Neil finally made an appearance. "Nice of you to join us."

"It's a long way up. Is Daniel all right?" Neil asked, concern stark on his face as he looked at Daniel's blank eyes.

I shook my head and glared at Arawn. "If you kill him, I won't help you. I'll let you burn. Let him go and I'll get my husband to feed."

Before Arawn could take his hand off of him, I made a shallow cut across my chest, pulling the shirt open so Daniel wouldn't be able to miss the sight.

When Danny came out of his stupor, he started moving toward the Hunter as though he'd never stopped. Then he caught my scent. His head snapped around and suddenly he was hunting me. I heard Nim's gasp as she watched the scene with great curiosity. There wasn't a lot of space to begin with and now there were a couple too many people with us. I moved toward the small pallet and sat myself down, watching as Daniel moved close to me. He looked ready to pounce, but I ran my finger along the cut and offered it to him, taking away his need to force me.

The vampire went down on his knees and sucked my finger into his mouth, his tongue whirling gratefully around the blood. He leaned over when he was done and ran his tongue along the cut, murmuring his appreciation. "Mine."

"Yes, Daniel." I did everything I could to soothe him, to reassure him. "I'm yours."

I let him pull me and push me until I was in his lap. My arms and legs wrapped around him, my throat pressed to his adoring mouth as he pulled me in. I didn't care about the others who were watching. I only cared that I could feed him. I only knew that I could nourish and protect him. I was his and it was heavenly.

I floated back to myself as Daniel held me close, licking long strokes along my neck and telling me how much he loved me.

"Impressive, companion." The death lord pulled me from that warm cocoon Daniel had wrapped me in. "He was far gone. It should have been a brutal experience, but you turned his violent impulses to gentleness."

"It isn't hard when you know what to do." I ran my hands through Daniel's hair.

"He loves her," Neil explained. "If he is given any kind of a choice, he'll always choose her pleasure over his base instincts."

Nim looked down at us with a tiny smile on her pixie face. "I want a vampire to bite me, Arawn. It looks like fun."

Arawn's smile was indulgent. "I'm sure if we survive the next few hours that Zoey would be happy to find a vampire to bite you, dear. You'll more than likely find the experience pleasurable, and I would like to watch you."

Daniel pulled away from me slightly. "Thank you, Z."

"Do you feel better?" I asked, searching his face.

He leaned over and kissed me. "I'll feel better when we're away from this place. I feel stronger though. The death lord won't need to kill me. I do want you to change your clothes as soon as possible. I don't like you smelling like another man."

"Then we should get moving," Nim said cheerfully. "Chima will have lots of clothes for Zoey to wear. She's close to your build. She's probably at the palace with her father, but she always leaves some stuff at her country home as well."

"Chima is King Angus's daughter?" I asked as Daniel helped me get up.

The Hunter nodded. "She's his only child and a great friend of ours." He looked at Arawn. "I still think it would be better if I took Her Grace and pressed on to the palace."

Daniel growled and shoved me behind him. Neil came to his side in a show of force.

"I don't think the vampire will allow it, Hunter. He seems to have had enough emotional activity for the night," the death god said. "Chima will have a way to contact her father at her country house. We'll have to settle for that. This should all be over tomorrow afternoon. Now let's move."

Neil looked back at me. "I just climbed all the way up here and now I have to go back down?"

I looked at him with sympathy because I hadn't been forced to climb and I would ride back down on Danny's back. "Sorry, buddy."

He shook his head as we began to descend. "When I get home, I'm going to hole up in the penthouse and eat ice cream and watch TV for a month. I won't get off the couch. I'll just sleep there, too."

"I'll be right there with you," I promised as Daniel did his best impersonation of Tarzan.

Chapter Twenty-Eight

I woke up and stretched, feeling every pull in my muscles. The night before weighed heavily on me. I hadn't slept well. Dreams of being separated from Dev had plagued me. We'd been gone for several days and I wondered if he was waiting for us to come back or if war plans consumed his every moment.

I glanced up, the daylight that filtered through the heavy curtains making everything seem a little gauzy and unreal. Daniel lay to my right, his handsome face relaxed in sleep though he made none of the little sounds or movements normal people made when they slept. Daniel didn't move. He didn't give off heat. I loved Danny, but I loved to sleep with Devinshea. He held me, moving beside me all night, keeping me warm and letting me know he was there. Daniel couldn't hold me. If he tucked a hand around my waist, I wouldn't be able to break free until he was awake. It was just another way we needed Dev to complete us.

I wasn't sure what time it was but guessed it had to be afternoon. We'd managed to make it to Chima's country house just before dawn. Country house was a misnomer. The place was huge and befitting the daughter of royalty. The staff had been asleep, but the steward had admitted us and given us rooms. They were apparently used to ascended gods joining the king's daughter in the middle of the night. We'd been told that Her Royal Highness was in residence but had gone to bed and would receive us in the morning. They tried to separate Danny and me from Neil, but we had set them straight. Neil was asleep on my left side, his senses ever ready to take care of anything that came our way.

"Go back to sleep, Z," he commanded when I sat up in bed. "It's too early to get up."

"Can't." I crawled out from between Neil and Daniel. I covered Danny back up with a comfy quilt. He didn't need it, but it made me feel like he was more comfortable. My stomach rumbled the whole time. "I'm too hungry. Danny got to eat and I saw you chase down that little furry thing while we were in the forest. I need food. You can stay here, sweetie. I'll just pop down to the kitchens and be right back."

Neil huffed and got up. "Not a chance in hell. Maybe if we were home I would let you run around on your own, but here you just get into trouble." Neil yawned widely and stretched his magnificent body. "Pass me my clothes. Yours are on the end of the bed. Apparently this Chima person is about your size."

Chima's style made me think *Xena: Warrior Princess*. I dressed in soft animal skin trousers, a linen shirt, and a matching vest. The clothes were functional, and they fit like they were made for me even in the chest. She'd even given me a pair of comfy boots. I was going to kiss Chima when I saw her. Neil and I were dressed in quick order and made our way down to the dining room.

This house was much more elegant than Arawn/Roarke and Nim's cabin. The wood floors gleamed with care and at places were covered with finely woven rugs. There were paintings on the walls that told me Chima had spent her share of time on the Earth plane. She'd collected a couple of Picassos I suspected some museums would kill for. I was looking forward to meeting her. Nim was nice but spent too much time looking at my boobs to be counted as a girlfriend. If I managed to get along with King Angus's daughter, that could only help Seelie/Unseelie relations.

Neil let his nose lead us. We entered the well-decorated dining room with high hopes for a decent meal.

"Hello." A strong feminine voice greeted us. She looked me up and down, and after a moment, she began to speak. "You're not Nim so I assume you must be Zoey Quinn."

"I am. You must be Chima." My hopes for good political relations vanished in an instant because I was pretty sure this was our hostess and she was not fucking happy to see me.

She sat at the head of the table and there was no questioning her regal manner. "I am, indeed. You have to forgive me, Your Highness. I've been in the country for the last several months and had not heard of your marriage until my steward mentioned it this morning. I wish you felicitations."

No, she didn't. She wished bad shit on me. I knew a jealous woman when I saw one. I was betting this one hadn't had a boyfriend to keep Devinshea out of her bed.

"God, Z," Neil commented in a quiet tone as he looked our hostess over. "She looks a lot like you."

She did. Though her facial features were not like mine, we certainly had the same body type. She had curves and nicely placed breasts that Dev would have loved. I wondered how often he'd spent time in her bed to make her so jealous of me. I tried to tell myself that I was the one he married and I should be magnanimous. I knew his time in the Unseelie *sithein* had been hard on him, so anything that brought him joy here should be celebrated, but it was difficult.

I put on a sincere smile and hoped charm worked on her. "Thank you. I have to admit, it doesn't seem quite real. It's hard to think I married a faery prince. Thank you for the use of the clothes, by the way. I found myself in desperate need of them."

"I'm glad to see they fit, Your Highness." She had wide sky blue eyes and they narrowed as she considered me. "I was surprised to hear you were human. The Seelie don't tend to take well to anyone who isn't exactly like them."

I shrugged and felt uncomfortable. I could smell the food and hoped she couldn't hear how much I wanted it because she might be bitter enough to deny me. "They don't like me all that much. Most of them seem to think I'm not worthy to have married a royal. The only person I made friends with over there was a troll."

She shook her head and silky curls escaped her updo. "Well, that's not surprising. What is surprising is that Miria allowed the marriage. I would have thought anyone not fully *sidhe* would be unacceptable."

I stood up to my full, if somewhat not imposing, height. I wasn't about to take that crap from anyone, even if they were my host. "My husband made it clear to his mother that she could accept me or we could go back to the Earth plane. He loves me. He doesn't care that I'm human."

"Lucky you, Your Highness." She pushed back her chair and stood up. "Please feel free to keep the clothes. I'll have more sent to you since they fit so well. We have a lot in common, as you will discover. Please sit and break your fast. I'll see you later, after the Hunter and Arawn have awakened so we can decide how to get you back to your loving husband with all due haste."

I couldn't think of anything to say to that obvious sarcasm except, "Thank you, Your Highness. I would love to see my husband as soon as possible. We're not used to being separated."

Chima bowed her dark head to me and exited with as much grace as she could manage.

Neil whistled as he looked over the buffet. "Bitter, party of one. Damn, what did Dev do to cause that?"

I watched the door she had exited out of warily. "I don't know, but he did it well. I have Gilliana on one side and now Chima on this one. It doesn't seem like there's anywhere I don't run into Dev's ex-girlfriends."

Neil inhaled and sighed in happy anticipation. "At least she didn't skimp on the food. It smells wonderful."

"I'm wondering if I should eat it." I looked over the enormous buffet with wild regret. I'd been living off of soldier's rations for days. Soldier's rations sucked.

Neil was already filling a plate. "Why wouldn't you?"

"Hello, I'm 'just drank poison' girl," I pointed out.

Neil frowned at me. "You have to get over that. It was a curse, not poison. I already checked your clothes for hex bags. I don't smell anything but deliciousness, and the vampire blood in your system should take care of anything anyone tries to get you with. You and Daniel did that last night, right?"

I nodded. While Neil had been readying himself for bed, Daniel had insisted I take an extra helping. He was worried about the red caps despite the Unseelies' belief that they would leave Angus's daughter alone.

"So eat up, sweetie," Neil said.

"Chima would never attempt to harm you in that way." Arawn entered, dressed richly in court clothes. He looked at me and I didn't like the sympathy in his eyes. "She might not appreciate your marriage, but she won't harm you over it."

"So she had an affair with Dev?" I wished I could be more cavalier about it, but I would never get used to being around women who had loved my husband, and there was no doubt Chima had. She wouldn't be so bitter if it had been a simple fling.

"It is none of my business, Your Grace," Arawn stated as he picked up a plate. "I've never discussed it with her, but I certainly think all of the evidence points to it. Devinshea is what he is. The miracle is that he married at all." Arawn laughed as he reminisced. "He always told me that when he found his perfect woman, he would settle down and enjoy being faithful. I thought he was joking. I never imagined he would do it. Chima has sacrificed much over the last several years. I ask you to be kind to her, as the woman who won the prize."

"He wasn't a prize to be won." I grabbed a plate because if we were walking more today, I would need a little strength. I glanced at a large grandfather clock that told me I still had several hours before Danny was awake and we could get a move on. It didn't look like I would be having any girl time with our hostess, so I decided to eat as quickly as possible and then avoid her for the rest of our time here. "Has anyone been able to contact the king yet?"

Herne entered the room. "I hope you slept well, Your Grace." He nodded to Arawn, who quickly allowed Roarke to take over the conversation. "Good morning, Roarke. Exciting couple of days, huh?"

Roarke sent his friend a pointed stare. "Yes, if you like complete and utter terror. You might get an adrenaline rush from being hunted down, but I don't. I was looking forward to a couple of weeks' rest out at the cabin, not fleeing for our life because Nim decided she needed something exotic."

A servant came in the room and Roarke finally got around to my previous question. The small goblin brought in an extra platter of something that looked like fried ham. I didn't ask.

"Has your mistress called her father this morning?" Roarke politely asked the goblin, who turned his red eyes on us.

"My beautiful mistress spoke with one of the king's advisors not more than an hour ago." All the love he had for his mistress showed in his eyes. It made a nice contrast when he turned angry eyes to me. "The king is busy with the war preparations. Chima was told her father will call her later today to decide what to do with that one."

Herne pulled the little goblin over and made sure the servant knew he was serious. "She is a Seelie royal. Have you forgotten your manners? Do you seek to shame your mistress with your behavior?"

The goblin bowed, but the distaste in his eyes didn't go away. "Of course not, My Lord. I stand ready to aid Her Highness in any way she might need me."

He gave me one last dirty look and then left the room. I wouldn't be asking him for any favors.

Roarke shook his head. "I apologize. Chima is good to her servants. She inspires loyalty in all who work for her. They hoped for a marriage between her and the priest. Even her father tried throwing Chima and Devinshea together when he was here. They were…disappointed it didn't work out."

I supposed that would have been a perfect match for everyone in Faery. Dev and Chima would have brought the tribes together and there would have been no question that Dev would fulfill his duties to his wife's people. I wondered why it hadn't worked out. At one point, Dev would have done anything to get his people's approval.

"Why do Chima and the goblin call Zoey 'Her Highness'? I thought the proper term was 'Her Grace,'" Neil asked in between plates of food. I hoped the kitchens here could keep up with a werewolf.

Herne took that one. "Zoey is the wife of a high priest and the proper title is 'Your Grace,' but Devinshea is also in line for the throne. He can use the titles interchangeably. The Seelies would never call her Your Highness, but we aren't so desperate for everything to have a proper title here."

There was a loud clatter outside the door and a small, black-haired child sprinted through the room. I smiled because his harried nanny chased him through. He was a bright ball of energy streaking across the floor.

"Sean, you stop that this instant," she yelled as he broke for our table.

The little boy named Sean screeched his pleasure at the game he was playing. He feinted left and right, and then ran headlong toward me. He ran straight into my chair and I reached down to pick up the child, who appeared to be no more than four years old. He held his head and began to cry.

"It's all right, sweetie." I hauled him into my lap, loving the soft weight of him. He was sweet and obviously used to affection as he immediately threw his little arms around me and cried. I soothed back his midnight black hair that was already at the top of his shoulders. I wondered if holding any child would always remind me of the ones I'd lost.

I heard the nanny's startled oath and looked up. The tall *sidhe* female put a hand over her mouth in abject horror as she looked at me.

"It's all right," Roarke said to the woman. "She won't harm the child."

I was confused. I'd tried to build a ferocious reputation but not as someone who would hurt little kids. I patted the boy's back. Maybe they thought because I was married to a Seelie that I would kill all Unseelie. "Why would I hurt a baby?"

Herne shook his head regretfully. "I'm sure it was something Chima never wanted you to know."

The boy shifted his face to me, and now it was my turn to be startled. Emerald green eyes and a perfect face stared up at me. This was what Devinshea had looked like as a child. It made my heart seize. It was easy to see why Chima hated me. I had the title of wife, but according to all Seelie laws, she was the real thing.

* * * *

"Zoey, are you sure you want to do this?" Neil asked as I stalked my prey through the elegant hallways of the country house.

"Just tell me which way to go, Neil," I growled at my wolf. He'd been trying to steer me off course since the moment I'd decided to have it out with Chima.

"Promise me no girl fighting. It's not pretty and it's undignified. All that hair pulling makes the stylist in me want to cry."

"Fine, I promise no hair pulling." I stopped and took a deep breath. I looked back at Neil with a frown. "I have no real intention of fighting with the woman, but don't you think we need to talk about this?"

"About the fact that Dev has a kid?" Neil posited. "Maybe not, Z. She obviously didn't want to push the marriage. All she had to do was show up at the Seelie palace with Little Dev and Miria would have approved their union. She didn't. How does the timing work because Dev's been on the Earth plane for seven years?"

I did the math in my head. "It's only been eighteen months here. Dev was seventeen when he spent the year here. Declan just turned twenty-two and the boy is roughly four. It works out. Dev got Chima pregnant while he and Declan were here for Declan's training."

"But Dev didn't leave the *sithein* for a couple of years after that," Neil pointed out. "Yet she didn't contact him. Leave it be, Z."

I willed myself not to cry. "I can't. Dev wants a kid so bad. He should know he already has one. It isn't fair to him and it isn't fair to the child to not know a loving father."

I could only hope it wouldn't change his feelings for me. I had to hope that he wouldn't feel like he needed to stay here, but I worried his sense of honor would lead him to that decision. If I thought about what this meant for all of us, me and Danny and Dev, then I would probably follow Neil's advice and keep my mouth shut. But I'd just lost a child. Summer was lost to Danny and me as well. I couldn't allow Dev to not know Sean. I couldn't allow our family to lose another child.

Neil shook his head and pointed down a hallway. "Chima is that way, and I think Nim is with her. I'll stay out in the hall unless you need me. Remember your promise about the hair pulling."

I nodded and forced myself to walk down that hallway and confront the woman who had borne my husband's child. I cursed myself the whole way. Who was I to upset this balance Chima had found? No one was trying to force Dev to acknowledge his responsibilities and yet I was ready to push the issue. I couldn't get the look in that little boy's eyes out of my head and I pressed on.

Nim and Chima were talking as I approached the balcony they were sharing tea on.

"I like her," Nim said. "I don't understand your problem with her. She's sweet and funny."

Chima snorted and tucked a stray piece of chestnut brown hair behind one ear. "You don't understand? How can you not? Think about it for a second, Nim. How would you feel in my position? He said his people would never accept me, but they'll accept some human? And why is she running around with a vampire?"

"Whoa, Chi," Nim returned in an affectionate tone as I walked onto the balcony. "She isn't…"

"I'm running around with the vampire because he's my husband, too," I said forthrightly. I met Chima's blue eyes head on. "Now that I answered your question, perhaps you can answer one of mine. Why haven't you told my husband he has a son?"

"Zoey," Nim began.

"Hush, Nim," Chima said, her lips a flat line. "This is between me and Her Highness."

I flushed with anger. "Don't call me that. You can't mean it as anything but an insult since by all Fae laws you're his wife and I'm a second, with only the rights you're willing to give me until I produce a child."

"I give them all to you, Your Highness," she said with a bitter laugh. "Please feel free to consider that bastard all yours. I wouldn't take him back if he dropped out of the sky and begged me on bended knee."

"He has the right to know his son." I stated my position as plainly as I knew how.

"Why does he have the right?" Chima attempted to stare me down. "Did he stay with me to see if I was pregnant? Do you want to know what your loving husband did to me? He told me he loved me one night and walked out and left me the next morning. He never asked about me when he returned to this *sithein*. He never visited me or glanced my way at a state dinner. When he was done with me, he left a lovely parting gift and a note telling me he was sorry it couldn't work out. Why should I share my son with him?"

"Because he should know his father," I insisted. "Whatever he did to you, I'm sorry you were treated that way, but it doesn't mean he wouldn't be a good father. He deserves a chance. He wants a child so badly. When I lost ours he went a little crazy. Knowing he has a son on this side of the *sithein* could stop this war. Have you thought of that?"

"Look, as I told you before, I've been in the country with my son for a couple of months now," Chima said, calming down a bit. "I'm truly sorry to hear you lost a child. I don't know what I would do without my son. Perhaps before we tear at each other over a piece of shit man, you should bring me up to speed. All I was told when you arrived last night was that there was trouble with the new Seelie royal. I've learned a little from Nim this morning, but I try to stay out of politics."

It was a reasonable request and I honored it. I told the future Queen of the Unseelie exactly what had happened during my stay in Faery.

"Declan believes that Herne was an Unseelie spy," I explained.

"Of course he does," Chima said, rolling her eyes. "Did you try to sway him?"

"Declan doesn't listen to me."

"And you said he was upset about the baby?" Her eyes stared straight into mine.

"Declan was upset," I agreed. "Not as upset as Dev, of course. Dev was…I've never seen him so upset and we've been through some serious crap in the couple of years we've been together."

Chima looked over at Nim, who pointedly stared at her friend.

"Devinshea was heartbroken when his brand new goddess lost their baby." Nim spoke the words slowly, as though speaking to a child. "Devinshea recently married."

"Devinshea…yes. Of course." Chima took a moment to process and then addressed me. "Your Grace," Chima said with an almost intense sincerity. She leaned across the table. "Please accept my condolences. I've behaved poorly as a hostess and as a fellow female. I apologize for any bitterness I've shown toward you."

Nim sat forward. "You see, Zoey…"

Chima stopped whatever she was about to say with a harsh look. "I have no excuse but one. I cared deeply for Devinshea. I was obviously not the woman for him. Whatever we had is completely in the past and I ask that you keep Sean a secret between us. I have no intention of making a claim on the priest. It would only put a strain on your marriage and make all of us unhappy if you mention it to him."

Nim seemed upset, and I was glad that at least one person understood my position. I was about to argue when Neil rushed into the room.

"Do you feel that, Z?" he asked.

A wind whipped across the balcony, making me balance against the table to remain standing.

"It's an eddy wind," Chima shouted over the roar. "And it sounds crowded."

I was sure I looked confused. Another strong wind whipped by, making my hair blow back.

Neil stared up, shaking his head. "It smells like goblins and some *sidhe*, maybe. It's confusing. There's so much in that wind."

Chima nodded. "I'm sure it's a messenger from my father."

But it wasn't. We watched as the eddy wind gave up its riders and the red caps appeared on the lawn, their heads dripping with blood. They stood in perfect formation, and there were more of them than before.

"Why has my father sent red caps?" Chima stared at the army in her yard.

"He didn't," Nim said in a tight voice.

One final figure fell from the sky and landed gracefully on the lawn, his sword already drawn. He was tall and bulky, his scarlet eyes betraying his goblin blood. When he opened his mouth I recognized the voice of the man who had taken me from Gilliana.

"Felicitations, Your Highness," Con said in his gravelly voice. "Your father has sent me on a grim errand. You are to surrender Her Grace to me. She will be executed forthwith."

Chapter Twenty-Nine

"That makes no sense," Chima called down to her father's advisor. "Why would my father wish to incense the Seelies by executing the priest's goddess? I thought my father wished to avoid war."

Nim took her place beside Chima, but she pushed me into the shadows. I was pretty sure that Con knew exactly where I was, but at least he didn't have a good shot at me. Though the red caps enjoyed close fighting, they would use arrows when it was expedient. Even as Nim had shoved me back, I saw the goblins notch arrows in their longbows and someone start a fire to set them aflame.

"Your father believes the time has come to take out the Seelie plague," Con explained, his raspy voice all rational logic. "They've threatened us too many times over the past few years. If Declan Quinn is allowed to take the throne in the future, he will do whatever it takes to kill us all. We must act now to ensure our continued survival."

"Con is a traitor, Chima," Nim said loudly.

"Now, Nim," Con began. "There's no reason to throw about such inflammatory words. I've served the king with everything I have. I've tried to protect him from those who seek to overthrow him, like your mate, the ascended god, Arawn. You can't trust them, Your Highness. I know this girl is pretending to be your friend, but she's plotting against you."

"Chima knows who her friends are," Nim insisted.

Con wouldn't let up. "You must ask yourself why a 'friend'

would put you at such risk. Why is Nim running about the countryside with not one but two fugitives? The Seelie royal is here to create trouble and your father has already declared Herne the Hunter an outlaw. Yet your good friend places your whole household at risk by bringing them here to you."

"Asshole," Nim shouted down at the king's advisor. "You're the one who sold Her Grace to me."

"She is filled with lies," Con protested, looking as innocent as someone with blood-red eyes could.

"Give me one good reason why my father wants the priest's wife executed," Chima said, ignoring Con's accusation about her friend. I admired her ability to stay calm and get to the heart of the matter.

Con stepped forward and the entire army moved with him. "Your father will have his revenge on the priest for what he did to you. He left you to bear a child alone. He has no honor, and he will have no wife since he dishonored you."

I saw Chima's head shake. She crossed her arms over her chest. "Oh, Con, you prove yourself a traitor with every word your lips form. My father knows the truth of Sean's birth. He would never seek to hurt Devinshea Quinn in this way."

This seemed to confuse Con to no end. I watched as his mind sought out another avenue to go down, his jaw tightening as he thought. He gazed up and chose to give up the game. "I don't understand and have no time to delve into your enigmatic words. Even now the armies are gathering on the battlefield. Angus has requested a meeting with the Seelie's bitch queen to try to avoid a blood bath. I don't want to avoid a blood bath. I need to make sure Her Grace's head decorates one of our pikes. Then there will be no way Miria will listen to anything he says. If you refuse to listen to reason, then I'll have to take a more direct route. Let us see what the truth of your son is now, Your Highness."

He motioned to someone I couldn't see, but I had a suspicion what was happening when Chima cried out.

Neil grabbed my hand and tried to pull me away. "Time to go, Z."

I fought him and slipped from his grasp. I walked forward and saw the horrible sight of that sweet little boy being hauled out in front of the army of red caps. His legs kicked as he fought with everything he had. They cheered as he was held up for his mother's inspection.

"He has already witnessed the brutal death of his nanny," Con said with a satisfied smile. "I think it scared him to have to watch her heart being ripped out. I told him that if his mommy loved him very much, maybe I wouldn't do it to him, too. How about it, Chima? Does mommy love him very much?"

"You bastard!" Chima screamed. "You let my son go!"

"As soon as Her Grace is in my custody," Con promised soothingly. "I'll exchange the boy you love for the human who means nothing to you. But Chima, don't think for too long. My offer will expire soon. The red caps are crying for blood. The blood of one so innocent is very sweet. I would hurry before they decide they would rather have his blood than hers."

Chima turned and her face had aged in those few seconds. All the safety and comfort of her world had been stripped away, and she had no choices left. Neil swore and he stepped between us.

"Not gonna happen, lady," he growled. I looked down and saw his claws were out.

"Chima, you don't have to do this," Nim said but she sounded uncertain. "Arawn…"

"…would already be here if he could," Chima completed the thought. She reached into a pocket on her trousers and there was a small knife in her hands. "They undoubtedly already have Arawn and the Hunter in custody or on the run. You know how they protect their hosts above all else. It's their primary instinct. We can't count on them."

"The vampire," Nim offered.

Chima laughed bitterly. "One vampire against two hundred red caps? I don't think so."

"You didn't see the way he fought before," Nim argued.

Brown curls shook. "No, Nim. He has spent too much time in Arawn's company. And it's daylight, if you haven't noticed."

"What do you mean he's been around Arawn too long?" I asked. "Daniel can daywalk. It isn't easy for him but he'll do it to save us."

"You don't understand anything, Your Grace. We're fucked,"

Chima bit out. "Nim didn't bother to mention that Arawn has been drawing energy from your vampire, did she? Has the vampire been overly hungry? Has he been on the edge of control? Has he made decisions that didn't always make sense? I can see from your expression that he has. It's because Arawn has effectively been feeding off him. Why do you think Nim wanted a vampire? Arawn likes the feeling. It's like a drug. The death god has been getting high and your vampire needs time to recover, time that we don't have."

I turned to meet Nim's guilty countenance. I could see the truth of Chima's words in her violet eyes.

"I'm sorry, Zoey," she offered weakly. "I didn't mean any harm. It wouldn't kill the vampire. It was just for fun."

"Everything is fun with you, Nim," Chima said sadly.

"I can come up with a spell." Nim nodded, determination on her face. "I just need a few things."

"We don't have that kind of time," I pointed out, hating what I was going to have to do. "Neil, you have to let me go with Chima."

Neil turned, his lovely face savage all of the sudden. "No. Why is he more important than you? Why do you have to sacrifice yourself for these people? They haven't done anything for you."

I smoothed back a stray blond curl. "Sweetie, I have to. That's a child out there. I can't watch them kill a child, certainly not one that belongs to Dev."

"Chima…" Nim implored.

"Not a word, Nim," Chima replied. "This is all your fault. You stay out of it. Her Grace wants to do the right thing."

"It's right for you," Neil shot back at her. He looked at me, his heart in his face. "Don't do this. Please. Dev wouldn't want you to do this. Dev loves you. Danny loves you. You owe them. I love you. Let's just run."

"And leave Danny behind?" I tried to soothe my friend with logic. "What do you think they would do with him even if running was an option? I'm sure they have the place surrounded. How far would we get before they ran us down?"

"We should try," Neil insisted.

I shook my head. "No, we shouldn't. I should go down there and while they're occupied with lopping my head off, the rest of you should run because he can't let you live." Con would need to hide his betrayal, and there was no way to do that except to kill everyone who could possibly talk. I turned and looked at Chima. "Are you ready?"

Chima nodded her head, and there was a terrible guilt in her blue eyes. She didn't like what she had to do, either, but she would do it for her son. She had no choice and I expected nothing less from her.

"I'm going with you." Neil stood beside me.

"No," I ordered. "You have to get to Danny. You have to get him up and moving. You know he can hear you. Tell him what's happening. If there's any way for him to move, he will. He's the only shot I have."

"All right." Neil pulled me into a tight hug. "I love you, Z. Don't you fucking die out there. I'm going to get Daniel up. We're going to come for you. Stay alive."

"I'll try," I promised. Neil turned to go. "Watch your back."

He smiled, a sad little thing and I hoped beyond hope it wasn't the last smile I saw from him. Neil slipped down the hallway, letting his senses lead him away from danger to his quarry.

"Let's go, Your Grace," Chima said, her voice filled with resolve. "You first and I will follow."

"I'm not going to run, Princess."

She moved close behind me. "I can't take that chance."

I walked into the hall and toward the stairs, praying all the while that Daniel would wake up despite what Chima had said. Daniel had done some impossible things when I needed him to. Chima followed and Nim walked in her wake, guilt making her cute pixie face look pale and sad. There was a lost look in her eyes, as though she'd finally figured out there was nothing she could do to stop what she felt she'd set into motion. I could have told her that if they hadn't used her it would have been someone else, but I just marched down the stairs. Every bit of will I had I used to keep my feet moving when what I wanted to do was run to Daniel and beg him to save me. I wanted to live. I wanted to go home with Danny and Dev and have those babies I'd been promised.

If I ended up on the Heaven plane, Oliver Day was going to get such an earful. He thought losing his bet would be bad? It was going to be my job to make that angel miserable.

We reached the bottom floor and I saw clearly why we'd had no aid from the ascended gods' contingent. Herne the Hunter and Arawn were each on their knees on the floor with their hands at the backs of their heads, fingers interwoven in the universal sign of "I got caught." The Hunter looked grim and after his eyes slid off of us, he went back to staring straight forward. Arawn turned to watch us as we moved. Each was guarded by three red caps.

"Are you all right, Nim?" Arawn asked academically, watching his girlfriend with hooded eyes.

"Besides horrific gut-gnawing guilt, I'm fine," Nim replied from behind me.

"If you get the chance to run, sweetheart, please do it," Arawn said. "If they kill Roarke, I'll find another host and look for you. It shouldn't take long. Go to the Earth plane and I'll meet you there."

Nim continued shuffling along. "I know the drill, Arawn."

"You're a bastard," I sneered as I passed the death god, who looked like he couldn't care less that a whole bunch of people were about to die a horrible death. Would he get off on all that death? Maybe it would make him strong enough to break free and save his host and his girl. "Nothing matters as long as you and yours are all right, does it?"

Arawn pondered that briefly. "No, I suppose not. It's not so different from your vampire. You can worry about the rest of the world, Your Grace. I've lived long enough to know that the rest of the world won't care that you made a sacrifice. They won't care that you're dead. They'll forget you quickly and another naïve idiot will take your place. There's an endless stream of women such as you who refuse to see the world for what it is." His eyes were cold as they turned from me and found his lover once more. "Do as I told you, Nim."

"Keep moving," one of the red caps ordered. His cap was dripping blood onto the formerly lovely carpet.

The door to the front lawn was open. It was nice to see the red caps weren't making it hard for me to walk to my execution. There wasn't exactly a red carpet, but it was pretty damn close. I looked across the lawn. There were so many men out there waiting on two small women, as Nim stayed in the doorway. It was just me and

Chima and an army of males. I swallowed audibly and hoped that the whole beheading thing was as painless as the experts said. Not like the experts knew.

I was about to find out.

Chima came up against my back, her hand hauling my arm into a painful position.

"I told you," I said, mad that she was making this harder. "I'm not going to fight."

That was a lie. I was going to fight like hell, but not until she had her son back.

I felt something small and cold press into my hand. "And I told you, I can't take that chance."

I closed my palm around the small knife Chima had been holding. If I held it tightly against my side, I might get away with it. It wasn't much but it was a shot.

"I am grateful to you, Your Grace," Chima whispered. "I wish there was some other way. If I survive, I'll tell everyone of your sacrifice. Arawn is wrong. We won't forget. My father will honor you, and I'll make it my mission in life to stop this war."

Con was getting impatient. "Are you going to bring the bitch to me or not, Chima?"

"I want my son first." Chima held me fast.

The goblin holding Sean moved forward at Con's gesture. Chima pushed me along to meet the guard in the middle. I could see Sean's eyes light up with hope as he saw his mother coming toward him, and I understood why Chima had to do this. He was so sweet and beautiful and he deserved to grow up. He didn't deserve to die a pawn in some idiot's war.

"Push Her Grace toward me and I'll let your son run to you." The goblin rasped his instructions. His claws were digging into Sean's arm, a thin trickle of blood already visible.

Without hesitation, Chima shoved me hard toward the goblin. I stumbled even as Sean streaked by me to get to his mother. The tumble allowed me to better hide the weapon Chima had given me. Most of it was hidden up the long shirt I wore, but all I had to do was move my hand to use it.

The goblin wasn't interested in my dignity. He strode up and, rather than waiting for me to get up and walk, he simply grabbed a handful of hair and started dragging me. Pain flared along my scalp and I scrambled. As I tried to keep up, I watched Chima wrap her arms around her son and join Nim. I saw the regret on their faces, but they disappeared around the corner of the house, attempting to make their escape.

I was alone with an army of monsters.

"Poor little human." Con looked down on me as my goblin escort tossed me toward him and I fell at his feet. "You just wanted a good lay and you end up here. I hope the fertility god made it worthwhile for you."

"Screw you," I spat, looking up into his red, alien eyes. His long white hair looked wrong on his body, far too soft for someone so hard.

He laughed, a sound that was somewhere between a guffaw and a rasping cough. "Unfortunately, I can't take you up on that generous offer. It's a shame because I would love to know what it is about you the sex god found so amusing he was willing to give up all those other women."

"Sounds like a damn good reason to keep me alive." I meant what I told the Hunter. I don't believe in death before dishonor. I believed in staying alive for just another hour and a half so Danny could wake up and kill this asshole.

"Tempting, but no." Con turned me down as he pulled me to my knees. His hand wrapped in my hair, holding me in place. I was going to have to rethink my hairdo. Too many times some asshole used it against me. "The war is about to start and I do want your head on my pike. Your husband will be the first to see it as I march across the field of battle. He'll sound the horn of war before Miria or Angus can even think to talk."

Con held my head at a rough angle as the red caps began to chant. I wasn't sure what they were chanting, but I was pretty certain it wasn't anything I wanted to hear. The hold Con had on my head hurt, but my throat was vulnerable and completely exposed. I could vaguely see Con hold up a hand to bring forward one of the goblins. He moved forward with a broad sword. It looked too heavy for the squat, fierce creature but he wielded it like it was nothing. All in all I was certain he'd been well trained as an executioner.

"I am merciful, Your Grace. I grant you a painless death. Your blood will stain their caps for our glorious battle," Con said with flourish as the goblin raised the sword to swing it in an arc that would separate my head from my body.

I let the small but sharp knife fall into my hand and as hard as I could, shoved it behind me, my aim finding that soft sac that all men carry at the center of their universe. I sank the knife in deep even as Con screamed and let me go. I felt the sword swing above my head as I hit the ground.

I was on my feet as quickly as possible while I still had the confusion of my actions and Con's girlie screams to give me a few seconds. I ran for the house, thinking to find a place to hide, but a strong wind forced me back to my knees even as I could see the door that might mean my freedom.

The goblins were regrouping, and Con was shouting my name. I didn't think he would be so merciful the next time he got his hands on me. I was being called everything a man could think of to call a woman he truly detested.

I fought to get up, but that wind was too strong. My heart sank as I realized it was another one of those blasted eddy winds that seemed to plague me. The goblins had sent for reinforcements. They had excellent timing as they had managed to neatly block my escape.

Bodies fell to the ground around me.

"Damn it," I heard a familiar voice growl. "That's the worst ride I've ever had. Who the hell taught you to drive? I think I'm going to be sick. Why don't you people just use cars?"

Even as he complained bitterly, Lee bounced up, ready to take down anything that came his way.

"I agree, brother." Declan's voice came next. "You are terrible at that. I am going to learn how to catch an eddy wind just so I never have to allow you to drive again."

"I didn't have any problem with it, boss. It was fine." I had never been so happy to hear Zack suck up.

I looked up and my husband smiled down at me, his hand held out to help me stand. "Hello, my wife. It looks like you could use some help."

Chapter Thirty

I launched myself off the ground and into his arms, sighing with pleasure as they wrapped around me. "You came for me."

"I will always come for you," Dev promised as he hugged me fiercely. "Even when I prove myself to be a stupid ass, I will always wake up and come for you. I realized that everything I loved was over here, wife. My future was here and I couldn't give it up for revenge. Please forgive me."

"Zoey, please forgive my brother later as we have an army of red caps ready to slaughter us, and I don't think they will wait for your tender reunion," Declan said even as he notched an arrow. He pulled the bowstring back to an impossible spread. I'd seen Declan use his weapon before and I believed his boast that he was the greatest archer in all of Faery.

"Zachary, Lee," a deep, soothing voice said. I looked up and saw Bris had taken over. He looked…angrier than I had ever seen him. Bris was gentle and kind. He was patient, but there was nothing of that Bris in his face now. "Please protect my goddess. Where is Daniel?" He directed his question at me.

Lee and Zachary began to lead me away from the fertility god as Declan started letting his arrows fly faster than any human would have been able to manage. "He's safe as far as I know. He's with

Neil."

The red caps stopped advancing as Con held his hands up. He looked over our small party and let out a hearty laugh. "Welcome, Prince Declan. I couldn't ask for a better guest to join us in these proceedings. And the priest was stupid enough to come after his bride."

"He isn't alone," Bris said solemnly. He stepped forward, his big body a target, but he stood in front of the group as though we were his to defend.

Con smiled, showing small, curved goblin fangs. "Yes, I heard you had ascended. Your time in the priest will be short lived, My Lord. So Prince Declan, you brought along a fertility god to fight a war. I'm afraid you're outgunned, unless you intend that we all fuck each other to death."

"Con," Declan acknowledged with a frown. It was obvious he knew the half *sidhe* and didn't care for him, but there was nothing new on that front. "I suppose Angus does not know about your treason." A terrible thought hit Declan and he blanched. "Please tell me you were not working with the Duke of Ain. Say it was anybody but him because you have to know that my sister-in-law will never stop saying she told me so. I will hear it as long as she has a voice to speak."

"I told you so," I yelled from behind my wolf guards. Declan was right about one thing. I would be saying those words a whole lot in his near future. If we made it out of this alive.

"Damn it. I hate it when she's right." Declan turned back to Con. "You will pay for your crimes. Tell me something before we kill you, Con. Where is the woman who owns this house? Was she in residence? Has she been taken prisoner as well?"

"She got away," I told Declan, who nodded and turned back to his task.

"How exactly do you intend to make me pay for my crimes?" Con asked arrogantly. He held his arms wide, indicating his men. "I have an army of killers willing to do my bidding. You have a fertility god, two men, and a helpless girl."

"I wasn't so helpless when I carved up your balls, Con," I pointed out.

Zack laughed out loud and seemed far too relaxed for a man who was facing down an army.

"Lee." Anxiety made my stomach churn because that nasty old Con was making sense. We were horribly outnumbered. "Shouldn't we get up there and help Dev? Tell me you brought guns and maybe a tank."

"We have everything we need, Zoey." Lee didn't take his eyes off the scene in front of him. "You stayed alive and you castrated a son of a bitch. You did your job, darlin'. Now let your husband do his."

"I'm going to kill you, bitch," Con promised. "And I'll make your husband watch when I take your head."

"You arrogant fool," Bris said darkly. "Those who deal in death always forget how powerful life can be."

There was a mighty rumble as the earth beneath us began to shake. I could see plainly that it wasn't an earthquake. Earthquakes don't just happen in a small area leaving everything else untouched. The house behind us was still, completely unaffected by the cracks that began to form in the ground beneath the army. I started to fall, but Lee held me up. The sound of all that dirt moving seemed to fill the yard as I had a sense of something big coming.

"It's all right, Zoey," Lee said.

The ground spat up a thicket of rope-like vines that came from seemingly every inch of the yard where a red cap stood. I watched as their red eyes popped open in surprise as they lost their footing. They tried to move away. They tried to run, but there was nowhere to go as the ground drank them up, hungrily pulling them under.

The goblins fought and tried to claw their way out, but the vines just pulled harder until there was no one left on the field. I was struck by the sudden quiet and how the ground shifted easily back to its formerly perfect state. It was like nothing had happened. No one who had not seen the deed could believe an entire army was now held in hard dirt.

"Damn," Zack said beside me, respect plain in his voice. "I'm totally not pissing Bris off."

Bris, however, was not through. He looked back at me. "Are there more, my goddess?"

I nodded silently before finding my voice. I was with Zack. I was impressed, too. "There were several in the house. Six, I think."

Bris held his hand up and a dozen thick vines with wicked thorns appeared from the ground around him.

"Bring them," he commanded, and I watched as they sank back into the dirt, their movement visible as the ground swelled above them. They raced toward the house to do their master's bidding. It wasn't long before the goblins in the house were pulled screaming into the yard to join their brethren in an earthy grave.

"Goddess," Bris commanded me, and Lee allowed me to go to him. "Was the man named Con the one who tried to harm you?"

"Yes," I replied, still coming to terms with what I had seen. "He thought if he killed me, he could make sure Dev wouldn't back down."

Bris arched an eyebrow as he walked out into the now perfectly kept yard. He moved methodically, as though he was looking for something. My attention was taken away from him as the Hunter and Arawn entered the yard at a run. They pulled to a stop as they saw our party.

"Zoey, what's happening?" Arawn asked. "The goblins guarding us were taken away by vegetation."

"Well, I didn't get beheaded, asshole," I said, looking at him with a frown.

Arawn wasn't taking my shit. He took me by the shoulders and shook me. "Answer me, Your Grace."

Lee and Zack growled and Bris looked up from what he was doing.

"I suggest you take your hands off my goddess, Death Lord, unless you wish to discover firsthand what I did with the red caps," Bris warned.

Arawn immediately let me go and took a healthy step back. "I apologize, Bris. I didn't realize you had joined us. It's been a trying afternoon." He looked back at me and I saw some emotion in those dark eyes. "Do you know where Nim is?"

"She took your advice," I told him shortly. "She's probably halfway to the Earth plane by now. I'm sure she will wait for you there."

He nodded and seemed satisfied. Bris stopped over a spot and seemed to have found what he was looking for. He held his hand low to the ground and then pulled it up in a sudden motion.

Con was spat from the ground and came up coughing. Before he could clear his lungs of the dirt, he found himself suspended in midair by thick vines. Bris looked up at him.

"What did you intend to do to my goddess?" Bris asked, his voice terse.

Con glared down at the fertility god. He wasn't one for begging or pleading. As the Hunter had explained to me the night before, the Unseelie were a direct lot. "I intended to have that bitch's head on my pike when I marched into war."

"Did you believe she was undefended? Did you think because my power is fertility and sex that I could not defend my own goddess?" Bris bit out the questions with barely contained rage. "Do you think a god like me is soft and will let what he loves go because he would rather not fight?"

"I don't give a shit." Con took a deep breath and seemed to ready himself. "Put me back in the ground. I'm immortal. I am Unseelie *sidhe*, and a few years in the dirt will do nothing but harden my resolve."

"Then you leave me no choice," Bris said evenly. "Though the truth is you sealed your fate the moment you laid hands on her."

The fertility god's hands twisted and a new vine popped up and wrapped itself around Con's throat. The *sidhe* struggled but he was held tightly and after a horrifying moment, I realized that vine wasn't attempting to strangle him. Bris was proving he didn't need a piece of steel to accomplish what Con had failed at. That vine squeezed until blood began to flow.

Con's head popped off with a sickening click and fell to the ground.

"Damn." Lee breathed beside me, his brown eyes wide with awe. He actually took my hand and pulled me back.

Bris looked down as Con's body disappeared into the ground once more, never to rise again.

"So much for your immortality," he said to the man who would never answer. Bris turned toward me, and I saw his face fall as he noted my wolf's protective stance.

"My violence has frightened you," Bris said in a quiet voice that made me worry he was ashamed.

I wasn't having that. My head was on my body and that was a win. Wins should be celebrated. I pulled free from Lee and launched myself bodily at my savior. Bris braced himself for impact and allowed me to wrap my legs around his waist as my arms found his neck and I kissed him with a laugh of great joy. I pressed my lips to his as I stroked his face.

His hands found my rear and cupped it. He returned the kiss, slipping me his tongue at the first opportunity. "Do I take it my violence has incited a need to mate, my goddess?"

I kissed him again. "The fact that my head is still on my body has made me joyful, Bris."

"I'm glad," he said sweetly. "My host is eager to greet you again, goddess. Know that I am happy to have rendered this service to you. I look forward to our next ritual."

"I look forward to it too, My Lord." He looked surprised but pleased as I used his traditional title for the first time. He had more than earned my respect.

Dev's smile was wide as he returned to me. "Hey, my lover, you're finally relaxing around Bris. This is a good thing."

"Yeah, well, I kind of love him today," I admitted. "And I definitely love you. Thank you for coming for us, baby. We should go and find Danny. He's weak. The death god has been feeding off of him."

Dev allowed me to slide to the ground beside him and took my hand as though he were afraid to let go of me. He turned his attention on Arawn, his mood becoming dark. "And how did you come to be here with my wife, Arawn? You have your own woman. Where is she?"

"I'm here, Devinshea." Nim rounded the corner of the house. She walked to her boyfriend and kissed him softly. "Please tell Roarke I'm so glad he is well."

Arawn nodded his head, shame in his eyes. "He's angry with me, love, not you. I'll let him tell you himself once I'm certain we're out of danger."

She nodded and turned to me. "Chima is behind me. She's just slower because of…"

Dev ignored her. "I want an answer, Arawn. My goddess's wolf was able to track her even through the eddy wind we rode. We tracked her from the entry of the *sithein* to your cabin. I know what you used that cabin for in the past. I spent time there myself. If you bought her as a slave then she better have been scrubbing your floors or we shall have a problem."

"He refuses to share his goddess," Declan pointed out. "Well, with anyone but the vampire. He is quite unreasonable about it."

Arawn smiled, an arrogant challenge. He seemed to be getting back on his feet. "She was purchased as a pleasure slave, of course. She's scarcely suited to kitchen work. She's obviously meant for the bedroom."

"Don't tease him, Arawn," Nim said with a tired sigh. The cute brunette stepped forward and faced Dev. "Arawn never touched her. I bought her for me. If you're upset then you should be upset with me."

I rolled my eyes as my husband clutched his heart. "Please, please tell me Daniel took video."

"I have it on the highest authority that he intends to embellish the tale with great relish," I offered.

Dev nodded, his eyes alight with anticipation. "I would do the same for him."

Lee looked up. "Someone's coming."

I saw Chima walking around the house. She hesitated for a moment and when she saw who was in the yard, she stopped completely. I had to tell him. There was no way Dev could look at the child in Chima's arms and not know. I needed to make it clear to him that I would accept his child even if I wasn't the child's mother.

"Baby, I found out something while I was here." I kept my voice low so only Dev and his brother could hear me. I was sure Declan knew about the affair since he'd been here at the time.

"Why is Chima carrying a child?" Declan asked.

"Dev, Chima had your baby." I spat it out before I could change my mind. "I don't know what happened between the two of you. I don't know why she didn't tell you."

"Oh, I can think of a reason." Dev turned to look at Chima, who was now walking boldly across the yard, her son on her hip.

Declan turned to his brother. His face had gone a stark white. He let his bow fall to the ground. "Zoey, move out of the way."

"Now, brother…" Dev began, but there was no stopping Declan. He reared his hand back and slapped Dev as hard as he could. Dev wasn't ready and he staggered back and ended up on his ass in the grass, looking up at his twin.

"Your choice of weapons, brother," Declan declared.

I shoved my asshole brother-in-law out of the way and knelt down by my husband. Several things were apparent to me now. I was glad I'd been so open and magnanimous or I would have been eating some serious crow.

"Are you all right, baby?" I asked. I looked over his face, which had an angry handprint on it now. I stared up at Declan. "Jerk."

Dev managed a completely angelic look. "I think I will be all right, my goddess. I can only hope my jaw isn't broken."

I rewarded his bad acting with a kiss. "So, I was wrong, huh? No baby with Chima?"

Dev grinned. "Not unless I have some amazing powers I was unaware of until now."

I stood up to my brother-in-law. Chima looked surprised that Dev was on the ground. Her mouth hung open so I decided to speak for her. "You're an asshole, Declan. And you don't deserve her."

Nim walked up to join me. "King of the Seelie? You aren't even brave enough to face your responsibilities. You should be ashamed of yourself. She's not good enough for you? Let me tell you what I think of that…"

I could tell that Nim had been holding that speech in for a good long while. Now that she was let off the leash, she let Declan have it. Declan looked truly frightened for the first time in our acquaintance as Nim and I cornered him.

"Why are the females berating Declan?" the Hunter asked. "I thought the priest impregnated Chima."

"No," I announced loudly. "The person who knocked up his girlfriend and then left her high and dry wasn't Dev, and I should have known that. Sorry, baby."

He winked. "I forgive you."

Chima bent her head apologetically my way. "I am sorry, Zoey. When you appeared on my doorstep, I thought you had married Declan, not Devinshea. As I explained, I heard only that the Seelies had a new royal. As Dev has been gone, I made a mistake and assumed wrongly. Please forgive my rudeness to you."

"Hey, I'm just glad we cleared that up." I couldn't imagine having to be married to that jackass.

"Do you want to know why Chima let the entire court believe she had Dev's baby instead of yours?" Nim continued to rail at her opponent. She had him backing up now. "She was ashamed. She only told her best friend and her father. She was ashamed she had taken you to her bed."

I hadn't thought Declan's face could fall further but it did. I felt Dev get up beside me as his brother looked at his former lover.

"Is this true, Chima?" Declan asked quietly, no arrogance to hide behind now. "Were you ashamed you slept with me?"

"I was ashamed I loved you," Chima admitted, her eyes misty.

Dev walked up to her, his eyes on the child. "May I take my nephew? You can't beat on my brother while you hold the child."

Chima actually managed a laugh as she passed her son to Dev. "This is your uncle, Sean. He's a good man."

"And I am not?" I heard Declan start to get his spine back.

Sean smiled as Dev took him and raised him high. "You're tall."

"And you will be too, Sean Quinn," Dev promised. "You'll be tall and strong like your father. It's a great honor to meet you. This is your Aunt Zoey. She's completely crazy and can tell you the greatest tales of her adventures. You'll have to meet your Uncle Daniel. He's a vampire."

"Really?" Sean asked, his eyes wide.

Dev put his arm around me and I saw him try to contain his emotions as he looked down on that sweet face. Our son would have had that face.

"We'll get our chance," he vowed even as Chima started in on her ex. They were screaming at each other but Dev and I were in our own world.

"We will," I promised. "And I definitely want twins."

"I shall work hard to see that you are satisfied, my goddess." He gestured to Nim, who took Sean. "Let us go and get our vampire so we can stop this war, take our revenge on the duke, and get to the part where we practice making Sean a cousin."

"What about those two?" I asked because they were going at it.

"What did you gain by keeping this from me?" Declan was swearing.

"Oh, I don't know, Declan. How about my dignity?" Chima shot back. "How about my self-respect and the ability to look at myself in the mirror?"

"Fuck your dignity now, Chima," Declan responded. "And screw your self-respect because we're married and there's no room for any of that in our bed."

"Married!" Chima screeched, and I was pretty sure the goblins buried underground could hear her.

"They'll be fine," Dev said, starting to lead me toward the house. "It's foreplay for them. Lee, if you would lead us to Daniel, I would appreciate it."

Lee took the lead even though I could have told him where our room was. Zack took our six just in case there was anyone hanging around. We turned the corner to go up the stairs just as Neil was coming down. He carried Daniel and his eyes darted around like he was expecting to get jumped any minute.

"Zoey! Thank god. I'm so glad to see you." Neil's face fell as he glanced down at the man he was carrying. "Zoey, I think he's dying."

Chapter Thirty-One

"Move him to the couch," Dev ordered Neil.

As Neil laid Daniel down on the large sofa, I dropped to my knees and reached for Daniel's hand. I was shocked at the terrible chill I found there.

"Oh god, Dev, he's so cold." I ran my hands along his chest and up to his face. Everywhere I touched was cold and dead. He was utterly limp on the couch, with no spark of animation to light him. Normally when he slept the way a vampire slept, he was stiff and unmoving.

Daniel was like a corpse. Nausea swamped me. I'd been here before. I'd seen him dead and laid out on an autopsy table. Tears streamed down my face. I couldn't handle this. He couldn't be gone.

Dev reached down and placed a hand on his arm. He initially shrank back from what he felt there, but then he forced himself to sink down beside me and placed his hand over Daniel's heart. "What the hell is wrong, Dan?"

"He wasn't like this before," Neil said, gazing down on all three of us, worry plain in his eyes. "He would get cool but not cold."

Neil was the only one of us who knew what Daniel had been like before he began his relationship with Dev and me, before Daniel had gained the ability to daywalk. Neil had been his servant for years after his turn. He'd protected Daniel when he was vulnerable. Neil was the only one who truly knew this wasn't normal. "His body would be cooler than it was when he was awake, but it was never like this. Z, I told him what was happening. I told him you were going to die. In the past he would have tried, at least. He could hear me and he would let me know by shifting just a little. I got nothing from him. It's like he's not there anymore."

Dev's face was a mask of guilt. "I stayed away for too long. His body has grown used to having more blood."

"That's not it," Neil insisted.

"He was used to feeding from my magic." Dev plunged forward. He was beginning to look a little desperate now. "I'm so sorry, Zoey. I should never have allowed us to be separated. He's grown reliant on both of us, and I was too selfish to see it."

"Dev, stop." Guilt wouldn't solve anything at this point. We needed to figure out how to wake Daniel up. He had to wake up.

"After you lost the baby, I knew he was hungry and I knew he wouldn't feed off of you because he thought you were too weak, but I was angry." Dev's face knotted in an expression of self-loathing. "I knew he wouldn't take blood from anyone else. I let him go hungry."

"Dev, this is not your fault," I said.

He shook his head. "This isn't the type of relationship where I can tell him to fuck himself and not talk to him for days. He needs me. He needs us."

"Stop it." I forced him to look at me. "This isn't your fault. I was with him for days, baby. I fed him and he was full. He was full of blood and he had plenty of sex. The two days he went without were uncomfortable but it wouldn't do this to him. Lee, bring the death god in here. This is Arawn's fault. Daniel was tired when we went to bed last night but he certainly wasn't cold. I want to know what that bastard did to my husband."

Dev pulled his Sig Sauer from the holster in the small of his back. "Zack, take Neil as well. Convince Arawn to join us by any means necessary. I'll protect us if it's needed."

Zack nodded, looking forward to a little intimidation. Neil and Zack followed Lee out the door.

"I'm so sorry, my love," Dev said, his arm going around my

shoulder.

I looked down at Daniel, praying there was some way to bring him back to us. It wouldn't mean anything to have come so far only to lose Daniel. I reached out again and clutched his cold hand. His body was a perfect slab of marble, as if Michelangelo had carved him. He was so still it reminded me of the last time I'd seen him this way. He'd been on a gurney in the morgue. I had needed to identify his body. I took a deep breath. He'd come back to me that time, and he would come back again.

"I'm coming," a deep voice said. "You don't have to push me and you don't have to point that thing at me."

"I don't have to." Lee growled as Zack continued to point his gun at the faery. "I'm just enjoying it. If you've killed the vampire, I think I'll enjoy taking you apart piece by piece."

"It wasn't me, idiot." Roarke's tone was harsh, a little gravelly. "All you'll do is kill me and it won't hurt Arawn at all. He'll just find a new imbecile to inhabit and he and Nim will go their own way."

"Roarke," Nim reached out for him.

"Shut up, Nim. You're just the same as Arawn. You both want to use me to your own ends. I don't want to talk to either of you." Roarke was pushed into the room, all three wolves surrounding him.

"Guys," I said to the wolves. "I don't think Roarke is going to do anything to hurt Daniel. It's the other one's fault."

Lee shook his head in annoyance. "I hate this whole sharing bodies thing. There should be a one person per body rule. I never know who I should beat the crap out of."

"Well, it isn't me," Roarke insisted. "How can I help you, Your Grace?"

I had a feeling the question had been directed at Dev. Roarke bowed his head to the priest with the greatest respect.

"This man is my partner," Dev said with quiet determination. "How has the death lord injured him?"

Nim stepped forward. I was a little sad to see her former light had dimmed. "Arawn can feed off the energy that comes from the reanimated dead. Usually there is little even from a vampire. Daniel's unique DNA makes him different. Arawn told me last night that he has an enormous amount of energy pouring off of him."

"Well, there doesn't seem to be much now, does there?" Dev stood and walked to Nim. He towered over her but he didn't seem to mind intimidating the small woman. "We've been friends, Nim. I've aided you at times. I know that you and Arawn have been lovers for at least a thousand years, so I understand how important he is to you. If Daniel dies, know that I will make it my goal in life to discover a way to destroy him."

"He didn't mean any harm, Devinshea," Nim insisted, her violet eyes pleading.

Dev shook his head, not moved a bit. This was a side few people saw of Dev. For the most part, Dev was calm and friendly. He appeared to be a rather soft, caring man while Daniel was the ruthless killer, but Dev was every bit as merciless as Daniel could be. He just hid it better. "I don't care whether harm was meant or not. If he dies, I will pursue my course and I won't stop until I've achieved it."

"I know what happened," Roarke said. "You don't have to scare Nim."

Nim tried to hug Roarke, but he pushed her away gently. "Not now, Nim. Arawn will be back soon and he'll be happy to hold you."

I frowned as Nim sank into a chair and looked pretty damn miserable. Roarke turned back to Dev.

"Explain this to me, Roarke," Dev demanded. "My goddess tells me he was tired but fine last night when they went to bed. Daniel should have been able to rouse himself when our wife was in danger. I have seen him do amazing things, take more damage than any being should be able to when her life is at stake."

Roarke listened for a moment to a voice in his head. "He was fine last night. Arawn had ceased his slow feed on the vampire. It was the danger he was placed in when the red caps caught up with us that caused him to drain the vampire."

"Drain him?" I didn't like the sound of that. Anytime the word drain is used in the same sentence as vampire, something has gone wrong.

Roarke nodded. "When Arawn is in danger, he tends to pull energy from anything he can feed from that happens to be within range. It's an instinct. This time he pulled so much energy from the vampire trying to fight off the red caps that it put the vampire in a comatose state."

"How do we get him out of it?" I asked.

Black eyes rolled forward and Arawn finally made an appearance. "You do not, Your Grace. I'm afraid I pulled far too much energy from the vampire. He won't come back from it."

My heart beat against my ribs. "What the hell do you mean?"

The death god had the good grace to look ashamed. "I thought we all were going to die. I reached out without thinking and by the time I realized what I'd done, it was too late. It didn't matter anyway. The goblins were prepared for death magic. They easily fought back against everything I tried. They had charms and spells prepared for me. They apparently hadn't planned on the fertility god showing up."

"Are you trying to tell us Daniel is dead?" Lee asked the question Dev and I could not.

"He isn't," Zack insisted. "I still feel him, Zoey. He's in there. He's just trapped and he's getting weaker by the second. Try giving him blood."

I turned to try because I would open all my veins if it would wake him up.

Arawn's hand came out to stop me. "It won't help. You'll merely weaken yourself. He won't be able to take the blood. You, wolf, try to feed your master. Your mistress won't believe until she sees it for herself."

Zack got a stubborn look on his face. He pulled the knife from his boot. "I'll feed my master. Once he has some blood in him, you'll see that he's still with us. I would know if he was gone."

Neil watched Zack with a compassionate look on his face. Zack quickly, and without a single grimace to show the pain he caused, drew the knife across his wrist. Blood welled, rich and thick and it spilled over Daniel's mouth. Even if Daniel had been in his sleep state, he should have reacted to that blood. His mouth should have opened and let the blood work its way down his throat. Daniel was perfectly still and Zack's blood ran across his closed lips and down his face. Zack cursed as his wrist closed and he tried again.

"Zack, it's no use." Lee said, his gravelly voice filled with sympathy for his only brother.

Zack frowned. "I have to try."

"No, Zack," I said quietly, feeling tears start to run down my cheeks. "We need to find another way." I wasn't willing to give up.

"He won't be able to feed," Arawn stated relentlessly. "He's only alive now because of what he is. Had he not been a king, he would be dead. As it stands, he will fade. It will not be painful for him."

"It will be goddamn painful for me." I hated him in that moment. I looked to Dev. "We have to get him home. Maybe Marcus knows something. Maybe Sarah knows something. There has to be a way to save him."

"Perhaps I can be of assistance, goddess," Bris's gentle voice offered. He stared down at me.

"You can't be serious," Arawn said, looking at the fertility god inhabiting Dev's body. "That's insane."

I ignored him. Nothing mattered except our little family. I looked into Bris's emerald eyes. "Can you help him?'

"I believe I can." He brushed the tears from my cheeks. There was the saddest look on his face as though he wasn't sure it would work and he feared what would happen if it didn't.

"Why?" Arawn asked, genuinely shocked at Bris's offer. "Why would you do this for them? You're an immortal god. They're nothing compared to what you have seen and done. Why risk it?"

Bris considered the death god with a sad shake of his head. "You have walked the planes of existence for millennia, Arawn, and yet you still have no comprehension of what it means to be alive. There is no point to life without love. Love, at times, requires risk. It would not be worth having if you never had to sacrifice for it."

"What are you going to do?" The way Arawn was talking made me think that whatever Bris was going to do would be hard on him.

"Make you smile again, sweet goddess." He bent down and planted a simple kiss on my forehead, then his hand shot out and he covered Daniel's chest with his palm.

Daniel's body jumped like it had been struck with electricity. Dev's body kind of crumpled to the floor as if all the life had gone out of it. I heard my little scream as I tried to figure out which one to touch first.

I dropped to my knees as Daniel's eyes flew open.

"Zoey," he said before he could see anything.

"I'm here." I put my hand over his heart. He was warmer now, so much warmer than he'd been before. Life had been rushed into his body, a warm wave that brought him back to me. Bris had done this. Bris had saved me and then brought Daniel back.

"What happened?" he asked, trying to sit up. "Why am I covered in blood?" He wiped his hand across his mouth and then drew his fingers onto his lips. He tried to focus, but I could tell it was hard. "Zack, are you all right?"

Zack smiled. "Yes, sir. I was just trying to prove a point."

Whatever Daniel would have said to that was lost as he realized Dev was with us. "Dev?" He forced himself to sit up. "Jesus, Z, what the hell is wrong with Dev?"

"I don't know." I panicked a little. I couldn't save one husband just to lose the other. I felt Dev's neck, trying to find a pulse. My hands shook.

"Zoey," Daniel said, taking my hand in his. "He's alive. I hear his heart beating. Why is he unconscious? He came for us?"

I nodded. "Lee led him here to save us. The red caps are gone, thanks to Bris."

"Really?" Daniel asked, not quite believing me.

"You're alive because of Bris, vampire," Arawn said, his voice almost accusatory. "He sacrificed everything for you."

Dev's eyes came open slowly. "Zoey, is Daniel…"

"I'm here," Daniel said.

Dev smiled weakly. "Thank the goddess, it worked."

"What exactly worked, Dev?" I asked.

Dev took a long breath, his chest rising and falling in a beautiful life-giving pattern. "Daniel had been drained by death magic. It put him into a comatose state, but it hadn't killed him. He couldn't move, couldn't feel, couldn't feed. Bris thought he could jump-start his system."

"With what?" I was afraid I knew the answer.

"With his essence," Dev said sadly. "I don't feel him anymore."

"He's gone?" I'd always felt odd around Bris, and now I wept his loss. Tears blurred my vision as I thought about the consequences of what Bris had done for me. For us. He was part of our family.

He'd done this for us.

"Yes, Your Grace," Arawn said bitterly. "All that power, all that magic is gone because he couldn't stand to see you cry. He might never be able to reintegrate with the priest."

Dev shook his head. "I don't know. He's strong and Zoey moves him. I believe he'll try again. He certainly intends to. He hopes that with the magnification the temple can provide that we'll be able to bond again, though it will be a while before he is back at his full power."

I suddenly felt a warm breeze flutter around me and I knew it was him. "He's still here. I feel him. He's surrounding me."

And it was about more than me. Bris knew how Dev felt about Daniel, too. There was a connection between them. I would have called it a brotherhood at one point, but I couldn't anymore. There was more to it. There was love between them. Bris understood that. Bris had sacrificed himself for that love.

Arawn huffed a little. "Yes, he's here. He is immortal but he is without a body. He's weakened and it will take a lot of magic to allow his taking of another host."

"Shut up, Arawn," Nim said suddenly. "You don't know him. You're judging him by your standards. He loves them. He will be determined to get back to them. Just because you're a coward doesn't mean he is."

"Nim!" Arawn looked at his lover, shocked at her outburst.

She stood up and looked strangely determined. "It's not that I don't love you. I do. I love you so much it hurts, and I have since the day I saw you so many years ago it would shock the people in this room. The fertility god was right. We have forgotten why we live in the first place. I used to have a job. I used to be important. Now I follow after you hoping that one day you'll let me try to have a baby."

"You know why I think that is a bad idea," Arawn argued.

"Yes, the child would more than likely be mortal." This seemed like an argument Nim probably had made many times. "I'm not afraid of loss. I'm afraid of never having anything. I didn't regret the child I adopted before. I had to watch him die and I loved him. I was richer for being his mother. He knew how to love, Arawn, even when it cost him."

"He committed treason against his king," Arawn muttered.

"For love." Nim took a deep breath and looked at me. "I know I have no right to ask anything of you, Zoey, but if you wouldn't mind, I would like to go back to the Earth plane with you. I think I know someone who can help your vampire with his heart trouble."

Arawn's face flushed. "Not him. He is out of our lives, Nim."

"He was never truly out of our lives. He can't be," Nim returned with a little fire. "He's the only one who can help, and I'm the only one who knows where I stashed him."

"Stashed him?" I asked, eyes wide. I couldn't help but stare at Dev and wonder if Bris would ever reintegrate. He'd given us everything. I wanted him back. I wanted him close. He'd proven himself to me. I could love and trust Bris, and now he'd possibly given us a chance to heal Daniel's heart.

Nim's button nose wrinkled. "He was an old mentor of mine. He was a handsy old goat. I kind of cursed him. He should be willing to help if I let him out. He's had twelve hundred years or so to think about bad touching and why he shouldn't do it."

"Okay. If you think he can help then you're welcome to come with us." I prayed Bris would come as well.

She bowed her head, a solemn gesture. "Thank you."

"What if I don't want to go to the Earth plane and look up your old flame?" Arawn asked.

"I didn't ask you, Arawn," Nim said sadly. "I'm leaving you. I need some me time."

The death god shook his head. "But I love you, Nim."

She walked to him and went up on tiptoes to kiss him softly. "Then understand that I need a little time. I love you, Arawn, but I don't like me much anymore."

Roarke's dark eyes looked down at her and he smiled. "We'll still be here, Nim. Go do whatever you need to do and I'll work on him. Love you, Nim."

Dev helped Daniel stand up. They both looked weak, as if they had halved their energy between them.

"Let's get you dressed, Dan," Dev said. "Unless you intend to stop a war in Superman boxers."

Daniel grinned. "They were a present from our wife."

"Yeah, you would never buy those on your own," Dev teased. He was suddenly serious, his mouth turning down. "Zoey, do you really think he's still here?"

Daniel reached out and Dev put his hand in his. There was no self-consciousness about it. Their hands melded together in a union I wouldn't have thought possible a year before.

And then my nipples went hard. Warmth enveloped me like a hug and a… "Yep, it's Bris. I think he just felt me up."

"That's him," Danny and Dev said at the same time. I watched as their hands squeezed together. There was heat and longing between them. Daniel understood his sacrifice. He pulled Dev close, though they didn't embrace. Still, there was no distance between them. They were so close, their heads together in peace, in stillness, in prayer.

"Thank you," Daniel let his cheek rest against Dev's. "Please let him know. Let him know we want him back. We need him."

I reached out to them. "Bris, don't leave us."

It didn't matter how long it took. We wanted him back. We needed him. He completed our little family.

A warm wind surrounded me again. It played on my skin. He was here. He would follow until he could join us again. He had no intention of leaving us.

"Help me."

I turned and was startled to see the Hunter standing in the hallway. Sean was asleep on his shoulder, his little mouth wide open and drooling all over the ascended god. The Hunter looked at me pleadingly.

"I do not know what to do with it," the Hunter said. "Its parents are still yelling at each other. They're circling each other and questioning each other's parentage. I tried to point out that both King Angus and Queen Miria were married at the time of their births but it didn't help."

I shook my head and took the child from him. Dev and Danny started up the stairs to get Daniel dressed. I sat back in the chair and let Sean sleep on as his parents proved they knew some dirty words.

"Don't get comfy, boys," I told the wolves. I still felt Bris close by. He gave me great comfort. “We have to head out ASAP. We need to get to the palace and stop Angus from meeting my mother-in-law.”

Lee put a hand on his belly. “I’ll skip lunch then. If we’re riding that wind again, I don’t want anything on my stomach.”

I sighed. If Lee was willing to give up lunch, I was in for one wild ride.

Chapter Thirty-Two

I held on to Daniel, my arms wrapped around him and not simply because of the way the eddy wind banged through the sky, tossing us all around. I held on to him because I could still see him lying there. The cloud moved violently, but Daniel's hands were gentle as he twisted this way and that way to take the brunt of the other bodies hitting us as Dev made wild turns.

"This is the spot." Dev had to scream over the winds and I could still barely hear him.

Daniel had no such trouble. He simply nodded and then kissed my forehead before stepping out of the mist that surrounded us and disappearing.

"You're next, Zoey." Dev gave me a little push. "Let Daniel catch you."

I fell from the wind, the outer edges roaring past my ears like a hurricane. I sped ruthlessly toward the ground and scrambled to get into a good position to hit the dirt because the way Dev had pushed me, I was going to land flat on my ass. I kind of screamed as I hit free-fall speed, and then I landed on Daniel with a resounding thud. He didn't catch me exactly but his body did stop my fall.

"He drives like crap," Daniel said, turning over and forcing me upright.

"It wasn't so bad." The actual ride had been fine. It was the takeoff and the landing that could use some work. Dev had to first find one of the winds that whipped through the Unseelie *sithein*, and then he had to time it just right to call the wind to sweep the party up. Being pulled into the wind was like being an ant sucked up into a vacuum cleaner. It had made me nauseous, and I had held onto to Daniel for dear life, practically strangling him in the process.

"God, Z, it made me want to puke and I don't do that anymore," Danny admitted, getting off the ground. He looked up, watching for the next person to fall. "Careful, baby. I don't want you to get hit."

The outline of the wind was barely visible, so we couldn't be sure just where the body would hit. Lee was kind enough to announce his position as he screamed when he fell. Lee hit the ground hard and came up growling.

"You could have caught me, Donovan," Lee groused.

"Do you have any idea how heavy you are, man?" Daniel shot back. "Besides, I thought you were all lone wolfie. You don't need anyone. Have your master there catch you."

I held my arms out with a welcoming smile. Lee grumbled as he rolled his eyes, but I saw his grin.

"That one is mine," Daniel said seriously as he caught Zack, who was scrambling even as he fell through the air. Zack was on his feet, smoothing out his clothes before Lee managed to catch his breath.

"I don't see what the problem is." Zack was completely unruffled by the experience. His attention was on the sky above as Neil came through and Zack caught him easily. "I think it's kind of fun."

Neil didn't look like he thought it was fun. My bestie was a little on the green side.

Declan landed on his feet and then caught Chima and Sean, who laughed the entire way down. Declan tried to hold her, but Chima insisted they be put down.

Declan looked at his son approvingly even as the rest of our party descended. "The boy is unaffected by his uncle's poor driving. He has a strong stomach. He will be a great warrior."

"What if he doesn't want to be a warrior?" Chima replied tartly even as Sean was trying to play with his father's bow.

"What else will he be, Chima? Are you planning to send the boy to butcher's school? Perhaps he will be a gardener?" Declan asked sarcastically. "He will be king one day. He could be king of both the Seelie and Unseelie. He will be a great warrior."

Dev hit the ground on his feet, his form perfect, and there was a smile on his face as he found me and Daniel. "It's good to see you survived the experience, you two."

"I landed on my ass, Dev," Daniel complained.

"I landed on Daniel's ass, too." I gave my faery prince an encouraging hug. Though it had only been a couple of days, it felt like forever since we'd been together.

"It's quiet." Nim glanced around the seemingly empty courtyard.

There was a silence about the place that I found disconcerting. The palace should be bustling with activity. There should have been soldiers and guards, but the entire place looked deserted.

"Too quiet." Chima managed to stop arguing with Declan long enough to look around the palace grounds.

I took my first glimpse at the Unseelie stronghold. King Angus's home stood roughly half a mile from us. Unlike the marble white of the Seelie palace, this one was done in dark stones. Dominating the landscape, it looked entirely medieval and highly fortified. It also looked deserted.

"Where is Grandpa?" Sean asked.

"I don't know." Chima shook her head, staying close to her son.

"The traitor said the war was about to begin," the Hunter noted. "Perhaps the king has joined his army on the battlefield."

Dev stared at the palace as though trying to see if anyone was there. "But Mother intended to talk to Angus first. They should have met at either our palace or here. Even if they chose a neutral location, the entire population of the Unseelie palace wouldn't be gone."

Lee held a hand up, getting everyone's attention. "We're not alone."

"Lee's right," Zack concurred. "There are people here. They're hiding."

Chima stepped forward. She held Sean on her hip. "Hello? Is anyone here? It's Princess Chima. I'm looking for my father. Please show yourself."

Declan tried to pull her back. "Chima, you cannot leave yourself open like this. Get behind me."

"These are my people, Declan," Chima said. "Why would they hurt me?"

I heard Declan's snort. "My lovely naïve wife…"

Chima shook her head. "Don't you call me that."

"It's what you are," Declan shot back. "And one of your people just tried to kill our son."

"With the help of your mighty duke," Chima replied.

"Yes." I was willing to look at the positive side of things. "See, the Seelie and the Unseelie can work together."

Dev laughed but Declan huffed. "I am merely pointing out that we are not so different. Both of our palaces are filled with traitors trying to kill us all. It is a piece of common ground that we can build on. That and my and Chima's undeniable sexual chemistry."

"We don't have any sexual chemistry, you idiot," Chima snarled at him.

Declan's green eyes narrowed. "We certainly had good chemistry when I fucked you in the yard during our argument."

Chima's lovely pale skin took on a distinct red tone. "I can't believe you just announced that."

The prince waved off her embarrassment. "It is faster that way. I was going to tell my brother, who would certainly tell the vampire and Zoey, who would immediately tell the gossipy blond wolf, who would tell Zack, who would mention it to the irritable wolf, who wouldn't care. See, they would all have known anyway."

"You didn't have to announce it in front of our son," Chima said.

"The boy should know his parents are passionate." Declan disregarded her concerns. "He should know they can't keep their hands off each other."

"You managed for years," Nim pointed out.

"Not because I did not want Chima." Declan's voice softened. "I stayed away because our relationship was not workable. But you should know, my lover, that every woman I have fucked since we broke up I have pretended was you."

"And that is an enormous amount of women, Chima," Dev offered magnanimously. "Really, it proves his devotion."

"Yes, I can see that." Chima turned to Lee. "Could you point me to where these people are hiding?"

Lee didn't need to because a brownie was rushing across the yard as fast as her small legs would carry her. "Your Highness!"

Recognition lit Chima's face. "Bridgit, thank the goddess. What's happening? Where is my father? Where is the court?"

Bridgit's small, flat face looked confused as she stared at us. "Princess, isn't that the Seelie prince?"

"Yes," Chima said impatiently. "It's Prince Declan and his brother and his brother's family. Now where is my father?"

Large brown eyes widened. "Miria called off all negotiations when she heard the news that her sons had been killed by our warriors. The battle has already begun. Miria has promised to kill all of us."

"Why does Mother think we are dead?" Declan asked. "She knew we were going to look for Zoey and Daniel. I explained to her that I had to go with my brother."

Daniel crossed his arms over his chest. "I'm sure the Duke of Ain saw it as a great opportunity to press his case. He controls the information that flows from gate to gate. Why wouldn't he lie about your death? Con was going to try to make it the truth."

Chima passed Sean to the brownie. "Please take Sean to our rooms."

Declan snapped his fingers and five guards appeared, twisting reality around them. I always wondered if they just sat in some magical waiting room. Declan looked at the warriors. "You will protect my son with your life. You will not pick a fight. You will remain silent unless absolutely necessary. Can the brownie be trusted?"

Chima nodded emphatically. "She raised me, Declan. Sean is like her grandchild."

Declan nodded. "You will follow the brownie's orders in everything. Consider her your temporary mistress."

One of the guards opened his mouth in obvious protest.

Declan stared him down. "He is my son. He will one day be your king. If you will not do my bidding in this then consider yourselves enemies of the state. I will consider your disobedience to be treason."

The guards bowed their head in acquiescence. They surrounded the brownie and her charge.

"He's serious," Chima assured the servant. "They'll follow your orders and keep you and Sean safe until we return."

The brownie nodded and her arms formed a protective circle around the boy. After saying good-bye one last time, the brownie started into the palace and the Seelie guards followed.

Chima turned to Declan. Her blue eyes were serious as she regarded him. "Thank you, Declan."

"I should have sent you with them, Chima." Declan watched the guard like he wanted to call them back. "I should have ordered them to keep you safe and not let you out of their sight, but I am trying. My brother's wife seems to find it irritating when her husbands try to keep her safe."

"Then I will have to thank Zoey for training you well," Chima said with a small smile. "But for the record, Declan, we're not married."

"We certainly are," Declan insisted, taking her hand. "And I shall call your father out for keeping my wife and son from me."

"You certainly will not!" Chima yelled.

Lee groaned and looked at Dev. "I'm ready to go in that damn wind again because that awful sound will drown the two of them out."

Lee didn't need to ask. Dev was already looking to the sky and taking my hand. In the blink of an eye we were riding the wind to the Unseelie gate and the battlefield.

* * * *

Our landing was smoother this time. Daniel managed to stay on his feet and he caught me in a neat motion. As the rest of the party made it to our destination, we were immediately faced with a problem. The gate to the plains was closed and heavily guarded.

Fifty armed Unseelie warriors stood as a phalanx against a possible Seelie invasion. They had been facing the closed gates but they turned and stared at us as we hit the ground.

"Shit, Z, get back," Daniel shouted as Lee landed behind us.

The minute he heard the worry in Danny's voice, he exploded in a mass of fur and claws. Lee and Daniel stood in front of me as the guard made their charge.

"Stand down!" Chima yelled when she made it to the ground.

Declan was already pushing her back. "Stay with Zoey."

"I'm their princess and they will follow my orders," she insisted.

Declan notched three arrows at once, splaying them between his fingers. He drew back and carefully sprayed the crowd, managing to avoid Daniel and all three wolves, who were fighting the guards.

"Or they will assume that the Seelie royals have taken you as a hostage," Declan explained, preparing his weapon for another assault. "They will attempt to kill all of us to protect you. Nim, get back here."

Nim scrambled to get back when she saw how Daniel was tossing bodies about. Dev hit the ground and his brother was immediately at his side.

"It is time for Bris to work his magic, brother," Declan ordered.

I saw Dev's face fall but he raised his hands and a sweat broke out on his brow as he attempted to call all things green to our aid. The grass around the fight grew but not to any height that would make a difference. I could see that my husband was tired. He would have to get used to using his magic without having Bris to call upon.

"What is wrong?" Declan asked.

Daniel wrestled a long sword away from one of the warriors, and that was all it took. After a moment, even the wolves dropped back to give the vampire room to work.

The Hunter watched from the sidelines. "He's a magnificent predator. No wonder Arawn found him fascinating."

Nim stiffened beside me at the mention of Arawn's name. I felt bad for the girl, but I was damn glad he wasn't with us. I didn't trust him and Daniel needed every bit of energy he had. With the grace of a carefully choreographed action film, Daniel danced through the men. One by one they fell to his sword. Some tried to get back up but Daniel quickly made sure it would be a while before the immortal warriors rose from the field. Night had fallen and Daniel was at full strength.

Nim stared at Daniel with wonder in her violet eyes. "I've only seen his like once before, and it was long ago."

"Did you meet the other vampire king?" I asked, curious as to the job Nim claimed she had before she met Arawn. I had to wonder what kind of occupations had been open to a girl back in the Dark Ages.

Nim shook her head. "He wasn't a vampire but he certainly was a king. I'm beginning to think it wasn't chance that brought us together, Zoey."

I frowned. "It wasn't chance at all. It was that asshole Con."

Daniel skewered the final faery and aside from the occasional groan, they were blissfully silent. Daniel looked up from his killing field and caught my eye. "You good, Z?"

I nodded, but we both turned at the sound coming from Declan.

"What do you mean?" Declan's question came out as a scream. He had his hand on his sword hilt.

Daniel was standing in front of Dev before I could even see him move.

Dev stepped in front of Daniel. "He's not going to hurt me, Dan. And you heard what I said, brother."

Declan squared off, his shoulders tightening. "You thought the vampire was worth killing our people's future?"

Dev was red in the face as he stared at his brother. "He's my partner. Bris was willing to save his life and I took him up on it. What was I supposed to do? Allow Daniel to die?"

"Yes," Declan declared. "You were supposed to think of your people first."

"He is my people," Dev replied as Daniel watched quietly, his mouth a flat line. He was waiting to put Declan on his ass if he laid a hand on Dev. I wasn't so sure Dev would appreciate Daniel trying to handle his fight, but Dev belonged to Daniel and there was no way Daniel would allow someone to harm him if he could stop it.

"He's still with us," I tried to interject. Bris wasn't lost.

Declan snarled down at me. "Oh, I am sure he is, Zoey. He is hanging around in a useless ghost-like form. This is your fault. You cried, I'm sure, and begged my brother to save the vampire. Do you understand what you have done, Zoey? You have taken away our only hope."

"Yes, because I certainly couldn't help anyone on my own," Dev said bitterly. "I have no power without a god to prop me up."

Declan's face twisted with anger. "Well, brother, as I am the only one of us to have proven his fertility with a living child, perhaps I should take over your duties as well. Don't try to tell me you got Zoey pregnant because we all know that was Bris. Hope your vampire was worth it, brother."

Dev's jaw locked, and I could see his rage was about to spill over. I took his hand and hoped the contact would help the way it sometimes helped Daniel. He took a deep breath and nodded to his brother. "Understood. I wish you luck in performing my duties. Daniel, there is a door to the Earth plane at the north end of this *sithein*. We'll find ourselves in Scotland, but I believe it to be the safest way to get our wife home. Zack, you will wait here until the battle is finished. When it's safe, please retrieve Sarah, Felix, and Albert. I will have cars awaiting you at the *sithein* door."

"What are you talking about?" Declan stepped in Dev's way.

"We're leaving, asshole," Daniel announced with a satisfied grin. "You're on your own."

"As I am no longer needed on this plane, I will retreat to my home with my family," Dev said, a chill in his voice. "Do not bother me again with your troubles, Declan. I wish you luck."

Chima stepped forward, her eyes pleading. "Priest, I don't care what the Seelie think. I promise you, the Unseelie desperately need you. We have kept your temple in all good preparation in hopes that you would return. Ascended god or not, we need you. As the goblins' princess, I beg you to reconsider. Our plight is desperate. Don't allow your brother's ignorance to cost my kingdom as well."

"Dev," I said, pulling on his hand. "We can't leave. Your mother is in danger. The duke intends to assassinate her during the battle. You can't walk away. It would haunt you forever."

Dev turned, his skin turning pale. "Daniel…"

Daniel nodded. "Whatever you need, man."

Dev looked to the door. "The battle can only be ended by each side blowing the battle horns. One is not enough."

"I'll find my father," Chima promised.

"You will not be going onto a battlefield, wife. You could be killed," Declan protested. His voice was slightly subdued as though he realized how much his previous actions might cost him.

Chima sighed and a weary look crossed her face. "Then I suggest that you defend me, Declan. I'm tired of fighting with you already. I am going to offer you a deal. You may take it or leave it. Though I worry a marriage to you will not be happy, I'm willing to accept your claim if it will bring our tribes together."

Something like hope lit Declan's green eyes. He took Chima's hands in his. "I love you, Chima. I have since we were children. I promise I will try to work with the Unseelie if it means we can be together. I want to know our son."

"Yes," Chima said. "You'll need him since it appears you've lost your brother."

Declan's face turned stubborn. "It is for my son that I wish my brother had not proven to be so selfish. He chose that goddess of his over our people. Perhaps he is not fit to be our priest."

"You'll work with him as he is still the Unseelie priest. He's the Unseelie's High Priest." Chima made sure to enunciate the honor she bestowed upon him and looked at Dev expectantly.

"My goddess and I will use our paltry power to aid you in any way possible," he promised. He got back to his battle plans. "Zoey, Neil, and I will make our way around the edges of the battle to try to get to my mother. Zack and Lee will stay with Daniel."

"And I will be?" Daniel asked.

"Providing one hell of a diversion," Dev replied.

Daniel smiled slowly, looking forward to the violence. "I might need to refuel during battle, depending on how long it takes."

"As long as you don't drain the warriors, they should survive the experience," Dev offered. "That's what Zack and Lee will be there for. They'll protect you should you be forced to take a lunch break. You should try one of the goblins. I've heard their blood is exotic."

"Never had one before," Daniel acknowledged.

"Hunter," Dev called. "You will join us?"

The Hunter nodded his assent. "I'll be ready should you desire to call upon me and mine."

Dev's face turned savage, and I knew he was thinking about the Duke of Ain and his family. "I'll be calling on you, Hunter. Make sure you are ready to ride. Now, Daniel, if you wouldn't mind getting that door open for us."

Running faster than I could track him, Daniel hit the enormous gates and they exploded outward under the force of his arms. The sounds of battle assaulted us.

Dev took my hand and we found ourselves in the middle of a war.

Chapter Thirty-Three

It was my first look at the plain that separated the *sitheins*.

"It's daylight." I started to try to reach for Daniel, but he was already running away from me.

"It's a magical light, Zoey." Dev's eyes moved across the plain, taking in the battle in front of us. "It won't affect him at all. It's always daylight on this plain. It's another defense mechanism."

I was certain that on a normal day, it was peaceful and beautiful. The grassy plain was flat and almost certainly would be a fertile green had it not become saturated with blood. The sounds of sword hitting sword rang across the field. Even as Dev pulled me along, I turned my head and watched as Declan led Chima and Nim to the back of the Unseelie war machine. There were several tents set up, and I could see what must be the king's advisors meeting underneath one. I didn't see anyone I thought could be Angus, but I hoped whoever it was would listen to Chima's reason. Dev, Neil, and I had the infinitely harder job. We had to do the same thing Chima, Nim, and Declan were doing, but we had to make our way across the entire length of the battlefield to do it and we would be doing it without the aid of eddy winds. It was far too dangerous with all the arrows flying around.

I didn't like the idea of those arrows rushing toward my

vampire. It wouldn't matter that they weren't silver tipped. Each one was a little stake flying through the air. He would have to be careful.

"Stay close," Dev yelled over the clatter. I followed his eyes as he spotted Daniel.

I caught my breath as Daniel ran onto the field and took a mighty leap. He jumped over the back lines of the battle and into the middle of the fray. It only took a second before the bodies started to fly and all attention was on the newcomer. The blood-soaked battlefield brought out Daniel's beast, and he was on full display. I'd never seen his fangs so long or his claws so sharp. Just the smell of all that blood was enough to put Daniel on the edge of his control. He cut through the lines easily, raining confusion down all around him.

I felt Neil running beside me, his pure white fur a dramatic contrast to the violence around us. We stayed close to the edges of the battle but it encroached. A Seelie *sidhe* battled a large male goblin. It was apparent they had been fighting for a while, hacking little pieces off of one another, but the *sidhe* was tiring and the goblin's strength held up. The goblin wielded a bloody cleaver and brought it down on the *sidhe's* arm. I shrank back as the faery's arm hit the ground.

"Don't look." Dev pulled me as far away as he could.

I tried to follow his command, but it was everywhere. Violence and bloodlust filled the world and it made me sick. I wanted to close my eyes and block the sights of people who should work together, cutting each other apart. In the middle of all of it I saw Lee and Zack, their magnificent wolf selves howling even as Daniel became a prime target.

Dev cursed and I found myself on the ground, his big body pressing me into the dirt. He held my head down and forced my torso under his as I heard a horrible sound. It sounded like water rushing violently toward us.

"Don't move." Dev whispered the words directly in my ear, and I could hear the worry in his voice. His body tensed as if in anticipation of some horrible pain.

All around me I heard the distinct thuds of arrows hitting the dirt. There were screams of agony as some of the arrows found warm bodies to lodge into. I felt Dev jerk against me and I heard him try to contain his groan of pain.

"Baby," I said quietly. "Where are you hit?"

"I'm fine. It's my right arm. Quickly, we don't have long before they send over another volley." He rolled off me carefully, protecting his left arm. "Zoey, pull it out or shove it through."

I wanted to protest that he was crazy if he thought I would do that, but there wasn't time and he was right. If I could get the arrow out, he would heal quickly and we would move much faster. Neil growled ahead of us, letting me know we had little time.

I studied Dev's arm briefly. The arrow had lodged in the muscle of his upper arm. With the flat of my right hand, holding his arm with my left, I shoved the arrow until the thick gory head was through. Dev groaned but didn't move as I managed to snap the shaft and pull both sides out.

Dev was on his feet before the arrow hit the ground. He flexed his hand and then handed me the Sig Sauer. "Sorry, sweetheart, that was my firing hand. Give me a few minutes and I should have the feeling back."

I didn't mind having the gun. It made me feel better and I was a damn good shot. Ahead, Neil was attempting to make a path through the warriors. The ones who wouldn't move I shot. The cold iron bullets were persuasive.

I could see the Seelie back lines now. Miria was dressed in trousers and a practical shirt. She stood high on a platform with a small guard surrounding her. She looked different than the last time I had seen her. Her perceived loss was visible in every inch of her skin. It was as though all the hope and joy had been drained from the Seelie queen and what had been left was a need for vengeance. She would never stop, never call off the battle because she believed her sons were dead and gone and she had nothing left. I had to get to her, had to let her know all was not lost.

Even as I ran toward her, I heard a mighty yell go up in the thick of battle.

Daniel was busy with one of those mid-battle snacks I knew he looked forward to. It was the only time he would ever allow himself off his self-imposed leash. He would never feed from anyone but me or Dev when the feeding was an intimate act, but there was nothing intimate or gentle about this. This was a predator pulling his unwilling victim down and glorying in the kill. This was a lion taking down a gazelle, though I'm sure the goblin would be offended by the metaphor. Luckily, this gazelle was immortal and would live to be pissed off by the experience.

The shout that went up came from a large, white-haired *sidhe*. It was Padric, his heavy sword coated in blood as he turned toward his queen. His pale eyes were confused as he began to run back toward the encampment.

"I'm sure they were told you and Daniel were dead, too," Dev yelled in explanation.

Miria saw Padric running toward her and hurried to the end of the platform. She ran down the stairs and met him at the back as he broke through the lines. As I ran toward them, I saw him whisper in her ear. She held on to Padric even as she then tried to get a good look at Daniel, as though she would not believe it until she saw it for herself. There was no question in my mind what she was asking him. She wanted to know about her sons. Padric shook his head.

They were so closely engaged that neither saw the men creeping up behind them. While Daniel was providing us with a distraction, it was also working for the bad guys. Much of the battle was now focused on the blood-soaked vampire who had been hit more times than any of them could count and still left a trail of bodies in his wake. The weapons makers of the faery world would be stocking up on silver in the near future. Cold iron didn't mean a damn thing to Danny. I was sure he would tell me it tickled.

Three men worked their way toward the Seelie queen. Even Miria's guard was distracted.

"Neil," I screamed, pointing toward the trouble.

He barked and took off. He was far faster than Dev or I could hope to be. He swerved and curved his way through the combatants.

Dev and I had more trouble than Neil. We had to stay on the outskirts of battle, making our way around the bloody fights that seemed to go on everywhere. Dev grasped my hand as we tried to get to his mother.

The assassins held cold iron knives in their hands, and they were smart enough to divide their forces. Two were making their way toward Padric while one was lying in wait. I could see the way the plot would work. The third assassin would wait until Padric was detained with fighting and probably murdering the other two. Then the third could easily slit the queen's throat and take her heart. It was likely a suicide mission, but the Duke of Ain had proven to have loyal followers.

"Mother!" Dev screamed, trying to warn her, but his voice was a small sound, easily missed amid the cacophony of death around us.

We ran hard, shoving our way past warriors. We were on the Seelie side, and now some of the warriors were beginning to recognize their supposedly dead priest and his also newly risen goddess. It made it easier. They didn't attempt to fight us as we struggled to get through the throng to make our way to Miria.

Neil had no such trouble. He twisted his way through. Very few people looked down to pay attention to the white dog working his way toward the royal. The moment he got a chance, Neil made a break for the queen. He barked a warning just as Padric was jumped. I watched in horror as both men managed to stick their knives cleanly into Padric's strong torso.

I tried to get a shot, but I was too short. I would hit the other bodies that were in our way.

Neil howled and stood between the queen and her assassin even as Miria pulled a knife from her belt and tried to help Padric. Neil leapt onto the killer at the queen's back but now the two who had been taking out the head of the royal guard divided their forces. With Padric bleeding profusely, one of the men started after the queen.

I tried to shove my way through, but I couldn't find a way out, and now the warriors were starting to notice us. It wouldn't be long before someone decided to keep things the way they were and make Dev's previous death into a reality.

"Give me a boost," I yelled to Dev.

"What?"

I pointed up. "I can't get a shot off. I need some height."

Dev leaned down, cupped his hands together, and waited to boost me up. I would have one shot, a mere second to find my balance and my target. I put my right foot in Dev's hands and he lifted me up and over the fray. Having a husband who tops six foot five is helpful when you need a lift.

I balanced on one foot and concentrated, allowing the world to fall away the way my father had taught me to. Time felt suspended as I blocked out everything else but the feel of the gun in my hand, the trigger a firm pressure against my finger. My vision narrowed to the man about to slit my mother-in-law's throat. I breathed deeply and let my focus pinpoint his head. In a heartbeat, I pulled the trigger gently and watched as a place right above his left eye exploded.

There were loud shouts and someone screamed to get "the woman." I was pulled roughly from my perch by strong hands. Yeah, I was apparently the woman in question. The force of being jerked around caused me to lose the gun that would have been helpful given I was being hauled off by an angry mob.

Dev screamed and I saw him fight against hands that held him. He kicked out, but there were too many of them.

It occurred to me as I was pulled in several different directions by vicious hands that perhaps my actions had been misconstrued. It was possible that the Seelie warriors I was currently being carried off by were thinking I was the assassin rather than the queen's savior. I was pulled down and circled by a group of warriors. The largest of my captors wasn't waiting on a fair trial. He shoved me to my knees and forced my head back.

It looked like everyone wanted to behead me.

A mighty roar filled my world, drowning out all other sounds. I was shoved forcibly to the ground. My chest and both arms hit the saturated grass as Lee stood over me, growling at the circle of would-be executioners. I managed to see the group that surrounded us take a healthy step back as Daniel landed on the ground in front of me. His clothes dripped blood and his voice was a low growl.

He stared at the men holding Devinshea back.

"If you have any wish to stay alive, you will release him." Daniel had to work to enunciate around the fangs in his mouth.

"It is an Unseelie trick," a warrior said. "The princes are dead. This is magic created to fool us."

"I am no Unseelie trick," Daniel promised. "Give him to me or I will no longer hold back."

"Hold back?" I heard someone mutter. If Daniel had been

pulling punches, I was pretty sure they didn't want to see him let loose.

I saw someone shove Dev forward, and he was quickly pulled behind Daniel. He was on his knees as Lee moved to guard our backs and Zack joined him.

"Are you all right?" Dev pulled me close. "I have to get to Mother…"

But even as he said it I heard the sound, the single blare of a great horn from the Seelie side. When we looked up following that blissful noise, I saw Neil in human form, pointing the way to us for the queen. Padric was back on his feet. He held his side but kept up with his queen as she made her way to us.

There was one more sound we needed to hear, and Dev tensed as he held me, waiting for it, praying for it.

It was farther away this time but no less beautiful. The Unseelie side answered and just like that, the battle was done.

Chapter Thirty-Four

"Devinshea." Miria shouted. Padric walked behind her, his face pale, but he seemed to be healing. The crowd parted for them, giving the queen space to move.

Dev got to his feet as Daniel stood down. They turned to me and each took a hand to help me up. Daniel's eyes were dark and filled with need as the bloodlust was receding and another lust took its place. I was sure I was his wet dream. I was soft and vulnerable, my heart racing from the adrenaline, and I was covered in blood.

"Zoey," Daniel groaned my name as he pulled me into his arms. "God, I want you so much."

This wasn't the time or place for public sex. It's sad that I've started to think there actually is a time and place for that, but I'd been with Dev for too long. We still had a few issues to work out, so I gave him the next best thing. I put my hand to his mouth, shoving my finger in, and he sucked it, drawing the blood from my skin. He fell to his knees at my side, carefully cleaning each finger as I ran my free hand through his hair, trying to bring him down to earth.

Zack took his place next to Daniel. Lee and Neil, who had

changed back to his animal form, rested at my side. The wolves preferred to stay in their strongest form until they were absolutely sure the danger had passed.

"Oh, thank the goddess," Miria proclaimed, allowing her tears to flow freely. She hugged her son close. "I was told you were dead. Your brother?"

"Is well, Mother," Declan announced, pushing his way through the crowd. "Surely you couldn't believe I would allow myself to be murdered."

Miria held her arms open for her eldest son. I don't think she noticed how Dev pulled back from his brother.

"As you can see, Miria, your boys are alive and well," a booming voice with a thick Scottish accent said. "I didn't have them brought to my palace and executed as your so-called intelligence suggested."

I followed Miria's eyes and caught my first sight of the Unseelie King. Angus dominated the scene. He was at least six foot seven with a broad muscular build. He was dressed savagely in animal skins and leather boots, likely all of which he'd killed himself. His face was covered in scars from previous battles and like his ancestor, Balor of the Evil Eye, there was a place on his forehead that was covered by a patch. His third eye. It was said that if Angus wanted to, he could kill a man with a single glance from that eye.

I couldn't look at the man and not think "yargh, me mateys."

"I can see that," Miria allowed. She frowned as she looked around at the crowd. It seemed to be finally sinking in that she had a traitor in her midst. She glanced back at Padric. "Have the Duke of Ain brought to me, by force if necessary."

"I will, my queen," Padric promised. He flicked his hand and five warriors followed him.

"I was so worried," Miria said to her eldest son. "I knew you were going to the Unseelie homeland to save your brother's goddess. I was told Angus had caught you and executed all of you."

"Nothing so dramatic, Mother," Declan explained, looking nonchalant. "It was simple. Zoey had been taken prisoner by the Unseelie traitor, Con. I was forced to rescue her and Angus's daughter Chima, who turns out to be my bride."

"What?" Miria's eyes widened as she took in the king's daughter.

Declan shrugged. "I might have been having a secret affair with the Unseelie princess. That affair might have produced a lovely, strong boy. I would not have named him Sean, but I suppose since the boy is used to it we shall have to keep the name."

Angus was rolling his not deadly eyes and looking down on his daughter. "Are you sure we shouldn't have lied and said Sean was the priest's son? I would have preferred him as a son-in-law. I'll most likely kill that one."

Dev made his way back to me. Daniel was still luxuriating in the blood on my skin. I heard him sigh every now and then as he moved from finger to finger and up to my wrist. I tried not to look at the Seelie warriors who watched him with unconcealed distaste. He might look like a monster to them, but he was a monster I loved dearly. Dev reached down and set his hand on Daniel's shoulder to let him know he was there. We were starting to take after our wolves. We preferred physical contact when we were together.

"There was one disaster I have to report, Mother." Declan's gaze turned to his twin. He didn't even try to hide his contempt for Daniel. "Devinshea chose to sacrifice Bris to save his wife's vampire."

A collective gasp was heard throughout the crowd. All eyes turned to us and even Daniel stopped what he was doing. The only person who looked vaguely happy with the turn of events was Angus. There was a small smile on his rough face, like he knew something the rest of us didn't.

Miria gasped, turning to Dev. "Is this true, son? Is the god truly gone?"

Dev cast his eyes down. "He is not gone entirely, but he was weakened. It might be a while before he is able to take a host again. My goddess still feels his presence. He will bide his time and attempt to reintegrate with me in the future."

"Of course Zoey feels his presence," Declan said, showing his skepticism. "Zoey is the reason you betrayed your people, brother. I hardly think I can believe a word she says."

"It was not a betrayal." Dev looked to his mother, willing her to understand. "I was saving someone I love. You would do the same."

"No," Declan said with great certainty, shaking his head. "She would sacrifice. She would do what is best for her people. She would never have chosen a monster over her family."

Now Angus's smile wasn't even small. He was deeply enjoying the prince's current occupation of deep hole digger. Miria, however, frowned and didn't deny what Declan was saying.

Dev bent down to help Daniel up. Daniel was in control again, and I could see that Declan's words were pulling out his sense of shame. He looked around, feeling the condemnation from Dev's people.

"Daniel just saved you," Dev said to his mother. "If it hadn't been for Daniel we would never have been able to make it across the field. Neil wouldn't have been able to keep the assassin off you long enough for Zoey to kill him. That's your monster, Mother. We all risked everything to stop this bloodshed and save you."

Miria's green eyes took in her son. "I understand, Devinshea. I truly do. I do not think the vampire is a monster. He is your partner and you have forged a life with him and your goddess. But Devinshea, the only reason the nobles were willing to take you back as our priest was Bris. While we need your power as a Green Man, it is inconsequential compared to what Bris could have brought us."

"I disagree," Angus interrupted. "I've had reports that since the priest bound himself to the vampire and his companion, he's left a wide swath of pregnant females wherever they sleep."

"Humans." Declan discounted the notion entirely. "They are intensely susceptible to sex magic."

Chima stepped forward. "It's not just humans."

Miria shook her head. "They will not accept him without the god. Hopefully, Bris will reintegrate soon and all will be well. You can take your place and the nobles will accept you."

A bitter laugh huffed out of Dev's mouth. "Fuck your nobles, Mother. I'm done with this place. My home is on the Earth plane now. I shed the title of priest and consider myself Seelie no longer. I'm Zoey's husband. I'm Daniel's partner. Goddess willing, I will be father to our children, but they won't be Seelie either. As soon as I finish my final task, I will trouble you no more."

"Devinshea," Miria began and I could see her heart was aching.

"Feel free to call upon me if you ever find yourself in Dallas," Dev said. "I don't seek to cut you entirely from my life, but I understand that you're a queen and must hold your standards high. I love you, but there is no place for a freak like me in your world."

"Ah, Your Grace, let's talk about my world." Angus's accented voice was pure honey. "Your mother might not have a place for you, but I certainly do."

Dev looked at the Unseelie King. "I meant what I said, Angus. I intend to stay with my family on the Earth plane."

"That doesn't mean you can't visit your people and bless them with your magic from time to time," Angus reasoned. "Any children you have will be faery children. We Unseelie have no problem with mortals. Many of us are mortal. I've found it just makes us tougher. You don't have to be born Unseelie, son. You just have to need a place to go." He turned to Daniel and there was great admiration in his eyes. "As for this beastie here, oh, he's more than welcome. My only worry is that he might fight me to take over, and the damn bastard might win."

Daniel's lips tugged up slightly. "Your throne is safe, Your Highness. I have my own waiting for me at home."

"Aye, King of the Vampires," Angus acknowledged with a solemn nod. "Now, you see, I'm thinking we could have ourselves an alliance. A man like you, Mr. Donovan, I think would make a powerful ally. You will find our nobles, that fucker Con aside, will have no problem with your fangs and your bloodlust. It'll match their own."

"Devinshea," Miria said firmly, "you cannot possibly consider his offer. You are my son. The nobles will accept you once you have ascended again."

"And my nobles don't give a shit if you ascend at all, Your Grace," Angus countered.

Miria pointed at Angus. "He is only making the offer on the gamble that you will reintegrate with Bris. Can you not see that, son? He is playing the odds that you will ascend again and then your primary loyalty will be to the Unseelie. Your own people shall be secondary then if you choose to take their High Priest post."

Dev looked at me, his eyes asking the silent question as they switched between me and Daniel.

"I'll go along with whatever you want, Dev," Daniel said. "They're your family. I can handle being called a monster. It's not the worst I've heard. I won't think less of you for wanting to wait to see if Bris comes back."

Dev snorted. "Like I'm going to do that. I meant what I said, Dan. I'm done with the Seelie. I was asking if you minded being considered Unseelie. They would consider you both Unseelie. Our children would be Unseelie *sidhe*."

"I know where I'm comfortable," I said sincerely. "I like wearing pants and being able to defend myself. Besides, I want our kids to know the faery side of their nature. I worry the Seelies would be even less welcoming to kids who have a human for a mother and a halfling and vampire for fathers."

Chima bowed formally our way. "I assure you, Your Grace, that I am looking forward to Sean having a cousin to play with. Tell us you accept, Devinshea. Allow us to be blessed once again with a true high priest."

Dev walked forward and placed himself in front of King Angus. "I promise to be your good priest," he said formally, even as his mother bit back a cry.

Angus bowed as well, the high priest the only noble the king showed that respect to. "And I will be your good king, Priest. I'll never deny you aid. You have merely to ask and the Unseelie will be there. Though we might have called the battle off, it seems to me the Unseelies have won this day."

The love fest was interrupted by Padric, who returned with the struggling duke. The duke fought the warrior, but Padric wasn't about to let his quarry go. He hauled the traitor to the queen and forced him to his knees.

"Braden." Miria looked at him as she might look at a worm. "Would you like to explain how my sons stand before me alive and whole when you swore they were dead? You set me on the course to this battle."

The duke's voice was tremulous. "I was obviously mistaken. I had bad intelligence. It was an honest mistake."

"Mistake?" He was going to try to play it that way? I wasn't about to allow that to pass. "Was it a mistake when you had your daughter sell me to the Unseelies as a sex slave? Was it a mistake when you cursed my unborn child? How about attempting to assassinate the queen?"

Miria turned to me, her skin going pale. "These are grave accusations. Are you certain, daughter?"

"I will prove our certainty, Mother." Dev glanced around until he found who he was looking for. "Hunter?"

A gasp went through the crowd and even Angus pulled his daughter close as if to protect her. Everyone around held their breath in bated anticipation of what was going to happen. Everyone, that is, except the Duke of Ain, who started to beg and struggle again. His eyes were wide with horror.

"Yes, Your Grace," the Hunter answered with a sly smile. His dark eyes glittered, his whole body seeming to swell with power.

Miria put a hand on her son's sleeve and even Declan looked pale. "Son, if you are wrong…"

"Dev," Declan said, "don't do this. We can just behead the bastard and be done with it. We don't need a hunt."

"Oh, brother," Dev said with great relish. "I prefer Unseelie justice." He turned and pointed at the duke. "I am Devinshea Quinn, High Priest of the Unseelie Fae. I accuse the Duke of Ain of crimes against me and mine. He plotted against his queen, betrayed my goddess, and cursed my unborn son. I demand justice, Hunter."

The Hunter strode forward. Even as he walked, he raised an arm and I could feel the sky above me opening up. "And you shall have it. We ride!"

Now there was panic as the crowd around us broke up and ran for cover. Padric released the duke and he began to run. He could run as fast and far as his legs would allow and it wouldn't matter. The hunt would find him. The hunt would have his blood.

A huge black horse, who I would have sworn was on fire, descended and the Hunter mounted in a graceful, fluid motion. The horse reared back and the heavens above seemed to open, unleashing a great army. All the monsters of the world, it seemed, had wings and teeth. They blacked out the sun as they moved toward us.

Dev pulled me close and Daniel covered my back. I was safe and secure between them, but I could hear the screams. I caught glimpses of wild nightmares come to life. They flew past with one thought in their collective brain—kill the Duke of Ain. Bring justice forth by spilling his blood.

"Don't watch," Daniel said, pushing my head against Dev's chest. "You don't want to see it, baby."

I wrapped my arms around Dev and let Daniel's body drown out the screams that seemed to go on forever. The sounds alone would haunt my nightmares. After the longest time, the cries died down and I felt the rushing of winged creatures as they went back to wherever they had come from.

Dev didn't release me even when the Hunter returned.

"Are you satisfied, Your Grace?"

There was darkness in my faery prince's eyes as he nodded. He didn't regret having called the Wild Hunt. "I am."

The Hunter bowed and dismounted. The horse took off to wait in the sky for his master to call him again.

"Come, Daniel. Let's return with King Angus and let our wife rest," Dev said. "It's been a hard few days. I would like to take you up on your previous offer, if it still stands."

Danny had offered to lay in bed together, warm and safe, and discuss our future. "It is always open, Devinshea," Daniel affirmed with a smile. "Though I'll need a bath before you let me into our bed."

Dev grinned down at me. I was every bit as filthy as Daniel. "I think we can all use a bath."

I perked up. I remembered how our last bath went. I stopped when I had a sudden, horrible thought. "Oh, god. The Blood Stone. Did that bitch get my stone?"

Daniel reached into his pocket. "They weren't brave enough to search me. It's been in my pocket the whole time."

"Then let's get to the part where we practice the whole baby-making thing. I could use a break." I looked down to make sure the wolves were following. I was sure Lee, at least, was looking forward to a nice long nap.

"I think you will like your temple, Zoey," Chima said with an eager smile. "I'll have everything in readiness for you. I'll make sure there is a great feast to welcome you home."

"Dev!" Miria shouted as we began to follow Angus and Chima.

Without looking back, Dev replied. "You should take care of Gilliana. She was in on the plot with her father. I'll be satisfied with her speedy execution. Please send her head to me with all due haste. If you do that, I won't call the hunt down again. I'll talk to you soon, Mother, but not today. As for Chima's husband, I prefer not to talk to him at all."

Chapter Thirty-Five

"What do you think it does?" Dev stared at the Blood Stone. It was strangely beautiful in the midday light. He lay on his stomach and I stared at his completely perfect ass.

"I have no freaking idea, man," Daniel admitted, kissing the back of my neck as he let his hands wander across my breasts. Even though he'd just come, he was already getting hard again.

I lay back against Daniel's chest, fairly exhausted. It had been hard keeping up with the two of them since we'd been safely ensconced in the Unseelie temple. We'd tried our hardest to bring Bris back to us but so far we'd had no luck. However, despite Declan's dark warnings, our fertility rituals had seemed plenty powerful. We'd performed several over the last two weeks and Angus had been pleased. Our volume might not be at a hundred and fifty like it had with Bris, but we were a solid ninety-five, and the Unseelie seemed thrilled with their priest. Tomorrow we would be heading home. I was going to miss this big, comfy bed we had barely left for two weeks.

"Goddess, Daniel," Dev said with an admiring smile. "I thought I was insatiable."

Daniel didn't stop his gentle assault. "Tell me you don't want to go again."

Dev set the Blood Stone aside and got up on all fours. I could see plainly he wanted to go again. His cock was standing at full attention.

"Hey," I said, pushing away just a little because I still hadn't recovered. "Nobody asked if I was ready to go again."

Spreading my knees and laying a little kiss on my stomach, Dev settled himself between my legs. "I'm not concerned with that, sweet wife. We can get you ready."

Daniel chuckled in my ear as he held a breast, offering it to Dev's mouth. He made sure my nipple was a ripe berry for Dev to suck on. "We can definitely get you ready."

A feminine voice interrupted us. "Hey, naked people, you have incoming," Sarah yelled from behind the door to the bedroom.

"Tell 'em to go away," Daniel growled.

Sarah opened the door slightly. "I already tried that. It's the king, Chima, and Nim. They're insistent about coming in. Just to warn you, the brat is with them."

Dev groaned and got on his knees. Declan had been hanging around the Unseelie *sithein*, getting to know his son and trying to talk to his brother. Apparently Miria had ordered Declan to make up with his brother and Declan wasn't going to let it go. Dev had ignored him so far.

"We're getting dressed," Dev yelled back. He sighed and we all got up to make ourselves ready.

Ten minutes later, we met with the king and the others in the parlor of the temple. Albert had set out a tempting little buffet and, after the morning's play, I was feeling hungry. Daniel held out a mini cookie for me and I playfully ate it from his fingers. Albert smiled at me as he poured my tea. Of all of us, Albert was probably the happiest with our new faery home. The cooks here came to him for advice and he reveled in the teaching opportunities.

"Well, we know you've been busy, brother," Declan said. "What you lost in power you have more than made up for in sheer volume."

Dev communicated with his brother in the only way he spoke to him anymore—with his happy middle finger.

The king shook his head. "Well, we'll be sorry to see you go. We look forward to your next visit. Nim tells us she is going to be journeying with you."

Chima frowned. She wasn't happy about losing her friend.

Dev inclined his head. "She's welcome to."

Nim smiled and clapped her hands. "I'm so excited. When Arawn used to take me back to the Earth plane, we spent a lot of time in nursing homes and retirement communities. He just felt more comfortable around the nearly dead. Sarah and Neil said they would take me clubbing."

"They would be the ones to do it." I was sure Nim would be a popular fixture at Ether.

Nim took a deep breath. "So, I wanted to talk to the three of you about something. I made a big decision. It happened when I saw Daniel on the battlefield."

I felt Daniel tense beside me.

"I think it was fate that brought you to me, Zoey," Nim said. "I think it was fate's way of reminding me that I have a job to do. You see, a long, long time ago I was tasked with protecting a special weapon. I was supposed to hold it until the right person came along and when he was done with it, I would hold it again until it was time for the next king to rise." Nim's eyes were cloudy with memory. "The last time kind of sucked because I had to wait around in this lake for four hundred years before the little bugger showed up."

Daniel sat up beside me, giving Nim his complete attention. "Nim, what's your full name?"

Nim smiled slyly. "I have been called by many names, Daniel. Nim is short for Nimue, but you might have heard me called Vivienne."

"You're the Lady of the Lake?" Daniel breathed the question with a reverence I hadn't known he was capable of.

Nim stood and walked behind the couch. She reached down where she'd placed something. "Yeah, like I said, hanging around in a cold-ass British lake kind of sucked, but it was where I met Arawn and a boy named Arthur."

Daniel stood up. He was slightly breathless. "Is that what I think it is?"

Everyone stared as Nim pulled a magnificent sword from its sheath. The sword caught every eye in the room. It was polished and gleamed brightly in the midday light.

"Excalibur." Nim turned the weapon, offering the hilt to Daniel. "I think it's yours for now, Daniel. Wield it well and always point it justly."

Daniel took the sword from Nim's small hands. He tested the weight and after a moment bowed to her. "I'm honored you believe me worthy of this sword. I promise I'll use it wisely."

I looked at Nim. "So this old boyfriend of yours?" I knew the stories.

She grimaced. "Yeah, Merlin. We might have trouble with him but he can fix Daniel's problem."

Dev sighed. "So we're going to journey to unleash the wizard Merlin from his prison with the Lady of the Lake and Daniel gets to play around with Excalibur. The first person to call me Lancelot gets beaten soundly."

"I hadn't even thought it," I lied with a bright smile.

"I had," Daniel admitted.

"He was a good boy. He just fell for a girl. It had nothing whatsoever to do with his odd upbringing." Nim shrugged. "I taught him to be a free spirit."

I recalled that Vivienne had adopted the mighty knight. It was hard to think of Nim as a mother.

"Well, now that everyone is happy, I would like a word with my sister-in-law," Declan announced.

"Not a chance." It was the first time since the battle that Dev had spoken directly to his brother.

"You are leaving tomorrow," Declan argued. "You will not speak to me so I am forced to speak to her."

I stood up. "It's fine," I said to Dev. I was interested to see what he wanted. He had been watching me for days with contemplative eyes. "I won't be more than a minute."

I followed Declan out to the front of the temple, thinking about the fact that we had Excalibur. How could we use it to take out Marini, beyond the obvious fact that he would look good skewered on it?

The breeze was warm and made me wonder how much time had passed on the Earth plane. What season would it be when we got home?

"I know your vampire is planning a war, Zoey," Declan said abruptly.

"It's none of your business." I had zero intentions of allowing him to piss me off.

Declan looked out over the courtyard, but the set of his jaw was angry. "I will make this succinct. I know my brother and I are estranged, but he is still my brother. I expect you and Daniel to keep him safe. If he is killed, I shall hold you responsible and we shall have a problem."

With that said, Declan turned and walked away, having nothing further to say to me.

* * * *

I sighed as I took in the door that would land us back in Texas. It had already been an exhausting journey. We had to travel from the Unseelie *sithein* through the Seelie *sithein*. The only bright spot had been seeing Miria and Bibi one last time. Miria had put on a brave face and tried to pretend nothing was wrong. Dev had managed a strained good-bye kiss for his mother.

"Tell me there's a limo waiting on the other side of that door," Neil begged.

Dev laughed. "We're in the middle of nowhere, Neil. A limo would have trouble with the terrain. I have a couple of jeeps coming for us. I promise, though, once we get to Austin, it will be nothing but first class all the way."

The door to the *sithein* shimmered and suddenly I could see rolling hills and cactus plants. Lee practically ran through the door and Zack was right behind him. Daniel looked so happy to be going home. Dev did, too, but I knew the trip had not gone as he'd hoped. I looked back and saw Felix helping his wife up. I thought about the secret she had told me last night, the one she had shared only with Felix and Neil.

Sarah was pregnant.

She'd cried and hoped it didn't upset me. I assured her it didn't, but I lied. It didn't hurt me because I was jealous. It hurt because I would miss her. I'd talked to Felix and he agreed with me that it would be best for them to distance themselves for a while. I didn't want anything to happen to Sarah or her baby and I couldn't promise she would be safe as long as she was close to me. Louis Marini had already proven he would use anyone I cared about as a pawn in our game.

Dev stood at the door. I hesitated for a moment. We had stopped a war on this plane, but I was walking through the door to home with the full intention of starting one this time.

Daniel took my left hand and I gave Dev my right, and as we walked through together, I had but one thought.

I prayed this was a war we could win.

Zoey, Daniel, and Dev will return in Steal the Night.

Author's Note

I'm often asked by generous readers how they can help get the word out about a book they enjoyed. There are so many ways to help an author you like. Leave a review. If your e-reader allows you to lend a book to a friend, please share it. Go to Goodreads and connect with others. Recommend the books you love because stories are meant to be shared. Thank you so much for reading this book and for supporting all the authors you love!

Steal the Night

Thieves, Book 5
By Lexi Blake
Now available.

She was born to be a thief. To save the world, she will have to become a queen…

Zoey Donovan-Quinn is growing restless. After months of searching, her crew hasn't been able to locate the resting place of the one man who could save Daniel. While they frantically continue their quest, Zoey is still struggling to recover from the devastating losses she suffered in Faery. In the midst of her grief and worry, Louis Marini appears and demands the Blood Stone he forced Zoey to steal. Zoey has no other choice than to hand it over.

When the giant ruby's true nature is revealed, Zoey discovers she has given their greatest enemy a weapon of unimaginable power. Equipped with the Blood Stone, Marini intends to dominate the supernatural world and, on a more personal note, claim Zoey as his companion.

Desperate and on the run, Zoey, Dev, and Daniel forge an unlikely alliance with an old adversary who claims he can lead them to the wizard who can free Daniel from Marini's clutches and help him claim his throne. As they race to solve a thousand-year-old mystery and gather their forces for the ultimate battle, Zoey prepares to do what she does best.

If Daniel and Dev are to have any hope of victory, she will have to do the unthinkable... surrender to Louis Marini and steal back the Blood Stone.

* * * *

After a long while, he went still and turned to us and a slow, satisfied smile crossed his face. "It's here, Your Highness."

Nimue went to stand next to the demon and gestured for Daniel to stand beside her. "We need the sword now." She took it in her hand and frowned, looking the slightest bit nervous. "Now we find out if I did my job properly."

"What do you mean?" Danny asked.

She tugged at her bottom lip with her teeth. "Well, there's always a test with things like this."

"Like the sword in the stone?" I remembered my Arthurian lore, or at least the Disney movie.

Nim nodded. "Yes, that was the test for the boy. I set up the test for this king a very long time ago. I didn't know exactly why I chose this method because at the time it seemed odd, but something told me this was the proper challenge."

"Why a test?" Neil asked. "You're the Lady of the Lake. Don't you just know who to give the sword to?"

"Think of it as a fail-safe," the nymph replied. "If I'm incorrect, Excalibur in the hands of the wrong person could prove very bad for us all."

"But Daniel already has the sword," Dev pointed out.

Stewart chirped up to answer that question. "Oh, he won't for long if he doesn't pass this test. If he fails, we all die. Well, all of you die. I just go back to the Hell plane and resume my former life. But I would mourn you all terribly."

"What's the test, Nim?" Daniel asked.

Nim smiled a secret little smile. "It's simple, Daniel. I thought at the time it was too simple, but now it's very fitting. I'm sure it will all work out. The world needed Arthur's strength so his test was one that proved it. The world needs something different from you."

Daniel sighed. It always came back to that. "Where am I supposed to bleed this time?"

"Take the sword, please," Nim instructed. "Give it to me and stand right here where the veil is the thinnest and the door can open."

Daniel did as instructed and the minute he was in place, Nim's hand came back and she sent Excalibur straight into Daniel's gut with a horrible twist.

All hell broke loose. Zack leapt forward, his semi pointed straight at the nymph's head. Lee pulled me back even as I tried to run toward Daniel. Dev made it to our vampire first. Daniel had fallen to his knees, his blood spilling all over the green grass, but before Dev could reach down to haul him up, he put an arm out to stop him.

"I'm fine," I heard Daniel growl, clutching his middle.

"She gutted you," Dev yelled as he turned his face accusingly to Nim. His gun was on full display. "Give me one good reason I don't put a bullet in your skull, Nimue or Vivienne or whatever the hell your name is."

"If you're going to shoot me, you should step back to do it, Devinshea," Nim announced even as I felt a wave of energy flicker across my skin. Lee cursed softly and I knew he felt it, too.

"The veil is opening," Stewart said. "Someone should get the king back unless he wants to be ripped in two."

Dev put his arm under Daniel's shoulder on one side and Zack took the other. They started to hurry him away from the site.

"Didn't I just get ripped in two? Sure as hell felt like it," Daniel muttered as they made their way to me.

Lee let me go and I went down on my knees even as Daniel hit the ground.

I knelt beside him feeling for the already healing wound. I expected it to be deep and still bleeding, but it was already closing. In moments there wouldn't even be a scar. "Do you need blood?"

He nodded. "Not you, baby. I already took my share from you."

Dev didn't hesitate. His sleeve was already rolled up, as though he anticipated the need, and he came in behind Daniel, offering his wrist. He didn't hiss at the pain. There was only a slight tightening around his eyes to show he felt anything at all as Daniel began to draw from him. I didn't even yell at Danny for not pulling Dev in. That was a private thing and they wouldn't do it in front of anyone but me.

"We have to hurry." Nim used her sweater to wipe the blood from the sword. She tossed it away when she was done and held Excalibur out for Daniel to retrieve. "The test has been passed. The king's blood has opened the veil and Merlin waits. I'm sorry for the violent nature of the test, Daniel, but it was necessary. There's no question now. You are the King of the Sword. Are you ready to meet your mentor?"

Daniel released Dev's wrist, licking the wound clean, and it quickly closed. He was on his feet and he helped Dev to his. Daniel looked down at his ruined T-shirt and sighed. He zipped up his leather jacket, covering the blood. Daniel looked down at me. He nodded to Dev and they each took an arm to escort me. It was how we had entered all state functions when we were in Faery. Daniel was signaling he wanted to continue the practice on this plane. "We are ready."

The demon held out his hand to stop us. "Please allow me to educate you in this. Your Highness, you should go first," Stewart explained. "It's tradition. This is a very important moment. It will be commented on and talked about. We must get it just right. The king enters, and then the queen, and then the rest of your retinue. You are at the center of this kingdom and we follow you."

Daniel actually threw back his head and laughed. "Stewart, you know nothing of my kingdom if you think I'm the center. I haven't been the center of my world for at least twenty years and I don't ever intend to be. As for tradition, well, it's time I made my own."

In between the two men I loved more than anything in the world, I made my way into the prison of Myrddin Emrys.

Dungeon Games: A Masters and Mercenaries Novella

Masters and Mercenaries, Book 6.5
By Lexi Blake

Obsessed

Derek Brighton has become one of Dallas's finest detectives through a combination of discipline and obsession. Once he has a target in his sights, nothing can stop him. When he isn't solving homicides, he applies the same intensity to his playtime at Sanctum, a secretive BDSM club. Unfortunately, no amount of beautiful submissives can fill the hole that one woman left in his heart.

Unhinged

Karina Mills has a reputation for being reckless, and her clients appreciate her results. As a private investigator, she pursues her cases with nothing holding her back. In her personal life, Karina yearns for something different. Playing at Sanctum has been a safe way to find peace, but the one Dom who could truly master her heart is out of reach.

Enflamed

On the hunt for a killer, Derek enters a shadowy underworld only to find the woman he aches for is working the same case. Karina is searching for a missing girl and won't stop until she finds her. To get close to their prime suspect, they need to pose as a couple. But as their operation goes under the covers, unlikely partners become passionate lovers while the killer prepares to strike.

A View to a Thrill

Masters and Mercenaries, Book 7

By Lexi Blake

A Spy without a Country

Simon Weston grew up royal in a place where aristocracy still mattered. Serving Queen and country meant everything to him, until MI6 marked him as damaged goods and he left his home in disgrace. Ian Taggart showed him a better way to serve his fellow man and introduced him to Sanctum, a place to pursue his passion for Dominance and submission. Topping beautiful subs was a lovely distraction until he met Chelsea, and becoming her Master turned into Simon's most important mission.

A Woman without Hope

Chelsea Dennis grew up a pawn to the Russian mob. Her father's violent lessons taught her that monsters lurked inside every man and they should never be trusted. Hiding in the shadows, she became something that even the monsters would fear—an information broker who exposed their dirty secrets and toppled their empires. Everything changed when Simon Weston crossed her path. Valiant and faithful, he was everything she needed—and a risk she couldn't afford to take.

A Force too Strong to Resist

When dark forces from her past threaten her newfound family at Sanctum, Chelsea must turn to Simon, the one man she can trust with her darkest secrets. Their only chance to survive lies in a mystery even Chelsea has been unable to solve. As they race to uncover the truth and stay one step ahead of the assassins on their heels, they will discover a love too powerful to deny. But to stop a killer, Simon just might have to sacrifice himself…

About Lexi Blake

New York Times bestselling author Lexi Blake lives in North Texas with her husband and three kids. Since starting her publishing journey in 2010, she's sold over three million copies of her books. She began writing at a young age, concentrating on plays and journalism. It wasn't until she started writing romance that she found success. She likes to find humor in the strangest places and believes in happy endings.

Connect with Lexi online:

Facebook: Lexi Blake
Twitter: authorlexiblake
Website: www.LexiBlake.net
Instagram: www.instagram.com